The Witness
of Music

The Witness of Music

of Music

80 Years of Pro Musica in Detroit

ALEXANDER SUCZEK

MARICK
PRESS

Library of Congress Cataloging in Publication Data

Suczek, Alexander
The Witness of Music. 80 years of Pro Musica in Detroit
Non-Fiction in English
Includes bibliographical references and index
ISBN 10: 0-9779703-7-X (bound)
ISBN 10: 0-9779703-8-8 (pbk.)
ISBN 13: 978-0-9779703-7-7 (bound)
ISBN 13: 978-0-9779703-8-4 (pbk.)

Edited by Peter Markus
Design and typesetting by Sean Tai
Cover design by Sean Tai

Cover art: Robert Eovaldi. Detroit Symphony Orchestra Archives
Printed and bound in Canada

For information about permission to reproduce selections from this book,
write to Permissions, Marick Press, P.O. Box 36253 GPF, MI 48236

Marick Press
P.O. Box 36253
Grosse Pointe Farms, MI
48236
USA
www.marickpress.com

Distributed by spdbooks.org

Table of Contents

Acknowledgements

To begin at the beginning, I am obliged to thank the key officers and members of Pro Musica who jointly directed me that I should document the story of the society before it could be forgotten. They made a strong argument that in as much as some of the most colorful details existed only as oral history they could soon be lost and forgotten. It was officers and board members like Alice Haidostian, Hershel Sandberg, Ann Kondak, and Ken Collinson who gave me the original impetus to proceed with this project. And it was the late Ed Frohlich, former treasurer, who enthusiastically encouraged me with an important quote and the first cash donation to help fund the project.

Meeting minutes and correspondence carefully saved and sorted by Alice, Ann and Historian Penny Soby were valuable resources. Then an amazing trove of Pro Musica's early history was made available to me through the efforts of Jeanne Salathiel in the Music and Performing Arts Department and the Burton Historical Collection of the Detroit Public Library where she and her co-librarians were wonderful at helping me to track down information not always easy to find tucked away in files and stacks.

In New York, Artist Managers Bill Capone and Carrie Feiner, and pianist Frederic Chiu who performed with and for us in recent years provided helpful perspective on the story's place in the national music world and its potential interest to professional musicians and their managers. They, along with additional Pro Musica members like Elaine Weingarden, Lorraine Lerner, and Stan Beattie read and critiqued the manuscript in its late form providing valuable suggestions and corrections. Of special value are the recollections of Lorraine Lerner and Ann Kondak which are incorporated as a part of the penultimate chapter plus a charming anecdote from Inge and George Vincent.

Acknowledgements

I am especially indebted to our graphic designer of print materials for helpful advice at every step of the process and his skill in digitizing photos and graphic materials to be used in the book. Kyo Takahashi has been an inspiring collaborator in the development of the entire conception.

There also has been an exceptional display of commitment to Pro Musica and what it stands for and determination to make sure that its story is not forgotten. A most loyal corps of officers and members, under the leadership of Lee Barthel and Fred McKenzie generously provided funding that was essential to bring this book to a point where a publisher would take it on. And finally, I want to acknowledge the vision and faith of publisher, Mariela Griffor, who recognized the historical importance of Pro Musica's story and its significance in the world of great music and musicians.

Book fund contributors

Doris Adler, Mrs. Doris Arms, Florence Arnoldi, Richard Banyon, Lee & Floy Barthel, Leslie & Rose Marie Battey, Jr., Ms. Margaret Beck, Stanley & Carol Beattie, Margaret Borden, Robert & Marcia Closson, Paul & Moira Escott, Edward P. Frohlich, Alice Berberian Haidostian, Lawrence Hands, Dr. Edward and Barbara Klarman, Nancy Komenaga, M. F. Huthwaite, Nicholas & Ann Kondak, Max Lepler, Leonard & Lorraine Lerner, William Liberson & Sarah Goldfaden, Dr. Kim & Mado Lie, Jan & Barbara Linthorst-Homan, Carol & Ray Litt, Ms. Katherine McDonald, Fred McKenzie, M. J. & Freda Mendelson, Mr. & Mrs. James North, Mr. & Mrs. Robert Roney, Hershel & Dorothy Sandberg, Arthur & Gladys Sweet, Kyo & Mary Takahashi, Stanley & Elaine Weingarden, Eric & Dina Winter, George & Inge Vincent.

THE BEGINNINGS

1927–1938

Chapter One
A Unique Concert Society Is Born and an Upstart Comes to Detroit – 1927

B ack in the roaring twenties, lovers of fine music in Detroit were very much aware of their needs and opportunities to develop the city's cultural life. Detroit was a boomtown riding a wave of dazzling growth and prosperity powered by the auto industry and a dynamic entrepreneurial spirit. Having built fortunes in lumber and cars, Detroiters were turning their eyes to cultural goals. Civic leaders had recently established a symphony orchestra, engaged Ossip Gabrilowitsch as Music Director, and built Orchestra Hall. They also were determined to have a fine museum of art. By 1927, the newly completed Detroit Institute of Arts was ready to open. In a couple of decades it was to rise to the rank of the fifth most important collection in the country.

Djina Ostrowska

Meanwhile, Djina Ostrowska, harpist with the Detroit Symphony Orchestra, learned that in the spring of 1928 a national organization based in New York and calling itself Pro Musica was bringing French composer Maurice Ravel on a concert tour of the U.S. Established in the early 1920s by pianist Robert Schmitz, the New York management's mission was to bring European composers and artists to perform for a chain of Pro Musica chapters in cities across North America. By 1925 the network is reported to have spread to more than 20 cities including Montreal, Chicago, Denver, Kansas City,

The Beginnings

Los Angeles, Minneapolis, Portland, St. Paul, San Francisco and Seattle. The New York management also sent American composers to perform in Europe.

Ostrowska immediately proposed to Maestro Gabrilowitsch that Ravel should be engaged to appear with the symphony. However, the conservative Russian pianist-conductor was not yet a fan of Ravel. He responded, *What? That upstart!*

Undaunted, Ostrowska brought together a group of cultural and civic minded supporters and organized a Detroit chapter of the national Pro Musica organization. Important and influential support came from the city's most venerable amateur music club of the time, The Tuesday Musicale. The first meeting was held at the Women's City Club on Saturday December 17, 1927. Ostrowska called on Mrs. Myron B. Vorce to act as permanent chairman and Edward G. Kemp as secretary. Kemp's minutes report that in response to Vorce's request for nominations, 32 names were submitted for the Board of Directors. In a wave of enthusiasm all 32 were elected (see Appendix B).

At the time of that first meeting, the Detroit Chapter already boasted 150 members. Ostrowska set a goal of 300 members and a three-concert season that would first bring pianist/composer Bela Bartok and then Maurice Ravel. Franz Prattinger, a member from Detroit's Hungarian community, expected that approximately 50 Detroit Hungarians would join for the Bartok concert.

The relationship with the national Pro Musica organization was flexible. The New York office would make artists and composers available at reasonable fees and approve programs. But a local chapter was free to engage artists and plan programs on its own if its officers and members wished. Each local chapter paid a small percentage of its ticket sale income to the national organization for management and mailing costs and received a fee for listing Mason and Hamlin as its official piano. Each chapter was still free to use a different piano for any concert.

Three concert halls under consideration were the Playhouse, the Twentieth Century Hall, and the Recital Hall of the newly opened Detroit Institute of Arts. Mrs. Vorce reported that the museum hall was not well ventilated and available only on Friday evenings, but the cost was only $50. Moreover, the museum's management, intending their institution to be a home for all the arts, offered a generous policy of support and cooperation for the new organization.

Louis Ling, chief copy writer at a Detroit advertising agency, and Miss Caroline Parker, daughter of a prominent businessman, were especially eager to help. A graduate of Harvard College (class of 1898) and Detroit College of Law, Ling was a man of many talents with a special love of music. He had previously been drama critic and city editor of the now defunct *Detroit Journal*. He was also active in the Detroit Symphony Society. With Ostrowska, he and Parker were appointed to form a temporary committee on organization. They would choose a hall, set admission prices and membership fees, and have tickets and promotional materials printed.

Enthusiasm ran high and the organization quickly took shape. Materials were printed and the opening concert by Bela Bartok was scheduled for February 19, 1928, in the museum's Recital Hall. Mrs. Walter C. Boynton became chairman of the membership committee. A draft of by-laws was the subject at the next organizational meeting. Vorce, Ling and Ostrowska were authorized to sign and acknowledge the articles of association. Everyone was in a mood to make Pro Musica happen.

For the first concert event, Bartok delivered a talk about his music and performed at the piano. On his program were a suite, a sonata and five short pieces, plus two pieces by his compatriot, Zoltan Kodaly. (see Appendix A)

With a sense of pride and achievement over being a part of the musical *avant garde*, few in the audience expressed any discomfort over the unfamiliar style of Bartok's music. The more sophisticated members, some of whom were active professional performers themselves, were excited to have the opportunity to experience what was then the newest trend in classical composition. The youngest member of the audience was a teenage music student names Esther Peters who served as an usher. After completing her education to become a teacher of music and piano, she joined Pro Musica and remained an enthusiastic member until her

Bela Bartok

death in December 2003. She was the last living member of the founding team.

Audience reaction was not the same throughout Bartok's American tour under the national Pro Musica sponsorship. In such cities as San Francisco and Chicago, the newspapers headlined Bartok as a musical heretic, giving the public the impression of an outspoken iconoclast. His appearance then as a slight, retiring composer disappointed those who expected a fire-breathing revolutionary. Commentators of the era reported that he left his audiences and critics puzzled. He was not what they had been led to expect.

All his recitals were prefaced with a short lecture in English. He talked mainly about the problems of a contemporary composer relating his music to the popular temperament and characterized his musical point of view as treating simple melody with correspondingly complex harmony. Seeking not to be too provocative, he did not program his newest and most controversial works.

In Detroit, having the composer present to speak about his music and perform it in the salon atmosphere of the Detroit museum's 395-seat Recital Hall gave the program an intimacy and a distinction that captured audience interest for the launch of the new concert society. Russell McLaughlin, writing in the *Detroit News* caught the mood in his column.

> In this music was much sturdy rhythm and a plain honesty in basic melody that was obviously vital and important…His dissonances were abrupt and harsh to a point of dizziness…Bartok is a first rate pianist with nimble fingers and an uncommon pedal-technique, reaching real dynamic contrasts on his keyboard. He is humorist of parts, also, for the Burlesque, which is supposed to indicate a gentleman slightly flown with wine, does so very divertingly…this music may be pioneering toward a great goal and therefore, whether it entertains or no, studious persons should hear and weigh it. Pro Musica does great service in making it available.

For the second concert, in March 1928, Maurice Ravel was at the piano in a program of his own music with an ensemble of Detroit Symphony musicians. Clarinetist Marius Fossenkemper, cellist Georges Miquelle, and harpist Ostrowska were among them. Song cycles like *Sheherezade* and *Chanson Grecq* that helped make Ravel famous were performed by

soprano Lisa Roma with Ravel accompanying. Ostrowska played the harp in Ravel's
Introduction and Allegro with string quartet,
flute, and clarinet.

Writing in the *Detroit News*, McLaughlin
reported that due to tremendous interest the
concert had been moved at the last minute
to the large auditorium at The Detroit Institute of Arts. He described Ravel as

diminutive, frail and gray-haired and his
music, modernism adrift from its moorings.
It was nonetheless logical, absorbing and
often exquisite...For the 'Introduction and
Allegro,' Ravel conducted members of the

Maurice Ravel

Detroit Symphony Orchestra with Mlle. Ostrowska on the harp. The
allegro was repeated as an encore in response to audience enthusiasm.

The critic for the Detroit evening *Times*, Ralph Holmes, who often
appeared to be influenced by the humorous writing style of Mark Twain,
provided an amusing personal impression of Ravel.

Looking for all the world like Johnny Dooley about to do an imitation of
a head waiter...he led an attentive audience into a Monet world. The
audience went quite mad over it.

Whichever way you look at it, the upstart had conquered Detroit.

For a third concert on April 20, several members gave a program of
instrumental and vocal chamber music. In keeping with the Pro Musica
policy of off-beat programming, it included a quartet of cellos, a suite for
flute, violin and piano, music for two pianos and two sets of art songs.
Danish soprano Povla Frisch and her accompanist, Celius Dougherty,
added prestigious international artists to the roster.

For that very auspicious opening season, memberships were sold out to
fill the 395-seat hall and the list of officers, board members and subscribers
of Pro Musica Detroit read like a roll call of the city's musical, social, and
civic leaders. In the process, they became members of an elite interna-

tional network. According to the November 1928 issue of the magazine *Michigan Woman*, the Detroit chapter of Pro Musica was one of thirteen in cities across the United States. The national organization, based in New York, was nine years old at the time and had a total membership nation-wide of nearly 9,000.

Detroit's remarkable opening season concluded on May 28, 1928, with the society's first annual meeting at the Statler Hotel. It was preceded by a dinner which has since become a permanent practice. Presiding was elected president Ling. Ostrowska was first vice president. Charles Frederick Morse, organist and choir director at Grosse Pointe Memorial Church, was second vice president. Mrs. Frank W. (Dorothy) Coolidge became corresponding secretary. Mrs. Irene Boynton took on the duties of treasurer. Founding patrons and contributors included Mrs. Edsel Ford, Mrs. Henry B. Joy whose husband was a founder of the Packard Motor Car Company, Mrs. Frank Murphy, wife of a prominent jurist, Mrs. Truman H. Newberry of one of the leading lumber fortunes and Mrs. Jerome Remick, wife of the Detroit music publisher.

In accordance with the by-laws, the Society elected 25 directors in three classes with three-, two- and one-year terms (Appendix B). The shorter terms were to change to three years as they came up for reelection.

Charter members included Detroit attorney Ned Ailes who was widely regarded as one of the three most cultured men in the city then and for decades to come, Margaret Mannebach who was staff pianist of the Detroit Symphony, and pianist Mischa Kottler, Music Director of Radio Station WWJ. Nearly four decades later, Kottler was to succeed Mannebach as official pianist of the Detroit Symphony. Also from the Detroit Symphony were Ilya Schkolnik, concertmaster, Georges Miquelle, principal cellist, John Wummer, flutist, and Marius Fossenkemper, clarinetist. Among the city's professional musicians at large was pianist Edouard Bredshall. He, Mannebach, and Kottler were the city's most prominent piano teachers. All three were active performers.

On April 20, 1989, 61 years later, Fossenkemper wrote me a letter recalling Ravel's visit:

> *During the season of 1927-28, March 28th, at the Detroit Institute of Arts, Pro Musica presented Maurice Ravel in his first and only appearance in Detroit...*

The Ravel concert was indeed history-making. We repeated the same concert in Ann Arbor for the Ann Arbor Music Study Club. Being a graduate of the University of Michigan, we had access to the dining room of the Michigan Union where we had our dinner. Mr. Ravel was most [eager]to address some pictorial postcards of the Ann Arbor Campus and did so. He spoke often of his niece, Laura, living in Paris.

Both on the trip over to Ann Arbor and back Mr. Ravel proved to be a jovial companion. At that particular time I spoke and understood the French language fairly well, enough to make conversation. Mr. Ravel himself was able to speak some English. Our own Georges Miquelle was able to unravel any mistakes we might have made when he joined us in Ann Arbor. My good friends of the ensemble helped graciously, especially John Wummer, our famous flautist, who always injected delicious humor into any situation.

Back in Detroit safely, Mr. Ravel, John Wummer and I had a hamburger together before saying "goodnight" and, as it proved, "goodbye," for I never saw him in person again.

Kottler was a member until his death in 1995 and performed in a number of concerts during the financially stressed 1930s and on special occasions in later years. When asked about the Ravel concert, he wryly recalled that while he greatly admired Ravel's music, he found the composer to be *a terrible pianist.*

Coincidentally, in June 1928, Robert and Charity Suczek celebrated the birth of their son Alex. I was, of course, blissfully unaware that I shared my birth year with Pro Musica Detroit and oblivious to the fact that I would one day become dedicated to its musical mission. But as I look back on it today, it seems like fate as the later years of this story will tell.

In the meantime, while I was comfortably nestled in my cradle, Pro Musica concerts were vibrant events in the Recital Hall of the Detroit Institute of Arts.

The first season had already established traditions. Everyone agreed on three concerts a season. Then in October 1928, at the first board meeting of the second season, Mannebach and enthusiastic member Margaret Coulter suggested a social gathering to follow every concert. Hostesses were invited to provide food and drink; their husbands were to act as hosts.

The Beginnings

With the energy and enthusiasm that had been characteristic from the start, they made it a highly congenial and gracious afterglow with refreshments in the museum's Romanesque Hall. Candelabra and flowers graced long tables loaded with hot hors d'oeuvres. Finger sandwiches and petits fours were served by hosts in black tie while their wives in evening gowns filled cups of tea and coffee from silver urns and a large brass samovar. Guests and artists mingled, made small talk and discussed musical issues. In the fullest sense of their role, the host couples each made a cash gift to defray the cost of the afterglow. That was a practice to last almost 50 years. After that the Society included the afterglow in the price of admission.

It was at that time, too, that Pro Musica made its first effort to collaborate officially with the Detroit Symphony. Ling contacted Victor Kolar, assistant conductor, about having the Symphony Choir perform at the second season's final concert. While no arrangement was made, it opened the door to future possibilities that would not take long to materialize.

For the time being, the prime attractions remained the brilliant musicians and composers that the national Pro Musica provided, although the outstanding local musicians who sometimes took part in the programs generally proved equally illustrious. Most of the visitors' appearances in our city were debuts. The intimate scale of the concerts and afterglows in the elegant atmosphere of the museum's small recital hall and Romanesque cloister exhibit were very special attractions.

The programs were far from conventional. Naturally, when a composer was the featured artist, it was his music that was performed (with a few exceptions). The composer was also expected to talk about his life and his work. When famous performing artists were featured, they were asked to program music from the pre-classical and 20th century periods. There was music on the Pro Musica Detroit programs never heard in other local concerts and rarely, if at all, in other cities at that time except at other Pro Musica chapters.

For the audience it was a great learning experience. There was a rationale for each program. Musicians talked about the music and works were programmed because they related to each other in some way. Yet the atmosphere was festive rather than educational.

Bartok and Ravel were followed by Ottorino Respighi in December 1928. Known mainly for his enjoyable, programmatic orchestral suites

-representing sights in Rome (*The Pines of Rome* and *The Fountains of Rome*, for example), this pupil of Rimsky Korsakov, also turned out a variety of operas, chamber works, and songs. Some of the latter were performed by his wife, Elsa Oliveri Sangiacomo, with him at the piano. Assisted by members of the DSO he concluded the concert with his suite for small orchestra inspired by three Botticelli paintings. Respighi conducted. Compared to some composers of the time, this was easy listening.

Ottorino Respighi

A month later came Arthur Honegger joined by a vocalist and members of the DSO. One of the famous group of French composers known as "Les Six," he was exploring his own musical horizons. His music reflects influences of his Swiss Protestant heritage, Gregorian chant, impressionism, jazz, and opera. He emphasized melodic and rhythmic relationships more than tonality. It was a concert that made audience members sit up and take notice.

Unable to conclude arrangements with the Symphony Choir, Pro Musica completed the season with a concert that McLaughlin described with glowing praise in the *Detroit News* as "See America First." Leading attraction was American soprano Greta Torpadie, reputed to be one of the finest lieder singers on the continent. With her came an equally illustrious group of Detroit musicians including composer Valbert Coffey, symphony violinist Allan Farnham, and the DSO's concertmaster, Ilya Schkolnik, serving as conductor. Unlike the programs provided by the national office, all the music and musicians were American. Reports in the Detroit press confirmed beyond doubt that Pro Musica on its own could put together top quality, highly appealing concerts with a creative mix of international stars and hometown artists.

The third season opened in November 1929, barely a month after the stock market crash. While this would eventually have a dramatic impact, it was still business as usual in the music world. The Society presented the young Russian tenor Gabriel Leonoff, assisted by the Detroit String Quartet (of DSO members) and pianist and board member Mannebach.

Alexandre Tansman

Leonoff had recently won major recognition for a performance with Leopold Stokowski conducting. In recognition of a visit to Detroit by Russian Composer Alexander Glazunoff, the concert was dedicated to him and included some of his works. For members still recovering from the challenges of Bartok and Honneger, chamber music and songs by Russian and Spanish composers must have been a relaxation.

It was a brief reprieve. The concert on January 22, 1930, brought Polish born Alexandre Tansman. Having lived in Paris since 1919, he was considerably influenced by the modern trends in music there, especially by "Les Six."

In reviewing the concert in the *Detroit Times*, Ralph Holmes anticipated a practice of relating the concert program to one of the museum's gallery exhibits that would become routine decades later.

On the walls of the [museum] hangs an exhibition of modern prints. They show a world of sharp angles, harsh lines, distorted perspectives… In the adjoining auditorium…we heard the musical equivalent of these pictures…from the authoritative fingers of Alexandre Tansman, himself an exemplar of these moods, a practitioner of these methods. It is, of course, easy to sneer and get flippant in the presence of such music as this where orthodox tonalities mean nothing, where the harmonies all seem beveled off and the forms of construction all twisted and warped. But there was something about Mr. Tansman that carried too deep a quality of sincerity not to be taken seriously…Not that this listener heard many things which moved him or left a desire to hear them repeated, but others of the audience seemed to…His music is not devoid of melody or the emotional impulses recognizable by average people…In a violin sonata we found ourselves in the presence of a familiar language with moments of old fashioned beauty. True, Louis Ling appeared on the platform and rather apologized for the lack of modernity, the trouble being that the sonata is relatively ancient having been written all of 12 years ago… In a sonatine for flute and piano, the fourth movement sings a charming song...while the second was such perfect jazz that it would make the Tin Pan Alley boys burn with envy...In a military march he was the ultra modernist, splintering the chromatic scale into a thousand new colors and lacerating our ears just as modern urban American life lacerates us.

For his audience, Tansman's music bridged the transition from romantic and impressionistic to the modernism of Bartok. He spoke eloquently about the nature of the changes and illustrated his comments liberally with his compositions. The supporting musicians were all local professionals and board members. Challenged though the audience was, it retained its enthusiasm.

Sergei Prokofiev on March 2, 1930, is another legend in the Society's story. Still controversial and not universally admired, his reputation was soon to grow immensely. Once again the Society's members would brag that they had heard him first, and, as with Ravel, on his only appearance in Detroit.

The weekly news magazine, *Detroit Saturday Night*, carried a perceptive report:

Prokofiev, whose works once impressed us as products of a disordered mind and an unsteady hand, sounded quite orthodox owing to the somewhat rigorous education we lately received at the hands of Messrs. Honegger and Bartok...His works are interesting offering a suggestion of this mood or that but never an emotion. Emotion, we are informed by the moderns, is hopelessly out of style but so, too, were the now prevailing long skirts. Prokofiev's music is humorous and clever (both are being done this year) teeming with virility and effective in an impersonal, coldly calculated sort of way. He is a very capable pianist and has a style that is perfectly suited to the exploitation of modern music... With the Detroit String Quartet and Roy Schmidt, clarinetist, he offered an Overture on Yiddish Themes which was so tunefully pleasing that it had to be repeated... He accompanied Lina Llubera-Prokofiev (his wife) in a song group of which his arrangements of two Russian tunes won the highest praise...Now, thanks to Pro Musica, we have first hand information on which to base our opinions of the composer of Love for Three Oranges.

The Beginnings

There was an air of triumph at the third annual meeting of Pro Musica members on the evening of April 16, 1930. The Society was setting the pace for musical adventure in Detroit. It was garnering widespread recognition. And it was paying its own way. President Ling reported on behalf of the treasurer that they concluded the third season with a net cash balance of $100. Nominations were made for eight board members to renew their expiring two-year terms and, while the ballots were being counted, there was lively discussion of plans for future seasons.

Those plans were in for some stress. The economic impact of the stock market crash was beginning to be felt by everyone and it was having its effect on the Pro Musica home office in New York. At a board meeting, Ling read a list of attractions offered by New York. There was much comment on the unsuitability of many of the artists and fees for services. The board decided to look independently for other attractions.

There was another surprise when the newly elected President, Hubert O'Brien, replacing Ling, declined the office due to the pressures of business. With Vice President Morse acting as interim president the board debated skipping a season due to the difficulty of finding suitable programs. This idea was, however, quickly dismissed. The ranks closed. Morse became President, Ostrowska became Vice President and the group carried on.

The committee responsible for selecting artists assured the board that they could get composer Hans Barth through the National Music League for a January date. Miquelle agreed to plan a second program and the third concert was left to be determined. Clearly, Pro Musica's leadership was strong. Since it included several widely recognized musicians, it was well informed about and connected to the international music world. The society was ready to set its own course. That was more important than they realized. Pro Musica Detroit soon would be forced to be fully independent.

The fourth season opened on January 16, 1931. Composer Hans Barth brought a perspective on the evolution of keyboard music. He performed first on a harpsichord, next on a conventional piano, and last on the quarter-tone piano he had invented. It had two keyboards, or manuals, which were tuned a quarter-tone apart.

Some listeners had the impression at times that the instrument was out of tune. At other times, they sensed a new delicacy and subtlety to the melodic and harmonic effects which brought new possibilities for a richer keyboard literature. Writing in the *Detroit Times*, Ralph Holmes, who always seemed well informed about current popular comedians, predicted a future for the quarter-tone piano "as an encore instrument for Will Mahoney's xylophone dance. With those two keyboards to work on Will could break his neck."

It was unquestionably fortunate that Pro Musica had so many outstanding professional musicians among its members who lived and worked in Detroit. When the society's program committee did not like the offerings from New York, artists like pianist Kottler, cellist Miquelle, and violinist Schkolnik planned programs in which they invited other artists in the city to join them. The next two concerts of that fourth season demonstrated that Pro Musica could proceed with confidence on its own. Cellist Miquelle led the parade in assuring that much remarkable music would be included.

Along with art songs, a contemporary violin sonata and string quartet, and much interesting piano music, the February 24 concert ended with *Four Pieces for Four Celli* by contemporary American composer Stuart Mason. The April 17 concert then featured nationally famous cellist Hans Kindler. Following a Debussy Sonata and Roussel's Serenade for flute, harp and strings, he introduced Pro Musica to another new composer, Paul Hindemith. The music was a Sonata for cello solo. It put the audience once again on the frontier.

They were informed in the program notes that "Hindemith is without doubt the most prominent and talented composer among the younger generation in Germany. This sonata was written shortly after the war (WW I) and has the same despair and bitterness as Erich Remarques' novel All Quiet on the Western Front. The entire sonata takes only ten minutes and because of its conciseness and comparatively unfamiliar idiom will be played twice."

The program ended with a less austere work for flute, cello and piano by French composer Gabriel Pierne. As a pupil of Cesar Franck and Jules Massenet, Pierne (b. 1863) it was composed in a musical style more oriented to 19th century idioms.

Chapter 2
New Leadership and Creative Finance in a Time of Crisis – 1930

T he first big changes in organization came when Charles F. Morse took over as president in the fall of 1930. Then at the fourth annual meeting on May 8, 1931, the news broke that Pro Musica's founder, harpist Ostrowska, was moving to New York to pursue a career as soloist. Board member Caroline Parker made the announcement. The members passed a glowing resolution of gratitude that granted Ostrowska permanent honorary membership.

In New York, Ostrowska appeared with the New York Philharmonic and frequently with Arturo Toscanini. Having heard her perform regularly, no one in Pro Musica expected less of her. Nor could they begrudge her departure. She had done her job well. Pro Musica's board could carry on with what was then an established tradition. Morse had already proven to be a strong president and Ling returned to the executive staff as vice president. Pro Musica moved ahead without missing a beat.

In one provocative departure from the practice of bringing in only European composers and musicians, Pro Musica engaged from the New York office a traditional Japanese ensemble to open the 1931-32 season. With only four performers they presented a program of exclusively Japanese instrumental and vocal music and dance.

The leader, Seifu Yoshida, played a shakuhachi, a flute like instrument formed

Seifu Yoshida

of a bamboo stalk with five holes. Its range of melancholy sound was described as deeply moving to the Japanese listener. Madame Yoshida played a shamisen. It is compared to a guitar or banjo and is used for both solo playing and voice accompaniment. She also played a koto. With thirteen silk strings stretched on a piece of paulownia wood, it is reminiscent of a harp. Koto is probably the most widely known Japanese instrument.

Some of the pieces on the program were extremely old having a status comparable to the music of Palestrina and Bach in western culture. Others were contemporary pieces by Mr. Yoshida but were played in traditional style.

The highlights of the program were two classical dances with shamisen and song accompaniment. One dating back 200 years was an example of Kabuki drama. The other had even earlier origins.

The appearance of mezzo soprano Eva Gauthier in the second concert that season, January 22, 1932, was solidly in Pro Musica's mission to present new music even though the artist was not a composer. Born in Ottawa, trained in Paris and schooled in dramatic interpretation by the famous actress Sarah Bernhardt, Gauthier had premiered much vocal music of Ravel, Stravinsky, Bartok, Hindemith, Schoenberg, Satie, Honegger, and Poulenc, some songs of which appeared on her Detroit program. Often described as a *diseuse*, her reputation was based as much on semi spoken interpretation as singing. Appropriately, her program included first performances of songs by American composers.

Meantime, finances were reaching a state of crisis. As a result of the stock market crash in 1929, the economy had come to a standstill. Michigan banks had closed, all accounts were frozen and the Society needed $100 to meet obligations for the final concert of the 1931-32 season.

Writing for the Pro Musica Detroit archives in 1965, Dorothy Coolidge described how they made it through that period. Her story was later published in *Impresario Magazine*:

> Alas, the national organization did not survive the bank holiday, all chapters disbanding except Detroit. We wished to give our third and perhaps final concert that season but needed $100 more. The banks were closed but I had read that small depositors would be paid first. Pro Musica had $140 frozen and the last concert was to be in May.
>
> I suggested to the Board that one or more of the directors should buy the $140 for $100 cash. This startling suggestion went through and

*four directors paid $25 in cash each. Our attorney on the board, Edgar
Ailes, drew up the legal contract stating that when the bank account
was unfrozen each of us would receive $35. Thus the third concert was
given.*

*In September the bank paid the $140. Not a bad investment, $35
for $25 from May to September in the dollars of that depressed era.
Mr. Ailes is always asking me to suggest other such quick and profitable
investments.*

With funds available for that last concert, the composer format resumed
on April 8 with the appearance of Dr. Ernst Toch in a program devoted
exclusively to his own music. Trained in Germany and an exponent of a
dissonant, modernist style, he had just fled the Nazi regime to write scores
for Hollywood films and compose chamber music in America.

He preceded the performance with extemporaneous remarks in which
he defended modernism's inclinations to discord. He reasoned that just
as women change the length of their skirts and their hairdos, so music
changes its styles but keeps on being music. The Pro Musica audience
by this time had established a congenial spirit that made every concert
a pleasant get-together of friends with a common interest. Whether they
found the music accessible or not, they had a good time.

Somewhat bemused by this, Russell McLaughlin reported in his column
that "The audience laughed heartily at things and seemed to have a fine
time."

At the annual meeting six weeks later, money remained scarce and
the Board debated whether they should skip a season. There was still dissatisfaction with programs offered by the New York office and members
proposed that the Board should suggest composers and musicians they
would enjoy hearing. President Morse had discussed such ideas with New
York and had not found them sympathetic.

Finances were the main issue. Morse described their position as precarious and suggested that the Board members might pay for the next
season in advance to help out. Instead, they passed the hat and collected
$14.00. After all, times were hard.

It seemed likely that the Toch concert might be the last they would
bring through the New York Pro Musica management. Filled with enthusiasm for the great musical experiences they were enjoying, the officers and

board of Pro Musica of Detroit were determined to continue and do it on their own if necessary. Even faced with limited budgets, they wanted the artists and programs to be the best.

For the sixth season, 1932-33, the New York management offered one more French composer, albeit minor, pianist Florent Schmitt. With the participation of the local stalwarts, he included his piano quintet which remains one of his most memorable works.

In two cases, the Pro Musica board made arrangements with the Detroit Symphony to program special symphony concerts expressly to suit Pro Musica criteria. This meant mostly pre-classic and contemporary music with as many Detroit premiere performances as possible. Joined by the Symphony's regular audience, members attended those concerts in Orchestra Hall as Pro Musica events. It was a cooperative arrangement that must have helped the budgets of both organizations during those lean years.

The first of these came on short notice when Victor Kolar, the Associate Music Director, offered a program to suit Pro Musica for January 1933. Pro Musica member and pianist, Edouard Bredshall, would perform the Detroit premiere of Ravel's piano concerto and the orchestra would premiere Jaromir Weinberger's Polka and Fugue from his new opera *Schwanda the Bagpiper*. Unwilling to cancel one of its regular three concerts already scheduled at the Museum, Pro Musica's membership attended the Symphony concert as a fourth meeting that season, making what was reported to be "one of the most satisfactory houses ever attracted by our young moderns at the Symphony." It took place, of course, in Orchestra Hall.

Columnist Herman Wise, in the Detroit Free Press, gave the evening high marks:

> *A surprisingly large audience, made up for the most part of musicians, was present to join in the somewhat carefree evening...In the Ravel Concerto for Piano...Bredshall and at least six first desk men in the orchestra contributed the outstanding individual performances...The concerto was played for the first time in Paris about a year ago and has since caused untold dispute...Mr. Bredshall won nothing short of an ovation ... Concerts such as this ought to be offered twice annually...*

The third and fourth concerts on March 10 and 17, 1933, were performed entirely by Pro Musica's cadre of local professionals from the Symphony and the community at large. The first concert featured three pianists and a cellist. Kottler and Miquelle played a Saint Saens cello sonata and Chopin's *Introduction and Polonaise*. Mark Gunsberg and Loretta Petrosky offered Rachmaninoff's *Suite for Two Pianos*.

Only a week later another cast entirely of local musicians gave what McLaughlin described in the *Detroit News* as a rather rich affair. That was his way of saying that it was a long program. Schkolnick and his outstanding pupil Beatrice Griffin performed a Handel sonata for two violins with Kottler at the piano followed by Griffin in pieces for unaccompanied violin with the flavor of the old South by American composer Albert Spalding. Baritone Cameron McLean offered a diverse group of songs. Kottler played pieces for solo piano including a gavotte of his own composition that had to be repeated by popular demand. Finally, he and Miquelle closed the program with a cello sonata by the little known French composer Joseph Guy Ropartz. About that sonata, McLaughlin observed that "when the attention could be directed toward the work's progress, it was discovered to flow down devious but interesting channels toward perfectly logical ends. So ended Pro Musica's year with an excellent demonstration of Detroit's own artistic resources."

McLaughlin also reported that in the face of financial restrictions, those local performers had waived their fees for a contingency arrangement to pay them if funds became available. In those troubled times, enthusiasm and dedication found ways to carry on. It was the music that mattered.

Chapter 3

Into the Booking Business – 1933

It may have surprised but did not dismay the board when they realized that French composer Florent Schmitt would definitely be the last attraction from the New York office. Short of funds due to the bank holiday and the Depression, the national Pro Musica closed its doors and local chapters across the continent followed suit. Only the Detroit group with its corps of virtuoso musicians, resourceful board and enthusiastic membership decided to continue on its own. Going it alone created a new challenge, however.

As Dorothy Coolidge described it, "The Detroit chapter, now an independent, informal group of music lovers known only as Pro Musica Detroit, found itself in the booking business. From that time forward concerts were arranged, three a season, by the Board of Directors negotiating directly with artists, composers and their agents."

The Board continued to turn to the outstanding musicians in our community, especially those who were members of Pro Musica. Schkolnick, Miquelle and Kottler led the parade. They had formed a piano trio that performed weekly on Detroit radio station WWJ. It was the first chamber music radio concert series to be syndicated for nationwide broadcast. They were artists of international stature and were pillars of Pro Musica programming.

The concerts were not exclusively local in personnel, however. More composers were engaged to speak, and to play if they could. When budget and availability made it appropriate, the music for the composer appearances was performed by the local cadre. When a visiting soloist or ensemble was engaged, they would sometimes share the stage with local musicians to diversify the program. One can only imagine what kind of creative financing was going on in the depth of the Depression in order to hold these concerts.

The Beginnings

At a Board meeting in October 1933, individual members agreed to make direct contact with composers for future dates. Miss Haas would contact American pianist/composer George Antheil who had just returned from 10 years in Europe where he studied with Bloch and Stravinsky. Bredshall would contact the American composer Roy Harris and Morse would contact Arnold Schoenberg. They were ready to try for the best.

After a few false starts, they were able to open the 1933-34 season with American composer/pianist Henry Cowell who was enjoying a very successful international career. He had already made several European tours including the first by an American in the U.S.S.R. He took new approaches and employed a complex rhythmic language. Following an *Informal Discourse on Modern American Music*, he introduced the Pro Musica audience to the new concept of tone clusters in ten of his recent works for piano. Audience and critics listened with mixed feelings as Cowell struck the keyboard with fist and elbow and plucked the piano strings with his fingers. The rhythms were exciting but the sound required some getting used to.

McLaughlin reported that Cowell, "as a lecturer on modern music, gave no hint of the monkeyshines he was subsequently to perform...He divided music into entertainment and serious and declared himself an apostle of the latter...Whereupon he proceeded to present the most remarkable gymnastics. Whether he intended it or not, the audience was entertained."

For the next concert Morse arranged with the DSO for Victor Kolar to conduct a program of all Detroit premieres. It opened with a work by Malipieri called *Concerti* for flutes, oboes, clarinets, bassoons, trumpets, drums and double bass. Gian Francesco Malipieri had studied in Vienna and was a teacher at the Liceo Musicale in Venice in the 30s. His compositions borrowed from the styles of 17th and 18th century music. *Concerto Italiano* by Mario Castelnuovo-Tedesco followed in a more impressionistic idiom. This was a violin concerto with Schkolnik as soloist. After intermission came *Canzone della Sera* by Victor Kolar with a trumpet solo played by the orchestra's principal trumpeter, Albert Mancini. The final touch was most exotic of all: *Three Hindoo Dances* from the Opera *La Festa di Gauri* by La Monaca whose identity seems now lost to posterity.

The English baritone John Goss was available to appear on the third program. He was accompanied by Mannebach in a set of old English songs. His performance, hampered by a bad cold, was less than inspiring. According to reports, the evening was redeemed by Bredshall and Kottler with music for two pianos ending with *Cinq Melodies Populaire Grecque* by a favorite composer, Ravel.

The end of that season also brought the society face to face with grim reality. The combination of a depressed economy and the fact that so much modern music was wearing thin the tolerance of the more casual listeners had reduced the membership that year to 96. A few concerts had been held at the Statler Hotel where the cost was less than at the Museum even though the largest expense remained the cost of the artists except when the local artists made major concessions. At the annual dinner meeting, some suggested holding concerts in private homes, but the consensus was that the ideal location was the Recital Hall at the Detroit Institute of Arts.

The situation did not improve. Barely 100 members came to hear French Contralto Jeanne Laval on December 7, 1934. That may have been a blessing since she was afflicted with a severe throat ailment that seriously affected her voice. A larger audience appeared for the Paris Instrumental Quintet in February 1935 and, according to the critics, was rewarded with an excellent evening of chamber music. Moreover, the program was traditional, balanced between music of Couperin, Mozart, late romantic composers like Gabriel Pierne and Joseph Jongen, and the impressionist Claude Debussy. The final program in March brought Pro Musica back to its avowed mission. McLauchlin wrote that composer Filip Lazar was "doubtless the most modern person ever to be brought to Detroit by Pro Musica. And that is saying a great deal."

He went on to report:

> *The concert ended with a trio (by Lazar) for oboe, clarinet and bassoon played respectively by Dirk van Emmerick, Marius Fossenkemper and Joseph Mosbach…leading exponents of those instruments…and conducted by Mr. Lazar…it sounded like a combination of London street cries, a fog horn and the old cylindrical phonograph record called "Barnyard Folk." …the polite and deeply serious Pro Musica membership laughed out loud at it.*

The core membership, in fact, displayed a remarkable tolerance and spirit of adventure. Its responses displayed a clear appreciation of the fact that they were often venturing into uncharted territory with a readiness to accept that it might be rough going, even distasteful. In one of his columns, McLaughlin described attending a Pro Musica evening as "something like a grab bag. You may get a tin whistle or you may get a gold watch and chain." The members showed that they could tolerate the tin whistles as long as there were also the rewards of some new music that they found interesting, stimulating and comprehensible. They were unselfconscious about showing their recognition of music that went too far by laughing or even complaining, but they were serious about learning to understand new music. A group of members even formed a gramophone club. They met at each others' homes and listened to recordings of modern music to gain appreciation through familiarity. On the other hand, there was a desire for some more traditional offerings to be included in the programs manifested by enthusiastic applause when they did appear.

A spirit of social congeniality was also developing. As chairman of the Social Committee, Mrs. Austin saw to it that an attractive array of finger foods and beverages were served in a beautiful and gracious setting. The members looked forward to greeting their friends and the musicians after the concert in the Museum's Romanesque Court, a reconstruction of a medieval monastery chapel. Attendance at a Pro Musica evening was acquiring the charisma of a very congenial and cultural social event. Conversations were lively and the artists were usually besieged with comments, questions and requests for autographs.

Facing the crisis in low membership and lack of funds, Dorothy Coolidge pushed through a plan to have a membership drive every summer. A telephone committee would make calls and sign up members so that by the time the season opened, they would have enough memberships to cover the season's costs. In recognition of her leadership on this plan, she was elected Membership Secretary at the annual meeting in 1935.

Mrs. Coolidge ran her committee with the determination of a drill sergeant. By the time of the first concert in November, she was able to report 234 members, 101 of them new recruits.

The opening attraction was Russian Soprano Olga Averino, described by Detroit Free Press critic Herman Wise as "both intelligent and musical." Her program was 26 songs by almost as many composers ranging from Christoph Gluck and Orlando Lassus to Igor Stravinsky and Alban Berg. According to McLauchlin,

Her program was not confined to odd things not heard elsewhere…Modernity, however, was served. But even in that debatable field, Miss Averino's choice was broad and reasonable, extending from a banshee wail by Alban Berg to logical and lovely songs by Ravel, Bloch and Casella…Her last group…all Russian…was one of her evening's great successes…the drama that lies in Russian song…needs an emotional and intellectual woman such as she to make its meanings plain…

Olga Averino

The accompanist who also won high praise was Pro Musica's own Margaret Mannebach.

When it came to balancing programs to make the most modern music palatable by surrounding it with more familiar selections, the Detroit musicians seemed to use better judgment than some of the visiting composers. A woodwind ensemble of the now familiar DSO musicians brought music that, according to Herman Wise, provided pleasure not only for the performers but also for those who listened. After one Quintet by Mozart, all the music was 20th century, but the audience was comfortable with pieces by such now familiar names as Prokofieff, Ravel and Debussy, and so found the patience to listen comfortably to music of Ibert, Scriabin, Poulenc and Schoenberg.

Chapter 4

A New Turn in Artist Selection – 1936

At the last concert in May of 1936, Pro Musica for the first time imported a rising young concert pianist who was not a composer. Hailing from Puerto Rico, Jesús Maria San Roma grew up in New England where he was discovered by Serge Koussevitsky who presented him many times with the Boston Symphony. Again, the program was wide ranging, this time from the baroque to modern, and was received with great enthusiasm. Charles Gentry wrote in the *Detroit Times*:

> All the nervous excitement and color which attends a bull fight was crowded into the unusual recital which the modern Spanish pianist gave for the final Pro Musica event last night at the Art Institute...everyone went away exclaiming over the brilliant technique and dazzling power of this young pianist...the third encore...a really splendid performance of the Bach "Italian Concerto" elicited a desire to hear this vital and capable young artist in an all Bach program.

That concluded a season that significantly influenced the Society's programming. In a way, the event opened a new era as Jesús Maria San Roma was to be only the first in a memorable roster of piano virtuosos in the years to come and programs would include an added touch of the familiar, tried and true. Pro Musica was beginning to find its way in its independence.

Flushed with success and financially solvent, the society celebrated the season of 1936-37 with four concerts. The opener in October was billed as a special recital of 20th century music celebrating Twentieth Century Arts Week. The Society's President, Charles Morse, took the opportunity to bring a more educational format to the event. He delivered a brief lecture on 20th century music which was followed by the Detroit Symphony

Woodwind Ensemble with pianist Edouard Bredshall performing music by Ibert, Prokofiev, Piston, Honegger, Scriabin, Copland, Ravel, Debussy and Paul Juon. Among these composers, three had already appeared in Pro Musica concerts and a fourth, Copland, was soon to follow.

Eight composers represented were already familiar to the audience. The finale brought a new name, Paul Juon. Born in Russia and resettled in Berlin, he taught there at the *Hochschule für Musik*. His music combines elements of Russian folk songs with the German tradition. Commentary on Juon's *Divertimento for Woodwind Quintet and Piano* praised its variety of tone and enchanting moods. The Society's president Charles Morse explained that while the program was all contemporary music, extreme examples were avoided. The audience found the program novel and pleasing and urged another appearance of the ensemble. In its progress to independence, Pro Musica was finding a formula for pleasing its audiences while still pursuing its mission to present new music. Morse would encourage use of the lecture concert format in forthcoming concerts as well. It had already been the practice of composers and would be offered as an option to any artist who wished to speak. Over the years, artists who were comfortable speaking from the stage rated the practice as extremely helpful in establishing rapport with Pro Musica's responsive and attentive audience.

That season continued with another important ensemble: the famous Budapest String Quartet, recent immigrants from Europe. They had already made five tours of the U.S. but December 14, 1936 was their Detroit debut. There was a poignancy to their visit. They had left Europe because preparations for war occupied everyone's thoughts on that troubled continent. There was no time for music unless it served a political purpose. In Detroit they finally gained a kind of peace. Violinist Josef Roismann and cellist Josef Kroyt revealed that all of them found it easier to sleep here. Away from the turmoil of Europe and with a break in the travel schedule, they could really relax. They admitted having slept most of the week in Detroit. "Ah, such a good sleep," sighed Kroyt. "We like to be rested before a concert."

There was no sleeping in the concert. Quartets by Albert Roussel, Bela Bartok and Paul Hindemith demanded every technical skill of the players and intelligent listening by the audience. One high point for the audience was the *Capriccioso* movement from Bartok's *Quartet No. 2* when the emotional power rose to a frenzied climax led by cellist Mischa Schneider. Many members noted with glee the generous use of novel effects like playing with the wood of the bow or on the strings beyond the bridge in the Roussel and Hindemith works. The Recital Hall was filled to capacity.

American pianist Eunice Norton in February 1937 found an audience quite responsive to her performances of Ravel's *Gaspard de la Nuit* and Stravinsky's *Petrouchka Suite* from his ballet score. Her opening presentation of Copland's *Piano Variations*, on the other hand, struck most listeners as "a perplexing series of sounds." McLaughlin noted that her energetic pedaling put vitality and drama into music of Charles Ives and Hindemith that might have otherwise sounded dreary.

That season ended with a return engagement by Danish Soprano Povla Frijsch who had sung at the Ravel concert of the first season in 1928. Her skill in communicating the texts with clarity even in the most difficult vocal passages added to the appeal of a program already easy to enjoy. With songs by composers from Bach and Schubert to Debussy and Ravel, there was something for everyone and plenty of new music, or at least almost new.

Chapter 5

Two Tenth Birthdays – 1938

M arking the Society's tenth anniversary year, reporter W. K. Kelsey, who was also a member, wrote in the *Detroit News* a three-column recap of the group's beginnings and achievements. His profile of the audience is especially revealing:

> *Pro Musica is composed…of eager and curious inquirers who believe that the art of music has not come to a standstill and jellied. Many are shocked by what they hear; many can't make head or tail of it and say so frankly. They don't go to a Pro Musica concert to fall into enraptured dreams, but to keep their ears and minds open and thus learn what the music of the Twentieth Century is trying to be and to say…And Pro Musica is solvent and going strong…All this reporter can add as he looks forward to [another] season as a member is that the concerts are a lot of fun. If they weren't, wild horses could not drag his feet off the home radiator on a winter night. And it doesn't cost a wad of money, either.*

Pro Musica and I were both ten years old in 1938 and the year brought my first real contact with that musical world. My parents, a pianist and an engineer/ mathema- tician/inventor, had both grown up in the Austro-Hungarian Empire. Charity was from Vienna. She had been immersed in Viennese musical tradition. Robert was Czech and played the cello. He had studied mathematics and engineering at the University of Brün. They enjoyed entertaining guests who were in the arts and sciences. Having heard and met Ilya Schkolnik at a Pro Musica concert, they invited him to a gathering at our home. That evening, after treating the guests to a superb performance of the Bach Chaconne that resounded richly in our living room, he responded to my request for his autograph with a greeting

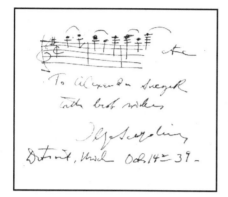

and musical notation above his signature. It was not until several decades later that I sifted through old mementos and found it as a reminder of just how far back I was in touch, however remotely, with the Society and the inspiring musical experience that it provided.

Seeking artists for the 1937-38 season, Board members again pitched in. Bredshall was negotiating with Hindemith and with pianist San Roma for a return engagement. Coolidge wanted to take advantage of the Roth Quartet being in Ann Arbor for a concert that year. DeWitt was in touch with soprano Ada McLeish. Composers Roy Harris, Aaron Copland, and Roger Sessions were also considered. The Board as a whole prioritized the list and authorized the individual members to make the bookings.

Jesús Maria San Roma returned on December 10 with a program carefully discussed and agreed to by the Board. It was nicely balanced with music by Bach, Haydn, Hindemith, Albeniz and a concluding work that delighted and fascinated the audience. That was *Ten Variations on Mary Had a Little Lamb* by Edward Ballanchine. Each variation was in the style of a different composer from Mozart to Liszt and San Roma treated it as a grand musical joke. McLauchlin reported that he rarely heard an audience laugh so heartily at a musical prank. Charles Gentry wrote in the *Detroit Times*: "San Roma proved that a serious concert pianist can have a sense of humor and burlesque his performance to completely win his audience so that he has to give five encores before he can go home." The performance was enhanced by the fact that in recognition of the artist's eminence, the Board had splurged on the rental of a concert grand piano at a cost of $22.

Even the afterglow made the newspaper. Along with describing the buzz of happy conversation about the pianist as entertainer, society reporter Judy O'Grady mentioned her discovery of doughnut holes among the post concert treats served by Mrs. Phillip Baker's Social Committee. "Look up the tray containing what you first take to be pfeffernusse. They're good!"

For the second con-
cert in February 1938,
Coolidge, who had by
now established herself as
an eager advocate of new
music, was able to book
the Roth Quartet for an
evening with a special
composer feature. Three
modernists were repre-
sented: Claude Debussy,
Alfredo Casella and Roy
Harris. McLauchlin lik-
ened the concert to a jour-

The Roth Quartet

ney down the path of modern music in easy stages. Compared to the music
by Harris, the Debussy was soothing. Casella, meantime, was an Italian
who trained in France with Faure, taught for a while in Paris and then
was influenced by Bartok, Stravinsky and Schoenberg. Returning to Italy,
he taught and composed there for the rest of his life where he turned to
making use of early Italian instrumental music and folk song styles. His
Three Pieces on the program that evening were from that last period of his
work and the concluding *Valse Ridicule* was such a successful burlesque of
all modern music that the audience cheered and demanded a repeat.

The Harris piano quintet brought McLauchlin's journey to its inevitable destination. The prestigious touch was that pianist Johanna Harris,
the composer's wife, performed the piano part bringing a kind of authority to the performance. It made little difference to J. Dorsey Callaghan
in the *Detroit Free Press* who called it a "harrowing experience." Reactions at the afterglow ranged from mystified to lost. Critics and audience
agreed, however, that the Roth Quartet was a virtuoso ensemble and the
discovery that Debussy's *Quartet Opus 10* was now pleasing to just about
everyone's ears left them with a satisfying sense of fulfilling Pro Musica's
purpose.

Most revealing of the impression such a concert made on the general
public is evident in an anonymous letter received by President Morse the
following week. He read it at a Board meeting where it was voted into the
archives.

The Beginnings

Dear Mr. President,

Well, of all things! Last night I strolled into the Art Institute up Woodward Avenue to see what this Pro Musica was all about and did I get an ear full!

I walked right in with all the musical Hoy-Paloy, sat me down and ses I, "Well, this looks as if it might be somethin'." Purty soon four real decent lookin' guys came out with three fiddles and one a big one, and set down and commenced to play some nice soft music by a feller named Debussy. I ses, "Those fellers can play." And I meant it too; and I guess every one else thought so at first, and I thought we was going to have a real good time. Then they played some pieces by a feller named Casella. I got my program here so I can spell the names. These pieces began soundin' sort of queer, but there was a part like a lullaby that warn't so bad, and then they started in on a waltz. They called it ridicule, so I guess they wasn't in earnest, but none of the men smiled while they was playin' so you couldn't tell exactly, they might have been in earnest. Anyways, I could hardly sit there. My back teeth got to actin' up so I was afraid folks might hear 'em. I guess the people all thought that was funny cause every body laughed too and would you believe it, they came out and did it again! I felt kind of sorry for them. I don't believe they knew they was bein' laughed at.

Well, after that every body got up and went out for a little exercise, they was all on edge so, but they all got over it, and we all went back in. I thought I might as well see it thro.

Purty soon a real nice lookin' lady all dressed in purple came out and sat at the piano, and the men all came out again and I thought now they will play some real nice music out of respect for the lady. But, by gosh! I never did see the beat of what they did then. Every fiddle played a different tune and when she tried to 'butt in' they all tried to drown her out. I think she could have played real well too, if they'd a let her. She had a real style to her and got in some good runs and things when she got a chance. Sometimes I thought she was a little mad the way she pounded the piano, but I didn't blame her.

They was a blond feller (Edouard Bredshall) turnin' the pages for her and he looked real scared too, as if he didn't know what they was a goin' to do either.

Honest to goodness, I got sort of uneasy and began lookin' around.

A feller can't tell nowadays what might happen. There might be a riot or somethin', but everybody seemed to be alright, I guess folks control theirselves purty well nowadays, they all have gone thro so much. Of course the players might have had some awful experience in some other town, or might have thought they saw one of the sixty families in the audience, or the C.I.O., this being Detroit.

After it was all over we was asked to have some tea and cakes and I thought I'd stay and see what the rest of the folks thought about it. And, would you believe it, they all acted as if they took it real serious, and they seemed to be sane sensible people too.

"Ho hum," I ses. "Rip, old boy, you better go home and sleep another twenty years, things ain't any better than they was."

Yours till things settles down,
Rip van Winkle

Another challenging modernist appeared in the 1937-38 season. It was Paul Hindemith who was making his first visit to Detroit. While his music was clearly difficult listening, at least the programming provided relief in its variety. Hindemith brought with him pianist Lydia Hoffman-Behrendt from New York and Pro Musica engaged tenor Eugene Conley and violinist James Barret from the music staff of Detroit's radio station WWJ. Mannebach, joined by Hindemith who was playing the viola, completed the artist roster. Violin and piano each had a sonata, the viola had two and Conley sang three of the composer's songs. The consensus was that Hindemith was a brilliant violist and, as a composer, was doing as much for developing the trend started by Debussy as any of his contemporaries. It was clearly an evening for intellectual appreciation of music, *not*, as Callaghan noted in his review, "solace for the soul."

The annual meeting in June 1938 illustrated the important growth and development of the Pro Musica organization. Five committees were carrying out the important work of the society and each worked independently under the strong leadership of its chairman. Edouard Bredshall headed the Program Committee; Mrs. Phillip Baker the Social Committee; Marcelline Hemingway Sanford (Ernest Hemingway's sister) did publicity; and Coolidge continued her iron grip of Membership, while Dorothy Tilly led the Gramophone Group. Morse continued as President, assisted by Vice President Ling, and Secretary-Treasurer John Coulter. The leadership was strong, dedicated and entirely voluntary. The fact that many of them were musicians helped assure that Pro Musica would not veer far from its mission to present new music. With that in mind, Bredshall presented a program recommendation that they bring the world's most influential teacher of composers of the time for a lecture recital. That, of course, was Nadia Boulanger from the American Conservatory at Fontainebleau, France.

There were many more good ideas, as well. Other members suggested the dancer and mime, Agna Enters; Gian Carlo Menotti's one-act opera *Amelia Goes to the Ball;* and the Roth, Pro Arte, Budapest and Kolish String Quartets all of whom were to tour the U.S. that season. Viennese composer Ernst Krenek, Ukrainian composer Maria Sokil and Russian Soprano Maria Kourenko (wife of composer Alexander Gretchaninoff), who was visiting Detroit with her husband, were also considered. In every case, a member had to take responsibility for locating and contacting the artists and negotiating with them for a booking and then obtain the board's final approval. Occasionally an artist could not or would not come. That a few had already heard of Pro Musica and were impressed with its mission was always helpful. Finding a mutually convenient date was often difficult. Negotiating an affordable fee was sensitive. Nonetheless, some remarkable contacts were made with rewarding results.

While neither Gretchaninoff nor his wife appeared for Pro Musica, my parents met them socially and took the opportunity to entertain them with a few friends at our home. After dinner, there was a pause in the conversation but no suggestion for anyone to play the piano. With the nonchalance of a ten-year-old, I marched to the keyboard and without introduction began to play *Waltz of the Flowers*. Gretchaninoff announced immediately,
"Tchaikovsky!" It seemed to energize him and when I finished, he took my place.

As Gretchaninoff began to play, Maria Kourenko alerted us softly to listen well.

"He is improvising. It is music we will never hear again."

He seemed to be in a trance and continued to play in styles and moods that ranged from soulful and pensive to lively and dance-like. We sat there enthralled for an hour until at last he stopped and smiled. It was only after a long, silent pause that everyone finally burst into applause. In retrospect I realize that it was a Pro Musica concert in our living room.

When new adventures were not possible, Pro Musica's history was now long enough to enable it to bring back past performers who had been very popular. Two such artists made return engagements in a December concert to open the 1938-39 season. Russian soprano Olga Averino and her accompanist Alexei Haieff shared the program with pianist Lydia Hoffman-Behrendt. They gave a combined recital of music by 11 composers who, with the exception of Modest Mussorgsky, were all living in the 20th century. The audience and critics found much to enjoy in music by composers whose work they had already come to know. Mme. Hoffman-Behrendt provided the high point of the evening with Prokofiev's Sonata No. 2. The scherzo was already widely considered one of his masterpieces. At the end of the concert, she repeated it as an encore by popular demand. The audience missed one special distinction, however. Averino's youthful (25-year old) accompanist, Haieff was a budding composer, a student of Nadia Boulanger and Karl Goldmark. He would soon make a name for himself as professor of music at the Carnegie Institute and Brandeis University. He would also create a very respectable body of orchestral, chamber and vocal music in a neo-classical style influenced by jazz. But at the time, that side of him passed unnoticed.

THE FORMATIVE YEARS

1939–1955

Chapter 6

Freedom in Art as War Looms – 1939

The second concert of that season scores as one of the high points of Pro Musica's history. In an event that many musicians today would give their eye teeth to have heard, the famed keyboard artist, composer, conductor and teacher of composers, Nadia Boulanger, came from Paris to deliver a lecture entitled "What Is Freedom in Art?" She illustrated her comments at the keyboard. That was on Friday, January 27, 1939.

Introducing her to the audience, Morse pointed out that she was the teacher or inspirer of almost all the musicians Pro Musica had presented in its eleven-year life. She was the first woman to conduct the London and Boston Symphony orchestras. She was the world's leading authority on counterpoint. He hailed her as the greatest woman in music of the day.

Her thesis was that a life is free "when one has the technique to employ; when one chooses the means one knows well". She defined art as "a point where thinking and feeling stop in a search for beauty. Stravinsky," she said, "illustrated the meaning of freedom in music." She called him "the greatest figure in music today."

Talking about modern music, she identified its two main tendencies. She rejected complexity in composition with the observation that complexity in any art form is never a sign of a great period. The other, leaning toward simplicity, was what she favored. As an example, she played a theme and variations by Faure. She then showed how Bach, Chopin and Ravel used the same formula of five notes to compose characteristically without departing from the simple formula. She praised songs that children can memorize and cherish as prime examples of freedom and simplicity.

According to Dr. Hugh Stalker, who helped Bredshall to bring Boulanger, "she was a musical personage who outranks most of the celebrated composers and performers who have visited here."

One can only speculate on the special significance of her choice to speak on freedom in art in 1939. Boulanger had been living and teaching in Paris at a time when all of Europe was grimly aware of the oppressive control of the arts in Nazi Germany and the Soviet Union. She described the times as sad and difficult, but she considered music to be flourishing. "Nowadays tears are from beauty, not false feelings," she said as though she felt that the tribulations of the world were helping composers to achieve a clearer vision. The comments were not lost on her audience, which gave her a standing ovation. The Society had already heard from the Budapest Quartet of their irrevocable departure from Europe's troubled environment. The topic must have been especially important to all musicians at that time.

In any case, Boulanger did not return to Europe until after the war. Following her appearance in Detroit, she and one of her favorite pupils, French composer Jean Francaix, performed the Mozart E flat Major concerto for two pianos with the New York Philharmonic. She remained in the U.S. to tour and to teach at the Harvard and Radcliffe colleges for the duration.

In more recent years, I had the opportunity to interview American cellist/composer Arthur Hunkins who studied with Boulanger back in Paris from 1957 to 1959. He summed up her approach as more like coaching a pupil to bring out his own talents and inspirations rather than trying to teach him what to do or how to compose. One of her special customs was to invite a group of a dozen students at a time to dine in her apartment for conversation and exchange of ideas. He found her to be a great lady.

The final concert of the year, in March, was no anticlimax. Among the four choices that the board had considered, it was the Pro Arte Quartet that came. McLaughlin reported that even as exponents of modern music, they offered "little of those discordant, experimental things...On the list stood Milhaud, Malipiero, Walter Piston and Ravel with a jolly little piece of cat's music from Schoenberg. The four quartets made a longer evening than usual but interest did not falter...[Pro Arte] is a perfect ensemble."

The annual meeting in May illustrated Pro Musica's continued growth and maturation. The Board was finally stabilized at 15 members in three staggered classes of five each. That meant that five members were elected each year for a three-year term. It became a permanent arrangement and has served well over the years. On a more mundane level, the society received gifts of china and tableware which could be stored at the museum for use at the post-concert social hour. They were donated by member Floyd Hitchcock who was an executive with the S. S. Kresge Company, where he obtained the simple but attractive cups, saucers, forks and spoons.

At this point, the availability of important and interesting composers seemed to be limited. The Board was pleased if they could bring in one composer per season. The program committee set to work to complete the series with outstanding new artists to give Detroit debut recitals. Thanks to the board's amazing perseverance, the quality never faltered and the programming continued a process of subtle change.

The 13th season opened on December 9, 1939, with a trio of musicians. Violinist William Kroll and cellist Victor Gottlieb were members of the prestigious Coolidge Quartet. They were joined by pianist Frank Sheridan in a program that was billed as more lyrical than the usual fare. A baroque trio sonata by Loeillet, followed by contemporary pieces by composers Frank Bridge, Claude Debussy and Maurice Ravel, filled the bill.

Following closely the concert with Nadia Boulanger, it was appropriate for her American pupil, Aaron Copland, to come to Pro Musica. His presentation in January 1940 was as much a lecture as a concert and provided some of the most illuminating explanations of the course of 20th-century music that the society had heard. Starting with the pre-WWI period in Europe and dealing with impressionism, dynamism and expressionism, he identified the factors that led to the break with 19th century romanticism. A column in the *Detroit Times* found his exposition somewhat elementary for a group that had already brought some of the most prominent modern composers: *To define and explain polytonality to an audience which has spent the last 10 years listening to, and digesting Milhaud, Poulenc and Hindemith, was something in the way of condescension.*

Writing in the *Detroit News*, J. D. Callaghan focused on Copland's description of composing film scores in Hollywood:

Music for the movies has certain inescapable handicaps. It is of necessity subordinate to the narrative and so is not heard by the moviegoer with full attention. The sincere writer, therefore, is bound to feel a little frustrated by the result.

On the other hand, many of the directors have a sincere appreciation of music and are willing to permit a composer to develop his music as he sees fit… There is a great opportunity for composers who write for the films to develop in a new medium and give expression to forms which other conditions do not permit.

Probably the best known film for which Copland composed the score was *Of Mice and Men.*

The composer also took a dig at symphony audiences. "They just don't seem to be willing to listen to anything which is unfamiliar."

He illustrated his comments at the piano playing samples of music by the contemporaries he was talking about. He traced the development of styles from Debussy, to the work of the important moderns from Ravel to Schoenberg. Then he sought to demonstrate how it all related to the music of the Mexican composer Carlos Chavez, the American Virgil Thomson as well as Copland's own creations.

Winding up that season in March 1940, French baritone Yves Tinayre gave a program of rare, primitive and modern songs. The Board was influenced to choose him by Oscar Thompson of the *New York Sun* who wrote of his New York recital: "He is one of the most accomplished and persuasive artists of our time, so exceptional is the singer's adjustment of his vocal means to the task in hand, so deep is his absorption in the music he sings, so sure is his technique and so secure his vocal poise."

McLaughlin made a significant observation regarding the program's division into half primitive masters of occidental music and modern French art songs. "It became apparent that the old devotional songs with their Latin texts frequently pursued the serpentine courses which nowadays we immediately call modern." Tinayre spanned the centuries from a 10th-century *Ode to Boetius* to 20th-century songs of Chausson, Debussy and Ravel.

Recalling this period, Coolidge wrote in 1965: "It became increasingly difficult to find performing composers, so the basic purpose of the organization was revised to include presenting, when possible, artists in their Detroit debuts in a Pro Musica type of program."

With the appearance of more performing artists and fewer composers, Pro Musica's programming was becoming less predominantly modern. Povla Frisch sang Bach and Schubert lieder in April 1937. Pianist Jesús Maria San Roma offered pieces from the Anna Magdalena Bach notebook and a Haydn sonata the following December.

In December 1940, the Coolidge Quartet included Beethoven's *Opus 69 No. 3* in a program with works by Milhaud and the English composer Eugene Goossens. The audience found the music comfortably accessible and brilliantly performed. Moreover, the appearance of the Coolidge Quartet was an item of special historic interest. Named for its sponsor, the great patron of music, Elizabeth Sprague Coolidge, the quartet was a reminder of Pro Musica's own Dorothy Coolidge (a distant relative) who at the time was still Membership Secretary. The *Coolidge* was reputed at the time to be the best quartet in America.

A few quotes from a review of their December 1940 concert have survived.

Milhaud Quartet No. 10: *The first movement is atonal in too many a spot and the slow movement strident and even downright vulgar. The second is lively, full of melody and the charm reminiscent of a dance.*

Goossens Quartet No. 2: *Vivid and vibrant harmonically, showing evidence of the influence of Delius.*

Beethoven Quartet, Op. 59, No. 3: *Consummate artistry, richly melodious.*

For encores, the quartet played a movement of *Wallenstein*, and Debussy's *Claire de Lune*.

Chapter 7
The War Years and a
Note of Patriotism – 1941

During his tenure as president, Charles Morse continued to influence the Pro Musica programming to favor an educational survey approach and, as America anticipated World War II, a patriotic theme as well. In January 1941, pianist John Kirkpatrick gave a concert entitled *A Grand American Fantasy*. It was devoted exclusively to works of "American composers arranged chronologically to exemplify American music of the past, present and future." The composers were Roger Sessions, Edward MacDowall, Carl Ruggles, Hunter Johnson, Charles E. Ives and Louis Moreau Gottschalk.

Reservations about modern programming were not limited to Bartok. After Kirkpatrick's concert, one critic wrote: " Whether Ruggles was evoking or being angelic or monotonously peripatetic, he devoted himself to crashing, ear-splitting dissonances which the pianist with a yeoman's will brought forth with all the effect of a set of crockery sliding downstairs on a tin tray." That was not the only view. Another critic said: "The audience liked Kirkpatrick's technique, his feeling and ability to interpret moods."

A piece called *The Union* by Gottschalk was the final work on that program. It was a combined concert paraphrase of the "Star-Spangled Banner," " Yankee Doodle" and "Hail Columbia," and it was described vividly in the program notes:

> *Though Gottschalk was from New Orleans, his sympathies during the War between the States were entirely with the abolitionists and this piece apparently aims to prophesy the rescue of the Union from the danger of the Southern secession.*
>
> *Noises of war and frantic gesticulations of "Yankee Doodle," culminating in a formidable outburst—the smoke clears away, revealing*

Bela Bartok and his wife

a mournful variation of "The Star-Spangled Banner" which ends resolutely—more noises of war—trumpet calls, echoes—from afar "Hail Columbia," accompanied first by zephyrs then by drum rolls advancing and receding—suddenly, simultaneously, "Hail Columbia" and "Yankee Doodle" whose combined efforts bring the war to a satisfactory conclusion.

There is no reference to "Dixie." Like many artists, Bartok took permanent refuge in the U.S. and so was available for his second appearance at Pro Musica in March 1941. He did not play only his own music. He gave a diverse concert that included Kodaly, Mozart and Bach. Some pieces were performed by his wife, Ditta Pasztory Bartok, and for a finale the two of them played the three-part suite, *En blanc et noir,* for piano, four hands, by Debussy.

Audience members and critics at this point were not always enthusiastic about so much contemporary music. Negative comments, lurking in the private conversations at the afterglow, sometimes surfaced for everyone to hear. But it was almost always with careful qualification to acknowledge the importance and value of Pro Musica's adventurous programming.

A review of the Bartok concert in the *Detroit News* observed:

The only orthodox voices were those of Bach and Mozart. It seems to this observer that an entire evening of Bartok and Debussy is a little too much to be absorbed at one sitting… One has the highest esteem for Mr. Bartok. He is a tremendous artist at the keyboard and a composer of more than ordinary ability; an earnest scholar and a great collector of the fascinating folk songs that abound in his native land.

On the other hand, from the *DetroitTimes*:

Mikro-kosmos includes everything from Chord and Trill studies and short technical pieces to variations on Hungarian Folk Songs. Some of the brief morsels, jewel-like in spirit and contrast, delighted and enter-tained no end.

This was a difficult time for Bartok. He had just escaped the war in Europe for the last time in a suspenseful journey across Italy, France and Spain to catch a ship in Portugal. His health was frail and, partly due to the poor reception of his work by critics and most audiences, he found it difficult to earn a living in the U.S. It was only through the intervention of prominent musicians like Serge Koussevitsky, Fritz Reiner and Josef Szigeti, along with executives at ASCAP that an appointment was arranged for him at Columbia University providing an income that he and his wife could survive on. Before starting work there, the pair made a transcontinental tour which included their stop at Pro Musica Detroit. Here they found the audience better prepared to appreciate his music but elsewhere there was generally a perfunctory response.

In continuing efforts to help him, Josef Szigeti and Fritz Reiner persuaded Koussevitsky to commission a new work for the Boston Symphony. Bartok's *Concerto for Orchestra* was finally completed and premiered in 1944 and seemed to open a door for the world to discover his genius. By 1948, American symphony orchestras were playing his music more frequently than that of any other 20th century composer except Richard Strauss and Sergei Prokofiev. From being one of the least accessible of modern composers, Bartok became one of the best known. It gave Pro Musica members an important sense of vindication in having presented him in concert twice and heard his music performed several times by other outstanding artists years before he finally achieved national recognition and acceptance.

Gratifying notes appeared in a program of the Detroit Symphony of December 30, 1953. The orchestra had programmed the *Concerto for Orchestra*. The conclusion of the program notes read:

Above almost any other man of music in the Twentieth Century, Bartok was the champion of new ideals of composition and the uncompromising battler for their purity and development. The world of music, belatedly, bestowed on him the honor of "discoverer."

Bartok, whose works were hardly known beyond his piano gems, "Microcosmos," rose suddenly to prominence within weeks after his

*death, when nearly fifty performances of his major works were pre-
sented.*

*Music lovers in Detroit will recall the visit here of the silver-haired
man of music under the sponsorship of Pro Musica, and the charm
of the evening of music provided by him and his wife. It is greatly to
that organization's credit that the composer was honored here during
his lifetime.*

Participation by board members continued to be enthusiastic and active,
so much so that the entire Board was serving as program committee and
suggesting artists for the next season. The prospects included Brazilian
soprano Elsie Houston, the Belgian Piano Quartet, two duo-piano teams of
Dougherty and Ruzicka, and Fray and Braggiotti, an All-American vocal
program, composer Samuel Barber, lecture recitalist Stanley Chappell,
composer Igor Stravinsky and many more. Charles Morse asked for a discussion of whether the Board as a whole should continue to act as program
committee and met with wholehearted approval. Everyone enjoyed playing a part. Dates were cleared and, in spite of the great number of suggestions, choices were made.

The 1941-'42 season opened in December with the Belgian Piano
Quartet playing music of two fellow countrymen, Jean-Baptiste Loeillet
from the Baroque era and Jean Absil from the modern era. According to
both critics present, the first was lyrical, the second upsetting. Nor were
they appreciative of the Tansman *Suite of Divertissement* that followed. In
contrast, they found the concluding piece, the *First Quartet* of Gabriel
Faure, a treat. The musicians were rated as highly gifted.

Half of the two piano team that followed in January was already known
in Detroit. He was Celius Daugherty who had appeared twice as accompanist to Danish Soprano Povla Frisch. This time, with fellow pianist Vincenz Ruzicka, they made a striking impact with a *Concerto for Two Pianos
Solo* by Stravinsky. Their previous success with this work in New York
had influenced the choice of these artists. Soothed in advance by music of
Mozart and Schubert and afterward by Ravel's tuneful pieces for children
and two-piano arrangement of *La Valse*, audience and critics acknowledged
the Stravinsky *Concerto* to be a powerful work using dissonance for accent,
volume for eloquence and savage melody. It was an impressive work and
played for all its worth.

Elsie Houston

For the last concert of that season, Pro Musica presented Brazilian soprano Elsie Houston. She gave the same program that she had presented as a substitute for Grace Moore in the New York Town Hall series a few weeks earlier and it was reported to be a great success on both occasions. The high points of her program were songs of Brazilian character. These included Villa-Lobos' *Carreiro*, with its weird cries of the ox driver and *Dansa de Caboclo* in which the music imitates a frog's croaking. She came to a spectacular conclusion with a group of four Voodoo songs to her own accompaniment on a finger drum. According to McLauchlin:

> *The lights were extinguished; she sat behind flaring candles and beat upon a drum in curious rhythms while she delivered in a purposely roughened voice a series of prayers and incantations designed to conciliate the demons and saints of the voodoo faith. It was Afro-Indian, primitive and blood-curdling and it was obviously expert.*

In the *Detroit Free Press* Callaghan added: "They were the calls of the primitive soul right out of the night and needed love song encores to remove the feeling of eeriness."

A report by Membership Chairman Dorothy Coolidge at the end of that season revealed new difficulties in selling enough tickets to pay the bills. Whereas the previous season had ended with 315 members, the present one had only 254. The loss developed after the disaster at Pearl Harbor on December 7. Attendance dropped at the second and third concerts. Coolidge's remedy was to offer very strong concert programs with more balanced appeal for the next season and to recruit an even larger summer committee to bring in new members from segments of the community that had not been reached before. Another of her strategies was to have a large group make phone calls to remind past members to renew. Since telephone marketing was in its infancy in those days, Coolidge seems to have been well ahead of her time. She also was an exceptional recruiter since her callers were all volunteers and the telephone committee in some years back then numbered up to 50.

The Board followed her suggestion. They brought for the 1942-43 season a nationally famous artist and two other world class attractions that had already proven popular with the audience in previous years.

Violist William Primrose and pianist Arthur Benjamin were the openers. Primrose was just emerging as an international star. Bartok, Milhaud and Britten wrote concertos for him. He played with leading orchestras and organized a string quartet under his name. The Australian Arthur Benjamin, who was then living in Vancouver, B.C., was similarly illustrious as composer, educator and pianist. Their program began with a sonata by a little known 18th century composer Pietro Nardini who had been a court musician in Florence, Italy. Sonatas by Hindemith, Benjamin and Brahms followed to round out a concert that was very well received. While a sonata by Benjamin was performed, little attention was paid to him as composer

The rest of the season brought back the Roth Quartet in January, and Danish soprano Povla Frisch, accompanied by the now familiar Celius Dougherty, in March of 1943. Both gave nicely balanced programs that seemed to meet membership chairman Coolidge's criteria. The Quartet spanned musical periods from 18th century Boccherini to contemporary Ravel and Shostakovich. Frisch enchanted her audience with art songs by 20 composers from Dvorak (*Gypsy Songs*) to Virgil Thomson (*Dirge*).

A letter from Frisch's New York management to Pro Musica's President Morse reveals the society's developing pattern of negotiation with artist managements. The manager explains that he could accept Morse's offer of a $350 fee if Pro Musica could accept a date when Frisch would be touring in the area. For a special trip later in the season, the fee had to be $400. Decades later, the negotiations remained similar but the numbers, of course, escalated.

The engagement of nationally and internationally famous touring artists through New York managements meant that the

Povla Frisch

services of local musicians who had been performing often for Pro Musica were now less in demand. Determined to continue their public recital activity, cellist Georges Miquelle and pianist Mischa Kottler independently produced their own joint concert at the Museum that season. Their opener was a sonata by little known contemporary Italian composer Ildebrando Pizzetti who joined with Respighi in urging a return to tradition in music. Sonatas by Shostakovich and Brahms followed. As a sign of the economic times, the admission was $1.10. Compared with Pro Musica's long established rate of $5.00 for a three concert season membership, it was obviously competitive. No public comments as to the impact on Pro Musica have survived.

By the time of Charles F. Morse's last season as president, 1945-46, a further pattern for the Pro Musica format had been set. The three concerts per season were allotted to a piano program, a vocal program, and an instrumental ensemble or solo recital accompanied by piano. A composer might replace any of these whenever a suitable one became available. While the format was not rigid, it gave a feeling of regularity to the series.

In Morse's final year, the opening attraction was the Guilet String Quartet with music of Schubert, Milhaud and Thompson. The second concert presented duo-pianists Dougherty and Ruzicka performing music of Schubert, Stravinsky, Czerny, Rieti, Dougherty, Milhaud and Richard Strauss (The Rosenkavalier waltzes, arranged by the performers). The final concert was a recital by Metropolitan Opera baritone Martial Singher programmed as a survey of three centuries of vocal music from the early baroque to the contemporary. His pianist was the young Paul Ulanowsky who later became famous as one of the world's greatest accompanists. Years later Ulanowsky released a long playing record of narration and music describing his art under the title, *The Unabashed Accompanist*. It remains to this day a bible of the art of accompaniment.

Chapter 8

A New President and A New Era – 1946

For 1946-47 season, Coolidge became president ushering the concert society into the post World War II era. Among the outstanding artists who came in this era are some who are now legendary. A few seem to be no more than footnotes in the history of the concert stage. But following the format that was then in place, Coolidge and the board members were diligent in seeking and distinguished figures. Some surviving clues suggest that even the now long forgotten performers must have been just as wonderful as those whose names we still remember. For a while, Coolidge and the Board even managed to increase the frequency of appearances by composers.

The opener of her first season in November of 1946 was lyric soprano Rose Dirman with a program including songs by some famous and some totally unknown composers. They range from Alban Berg, Joseph Marx, George Bizet and Enrico Granados to such mysteries as Johann Hasse and Henry Hadley.

The Pasquier Trio at the second concert sounds especially intriguing. Making its debut in Detroit, the trio was composed of three brothers from Tours, France. According to the program notes:

Jean is the violinist, Pierre plays the viola and the cellist is Etienne. While studying at the Paris Conservatory each became a member of one of the leading orchestras of Paris—Jean with the Pasdeloup; Pierre with the Lamoureux Orchestra; Etienne with the Colonne Concert Association. They made their debut as a string trio in Paris March 18, 1927, and have devoted themselves to this field ever since. Concerts all over the world, including two American transcontinental tours, have established their international reputation. Many modern composers have written for and dedicated works to the Pasquier Trio.

Duo pianists Arthur Gold and Robert Fizdale who gave the season's final concert were soon to become world famous. Both were native to North America, born into families that had come from Russia. Gold studied in New York with Josef and Rosina Lhevinne and Fizdale in Chicago with Ernest Hutchenson. Their New York debut at Town Hall in 1946 garnered a rave notice from Virgil Thomson in the *New York Herald Tribune*: "Duo pianism reached heights technical and artistic hitherto unknown to the art." The pair performed many of their own two-piano arrangements of works by Paul Bowles, Virgil Thomson, Stravinsky and other modern composers.

Their performance made such an impression in Detroit that Pro Musica brought them back several times during Coolidge's tenure as president. Inspired by their artistry and success, more two-piano teams began to concertise nationally and amateur pianists among Pro Musica members were prompted to try their hands at the art.

Coolidge's third season was exceptional, even for Pro Musica. It opened November 26, 1948, with French composer-pianist Francis Poulenc and baritone Pierre Bernac. They lavished a broad range of French vocal music on their audience. There were arias by Lully and art songs by Duparc, Debussy, and Faure. The concert culminated in Poulenc's performance of four of his studies for piano solo and six songs in his distinctive contemporary idiom.

In the notes for that program, Pro Musica members were reminded of the appearance of French composer Arthur Honegger in 1929 and alerted to another Frenchman who would soon join the Pro Musica roster, Darius Milhaud.

Francis Poulenc, one of the greatest of contemporary composers and one of 'Les Six,' the cardinal group of French moderns for two decades between the two wars, was born in Paris in 1899. He studied piano as a child and following World War I, in which he served as a soldier in the French Army, he turned to composition.

Besides Poulenc, the members of 'Les Six' were Milhaud, who is in California, Honneger who has visited the States, and Germaine Taille-

ferre, Louis Durey, and
Georges Auric. They are
all under the influence of
Eric Satie, the rebel composer who was their mentor
and spiritual guide.

Les Six were rebels
against Debussyan im-
pressionism and Franck-
ian romanticism, stressing
simplicity and brevity and
exploiting fresh idiomatic
material.

Poulenc has written
in various forms—ballet,
songs, choral and instru-
mental works. Probably

Francis Poulenc and Pierre Bernac

his most popular work with American audiences is his concerto for two
pianos and orchestra introduced by Stokowski in 1936 and now recorded. (It was years later that his opera Dialogue of the Carmelites
was added to the repertory of New York's Metropolitan Opera.)

Pierre Bernac (Edouard Bertin) was also born in Paris. He received
most of his musical education there at the Conservatoire. As a lieder
singer, he has been acclaimed for his artistry and has few equals in
Western Europe. He is probably the best known exponent of Poulenc.
America knows him through his recordings.

Detroit is one of the few U.S. cities chosen for the appearance of
these distinguished French artists on their first trip to this country. Pro
Musica can chalk up one more honor to its credit in acting as host.

Exclusive as the honor was, our city was in good company. Only two weeks
earlier the Poulenc-Bernac team had performed in New York's Town Hall.
Excerpts from the New York Herald Tribune review by Virgil Thomson
convey the significance of their appearances in both cities.

Francis Poulenc, who accompanied Pierre Bernac at the Town Hall
Sunday night in a recital of his own and other songs, is without question

*the greatest living writer of concert songs; and Mr. Bernac is his au-
thoritative interpreter. Mr. Bernac is also an interpreter of great musical power when dealing with the works of other composers... And Mr.
Poulenc, accompanying the singer in all these works, wins the season's
prize for playing beautiful accompaniments in a season where that has
been running high.*

*Mr. Bernac, like most of the other great lieder singers, has little to
offer of sheer vocal abundance. His voice is small in size and range,
though not unpleasant. The skill of his use, however, is enormous. With
an enunciation literally perfect, a musicianship that is impeccable and a
dramatic projection of immense power, he speaks his poems on the key
rather than really sings them. And if the art of the diseur is considered by
some (incorrectly, I think) an inferior one, it would be hard for anybody
not to find Mr. Bernac's musical communication a richer and more
authentic one than is at present available from any of the more resonant
vocalists...*

*Three airs from Lully which began the program were refreshing to
hear and sweet as cool water. Debussy's Three Ballads were less poi-
gnant...The two sets of Poulenc songs...were a delight both as composition and as rendering and in no way less richly fanciful than the
masterworks that had preceded them...*

*'Chansons Villageoises' on words by M. Fombeurre, which ended
the evening, are gay, gallant and boisterous. They give us the Poulenc
most musicians know best and they are of their kind perfect...an occasion for an audience containing many musicians to offer something of
an ovation to a composer, as well as to an interpreter that it is a privilege
and a joy to have among us.*

The second concert that season presented the newly organized Juilliard
Quartet which has since made its own history on the chamber music stage.
The group was founded with the aid of the Juilliard Musical Foundation
to stimulate the development of chamber music. The Quartet was in residence at the Juilliard School of Music in New York and its musicians were
members of the ensemble faculty there. Juilliard's Pro Musica program
of Beethoven, Webern and Bartok fulfilled their mission *to perform great
works and bring to contemporary music the painstaking musicianship usually
reserved for revered works of earlier periods.*

To end the season, Gold and Fizdale returned, having played nearly 200 highly acclaimed recital and orchestral concerts in the intervening two years. A highlight of their program was a *Concerto for Two Pianos Alone* (1947) by American composer Paul Bowles.

Chapter 9
A Knack for Signing Artists and Composers – 1949

I n spite of the scarcity of suitable composers, Pro Musica was doing quite well in that department. Enthusiastic and active member Dr. Hugh Stalker was elected first vice president. He traveled widely and was an avid concert and opera-goer. Wherever he went, he made contact with composers and performers and learned the names of their managers. He then attended Pro Musica board meetings armed with contacts for bringing new attractions. Examples of his correspondence in the Burton Historical Collection at the Detroit Public Library, display a fluency at charming artists and their managers into accepting Pro Musica bookings more for the prestige than the money that such a small organization could afford. He also accumulated a remarkable collection of programs auto-graphed by the artists during his active years in the society. Yet he was just one prominent example of the enthusiasm for this musical mission that infected all of Pro Musica's board and audience.

Perhaps the most perceptive appraisal of Pro Musica's accomplish-ment from its inception and over the course of its history was made by Ed Frohlich who became a member of the board in the 1950s, treasurer of the society in the 1960s and a right hand to Dorothy Coolidge in the last decade of her presidency. Ed was an attorney by profession but his heart belonged to music. He was an accomplished pianist and major supporter of such institutions as the Interlochen School of Music, The Detroit Sym-phony Orchestra and, of course, Pro Musica. In a conversation with me less than two years before his death in 2002 Ed said:

It is easy to look back and remark upon the great artists that Pro Musica presented in their Detroit debut recitals. But in almost every case those artists were still on their ascent to fame and often regarded the way

Gabrilowitsch characterized Ravel, as up-starts. Pro Musica's achievement has been its remarkable persistence over the decades in picking artists and composers for their great potential rather than for their approved and often belated stardom.

The next composer to come to town with Stalker's encouragement was England's Benjamin Britten and with him came his most famous interpreter, tenor Peter Pears. Their biographies from the program tell their stories.

Benjamin Britten

In Aldeburgh, a little town on the North Sea, in a house facing that sea, live Benjamin Britten and Peter Pears, our artists of this evening. The former is the composer-pianist-conductor who has given us the operas Peter Grimes, The Rape of Lucretia, *and* Albert Herring. *This fall his cantata* Saint Nicolas *will be presented in a one-hour performance over the Canadian Broadcasting Network. Last August 13 at Tanglewood, his Spring Symphony, dedicated to Serge Koussevitsky, was given its American premiere by Koussevitsky and the Boston Symphony Orchestra with the Berkshire Festival Chorus. He established the English Opera Company, now in its third year, that gives performances of the highest distinction both in England and on the Continent.*

Peter Pears, a former school master, gave up teaching in the middle 1930s to become a singer. As a tenor, he is now one of the most notable singers of his generation and has appeared in all of the operas of Mr. Britten, the performances of which have received ecstatic praise in many countries of Europe and everywhere they have been heard.

Their program opened with Elizabethan songs, one by John Dowland, three arias by Henry Purcell and Britten's realization of *Three Divine Hymns* from Purcell's *Harmonia Sacra*. The second half presented Britten's settings of seven touchingly beautiful love sonnets of Michelangelo and concluded with his widely popular arrangements of folk songs of the British Isles.

An interesting facet of musical life in America appeared in the opening program of the 1950-51 season. The artists were violinist Louis Kaufman and his pianist wife, Annette. Both were born and educated in America though Louis took up the violin as a child during a two year sojourn with his family in Romania. Back in the U.S. he continued his studies and became a child prodigy. By 1928 he had won the coveted Naumberg Award and made his debut at New York's Town Hall. But he made his home in Hollywood where he became known as the *Great Unseen Violinist*. He recorded violin scores for more than 400 movies including *Gone With The Wind*, *Wuthering Heights*, and *Of Human Bondage*. On the concert stage, he introduced new works of Katchaturian, Copland, Milhaud, Toch and many other living composers. Of the nine composers on his program for Pro Musica, eight were still living. A long lost manuscript of the piece by the ninth composer, Guiseppe Tartini, had been discovered only 12 years earlier in Vienna. The entire program was a Detroit premiere performance.

Norman Dello Joio then joined the ranks of composers who appeared in the series. He performed his third piano sonata and accompanied soprano Gladys Kuchta and baritone Robert Goss in a group of his songs. They also performed all the major arias and duets from his opera *The Triumph of Joan*. We hear so little of him today that it is worth including some biographical information from the program notes:

Norman Dello Joio was born in New York, January 24, 1913. His father was an Italian church musician and his ancestors for three generations had been organists at Gragnano, near Naples. He grew up with the traditional Catholic liturgy and Gregorian chant. He had two distinctly American enthusiasms, as well, baseball and jazz. At 16 he was playing in a band and soon had one of his own. He mastered piano and organ and could read anything at sight. He studied organ with his godfather, Pietro Yon, organist of St. Patrick's Cathedral. In 1939 he had a fellowship at the Juilliard Graduate School and his Piano Trio won the Elizabeth Sprague Coolidge Award. His best music, for all its contrapuntal texture and structural complexity, is simple. And for all its dissonance of harmony and boldly unorthodox thematic materials, his music is tender because he is a born melodist and a humanist. His major influence has been Paul Hindemith with whom he studied for two years at Tanglewood and Yale. He has written for orchestra,

chorus, chamber ensemble, solo instrument, and voice with equal in-
terest and ability...

That season closed with the Detroit appearance of Suzanne Danco, soprano from Milan, Italy's La Scala Opera Company on her American
debut tour. And who should accompany her but the increasingly famous
Paul Ulanowsky. At that time, Ms. Danco was already widely known in
Europe and had sung with many of Europe's leading orchestras under eminent conductors.

Chapter 10

A Silver Anniversary – 1951

banner season followed in 1951-52 to celebrate Pro Musica's coming 25th anniversary. No effort was spared to make it memorable. The Society was enjoying overwhelming success and popularity. Membership was oversubscribed and fit in the intimate recital hall only because not every member attended each concert. Single tickets were no longer available at the door.

A major factor in the Society's success at this time was the stature of Dorothy Coolidge who was active in the city's most important musical organizations. She was a member of the Detroit Symphony's Board of Directors, vice president of the Detroit Opera Theater, and board member of the Chamber Music Society. She was president of the Michigan Federation of Music Clubs, a past president and life member of The Tuesday Musicale of Detroit, and was honorary vice president of the Women's Association of the Detroit Symphony. In all of them she was a dynamic leader and always drew attention to Pro Musica. In the local press, she was often identified as *Mrs . Music*. Meanwhile, Dr. Hugh Stalker, who was then first vice president, was making it possible to engage more prestigious artists.

The season opened with an unprecedented return engagement, the third appearance with Pro Musica of the now internationally renowned duo-pianists Gold and Fizdale. Their program of Satie, Bizet, Stravinsky, Hindemith and Milhaud was ideal for Pro Musica. For their musical sensitivity and technical mastery they were hailed as *Redeemers of the two-piano medium as an art*.

The second concert brought French baritone, Gerard Souzay, pupil of Pierre Bernac and graduate of the Conservatoire de Paris. With pianist James Shomate he gave a program dominated by Faure, Poulenc, and especially Ravel, including Ravel's last three songs titled as a group, *Don Quichotte a Dulcinee.*

This was only prelude, however, to the anniversary season's grand celebration, a whole weekend of two concerts and a banquet and ball. It was time to relish and celebrate a remarkable record of achievement—75 concerts that kept the Society's membership abreast of some of the most important trends and composers of 20th century serious music. It had brought to Detroit more debut appearances of the most important living composers and emerging world class artists than any other venue in the Midwest. And it was the sole continuous survivor of the original national Pro Musica network.

The celebration began on Friday April 18 with the third regular concert of the season. The artists were the Albeneri Trio whose national origins emphasized the cosmopolitan character of the music world and the status of America as a mecca for great musicians. Pianist Erich Kahn was German, violinist Giorgio Ciompi was Italian, and cellist Benar Heifetz hailed from Russia. Each had impressive careers and associations with such figures as cellist Pablo Casals, Romanian composer Georges Enesco, and conductor Arturo Toscanini. They gave Pro Musica a program entirely of 20th century music by Martinu, Faure, Piston and Ravel.

The banquet was held on Saturday evening at the Statler Hotel. There was a welcome by the banquet chairman Mrs. W. Terrance (Betty) Bannan and commentary by toastmaster Phillip Baker. President Dorothy Coolidge reflected on the achievements of the previous 25 years and special guest, the music critic Paul Hume of the *Washington Post*, expressed thoughts on the future of serious music. The occasion stirred national recognition but the celebration was not over.

Back in the Museum's Recital Hall on Sunday evening an overflow crowd came to hear one of the world's most famous singers of the era, coloratura mezzo-soprano Jennie Tourel. Her program was an example of remarkable diversity and versatility ranging from art songs by Purcell and Beethoven to music of Debussy, Respighi, Gretchaninoff and Villa-Lobos. *TIME Magazine* had recently hailed her as "one of the four top recitalists singing in the United States today and probably the most versatile." Virgil Thomson wrote in the *New York Times*: *"Tourel is a singer in the great tradition. Her voice is beautiful, her diction clear, her tone impeccable and her musicianship tops."*

The afterglow in the Romanesque Hall was a glittering birthday party complete with a large cake. Tourel cut the cake.

The report by McLaughlin in Monday's *Detroit News* captures the spirit not only of the event but of the organization's very soul.

> *The anniversary doings which the society called Pro Musica engaged in over the weekend were the sort of festivity you would expect of a 25 year old group which inclines toward the modern dispensations, has a great record behind it and has always combined musical exploration with a good time. The concert Friday evening by the Albeneri Trio has been reported. There followed the anniversary dinner-dance at the Statler Saturday evening, and Jennie Tourel's private recital, a 'bonus' to the membership, Sunday evening.*
>
> *The banquet speaker was Paul Hume, music critic of* The Washington Post, *head of the music department of Georgetown University and a distinguished collector of presidential holographs.*
>
> *Mrs. Frank W. Coolidge, Pro Musica president, spoke of the record of the society in arranging Detroit debuts of great musicians before their greatness was recognized. Louis Ling, the society's first president, brought greetings from Djina Ostrowska, the founder, and from Charles Frederic Morse, former president. The toastmaster was Philip Baker and greetings were expressed by Mrs. W. Terrance Bannan. Hume was introduced by Dr. Hugh Stalker. His topic was 'Looking Forward' and he disclaimed authority in that direction before a group which, he said, had recognized Bela Bartok's genius 25 years ago. He told his hearers that we are faced not by revolutionary trends, but by the consolidation of such trends in the recent past. The desideratum used to be, he said, 'anything new.' The composition of today is the orthodox evolution of the novelty of yesterday. He did not prophesy any all-but adoption in America of the 12-tone scale, popular in Germany and Austria.*

On his return to Washington, Hume published a column in *The Washington Post* expressing his reactions to the event.

> *Detroit, Mich., is the home of a remarkable musical organization called Pro Musica. Several weeks ago this group of 400 people celebrated their*

twenty-fifth anniversary. Since 1927, without interruption, Pro Musica has presented a series of three concerts each year devoted to contemporary music. By contemporary, we do not mean music by composers who died in the early 1900s.

The first program was played by Bela Bartok. That was in 1928 when Bartok's name was hardly known even to musicians. Its second program was given by Maurice Ravel.

Pro Musica has a policy of engaging composers to present their own music if possible. If the composers do not perform, then Pro Musica engages artists known for their performances of contemporary music.

There are 400 members of this powerful and musically alert organization. Four hundred is the limit because the concert hall of the art gallery where the concerts are given will hold no more. And what do you think this costs the members of the organization?

Six dollars—count'em—$6 a year. For three concerts a season by some of the greatest artists and musicians in the world.

Jennie Tourell, Martial Singher...and dozens of other names are found on the list of artists who have honored the programs of this, one of the finest musical institutions in the country.

In a day when the cause of contemporary music is being relegated more and more to our music schools and colleges, with our orchestras and solo artists playing almost the most backward role in their history, it is encouraging to see a group carry on such a program without any suggestion of change.

...Members of Pro Musica are doctors, teachers, real estate operators, bankers, married couples drawn from all kinds of backgrounds. They have not come out of any different musical heritage than you or your friends.

They just have brains enough to realize that music has always been contemporary at some time in its life, and to want to hear the great music of tomorrow today...

How do they do it on 400 members at $6 a member? Easy.

Their hall comes to them for a very low rental. They engage their own artists, paying no middle agent for services not needed. You can engage many of the world's best artists for $500 a concert if you let them play what they want to play, rather than what they are told to play by

their big business managements who think they know better than anyone else what the buying public wants to hear...
Washington could do with a Pro Musica...

The text was distributed to every member and Hume's perspective greatly strengthened the Pro Musica members' appreciation of what they had, not to mention their resolve to continue.

Chapter 11

A Triumph of Volunteerism – 1952

A look back at that anniversary celebration and how the Society managed to arrange it reveals more than musical achievement. To produce that very special pair of concerts, fill the hall with appreciative audiences, entertain graciously at the afterglows, hold a triumphant banquet with a nationally famous guest speaker and balance the budget was an undertaking of major proportions for an informal group of non-professionals. Pro Musica did it elegantly and at a moderate cost because it had matured into a smoothly functioning team of dedicated members who took on responsibilities and did their jobs. The spirit of volunteerism, which was intensified by Hume's comments, reached a peak of proficiency in the preparations for the celebration that year. It was a clear indication of the ongoing devotion and involvement of Pro Musica's officers, board and loyal members. Nowhere is this more evident than in the reports delivered at the annual meeting of May 25, 1952, at the Women's City Club of Detroit.

> ...Applications for membership for our Birthday Year exceed our 400 limit. There were 431 acceptances of which 110 were new members... Florence A.Miller, Membership Secretary.
> ...This season, Pro Musica gave $85.00 to the Social Committee for each evening's social hour which was supplemented by Host and Hostess donations. The first social hour, for Gold and Fizdale, cost us $143.87. This was a gala night and we provided more than abundantly to make it festive. We found ourselves $3.62 in the red.
> The second social hour cost $132.49. We made up the previous deficit and were 24 cents to the good. Our third social hour, for The

Albeneri Trio, cost $138.13, again in the red by $5.43. However, donations put us ahead by $27.90 on the last night.

The unknown quantity of how much the hosts and hostesses will contribute, the price of the sandwiches which varied from $75 to $80, whether we have food left to sell, and if folks wish to buy any, the fluctuating price of the staples, and the size of our audiences make an accurate estimate for each evening impossible.

It is amazing how many people contribute to the success of a Pro Musica concert social hour. First and foremost is the fact that Pro Musica is permitted to entertain in the Art Institute and can depend on the cooperation of staff members Mr. Shaw, Mr. Engly and the Institute Guards to arrange the tables, open up the kitchen, start the coffee water, carry in equipment and supplies and after all is over, lock up our valuables.

The members of the social committee, Mrs. Vernon L. Venman and Mrs. W. Barclay Deyo, took the responsibility of buying the napkins, doilies, sugar, cream, lemons, coffee and tea for each affair. The flowers have to be ordered and matching candles provided. This year, for three concerts, Mr. Breitmeyer of Connors and Laidlaw delivered flower arrangements and even candles for two of the concerts to the Art Institute free of charge. Pro Musica can thank Mr. and Mrs. W. Barclay Deyo for this...

Telephoning for each host and hostess list was done this year by Mrs. Harold William Mohr. We are grateful for the many hours she gave to this and sending notices to the newspapers and to Dr. Stalker for the programs and for seeing that the coffee and tea service was presided over each evening— and for handling contributions of the hosts and hostesses.

The doughnut balls were made by Hagelstein Bakery in Royal Oak. Your chairman picked these up for each concert.

Sandwiches were made by Mrs. A. V. Baker of Ferndale. She takes great pride in making these for Pro Musica. 1400 to 1500 were picked up by Mrs. Kenneth Turner of Birmingham the first night, by Dr. and Mrs. Palmer Sutton of Royal Oak the second, and John Nelson of Dearborn the third night. John reported that Mrs. Baker kept making them up to the moment he arrived to be sure they would be fresh.

Hosts and hostesses (up to 16 per concert) saw that our guests were *served quickly and smoothly. For their generous contributions to the Social Hour, we thank Mr. and Mrs. Mischa Kottler, Mr. and Mrs. Arthur L. Miller, Mrs. Arthur Maxwell Parker, Dr. and Mrs. Hugh Stalker, Mr. and Mrs. J. Leslie Barry, Dr. and Mrs. I. Gellert, Dr. and Mrs. Warren Cooksey, Mr. Dudley Harwood, and Mrs. Henry B. Joy.*

Server Nancy Smith sees that there are four girls as maids. When I call her, Nancy says Don't worry Mrs. Nelson. I'll call the girls and we'll be there. We pay them each $8.00 an evening plus car fare of 30 cents. Nancy was given an extra dollar on the last night for her fine work and dependability. She also makes the coffee and tea.

We also thank Mrs. Berry for the publicity for the birthday weekend and write-ups for the last two concerts. Respectfully submitted, Violenda (Mrs. John) Nelson, Social Chairman

Treasurer Fred Sevald reported that the Society opened the season with a net balance of $1,595.57, spent $2,383.02 and ended the season with a net balance of $1,805.14 before the anniversary banquet and Tourel concert. Expenses for those events, including a fee of $1,001 for Ms. Tourel, exceeded subscriptions, leaving a final net balance of $720.52.

Notwithstanding her opening assurance of brevity, President Dorothy Coolidge had a lot to say.

...I shall be brief in my President's report and report only features of the past season not included at length in other reports...For the 25th anniversary year, the Board appointeed a special committee to plan a three-day festival weekend. Margaret Mannebach and Mischa Kottler were appointed with the President and we met first in May 1951.

The plan, presented at a June Board meeting, was for a Friday night concert, April 18, a banquet and speaker on Saturday, April 19 and a great artist like Jennie Tourel or Claudio Arrau for a Sunday, April 20, concert...At the Art Institute, the Arts Commission gave Pro Musica the two evenings rent-free as an anniversary present.

...To obtain Gerard Souzay on his short American tour, a contract for the season's second concert in February 1952 had been signed in March 1951. The opening concert in the fall of 1951 was to have been given by Lucas Foss, American composer. Six weeks before his concert date, Mr. Foss cancelled. Duo pianists Gold and Fizdale were approached because

*they were preparing a New York Town Hall recital which would mean
many contemporary works well prepared. Fortunately, they were able
to make Pro Musica's date...They are the only artists to perform three
times for Pro Musica...*

*A separate banquet committee was appointed... with Elizabeth
Bannan as Chairman and Louis Ling and Mrs. E. W. Austin as
vice-chairmen...Hugh Stalker printed his usual fine programs for the
four concerts and was instrumental in agreeing on the Tourel program
content...The banquet committee developed the handsome silver program...Your president requested the photographer for the Tourel social
hour...General newspaper publicity for the four concerts was handled
by Philip Marcuse, and Mrs. Nelson took over social committee publicity. Mrs. J. Leslie Berry was appointed social publicity chairman for the
Festival weekend, and by careful team play, there was no duplication in
items submitted to the press...*

*Virgil Thomson, American composer and critic, was to speak at
the Birthday Banquet. His promise had been obtained in July 1951.
Nine days before the banquet, he cancelled...because of conducting his
own opera...opening in New York that week. Since obtaining a speaker
by long distance telephone during telephone and telegraph strikes is the
work of one person, I undertook the job. Six days and six nights I tried
to reach possible speakers. Louis Ling, who was in New York, spent
hours to produce an amazing number of unlisted telephone numbers of
celebrities. I talked to William Schumann, President of Juilliard, Aaron
Copeland, Gian Carlo Menotti, Samuel Barber, Leonard Bernstein,
Howard Hanson, Claudia Cassidy, Edward Johnson, Sir Ernest Mc-
Millan, Rudolph Ganz, Felix Barowski, Thor Johnson and Irving Kolo-
din, to mention some. All were interested. Many knew of Pro Musica
but all were tied up. Several persons gave me the name of Paul Hume,
Music Critic of the* Washington Post. *I knew him as the man who
wrote the able reviews...of the two Coolidge Chamber Music Festivals
I attended in Washington and... his "tilt" with President Truman.*

*At quarter to one, Thursday morning, two days before the banquet,
Mr. Hume was reached by former board member Harry Seitz. I had
asked him to call since he was personally well acquainted with Mr.
Hume. Our guest speaker agreed to come and a vigil of six days and
nights was over...*

*I want to mention the inevitable conflict of dates with other music
activities. Our type of artist and ensemble comes to America for a short
tour. We must take them and obtain a reduced fee because of our size
if, when, and as we can... on an "open night" at the Detroit Institute of
Arts... We must book these artists eleven or twelve months in advance.
Their managers approach us with a tour that is almost sold out even a
year in advance. Is it any wonder that our dates often conflict with dates
chosen four or six months later by the Masonic Temple Series? I am now
giving every date in advance to the library and the other series manager,
but our closed society of 400 members means nothing to a big series...*

*You will not be surprised when I tell you that complete unity, coop-
eration and happy comradeship characterized the society's every effort...
The nicest people in the world belong to Pro Musica and it took all of us
together to make our 25th the brilliant and satisfying anniversary it was.*
Gratefully, Dorothy D.Coolidge, President.

For the 1952-53 season, operations returned to normal and, of course,
remained unique. The opening concert in November presented baritone
John Langstaff accompanied by the Berkshire String Quartet. That combination itself was probably a first for Detroit as were all the program
selections. It was largely because the Board felt that combination would
be interesting, and because the Berkshire group had a reputation for doing
contemporary music that the choice was made. The vocal music, including 15th- and 16th- century French chansons and Samuel Barber's 1931
opus *Dover Beach*, was specifically requested and sandwiched between
works for string quartet. *Rispetti e Strambotti* brought music by little known
composer Malipiero to Pro Musica for the last time, and little has been
heard of him since. The closing work was Prokofiev's challenging *Quartet
No. 2, Op. 92*. Surviving commentary suggests that the audience was quite
up to the challenge.

Viennese pianist Robert Goldsand offered a program that on perusal
sounds even more challenging with works by Prokofiev and Berg. *Detroit
Free Press* music critic J. Dorsey Callaghan, however, found the program
overall to be "deeply satisfying" and an example of how music from different eras can have much in common, so that "composer speaks across
the centuries to composer in delightful recognition." His examples were
Samuel Barber's *Passacaglia* and sonatas by Handel and Scarlatti. He even

described the Sonata in B minor by Alban Berg as "surprisingly conservative, almost romantic in its developed melodic lines and pleasant harmonies." He was most impressed, however, by the Prokofiev *Sonata No. 7.* "The Sonata is infrequently played and Goldsand left no doubt as to the reason. The final movement, marked precipitato, is just about the most dazzling experience in keyboard music."

Callaghan was equally approving of that season's last concert by one of the Metropolitan's most popular mezzo-sopranos of that decade. Famous for her interpretation of *Carmen*, Blanche Thebom treated Pro Musica to a mostly non-operatic program including five songs in vocalese (singing without words). The last was "Tarantella by Panofka which she performed in the killing manner of a diva of the "good old days." It was a nice bit of buffoonery, gorgeously sung."

This was during the period when I was in the Air Force. Home on leave at the time, I was able to attend Thebom's concert which I greatly enjoyed. Nearly ten years earlier, I had seen her perform *Carmen* with the New York City Opera on tour and so I took the opportunity at the social hour to tell her how much I had enjoyed that too. Thebom was especially pleased by my comment and I realized how meaningful it is to an artist to have that kind of face-to-face feedback. At a subsequent board meeting, however, Dorothy Coolidge described the task of putting on Thebom's concert as "hectic. No more opera stars!"

Otherwise, confidence reigned. At the annual meeting a short time later, the Board even proposed making a gift to the Detroit Symphony out of the Society's small operating surplus. At the same time, they raised the annual membership fee to $7.50.

By this time, the programming for Pro Musica concerts had settled on a balance between modern and traditional selections, sometimes even from concert to concert. This satisfied the new music mission without provoking complaints of excess. In opening the 1953-54 season, for example, the Quartetto Italiano gave a program that seemed almost conservative. A few modernists raised their eyebrows, but no one complained. The quartet was a post-war organization that had been extremely well received on its first U.S. tour two years previously. This was its debut appearance in Detroit. According to an unsigned note in the Society's archives, they performed their program of music for strings by Giardini, Busoni, Turina, Wolf, and Debussy superlatively well.

The February 1954 concert brought another interesting combination. Pianist Eugene List and violinist Carroll Glenn were joined by the Oberlin Conservatory (string) Quartet in a program that ranged from contemporary solo piano and violin sonatas to baroque concerti. List and Glenn were rated among the most outstanding young talents of the time. Of the six composers represented, Ravel, Prokofieff, Bartok, and Dello Joio had appeared at Pro Musica. Works by Haydn and Vivaldi were included. Callaghan reported in the *Free Press* that the quartet was "added to the evening by the soloists as a gesture of admiration to the sponsoring organization." McLauchlin in the *Detroit News* called it *"one of the liveliest programs of [Pro Musica's] recent history...Most of the works were novelties..."*
Callaghan's comments were quite descriptive.

With the quartet serving as a foil for the solo violin in the Vivaldi Concerto, Il Riposo, and for violin and piano in a Haydn double concerto, an effect of piquancy was gained...With the piano version of Ravel's Le Tombeau de Couperin, *the pianist recreated the gentle tribute in all its delicacy...Miss Glenn was heard first in the Prokofiev sonata for solo violin, a most unpleasant work...There is considerable beauty to be discovered in the slow movement but the sonata closes with much the same unrelenting spirit as the opening...Other works...were a set of five amusing miniatures, violin duets (by Bartok) in which Miss Glenn was joined by the first violinist Nathan Gottschalk.* Responding to audience enthusiasm, McLaughlin added, *"List played three satirical and highly amusing* Perpetual Motions *by Poulenc... The family (List and Glenn who were husband and wife) did the dance from Leonard Bernstein's* Violin Sonata.

Chapter 12

The Suspense of Booking Composers – 1953

While attractions like the Quartetto Italiano and List and Glenn were booked well in advance through managements, booking a composer was often a cliff hanger. With the 1953-54 membership already sold out and the Quartetto concert coming in two weeks, Coolidge still had not signed a composer for the season's finale. She had been trying to get Gian Carlo Menotti. Failing that, she finally came to terms with Aaron Copland. His countersigned copy of her letter contract, negotiated by a series of letters and long distance phone calls, finally reached her a week before the November 19 opening with his agreement to appear with the famous soprano, Patricia Neway on March 19.

An unsigned report in the *Detroit News* of March 20 described the evening in detail:

> Copland had the first half to himself, delivering an address of 45 minutes or so, entitled "The Composer's Experience." Then Miss Neway came forward with Copland at the keys and she sang some memorable songs.
>
> First came a full dozen of Emily Dickinson poems, set by Copland three years ago. Then there were three by Gauthier, set by Berlioz in the middle of the last century. Finally, she sang the moving aria of Magda, from "The Consul." That was the remarkable musical drama by Menotti in which she made her famous stellar bow to Broadway in 1950.
>
> Copland told the crowd that "great poetry is self-sufficient and seems not to need music." But Emily Dickinson's verse he found full of musical suggestion and, intending to set but one, he soon found himself the composer of a cycle.

He lamented the coldness which America exhibits toward "serious" music composed by its sons and he estimated that five percent would cover the amount annually performed by American symphony orchestras.

"It is still curious to the United States public," said the Brooklyn born Copland, "that an American should devote his life to a work at which he cannot hope to make money."

His settings of Dickinson's strange, sentimental, picturesque and oddly devout verses— with their broken rhymes and their strictly personal technique— reach back in modern musical speech to the forward reachings of Emily's own fashion and are, therefore, of a peculiar propriety.

Copland's scorn of the tonic chord is identical with Emily's contempt for a conventional rhyme; each is very well occasionally, but neither is worth consistent obeisance.

So he seeks to underscore her emotion, without trying to fit her into the pattern of key; most successfully, I would say, in the one called "Heart, We Will Forget Him," in "Sleep Is Supposed to Be," which belongs definitely in the recital repertory, and in the concluding "The Chariot." Miss Neway sang them all in her rich, emotional voice...as if she loved every syllable...in closing, her pure, dramatic and disturbing quotation from "The Consul" was the foremost musical delivery of the evening. Called Magda's Aria, it says My name is woman and my eyes are the color of tears, ending the concert on an overwhelmingly powerful dramatic note.

Booking a composer for the 54-55 season was even more suspenseful. Opening and closing attractions were signed well in advance. The New Music Quartet was to be on December 3. Soprano Phyllis Curtin, who had just signed with the Metropolitan Opera would appear on May 13 after the Met's season had ended. For mid-season, Dorothy Coolidge was determined to bring French composer Darius Milhaud. At a Board meeting in May of '54, she expressed her intent with the forewarning that Milhaud's official fee was $1,000 and pianist Zadel Skolovsky, who would perform his music, normally charged $8,000. Dorothy planned to offer $800 for both, plus the prestige of playing for Pro Musica. Everyone already knew she was a good salesman but this sounded too ambitious. On the other hand, Dorothy had good connections.

She enlisted the interest of Richard Leach, vice president and director of the Aspen Summer Institute in Colorado and a good friend of Milhaud. He urged her to come to Aspen in July when she would be attending a board meeting of the National Federation of Music Clubs in Denver. Milhaud would be there then. Leach guaranteed her a personal meeting with the composer. That was followed by months of correspondence which finally concluded with an agreement for Milhaud and Skolovsky to appear in Detroit. It was only confirmed by a telegram from Milhaud on September 28 that he would be there on December 10th during the winter break at Mills College in California where he was a member of the faculty. Dorothy swallowed hard over having two concerts one week apart but it was nonetheless a triumph. To do it, Skolovsky, who wanted very much to appear with Milhaud, cancelled a tour to Portugal while Milhaud added Detroit to his itinerary en route to Milan, Italy, for a performance of his *King David* at La Scala Opera. To supplement Pro Musica's fee, Dorothy arranged a second appearance for them at Michigan State University.

The series was a sensation.

In the *Detroit Free Press*, Callaghan praised the New Music Quartet for "sensitiveness to expression and nuance and its ability to create tonal beauty." He also commented approvingly that their name did not mean that they were devoted exclusively to new music. He found their performance of Villa Lobos' *Quartet No. 7* "filled with beauty and interest...a second movement is an andante...a nostalgic melody and basso ostinato which underlies most of the movement and is carried by the second violin." Music in the first half of the program was from the 17th and 18th centuries.

A week later Milhaud, who was a semi-invalid, relaxed in an easy chair on the small stage and talked about the role of music in modern society and the influence of jazz on his composing, giving the example of *Le boeuf sur le toit* (the bull on the roof). In recent years we have seen the phenomenon of what is called the *crossover* program in which classical and popular music blend, or classical musicians perform jazz or popular pieces. Here we had an example at Pro Musica in 1954.

Having officially joined Pro Musica only that season, this was the second concert I attended as a regular member. I recall especially Milhaud commenting on how amateur performance at home and in small casual groups, or even in community orchestras, was the real life of music. He spoke enthusiastically about his friendship with his former pupil, jazz pianist Dave Brubeck and its influence on his music. Brubeck had worked with the Frenchman at Mills College. They collaborated on synthesizing the jazz and classical idioms. Meanwhile, Skolovsky illustrated Milhaud's points at the keyboard. The composer's commentary continued almost seamlessly at the afterglow as people raised questions stimulated by his remarks to complete a memorable evening with a great figure in music. Many in the audience observed that the appearance of Milhaud made music history in Detroit, yet no press reports of this concert have survived.

More of Pro Musica's magic was evident in the arrangement of the end of season concert by Phyllis Curtin. Dorothy signed it at an affordable fee a year in advance. Within days of the signing, Curtin left the Colbert Management to join Columbia Artists, signed a contract with the Metropolitan Opera, and her fee skyrocketed. But Pro Musica already had its contract.

I had heard and met Curtin while I was a student at Harvard where she appeared in Sanders Theater concerts while still studying with Olga Avierino and Boris Goldovsky. She made a specialty at that time of singing songs by Daniel Pinkham, one of which was included in her Pro Musica program. Pinkham was also a fresh young talent who became friends with her during collaborations in the Boston/Cambridge music community.

Most pleasing to the Detroit audience, her program had popular appeal while still meeting Pro Musica criteria. As she was credited in the *New York Times*, it consisted entirely of unhackneyed selections. Special among them were the *Hermit Songs* by Samuel Barber and five Argentinian songs by Alberto Ginastera.

All three concerts were Detroit debut appearances of the artists. Coolidge was exultant at the next annual meeting. Her goal for the next season was to match the quality and avoid the scheduling problem of two concerts only a week apart. Ready to plan with the Board, she had a list of ten composers, four two-piano teams, fourteen pianists, four women singers, three men singers and twelve ensembles. The Board voted to bring Metropolitan Opera baritone Martial Singher, the Totenberg Ensemble of nine musicians, and English pianist Moura Lympany who was known to Detroiters through her recordings. Dorothy's report to the Board tells the story:

In New York I was able to obtain Singher's telephone number and talked directly to him. I had many interesting times at Aspen last summer with him and his charming family. He agreed to my fee—half his quoted fee—if he could obtain any other engagement en route and if Rudolph Bing (Metropolitan Opera General Manager) would give him a signed release. Within a week, the date of November 18 was chosen, the Bing letter received and the Singher manager began efforts to obtain en route engagements. The Totenberg Ensemble made a cut in its fee and submitted a mouth-watering program of Pro Musica caliber in order to make a Detroit debut under our auspices January 27. The English pianist took the longest to decide to cut her fee in half—watch for her debut at the Hollywood Bowl next year—but did so with en route possibilities and the Detroit debut in mind for March 9.

The fee reductions were not unique. Artists and their managers recognized that they had to accommodate smaller venues with lower budgets and were happy to do so when it helped to fill out a tour schedule. The artists particularly valued the special program opportunities and Pro Musica's reputation as a distinguished, even unique series. The manager invariably wrote into the contract that the fee was special and confidential. For Pro Musica it was routine as Coolidge was relentless about driving bargains.

The Pro Musica audience had also gained a reputation for its warmth, enthusiasm and musical sophistication. That was a factor in Martial Singher's readiness for a return engagement. And his audience was delighted with his song recital that ran the gamut from early baroque (Lully and Rameau) and classical (Mozart) to contemporary (De Falla, Milhaud and Poulenc).

Headlines as glowing as the one on the *Detroit News* report of the Roman Totenberg chamber group–"Ensemble is Cheered"—appeared with regularity. Of course, with selections like the *Summer* and *Winter Concertos* from Vivaldi's *The Seasons*, and the Bach *Brandenburg Concerto No. 5*, a virtuoso performance was bound to please. Hindemith's *Funeral Music*, Bartok's *Romanian Dances*, a suite by Milhaud and Ravel's *Tzigane* simply added spice to an already satisfying program.

The Detroit debut by pianist Moura Lympany was particularly timely. She had appeared first in New York only two seasons earlier. Noel Strauss in the *New York Times* praised her "refreshing wholesomeness, freedom from exaggeration, impeccable taste and first-rate virtuosity". He especially mentioned Ravel's Toccata which he "had never heard performed with such spontaneity or...exquisiteness of finesse in articulation." She played it in Detroit as well with similar reaction by Josef Mossman in the *Detroit News*.

At the annual meeting in May of that year the Society was again riding a wave of success. Membership chairman Esther Chase reported a record 462 memberships which she credited to the initiative of members, especially Board members, in bringing in new subscribers and winning back old ones. Her records indicated a 30 percent turnover from year to year. Coolidge set the record in recruitment with eight renewals and 12 new members. There was no advertising. Press releases published in the newspapers announced the season program and mailings to present and past members invited subscriptions.

Treasurer David Sutter, an executive of the St. Clair Shores National Bank, reported a healthy balance sheet. Artist fees for the three concerts had amounted to $2,100 while production, printing and other expenses amounted to only an additional $794. For the year there was a $570 operating surplus to add to a previous balance leaving $1,566 cash on hand. This, plus reputation, good will and membership loyalty was the sum total of Pro Musica assets. The Society was on a zero budget balance basis and paid its way with membership sales only from year to year.

The sense of having a good time at a Pro Musica concert or business meeting was enhanced by the flush of success and added to by Sutter who built small jokes into his treasurer's report. His most persistent year after year detailing was to report the exact number of doughnut holes consumed at the afterglows. He always got an appreciative laugh. The doughnut holes had become one of Pro Musica's treasured traditions.

Artist selection was no longer a committee project in terms of the search, however. Coolidge reported that she made a practice of combing the music section of one of the New York papers every Sunday along with scanning the hundreds of brochures sent to her by artist managements. She would then arrive at a Board meeting armed with a list of suitable prospective artists to choose from.

At the 1956 board meeting, the list included nine composers, four two-piano teams, six solo pianists, five ensembles and four singers. In this way she was assured of being able to give the board the most exciting options

among available composers and emerging world-class artists. The board members then prioritized three choices for their president to seek dates and contracts. For the 1956-57 season, the choices were the 14-member ensemble,
I Solisti di Zagreb, composer Lukas Foss and soprano Lois Marshall, all of whom Coolidge proceeded to book.

That was also the annual meeting when I was first nominated for the Board. I was not elected.

OLD WINE IN NEW BOTTLES

1956–1974

Chapter 13
Discovering the Ultimate
Musical Experience – 1956

Coming from a major cultural center (Zagreb) in Yugoslavia, cellist Antonio Janigro and his ensemble of solo virtuosos had just taken the concert world of Europe by storm. The ensemble was received with wild enthusiasm in 1955 during its inaugural tour of Austria, Germany, France, Holland and England. Pro Musica was again very timely in being able to present I Solisti on its first tour of the U.S. for the Society's 30th season.

I recall that concert vividly. The 14 musicians were overflowing the tiny recital hall stage with conductor and solo cellist Janigro practically in the laps of people in the front row of the packed hall. And that was where I sat, barely three feet from the cellist as he played the Boccherini Cello Concerto that opened the program. The intimacy of the situation was indescribable. I became aware of the overwhelming beauty and intensity of the experience. It awoke me to one of Pro Musica's most important features. .

There is nothing to compare with hearing the world's greatest artists perform in an intimate salon where the listener can sense every subtlety of expression of the performers. The DIA's Recital Hall, even though its acoustics are not superb, affords that experience. You can hear everything. From any seat in the hall you are close enough to note every motion, every expression. You are aware of the artists' intense effort and share their total involvement in the music. It is almost like having the performance at home in your living room. It outclasses the experience of listening to even the greatest artist in a large hall (or in a stadium with amplification) or even the finest recording on the most perfect sound system.

Coolidge and the Board immediately booked Janigro and his ensemble for a return engagement the next season.

Old Wine in New Bottles

For the appearance of composer/pianist Lukas Foss, the Society revived an early practice. The first string players of the Detroit Symphony were engaged to join in performing Foss' music. They were a formidable group. First violin Mischa Mischakoff had been concertmaster of the NBC Symphony under Toscanini and now held that post with the DSO. Second violin was assistant concertmaster Gordon Staples who was later hand picked by Mischakoff to succeed him. Violist William Preucil was a leading member of his section in the orchestra and Paul Olefsky was the virtuoso principal cellist.

Writing in the *Detroit News*, Mossman described the opening string quartet composed in 1947:

> A *rhapsodic work which often soared both emotionally and intellectually...The quartet had some moments when it could be doubted that Foss had much to say, but still he said it charmingly and ardently...Foss appeared as piano soloist playing a group of his own works and in his* Two Part Inventions *the content was just as remindful of Bach as the title...Next Foss appeared as accompanist in his* Capriccio *for a cello played by Olefsky who on the previous night had scored a success as soloist with the Detroit Symphony...The Capriccio was a lilting pleasure, definitively played by Olefsky and the composer. For the finale, Foss joined the quartet in Bach's F minor concerto for piano and strings, lesser but still exuberant Bach.*

Foss also spoke at length under the announced title of *Some thoughts on the Writing and Understanding of Modern Music*. In reporting his comments, Mossman mentioned that Foss drew long, loud laughs from the audience.

> But for all his humor, Foss spoke with searching good sense of the progress and building of music, examining the emptiness of cant phrases like 'self expression' and 'inspiration,' concluding that talent means the ability to work hard and, paraphrasing Bach, to comment that the talented work; the less talented just keep busy... Foss paid high tribute to his colleagues of the evening, adding that he had arrived in Detroit in time to hear the Detroit Symphony Thursday night and had no idea that Detroit had such a magnificent orchestra. He also remarked that he had learned to know many of the great symphonic works during his student

days in Paris at the Concerts Colonne under Paul Paray, now conductor of the Detroit Symphony.

Lois Marshall

On hearing the season's final concert, Harvey Taylor, Music Editor of the *Detroit Times* described soprano Lois Marshall as "the brilliant Canadian soprano who could give music lessons to most of the brighter stars at the Met." In the *Detroit News*, Mossman alluded to her inspiring personal story: "a young Canadian who triumphed spiritually over a crippling attack of polio to become a concert singer of almost legendary power and precision...Miss Marshall was at her best in Constanze's aria from Mozart's Abduction from the Seraglio...In response to the enthusiasm of the audience which filled the hall, she added songs by Mahler and Schubert and three 16th century airs arranged by Arnold Dolmetsch." As usual, the Pro Musica Board had been prescient in choosing her but it was not a difficult choice. Marshall had won the Naumberg Award and the unqualified praise of conductor Arturo Toscanini.

I Solisti di Zagreb returned in the fall of 1957 and their performance was, if anything, even more satisfying. Composers on the program ranged from Corelli to Hindemith. In appearing two seasons in a row, they joined a very slim roster of artists who appeared for Pro Musica more than once.

Capitalizing on their skill at catching spectacular new artists, Coolidge and the Board followed with the brilliant, young pianist Grant Johannesen. He had studied in France with Robert Casadesus and Egon Petri and had just completed a triumphant concert tour of Europe with Dimitri Mitropoulos and the New York Philharmonic. On his visit to Detroit, he performed with Paul Paray and the Detroit Symphony as well as giving a concert for Pro Musica.

American pianist/composer Paul Creston, who was enjoying a nationwide wave of popularity, ended the season. His name was already familiar to Detroiters who had heard two of his symphonies performed by Paul Paray and the DSO in the past season. At the Board's suggestion he brought with him soprano Marjorie McClung. In accord with Pro Musica's evolving policy, the first half of their program included Bach, Vivaldi, Lully and Gluck. In Creston's talk after intermission, he described composing as *not the mystery people think it is. Each composer has his own reasons and inspirations. My composing is a form of religion and a method of prayer.* He and McClung then concluded with groups of his piano pieces and songs.

Chapter 14

The Makings of an Impresario – 1958

That year I joined with DSO assistant concermaster Gordon Staples and principal cellist Paul Olefsky in launching the Grosse Pointe Summer Music Festival. Together with award winning (Queen Elizabeth of Belgium, Naumberg and Leventrit) pianist, William (Skip) Doppman, they constituted a superb artistic core for the festival. Olefsky and Staples invited me to perform a group of art songs accompanying myself on the classical guitar in a concert featuring violin-cello duos as one of the planned three concert series.

I had the connections to arrange the location and organize a committee to promote it. Already impressed with Dorothy Coolidge's powers at drawing audiences to Pro Musica, I persuaded her to take on the position of ticket chairman for the new festival. She launched us well. While she became honorary chairman and passed the job to a successor two seasons later, the festival continued presenting chamber music under the stars year after year. It was a happy summer interlude somewhat reminiscent of Pro Musica and partly inspired by it. It also raised interest in my own musical abilities among Pro Musica members.

The young American pianist John Browning, born in Denver, who opened Pro Musica's 1958-59 season, was the subject of an unusual controversy. His career was blossoming with widespread recognition. He was a hit in the Hollywood Bowl with the L.A. Philharmonic. Then he was overshadowed by his contemporary from Texas, Van Cliburn, who had just won the Tchaikovsky competition in Moscow. But Browning's career flourished and was built on a wide repertory that included much contemporary music appropriate for Pro Musica. He was regarded by many critics as the superior pianist even in the Tchaikovsky repertory. Time and notoriety gave Van Cliburn the edge, but Browning appeared at Pro Musica.

The composer/pianist that season was a relative unknown. Fr. Russell Woollen was a prime mover in the musical life of Washington, D.C. who specialized in vocal music. With tenor Leslie Chabay he provided a diversified program that included much vocal music of religious significance. Most noteworthy was a suite for high voice on poems by Gerard Manley Hopkins, composed for and dedicated to Pro Musica.

At this time, there seemed to be fewer suitable composers available and those that were approached were frequently too busy. Samuel Barber, for example, demurred because of his preoccupation with the production of his opera *Vanessa*. After Fr. Woollen, no composer appeared at Pro Musica for the next four years. Instead, the Society focused on bringing the brightest emerging performing stars. The choices were invariably top quality as was evident with the final concert of the season.

The brilliant chamber orchestra from Italy, I Musici, came in March of 1959 on its third American tour. This unusual ensemble had been formed by 12 young virtuosi in 1952 at the Accademia di Santa Cecilia in Rome. They were individually acclaimed in Europe but instead of pursuing solo careers they chose to revive a virtuoso ensemble tradition of the 17th and 18th centuries. This meant playing without conductor, each member taking turns in solo and section parts. The unanimity and elegance of their performances were contributing at this time to a renewed popularity of baroque music. Arturo Toscanini reacted to them with *Bravi, bravissimi. A perfect chamber orchestra.* The success of the concept was demonstrated at Pro Musica's concert when I Musici violinist Felix Ayo and cellist Vincenzo Altobelli stepped forward as soloists in a concerto by Vivaldi, and then two violinists, Roberto Michelucci and Anna Maria Cotogni, did the same in another. True to Pro Musica's policy, however, their program included contemporary music as well, ending with *Concerto Lirico* by Valentino Bucchi and Benjamin Britten's *Simple Symphony.*

At the annual meeting in May, 1959, the social chairman's report contained a particularly illuminating paragraph that stole treasurer Sutter's thunder:

> *This past season, we served 5,321 sandwiches and 1,104 doughnut balls for which we paid $275 and $33.18 respectively; we poured 6 quarts of cream into over 15 pounds of coffee and an unknown quantity of tea; and enjoyed $38.32 worth of gorgeous flowers and candles.*

Then we paid $124 to keep our own pretty manicures out of dishwater, get the coffee made, the sandwiches served, and the thousand and one details that Nancy Smith and her three helpers handle so smoothly in the kitchen.

The election committee again put my name in nomination for the board. In recognition of my having sold 10 memberships for the previous season and a reputation as the impresario of the Grosse Pointe Summer Music Festival, the members voted me in.

Chamber orchestras from Europe had proven to be very popular in recent seasons with I Solisti di Zagreb and I Musici making stupendous impressions. Not to be outdone, America provided its own virtuoso ensemble to open the very next season in November 1959. Camera Concerti had only recently been organized and had a more conventional format. It was directed by a great French horn virtuoso Joseph Eger who was at the time a faculty member at the Peabody Institute of Music in Baltimore. Concertmaster was violinist Charles Treger who was already well known in Detroit for making his debut here and becoming, at the age of 16, a first violinist and soloist with the Detroit Symphony. The group specialized in great concertos for horn, viola and viola d'amore.

In the *Detroit Times*, Frank Gill credited the soloists Treger and Eger as playing with great feeling and expertise, and the ensemble as polished. He highlighted in particular *Eger's chance to shine—and shine he did—*in Robert Kurka's Ballad for French Horn and Strings.

Kurka was born in Cicero, Illinois, in 1921 and died at the age of 36. He was a pupil of Darius Milhaud and is one of many little known composers whose works appeared on Pro Musica programs often arousing curiosity to hear more of their music. Among Kurka's major works are symphonies and an opera based on Karel Capek's famous satire, *The Good Soldier Schweik*. Its style is said to be reminiscent of Kurt Weill, all of which generates more curiosity. Board members sometimes speculated on the possibility of programming more of these discoveries, but the financial risks and logistics of staging an opera were too daunting.

Even in the face of audience conservatism, the chance to present new music was always high on Dorothy Coolidge's list of priorities and she wielded a strong leadership on the subject. It was not always well received, however. At the second 1959-60 concert in February, pianist William

Old Wine in New Bottles

Masselos, graduate of Juilliard and a Ford Foundation Grant recipient, presented a new work by his close friend and collaborator Ben Weber. At the time, Weber was highly regarded as a promising American composer. With Weber's *Fantasy*, Massellos brought back memories of a concert by Henry Cowell two decades earlier who treated the society to *tone clusters* played with his elbow on the keyboard. Massellos pounded the keys with his elbows and fists. Coolidge was besieged with complaints. Her response was characteristic. "As Charles Ives' father told his son, you have to stretch your ears!"

Meanwhile, the French connection that began with Maurice Ravel in 1928 was still strong. The 1959-60 season brought another tenor from the Paris Opera, Opera Comique and Conservatoire National de Paris. Michel Senechal was a lyric voice specializing in the music of his homeland and of Mozart whose operatic literature he mastered during a long and successful sojourn in Vienna. Interestingly, his program included arrangements of French songs by English composer Benjamin Britten and no Mozart.

Chapter 15

A New Kind of Bargain – 1960

I n the 1960-61 season, a welcome phenomenon appeared in Pro Musica's selection of artists. It was the nationally sponsored ensemble from a foreign country. Coinciding with a U.S. visit by the Danish Monarch and his Queen, the Danish government sponsored a U.S. tour by the Royal Danish String Quartet. With members who were all Danes and three of them graduates of the Royal Danish Conservatory, the ensemble had already earned an enviable reputation in the concert halls of Europe and toured here as cultural ambassadors of their country. From a practical point of view, it was a boon for Pro Musica since the sponsorship made possible an affordable fee for the society. It would not be the last of such opportunities.

The Danish quartet included on its program a work by their countryman Niels Viggo Bentzon. He was a faculty member at the Conservatory of Copenhagen as lecturer and concert pianist. Two years earlier he had made a three-month tour of the U.S. His more
than 130 compositions include everything from symphonies and chamber music to radio, stage and film scores.

An unprecedent return engagement marked the second concert that season and was hotly debated for that reason before the board finally assented. Duo-pianists Arthur Gold and Robert Fizdale made their fourth appearance with Pro Musica. They were hailed as the finest duo on the current scene. Most of the leading contemporary composers had written works for them. One, a Sonata for Two Pianos by Poulenc, was dedicated to the artists.

Another sentimental return concluded the season. Jennie Tourel, who had helped Pro Musica celebrate its Silver Anniversary nine years earlier, gave a recital that demonstrated again her remarkable versatility—from

Monteverdi to Leonard Bernstein with a substantial group of eloquently soulful Russian songs.

Dr. Hugh Stalker wrote effusive program notes describing Tourel: "... the full low tones of a contralto, the top range of a soprano, the flexibility of a coloratura, the languor of a Puccini specialist... subtle in French, expert in contemporary composers, sweepingly emotional in Russian, and sings Spanish songs like a gypsy... powerful, charming, engagingly humorous ..." You might guess he was totally smitten, but as I recall that concert (especially the Russian songs), the whole audience was too. I certainly was.

The following year, 1962, was Pro Musica's 35th and the artistic attractions were suitably special. The season opened with the society's recognition of a Detroit born artist whose studies with Mischa Kottler in Detroit, then at Philadelphia's Curtis Institute, and successes in New York and Europe had made him a concert star. Many in the audience remembered with pride hearing Seymour Lipkin's first public appearance in Detroit at the age of four when he played one of his own compositions and effortlessly transposed other works into different keys suggested by members of his audience.

Then came another nationally sponsored ensemble, The Netherlands Chamber Choir of Amsterdam, a program that stands out in my memory. From the haunting 16th century *Sanctus* by Jacobus Clemens Non Papa and Palestrina's Stabat Mater, to Dutch and Flemish folk songs, it was a unique and exquisitely beautiful musical experience.

The Choir was followed by the Beaux Arts Trio, then a new attraction on the concert circuit but already hailed as pre-eminent. Their program was distinguished for including works by two other contemporary performing artists, French pianist Robert Casadesus and Russian violinist Boris Koutzen. The program closed with a work that by this time was 'old hat' to Pro Musica: Maurice Ravel's *Trio in A minor*.

My new status as a board member was quickly recognized with an assignment. Stalker was taking an extended tour of Europe that year. In his absence I was given the address of his printer and the responsibility for printing the programs. With no further instruction, I produced the simplest program containing minimal information. It was only gradually over a number of years that I awoke to the importance of a fully informative program. I am even more aware of it as I review the programs as historic documents for the writing of this book.

The season of 1962-63 was distinguished by the honoring of a hometown artist who had achieved world class status and, at last, another composer. Ruth Meckler, like Lipkin, had studied with Mischa Kottler and then gone on to study with Rudolph Serkin at the Curtis Institute in Philadelphia. Recently married to violinist Jaime Laredo, they came to Pro Musica with cellist David Soyer. Their program included violin/piano sonatas by Bach and Hindemith, a Barber piano sonata, and a duo for violin and cello by Kodaly. Josef Mossman gave them a very favorable review in the *Detroit News*.

The composer was Leon Kirchner with the Lenox Quartet presenting three of Kirchner's works with commentary by the composer. They performed his first and second string quartets and a piano trio with Kirchner at the piano. As a pupil of Toch, Schoenberg, Bloch and Sessions, and influenced by the second Viennese School, his compositions were not particularly accessible to the audience. Some wished to hear the program again. Others found it simply unmoving. Coolidge became disheartened about bringing composers. There were no more for the duration of her presidency.

The young Canadian baritone, John Boyden, brought the season to a happy conclusion. Dorian Hyshka wrote in the *Detroit Free Press*:

> *The audience heard the 28 year old artist range with equal finesse through songs by Schubert, contemporary Swiss composer Frank Martin, Debussy and the late Gerald Finzi...studied on scholarship with Elizabeth Schwarzkopf...is all voice, a master of enunciation whatever the language... Boyden has lived up to the responsibility of the artist—to communicate the composer's work as fully as possible.*

John Boyden

A few years later, in a restaurant in Stratford, Ontario, our waiter turned out to be an aspiring baritone studying with Boyden. On learning that we were linked to Pro Musica Detroit, he confided that Boyden had described that concert as the most perfect program he had ever performed and Pro Musica as the most appreciative audience.

At the annual meeting that year there were a number of interesting announcements. Coolidge reflected on the dominance of her leadership with the amusing revelation that programs for the season were selected in the president's bedroom (where she read the arts sections of the New York papers) and that other organizations were bemoaning the fact that *What Mrs. C. wants, Mrs. C. gets.* That was certainly true in so far as the next season's concerts were all Detroit debuts by very notable artists.

Other items reflected changing times. The dues had been raised to $10. Publicity Chairman Thornton Zanolli reported that all newspapers were receptive to his news releases but not willing to print them. In addition, critics were not always available to review the concerts. Meanwhile, the renewals committee was having more difficulty filling its quota. The season had fallen 50 memberships short. Looking for remedies, the Board and Coolidge took special notice of letters from members indicating that ensembles were their favorite programs.

The ensuing 1963-64 season opened in December with the Paris Chamber Orchestra. Following a Coolidge recommendation regularly made but not strictly enforced, their program was split between music of the baroque and contemporary periods. I recall the performance as beautifully played and well received but the almost full house did not include a critic.

Pianist Charles Rosen, the second artist that season, was billed as a phenomenon. Along with highly individual virtuosity as a performer, he

Regina Sarfaty

was a Phi Bet Kappa graduate of Princeton University with degrees in French literature. Again the Coolidge rule was observed. His program was a stunning performance of Bach and Ravel.

Past problems with presenting opera stars recurred at the end of that season but were surmounted. Mezzo Soprano Regina Sarfaty had to postpone her date from March to April because of her spectacular success at the Vienna State Opera. More performances were demanded of her in Europe. For Pro Musica she sang art songs by Bellini, Poulenc, de Falla and Rorem, and one aria by Stravinsky from his *Oedipus Rex*. Already impressed with her rave reviews from Vienna, Amsterdam, London and New York, the audience was prepared to love her and they did.

The pattern continued. For the '64-'65 season Coolidge picked another promising young pianist, Ronald Turini, The Paganini Quartet and a state sponsored attraction on U. S. tour, the 29 voice Coro do Brasil. The choral program ranging from Renaissance polyphony to Brazilian folk songs matched the chamber orchestras in popularity. For '65-'66, there were Metropolitan Opera baritone Theodore Uppman, The Clebanoff Strings chamber orchestra and rising young pianist, Richard Cass. The season to follow would be Pro Musica's 40th.

Chapter 16

A New Period of Transition – 1966

The '66-'67 season was Coolidge's 20th as president and they had been glorious years. The volunteer organization enjoyed an esprit and dedication that would be hard to match with professionals or volunteers.

For 16 of those years, Dr. Hugh Stalker had been first vice president and added enormously to the vitality of Pro Musica. Along with helping to identify and book outstanding artists and composers, he had prepared the programs for printing and enriched them with biographies and notes on the artists and music. He often added recollections from earlier concerts. His notes were both informative and entertaining and his recollections often quoted from the reviews of concerts a decade or two earlier. He took care to include explanations of the music that had been performed as reminders of the unique character of Pro Musica programs and artists.

Second vice president was Mrs. W. Terrance (Betty) Bannan, avid music lover and devoted friend to Dorothy Coolidge. For most of that time, the secretary was Mrs. Arnold W. (Alice) Lungershausen who held the position of official harpsichordist to the Detroit Symphony.

Treasurer was attorney Edward P. Frohlich, accomplished amateur pianist and lifelong member of The Bohemians (a Detroit club of professional people in the arts). Ed's relationship with Dorothy Coolidge was so special that she borrowed her pet name for him, *Edward My Son*, from Queen Victoria. As important as any of them for holding the organization together was membership secretary Mrs. John M. (Esther) Chase, a pianist and music teacher. Her son was a member of the Detroit Symphony trombone section. It was a musical group in every sense.

Subtle changes were taking place. Miss Marie Marti replaced Alice Lungershausen as Secretary. The audience displayed less interest in hearing contemporary music although there was general enthusiasm for the music of composers who had already appeared on the series. And the Board's participation in the selection of artists was simply a matter of approving a trio of attractions that Coolidge had already chosen.

The artist management world had matured as well. The Society found itself dealing almost exclusively with managements instead of contacting artists and composers directly. Coolidge often took suggestions from the managements instead of following the news in the music world to identify appropriate attractions. And she had burned out on the mission of finding composers with appeal for the audience.

An important change came in 1965 when Dr. Stalker found it necessary to retire as first vice president, remaining only on the board. The ill health that prompted this change also prevented him from fulfilling an unnoticed role of preserving copies of the concert programs, many with artist autographs, and depositing them in the Detroit Public Library's Burton Historical Collection. It created a gap in the record of that time.

The change became common knowledge at the annual dinner meeting in June of '66 when I innocently accepted the nomination for his position and was elected first vice president. My only task was to arrange for the printing of the programs for our concerts. This time the job was permanent. Having received no more guidance or instructions than to get the programs printed, I again accomplished this with far less imagination and style than Hugh Stalker.

Solid in her position, Dorothy Coolidge alone chose artists, dealt with the New York managements, and presented each year's program to the Board as a *fait accompli*. She also set a standard by bringing in at least 10 new members every season and let the other officers and board members know, in no uncertain terms, that she expected them to do the same. Few even came close. Her system for solvency was the formula she had introduced nearly 30 years earlier, to have the membership sold out before the opening concert. Increasingly, she found herself obliged to call committee meetings and send letters to board members to remind them of this essential activity. Filling up the membership was always close in those years and more often than not fell short.

It was a relief to me that she was a one-woman show and gave me no more responsibility. I was still very busy with my career and my continued moonlighting as guitarist, troubadour and director of the Grosse Pointe

Summer Music Festival. I now produced as many as five outdoor concerts in July and August at the Grosse Pointe War Memorial in Grosse Pointe Farms with the enthusiastic support of the War Memorial's inspirational director, John Lake. I usually performed in one concert per season as well. This involved year-round planning and preparation. Along with outstanding chamber music performances, there were chamber opera, dance and occasional orchestral programs with the Detroit Symphony on the terrace overlooking Lake St. Clair.

The success of the Festival and its appearance of long term continuity undoubtedly influenced the vote of the Pro Musica Board to make me their first vice president. But I gave little thought to the possibility that I might one day have to succeed Coolidge. Pro Musica was going strong and she was the force behind it.

The search for emerging world class artists did occasion some near misses. One occurred with the booking of Metropolitan Opera soprano Helen Vanni for the opening concert of the '66-'67 season. She had won her first major engagement while studying at Tanglewood. It was the lead in the American premiere of *Albert Herring* by Benjamin Britten. A highlight of her career shortly before her appearance in Detroit was to record an album of songs by Arnold Schoenberg with pianist Glenn Gould. By the time of signing Vanni's contract, Gould was beyond Pro Musica's reach.

A major chamber orchestra from Switzerland was not, however. With a subsidy from its government, the Zurich Chamber Orchestra with eminent conductor Edmund De Stoutz and two outstanding soloists were captured by Coolidge as a special attraction for the 40th anniversary season. To accommodate the large ensemble and attract new friends and supporters, the concert was held in the Auditorium of The Detroit Institute of Arts. The main floor was filled with double the capacity of the Recital Hall.

The culmination of that milestone season was a banquet at the Grosse Pointe War Memorial in place of what would have been the third concert. Once again Mrs. Bannan, as chairperson, gave a welcome. Toastmaster was Dr. Stalker and main speaker was President Dorothy Coolidge recalling highlights of the first 40 years.

The evening was not without a concert, of course. While the celebration was not as flamboyant as the 25th had been, nothing could have been more appropriate than to have Detroit's pianist laureate and charter member of Pro Musica, Mischa Kottler, provide a musical offering for that 40th birthday party.

Kottler had rejected the peripatetic life of a touring concert artist, but he possessed every bit of the artistry, showmanship and charisma needed to captivate audiences. His talent was evident that evening in a performance music by Bach and Schumann for an audience of lifelong friends that was a fitting anniversary celebration.

Chapter 17

Strumming While Detroit Burned – 1967

T he summer of 1967 was a fateful time. It was the 10th year of the Grosse Pointe Summer Music Festival which was to have a special celebration of its own. An extra concert at the end of the series was billed as *A Guitars and Candlelight Cabaret*. Star artist was guitar virtuoso Gonzalo Torres from Mexico City, who switched with consummate skill from classical to bossa nova to Mexican trio style. Joining him were the talented classical guitarist and singer Ron Scollon and myself. We prepared an exuberant program of all those forms of music. Gonzalo and Ron performed classical duos, Gonzalo improvised bossa nova variations, and the three of us together played and sang popular songs in the vibrant Mexican trio style of the 1950s and '60s. Gonzalo provided the elaborately decorative tenor guitar (requinta) part.

That concert could not be performed on the night scheduled. It was preempted by a devastating civil disturbance in the city of Detroit that drastically and permanently altered our view of life in the United States. Instead of performing, Gonzalo, Ron and I were confined by martial law to my home in Grosse Pointe. There, in the backyard, we practiced our program by the light of a burning city reflected in the sky.

My fiancée Marybelle Riley, who was living down in Cuernavaca, Mexico, studying Spanish, watched on TV as the tanks and half tracks of the National Guard took control of Detroit. Learning that our *Guitars* concert was postponed for a week, she hurried to make the trip home in time to hear it. In the aftermath of the riots, the atmosphere at the concert was electrifying. Marybelle and I were married three weeks later. It was, indeed, a fateful season. And we had little foresight as to the long term impact of the riots, on the city, on politics, on our lives and on Pro Musica.

Life resumed its familiar course. At Pro Musica, following concerts by tenor Charles Bressler and pianist Abbott Lee Raskin, the season of '67-'68 concluded with yet another fine ensemble, The Munich Chamber Orchestra. It emphasizes the formula approach to programming that Coolidge had adopted to note that the Munich group was the 11th large ensemble, vocal or instrumental, that Coolidge had chosen to book in as many years.

In 1968-69 there were three pianists booked. Jean Paul Sevilla gave a solo recital followed a month later by a duo performance by Stecher and Horowitz. Mezzo soprano Lili Chookasian, famous for her role as Azucena at the Metropolitan Opera, accompanied by the Chicago Symphony String Quartet, completed that season.

At the annual meeting, Alice Lungershausen retired as secretary. She was replaced by Alice (Mrs. Berj H.) Haidostian who was emerging as another key figure in the organization. Haidostian is an outstanding example of Coolidge's effectiveness in recruiting. They met when Haidostian became a member of The Tuesday Musicale. Coolidge wasted no time in advising her that this obliged her to join Pro Musica as well. In truth, Dorothy Coolidge had invented the rule and used it to net more members for Pro Musica.

In 1969, international publicity triggered by a cover story in TIME Magazine turned the Guarneri Quartet into the world's pre-eminent ensemble and put its fee out of Pro Musica's reach. But only two weeks earlier Dorothy Coolidge had already signed a contract to bring them to Detroit. In spite of their subsequent success, the Guarneri graciously returned at the same low fee for repeat engagements in 1971 and 1973. A Detroit debut with Pro Musica does count for something.

The quartet's cellist, David Soyer, was already known to Pro Musica having appeared with Jaime and Ruth Laredo in 1962. And their program of Mozart, Berg and Ravel was the subject of a rave review by Collins George in the *Detroit Free Press*.

Along with the Guarneri that season came soprano Karen Armstrong and tenor Anastasios Vrenios in a rare joint recital including duets from *Don Pasquale* and *La Boheme* and, as a finale, from *Kismet*. Collins George described them in the *Detroit Free Press* as "two very talented…attractive singers…on the threshold of the big time." In fact, Armstrong was already a regular at New York's Metropolitan Opera and Vrenios was in demand at every other major U.S. opera company including San Francisco and Chicago.

But it was obvious by then that in comparison to the contemporary music mission that ruled in earlier decades, the program philosophy had changed considerably. Even the piano recital of Jeffrey Siegel that ended the season could be considered conservative for 1970—Mozart, Brahms, Ravel and Stravinsky whose *Three Dances from Petrouchka* are among his least startling and most comfortably listenable pieces.

The change was described forthrightly by Esther Chase who had been membership secretary since 1954. In an interview with the *Grosse Pointe News* she explained that:

> *Pro Musica was originally established to promote ...music by current composers, and originally tried to have the composers present their own works. Originally they did. Bela Bartok in '28 and '41, Paul Hindemith in '38, Darius Milhaud in '54, to name a few examples. But this position was gradually abandoned because, frankly, some people can be marvelous composers but not so good performers, and because some of the new music is so far out people won't pay to hear it...*
>
> *We found that people enjoy a balanced program, one that's not exclusively ultra modern. They don't mind a certain amount ...But they'll walk out on a whole evening... So Pro Musica modified its position... will present, as it did last month, the Guarneri String Quartet in a program that does not include one ultra modern selection.*

By this time Pro Musica was more than 40 years old and Dorothy Coolidge had been president for two decades. She provided leadership that was both strong and distinctive and by adapting, she and board members like Esther Chase managed to keep the Society strong. For most of her tenure, the Society's social status was almost as high as its artistic standards. During its years of sold out membership it had acquired the image of an in-group. Attendance still hovered near and sometimes over capacity with the sale of single admissions which worked only because some members did not make all the concerts. Occasionally, extra chairs had to be set up in the hall.

If the membership sold out before the start of the season, Dorothy knew in advance the budget she had to work with left little to chance. Members from that era remember well her annual welcoming speech in which she compared Pro Musica to her New England farmer ancestors. "They always had their hay in the barn before the fall season began," she explained. At each opening concert she would tell the story and announce proudly that Pro Musica, too, had its hay in the barn.

But as program content had to change, times were also changing. More musical series were being offered to compete with Pro Musica's three-concert schedule. As the media gave coverage to other concert series, they gave Pro Musica proportionately less. The general music audience became less aware of the society's unique role. For the casual concertgoer, Pro Musica seemed like just another chamber music series. And people moving to the suburbs in increasing numbers, partly in reaction to the '67 riots, resisted coming back into the city for a Friday evening recital.

In response, Dorothy became even more conservative in her selection of artists and more dependent on the guidance of the artist managers. For the 70-71 season pianist Malcolm Frager gave the opening concert with a program ranging safely between the music of Handel, Beethoven and Brahms to Prokofiev. Winner of two of the world's most important awards, the Leventritt and the Queen Elizabeth of Belgium, Frager had already garnered standing ovations and rave reviews across Europe, the Soviet Union, and South and North America. While his reputation and virtuosity were enough to satisfy the audience, his inclusion of the

Malcolm Frager

Prokofiev *Sonata No. 3* was more than enough to satisfy the modern buffs as well. In the words of *Detroit Free Press* critic Collins George:

> His approach to the piano is very clean. He has immense power...perfect control...a sure sense of the dynamics of a work...one of the many incredible young piano talents...opened with an Aria and Variations by Handel in which he evoked harpsichord tones...then performed the massive Variations and Fugue on a Theme of Handel in which Brahms uses the same Handel theme...a clever bit of programming...two encores...Liszt and Chopin...fully meriting the standing ovation.

Old Wine in New Bottles

The second program featured soprano Helen Boatwright. In her mature career stage as voice teacher at Syracuse University, Boatwright was no longer a new, young artist. On the other hand, she had earned high praise for performances of works by Ives and Hindemith. Her program included songs by contemporary American composers Ernst Bacon, Normand Lockwood, Roger Sessions, her husband Howard and Charles Ives. Those songs were mingled discreetly with melodies of Schumann, Mozart and Debussy. There was an important sense of continuity in the educational backgrounds of the new composers. Bacon had studied with Bloch, Lockwood with Respighi and Boulanger, and Howard Boatwright with Hindemith. Roger Sessions was a pupil of Bloch and the Juilliard School, and had co-produced a concert with Aaron Copland. With the audience hardly realizing it, Boatwright's program had moved the Society into a succeeding generation of contemporary composers.

Chapter 18

Decline and Revival – 1971

T he '70-'71 season closed with the Orford Quartet from Canada. This superb, fast rising ensemble treated the Society to a beautifully balanced program of Mozart, Bartok and Schubert. Like a mirror image, the Guarneri Quartet opened '71-'72 with another outstanding quartet performance, their second for this audience. While the program was more conventional, featuring Mozart, Sibelius and Mendelssohn, Pro Musica members would have been grateful even to hear that eminent group play scales.

The season ended with a recognition concert for Detroit born pianist Ruth Meckler Laredo. After studying during her Detroit high school years with Pro Musica's charter member Mischa Kottler, and with support from the local Music Study Club, she had completed her training with Rudolph Serkin at Philadelphia's Curtis Institute and was winning recognition as America's first lady of the piano.

Known familiarly as *Ruthie* to many in the Society who had watched her grow up, she shared her current interest in Scriabin. The performance focused on two of his sonatas and a picquant lecture describing the composer's self-image as a religious prophet and its reflection in his music. It was an entertainment that evening to listen for such indiosyncratic touches as Scriabin's *mystic chords* (consisting of various types of fourths) which recalled other occasions when the Pro Musica audience found artists and composers talking from the stage to open new windows for them in hearing new music.

The opening concert for '72-'73 gave me a lesson in respect for the artist. On this occasion it was baritone Ronald Holgate. In preparing the program to be printed, I revised the order to open the program with a group of Britten's arrangements of *Songs from the British Isles*. I wanted to end the concert with what I thought would be the crowd pleasing Count's aria, *Un bacio di Mano*, from Mozart's *Marriage of Figaro*. Mr. Holgate would have none of that, however. His program had to be in chronological order which he announced emphatically from the stage. I felt chastised. Coolidge said nothing and the audience took it in stride.

The members were also suitably enthusiastic about Coolidge's practice of the safe artist policy that season. She brought back proven, sure-fire hits for the next two concerts. They were duo-pianists Gold and Fizdale in their fourth appearance, and the Guarneri Quartet in its third. Both paid suitable homage to the society's tradition. The pianists offered a Poulenc work written for them in '53, four years after that composer's appearance with Pro Musica. They concluded with a Debussy Capriccio (*After the Masked Ball*) dated 1952.

To end the season, the Guarneri highlighted Bartok's last quartet between great quartets by Mozart and Smetana. Bartok had completed his 6th quartet in 1939, two years prior to his second appearance at Pro Musica.

Those were the last performances by both groups for the Society although the Guarneri has appeared in Detroit many times since for other venues. This was a fairly common experience for artists who made their Detroit recital debut with us.

A trio of prominent soloists, violinist Berl Senofsky, pianist Ellen Mack and cellist Laurence Lesser opened the '73-'74 season calling themselves the *Senofsky, Mack, Lesser Trio*. Their program paid modest respect to the contemporary music mission with Ravel's now familiar *Trio in A Minor* flanked by Mozart and Schubert. Dorothy had engaged them through one of the most prestigious managements in New York with the manager's personal assurance of the trio's quality. Reading the *Detroit Free Press* the next morning, experienced members of the audience tended to share Collins George's judgment:

> The trio takes its name from the artists who compose it, all gifted musicians with thorough training and a wealth of experience...The program, while conservative, was an attractive, appealing one...one might have reasonably expected a glorious musical evening. But while there were some fine moments and the expertise of the players was clear, this glory was never achieved...

The headline read: *Three FineMusicians do not a Fine Trio make*. It provided a valuable criterion for booking ensembles made up of recognized soloists: a proven record of performing together.

In engaging pianist Eugene List for that season's second concert, Dorothy displayed one of her most important talents. For one of the most prestigious artists of the time, she persuaded his management to accept a fee suitable to a small concert society. In a career that began during the 40's, List had played more than 2,000 concerts on four continents before sold out houses. He performed for Truman, Churchill and Stalin at the Big Three conference in Potsdam and then was repeatedly invited to play at the White House for the next five presidents.

For the '73-'74 season, Dorothy picked up a lead from the music school at Indiana University, made direct contact with three excellent singers on the faculty of their opera program and brought them in as an operatic trio. The program of 15 selections included five trios and amounted to a survey of operatic styles dating from the time of Henry Purcell to contemporary Benjamin Britten. While the program offered little new music, it did include some fascinating musical rarities like a trio by Heinrich Schuetz, a duet from Purcell's semi opera *Oroonoko*, and the aria *Lamento di Federico* from Cilea's *L'Arlesienne*. In terms of the mission to bring emerging artists, it may be viewed as having achieved that in giving recognition to the development of Indiana's music school. At that time it was emerging as one of the nation's finest.

As plans proceeded for the 1974-75 season Coolidge dropped a bombshell. That year, she announced, would be her last as president. It was the year of her 80th birthday and her health was failing. Faced with this abrupt decision, a few board members and I looked around us and realized that the Society had grown old with her. Many members, like her, would also soon be departing from the scene.

Coolidge made no recommendation as to who would succeed her. I made no assumptions. Nor did I hear any plans or suggestions from other members. There were several prospects among the members of the board. Prominent among them was John Miller, an English teacher at Grosse Pointe North High School who was a great fan of opera and theater. He helped Coolidge choose Metropolitan Opera star Gail Robinson for that year's opening concert in November of '74 and she proved to be a popular choice. Three seasons earlier, the soprano had substituted for an ailing colleague in *Lucia di Lammermoor* in a performance at the Masonic Temple with the Metropolitan Opera on tour in Detroit. She was hailed for a stunning debut. Coolidge and Miller rightly counted on the name recognition to sell tickets. With similar strategy, Coolidge completed the season with a return visit of the Orford String Quartet and one of the top pianists of the day, Gary Graffman.

The Toronto based Orford Quartet was making its second appearance for Pro Musica and included a work by Canadian composer R. Murray Schafer. Totally original in style, it is scored intensely for all four instruments with a long mid section in unison that builds into what the composer describes as *ferocious intensity* and finally comes *to a curiously surrealistic close*.

For that pivotal season, the officers and board included Mrs. W. Terrance (Betty) Bannan as 2nd vice president, Mrs. Berj (Alice) Haidostian as secretary, and Edward P. Frohlich as treasurer. With Dorothy Coolidge's retirement pending, the ranks were soon to undergo a major reshuffling.

NEW WINE IN OLD BOTTLES

1975–1987

Chapter 19
On-the-Job Training for
a New President – 1975

The question of replacing Coolidge was not faced openly until the annual dinner meeting in May. But there did not seem to be any contest. Unanimously the Board elected me president and assured me of their vigorous support. While I had never thought seriously of seeking the position, I also felt I could not refuse. Considering the remarkable history of Pro Musica's achievement and the solidarity of the Board and membership, I felt as though I were being handed a holy grail.

As we discussed carrying on, we all acknowledged that we faced a serious challenge. Attendance was falling and our mission was no longer clearly fulfilled. Although I was only faintly aware of it at the time, the society needed to come up with a sense of revival.

Other concert series were moving their events to the suburbs. While the majority of Pro Musica members now lived in the suburbs and many expressed a growing reluctance to return to the city for an evening concert, the idea of making that move was never an issue for Pro Musica. The board affirmed its commitment to stay put at The Detroit Institute of Arts.

Security became an important consideration. Betty Bannan's brother-in-law, who was an executive in the Detroit Police Department, assured us of patrols around the DIA on concert nights. Moreover, we had only two incidents, both of which were minor. In one case, a spry senior member fought off a would-be mugger and sent him retreating down the street. In another, a swift, young thief snatched a member's purse containing only a lipstick, hanky and her ticket. Unfortunately, he did not use the ticket.

As it always had, the Board closed ranks and pulled together to surmount the challenges. The Society had an able treasurer in Ed Frohlich. Tom LoCicero took on the first vice president's post. Maxine Zeitz became 2nd vice president and Alice Haidostian remained as secretary. On the

Board, attorney Pierre Heftler lent advice. Both LoCicero and Heftler were key figures in the management of the Detroit Symphony Orchestra, while Alice Haidostian was a prime mover in the DSO Women's Association and in The Tuesday Musicale. Pro Musica remained networked with the most important musical organizations in town.

But efforts had to be made to enlarge the team, recruit new members and preserve the unique ambiance of the concerts and afterglows. There was little cash to work with. Pro Musica was solvent but had only $1,000 in the bank.

Most intimidating of all, I faced the challenge of taking the lead in selecting and booking artists. To say I was unprepared for my new role is a gross understatement. I had never spoken to, much less negotiated a contract with an artist manager in New York. And as new president, I received no help from the ailing retiree. Moreover, I still had only a limited appreciation of the Society's historic significance. Yet a historical memory was critically important for the perpetuation of Pro Musica's unique musical mission. It was the loyal Board that I depended on for support and guidance, and one artist manager in New York named Harry Beall.

After many years as a manager at New York's largest artist management company, Beall had set up his own independent agency with a small but very distinguished roster of artists. He also understood Pro Musica's unique position and needs. He offered us outstanding artists at fees appropriate for our size and provided valuable counsel.

Then I discovered that Pro Musica was not even incorporated. After the national management had gone bankrupt in 1932, Pro Musica Detroit functioned as an informal group for all those years exposing its officers and board members to personal liability for every obligation. That was corrected by LoCicero immediately. Pro Musica became a non-profit Michigan Corporation in 1976.

The next key step was for board member Jim Diamond, newly retired IRS Auditor, to apply for 501(c)(3) status allowing income tax deductions for contributions. That was granted a year later. Soon after, we established a long term basis for Pro Musica's survival by creating an endowment fund. We launched a campaign among members which created a comfortable nest egg that is still growing. It provides security against financial shortfalls and a small income to supplement receipts from memberships and ticket sales.

Single ticket sales, in fact, had become an important factor. With the change in attendance habits, people began to purchase tickets to individual concerts instead of the season membership. The hay was no longer in the barn before the season began. Pro Musica had to promote each concert and compete with other events in town on a date by date basis. It became increasingly evident that we were up against difficult competition.

The public is bombarded with promotion and publicity for cultural superstars and pop superstars and flock to their concerts. Anything less gets little attention and less response. Pro Musica was selling appearances of artists on the premise that one day we would brag about having heard them first. It was no idle claim. The record was rich in musical attractions whose names had become household words after appearing early on for Pro Musica. A New York artist manager to whom I showed our list for the first time gasped and repeated what had become a familiar response: "That's Who's Who in Music." Nevertheless, it was not an easy sell. On top of that, the momentum for presenting new music had slackened. There had been no composer on the program for more than a decade. It had been easier to present attractions with the most immediate popular appeal.

True to their word, Board members gave advice and guidance. Tom LoCicero let me know that the winner of the first Van Cliburn competition in 1962, pianist Ralph Votapek, was artist in residence at Michigan State University and was available. I was able to book him for our opening concert in November 1975. His program had audience appeal and acknowledged the mission for new music with a piano sonata composed by Aaron Copland in 1941, the year following Copland's first appearance at Pro Musica.

Prompted by another board member, an enterprising assistant at one of the most prestigious managements in New York called me to offer the spectacular young violinist Eugene Fodor. My explanation of Pro Musica's mission and history resulted in a program that ranged from Bach to Penderecki.

Fodor's career had been meteoric. After studies with his violinist father, he attended Juilliard, won a scholarship to study with Jascha Heifetz, then went to Indiana University's prestigious music school. He triumphed at the Tchaikovsky competition in Moscow and was the first American in 21 years to win the International Paganini Competition in Genoa.

His performance for Pro Musica was brilliant. Then, instead of his name becoming a household word, he seemed to burn out in a few seasons as the strains of touring took their toll on his artistic temperament.

I learned two lessons from this experience. Even the most promising performer may stumble. And most important for my task, artists and their managers constantly need to be reminded of Pro Musica's distinctive mission so that they can respond appropriately to our goals regarding artists and programs. It became my job to explain this in detail at every opportunity.

Mezzo Soprano Sofia Steffan ended the 1975-76 season with a novel program ranging from Purcell to Honneger and Poulenc. Both she and Fodor also coped with last minute date changes so that Pro Musica's concerts would not conflict with Artur Rubinstein's appearance with the Detroit Symphony.

Recalling Pro Musica's mission, Board members began to come up with highly appropriate suggestions and artist managements followed suit. For the opening of the 1976-77 season, Alice Haidostian urged us to book *Tashi*, an avant garde quartet of rising stars: pianist Peter Serkin, violinist Ida Kavafian, cellist Fred Sherry and clarinetist Richard Stoltzman. They gave us the Detroit premiere of Messiaen's *Quartet for the End of Time*. It had already gained icon status with hip audiences at a venue in New York's Greenwich Village.

The rest of the season was top quality but less adventuresome. Baritone Leslie Guinn from the Music School faculty at the University of Michigan gave a balanced program that included stunning song cycles by Arnold Schoenberg and Hugo Wolf. The season's third concert presented Bulgarian pianist Juliana Markova in her first year in the U.S. Educated at the University of Sofia and the Giuseppe Verdi Conservatory in Milan, her awards included the George Enesco Competition in Bucharest and the Marguerite Long Competition in Paris. In the same season she was appearing with the leading orchestras in such cities as Boston, New Orleans, and Los Angeles and giving recitals in New York, Houston, Atlanta and Omaha.

That year, 1977, provided an excuse for one of Pro Musica's less frequent but important traditions—a good party. The society's 50th anniversary was upon us and given all the challenges of change, a celebration was most welcome. The gala event took place on April 22 in the Crystal

Ballroom overlooking Lake St. Clair at the Grosse Pointe War Memorial.

Hosts and hostesses poured champagne at the reception and sat down to a dinner designed to match the quality of the Society's musical eminence— avocado and seafood, roast prime rib, freshly prepared hollandaise sauce for the broccoli and potatoes with chive sour cream. A Korean salad with sweet-sour tomato dressing led to a Bavarian strawberry pie. Appropriate wines accompanied the courses.

Mistress of ceremonies was Alice Haidostian but no long speeches were needed. Everyone knew why they were there—music. Before dinner, Ralph Votapek gave a musical offering in the Fries Auditorium, below the ballroom, with an all-Gershwin program for which he was already famous. After dinner, Gordon Staples, violinist and Concertmaster of the Detroit Symphony, performed a Bach Chaconne and a romantic pastiche of Viennese light music.

Making the celebration serve also as a business meeting, Barnard C. Perzyk conducted the society's annual election with dispatch and turned the evening once more back to music. For an afterglow, Marybelle and I performed three of our favorite Viennese Songs (*Wiener Lieder*). Using arrangements we had acquired in Vienna, she accompanied me on her accordion as I sang in Viennese dialect, self-accompanied with my guitar. The evening ended in that sentimental mode with a reminder of the society's custom of having music made by members.

The 1977-78 season was distinguished above all by adherence to the combination of a piano, an ensemble and a vocal program for the year's attractions, and, of course, the quality of the artists who were promising new figures in the concert world. Their programs were traditional, however. Pianist Lydia Artimew offered music of Mozart, Schubert, Schumann, and Chopin. The Marlboro Trio played Haydn, Dvorak and Ravel.
Soprano Valerie Girard's program included nothing later than Moore's *Willow Song* from *The Ballad of Baby Doe,* and the vocalise written for Bidu Sayao by Sandoval intermingled with several rarely heard art songs by Schoental, Turina and Obradors.

We were saddened on February 21, 1978, by the death of Dorothy Coolidge. She had been secretary for the first 20 years of Pro Musica's life and president for the next 28. Clearly, her most lasting and influential bequest to all of us in Pro Musica, was a commitment to bringing composers, their new music and new artists to Detroit. She had never strayed far from the path, and she left us with a determination to stay the course.

The next season proved to be a powerful fulfillment of her legacy. It was rife with risk, adventure and musical triumph and recalled the original goals. It featured two composers, one already famous but controversial, one quite unkown, and a third who cancelled at the last minute.

The opener was composer George Crumb in October of 1978. Violinist Lewis Kaplan, leader of the Aeolian Chamber Players, had contacted me with the tempting information that most of Crumb's chamber music had been commissioned for his group. At the time, Crumb's symphonic works were being performed by the New York Philharmonic and other major orchestras. It was clearly an opportunity that Pro Musica could not miss. I called Crumb at the University of Pennsylvania and arranged for him to come to Detroit.

I was aware that his music might meet misunderstanding, perhaps even rejection. But preparing for that concert had even more difficulties in store.

Press relations chairman Franziska Greiling wrote a press release that gave a rationale:

> Until this year Detroit has not had a program of Crumb's music despite his growing international reputation. In 1968 he won a Pulitzer priz for his symphony Echoes of Time and the River. By May 1977 his choral symphony Star Child was part of the penultimate concert of the New York Philharmonic season. He appears this year in Detroit for Pro Musica...a fact that has amazed at least one member of the musical establishment.
>
> " You're going to have an entire program of Crumb's music? My, you are brave," commented former Detroit Symphony Orchestra Conductor Sixten Ehrling to Pro Musica President Alex Suczek.
>
> Ehrling's remark echoes one made in 1927 by another symphony conductor, a comment which brought Pro Musica into being: Conductor Ossip Gabrilowitsch called Maurice Ravel an Upstart.
>
> According to Lewis Kaplan, Crumb has an emotional statement to make and he has the intelligence and knowledge to make it. In his own way, Crumb requires a virtuosity that equals that of earlier composers. He makes the musician extend his musical vocabulary.

" I'm a traditional composer," says Crumb. "My interest in a wider dynamic range for sounds and the color possibilities of voices and instruments relates me to Debussy and the whole rhythmic side of music."

With no advertising budget, we looked for additional ways to promote the concert. Seeking recordings of Crumb's music to use in public service radio publicity, press relations chairman Franziska Greiling found the record stores sold out and all copies at the library either checked out or stolen. Further investigation revealed that a generation of marijuana users favored Crumb's music for their turn-on parties creating a shortage of his recordings.

As it developed, the George Crumb concert was the first Pro Musica event to welcome a substantial part of its audience dressed in sweaters and jeans and perfumed with canabis. So much for the black tie tradition!

There was still more suspense. The Aeolian Chamber players of New York arrived on tour from the West Coast. The trunk containing their extensive battery of percussion instruments required for Crumb's music was supposed to be following by Greyhound bus. On the morning of the concert it was learned that the shipment had gone astray. George Crumb and I spent the day combing the city of Detroit for the exotic wood blocks, chimes, gongs and cymbals needed for the performance.

Amazingly, all were found. The last was a set of Crotale cymbals that the DSO tympanist had loaned to a touring performance of *Kismet* at the Fisher Theater. Barely 15 minutes before the concert, Crumb emerged from the Fisher Theater stage door, cymbals in hand. I rushed him to the DIA just in time.

Crumb himself was the secret of the concert's great success. Speaking with engaging wit and charm, he told anecdotes about his music that provided signposts to its comprehension. As he spoke from the stage, you could not help but like the man and his music.

That music had a mystical air. One of the three works on the program was *Vox Ballaenae* (Voice of the Whale) which called for flute. The flutist was Ervin Monroe from the Detroit Symphony since the Players did not have their own. The flutist was required to sing a note even while he played his flute. The pianist paused at the keyboard to reach into the piano and strum the strings with his fingers. There were significant moments of silence. Crumb held up a sheet of manuscript written in a circle as an illustration of one of his composing devices.

At the end of what must be considered another ear stretching experience, the Pro Musica audience rose and gave composer George Crumb a standing ovation.

An executive artist of another local concert series had presented *Vox Ballanae* the previous season and had also engaged Monroe for the flute part. Having learned from her of Monroe's familiarity with the music which led to our engaging him, we invited her to the concert. At the afterglow she confronted me with the comment: *Alex, I don't know how you do it. When we performed that piece last year, my audience booed and walked out!*

It was not for his remarkable success as an artist alone that we presented James Tocco. He was a native Detroiter. He also had a working relationship with the rising young American composer John Corigliano who agreed to attend and offer commentary on his new composition *Etude Fantasy* (1976) on Tocco's program. The demands of his schedule in New York forced Corigliano to cancel at the last minute, but a hall packed with Tocco's friends and relatives applauded his performances of the Corigliano and the Beethoven and Chopin that flanked it. Pro Musica was proud to recognize Tocco's well earned international fame.

Cuban-American bel canto tenor, Cesar-Antonio Suarez was described informally by his management as "our little Pavorotti." With him came pianist/composer Frank DiGiacomo for the last concert in April 1978.

Suarez was a Juilliard graduate and had made his U.S. debut only two years earlier as Arturo in *I Puritani* opposite Beverly Sills at the San Francisco Opera. He had also won the Giuseppe Verdi prize for young opera singers in 1976.

DiGiacomo debuted as a composer of opera with *Beauty and the Beast* which premiered in Syracuse, New York, in 1974 and was subsequently recorded. He also composed many art songs using texts by poets ranging from Shakespeare to Ugo Foscolo and D. H. Lawrence.

The program encompassed an array of songs and arias from the Baroque era to contemporary. There were some rarely heard treasures among them. On the one hand, the audience was charmed by the pure quality and tender expressiveness of the tenor's singing. On the other, it was invigorated by the energy and emotional force of Di Giacommo's description of a new, still unfinished opera as he told the story and played excerpts from the score.

This was one of the first occasions when the artists were our house guests. It began as a convenient way to save the expense of a hotel. It was quickly apparent, however, that there were unanticipated benefits. There was the important opportunity to become better acquainted with our guests and they seemed to develop a stronger personal interest in Pro Musica. Moreover, our attentive hospitality seemed to motivate them artistically. A special reward was Cesar's dedication of his encore, *Danny Boy*, to Marybelle in honor of her Irish roots.

Chapter 20

The Care and Feeding of Artists – 1979

I n keeping with the tradition of adaptive innovation established since the beginning by Ling, Morse and Coolidge, I awoke to the realization that taking good care of the artists was an obligation of the impresario. The artists live like gypsies from hotel to hotel and are expected to play or sing their hearts out for us. The least we could do was to make them feel as comfortable and as appreciated as possible. Besides, it provided another assurance of a great performance. Marybelle and I began a tradition of giving them red carpet treatment by meeting them at the airport, chauffeuring them wherever they needed to go, and hosting them as our house guests which included feeding them very well and offering them vintage wines from our cellar. When we ran out of bedrooms, we recruited other Pro Musica members as hosts.

If they asked about our musical activity, we sometimes even entertained them with our *Wiener Lieder*. The arrangements for guitar and accordeon were published in Vienna. The lyrics are in that city's unique dialect which I learned in the Austrian capital. The songs have undeniable charm. Our guests invariably appreciated the turnabout treatment of having us perform for them.

Our hospitality has proven to be a very welcome and rewarding practice. Glowing expressions of appreciation precede the signatures of world famous artists in our guest book. Managements report appreciation for exceptional hospitality. It would also give rise to amusing incidents.

Meanwhile, I was barely aware that my mother, Charity Suczek, had adopted a policy that I eventually came to think of as the care and feeding of new members. Among the many friends and fans she would acquire in her professional role as a teacher of gourmet cooking, she would recruit new members for Pro Musica and seal the bargain with an invitation to dinner before each concert. Having always been busy taking care of the artists on the evening of the concert, I never attended one of these events but I heard regularly that they were good parties. Charity Suczek had a reputation for fostering interesting conversation as well as serving outstanding food. Along with new recruits, many of the guests were Pro Musica regulars and one might well wonder whether the party or the concert was the bigger attraction. In any case, year after year we would see her arrive at the Recital Hall with a jolly entourage in tow. Occasionally we delayed the concert waiting for them to arrive. Woe to me if I started before they got there. It was impossible to audit the ticket sales that she generated but they certainly must have been considerable.

During a period of renewed international tension in 1979, politics created a minor problem. Russian pianist Alexander Toradze was refused a travel visa by his Soviet government and could not fulfill his Pro Musica contract. In his place, we were able bring Andre Michel Schub. The quality of our choice was confirmed a few years later when Schub became a winner at the Van Cliburn competition. His program was conventional but revealed his exceptional virtuosity with his left hand. It occasioned considerable comment among pianists in the audience. Their question was answered at the afterglow when he acknowledged that he is left handed.

Russian talent was represented at the February 1980 concert but no visas were required. Cellist Tanya Remenikova and pianist Alexander Braginsky were new U.S. residents. They had teamed up with clarinetist John Anderson at the University of Minnesota in the Musica Camera Trio. For Pro Musica, they brought American composer Barney Childs and performed his 1972 trio. At the time, Childs was professor of composition at the University of the Redlands. Copland had been one of his teachers. Trios by Beethoven and Brahms and a cello sonata by Franck completed the program.

Writing in the *Detroit News*, Jay Carr gave us welcome recognition:

Pro Musica makes a point of presenting contemporary works and Friday, it was Barney Childs' 1972 Trio for Clarinet Cello and Piano. The composer...was present and described the 12 minute single movement work chiefly as a long series of solo lines mostly alternating between cello and clarinet...the musicians choose their own tempo. The mood is primarily one of agitation. Hardly surprising given its essentially despairing view. Eventually the music dissolves because, in the composer's words, music becomes inadequate.

Then the players begin to speak (some of the lines are from poems by Paul Blackburn to whose memory the piece is dedicated) in overlays of fragments reminiscent of Berio's Sinfonia until human speech, too, breaks down, leaving only silence as the isolation of human experience dawns on them. Childs has enough of a philosophical turn of mind not to recognize and perhaps relish the paradox at which he has arrived. He is expressing the futility of expression.

On the technical level at least, it was anything but child's play and the performance was clean and urgent. These young instrumentalists, based at the University of Minnesota and a trio since 1976, displayed several strengths…[they] produce big, assertive, sometimes raw sounds with Remenikova seeming the most sensitive…a lithe performance of Beethoven…Anderson's tone is round and bright and despite an occasional slip, he wove his lines sinuously around those of the other two.

It was Pro Musica's good friend, Harry Beall, who made it possible to bring Jessye Norman for her Detroit recital debut to end that season on March 28. He called and advised me that for one more season he could still give us a contract for the already famous soprano at a price we could afford.

Jessye Norman came to our home for dinner but preferred to stay in a hotel. She soon regretted it. Some work being done in the hotel produced unpleasant fumes which bothered her throat

Due to her already considerable fame, Pro Musica presented her concert in Orchestra Hall with its famous acoustics and large capacity. On stage for rehearsal, Ms. Norman complained to me that the air was dry. She asked if someone could turn up the humidity. But the hall was still being restored. With the building partially open to the outside and totally lacking any air conditioning or heating system, that was impossible. My solution was to go home for my garden sprayer and moisten the newly replaced stage, still raw wood, with water.

When Ms Norman came back on stage you could feel the rising damp. She smiled with satisfaction. And her performance was ravishing. Norman's pianist was Dalton Baldwin.

The project was a challenge for our organization. While Harry Beall was charging us a very special fee, it was still the highest we had ever paid and we were anxious about selling enough tickets. There were other new expenses as well. For the first time in our history Pro Musica bought display ads in the daily papers since we had contracted to present the concert in Orchestra Hall to accommodate a larger audience than the recital hall at the Detroit Institute of Arts. Tickets were sold by our members and the Orchestra Hall box office. Despite some confusion about total sales, the 1200 seats downstairs in the hall were filled to bring us a small surplus.

The audience showed enthusiastic appreciation of Norman's program which included a group of songs by Poulenc who had appeared for Pro Musica in 1948. The society also made a number of new friends that evening who expressed interest in membership at the afterglow. That was held on the stage immediately following the performance. And there was this review.

> *If there is at the moment a darker, more opulent, more glorious soprano voice than Jessye Norman's, I can't imagine whose it might be,* wrote Carr in the Detroit News... *You find yourself thinking of burnished woods. Friday she came to Detroit's Orchestra Hall on behalf of Pro Musica, sailed onstage with warmth and stately magnificence and sent people home smiling.*
>
> *Given Norman's caliber of voice, not a soul would object if she were to concentrate exclusivedly on opera, but to her credit, she has worked hard at lieder and chansons and her recital (the ever reliable Dalton Baldwin joined her at the piano) was devoted exclusivedly to this repertoire where the size and luster of her voice do not give her any particular advantage...*
>
> *She performed Brahms, Poulenc and Richard Strauss after opening with a Haydn Cantata. Art songs are microcosms of emotion and interpretations of them can turn on the inflection of a single syllable. It takes years for an artist to work his or her way into this repertory, even one born to the language as Miss Norman is not (she was born in Augusta, Georgia)...In the Richard Strauss group, where sensuous tone counts for more than poetic imagination or depth, her voice broke over the horizon like a sunrise...in Brahms' Wie Melodien zieht es she seemed to take her cue from the lyric which speaks of drifting like a fragrance...the effect was radiant, beguiling.*

In Poulenc's Voyage a Paris Norman's voice sounded almost too op-eratic, missing Poulenc's charm and debonair lightness. In the other two songs based on Appolinaire, Montparnasse and La Grenouillere, one got merely a generalized mood of tristesse and not enough of the insight-ful phrasing and finely graded colorations that give song interpretations their character and individuality.

With perhaps one tenth of her vocal resources, Ms. Norman's teacher, Pierre Bernac, used to invest these songs with much more mean-ing. But Ms Norman did shine in the final Poulenc song Les Chemins d'Amour not so much when she opened up her voice as when she seemed to be crooning reflectively to herself. Evidently she felt most comfortable with this song for she offered part of it as her encore and sang it much more freely than she did the first time round with more of a flavorful cabaret approach.

A few of us in the audience were reminded of Pierrre Bernac's performance of Poulenc's songs when he appeared for us with the composer in 1948. We had already become accustomed to taking that kind of historic linkage in our stride and satisfaction in the insights it gave us. We appreciated the information from Carr that Norman had studied with Bernac. It amounted to another verification of Pro Musica's mission to have such a great artist perform Poulenc's songs three decades after the composer and his leading contemporary exponent had performed for us.

That did not end the season, however. Antal Dorati, music director of the DSO, wanted to present a chamber music program as a part of his Brahms Festival for the orchestra. Pro Musica welcomed the opportunity to collaborate once again with the symphony. Three Brahms sonatas were performed by pianist Ilse von Alpenheim and violinist Igor Ozim for this special finale to our season. It was an especially welcome occasion as it reopened the working relationship with the symphony that Pro Musica had enjoyed in its early years.

Apparently we had really captured Jay Carr's attention. About the Brahms Festival concert he wrote:

Brahms wrote a total of three sonatas for violin and piano, all within the space of a decade and they were able to fit handily into a single recital sponsored by Pro Musica Friday at the Detroit Institute of Arts. Ilse von

Alpenheim was the pianist and the violinist was Igor Ozim, a 48 year old Yugoslavian making his local debut…They began with Sonata No. 2 in A major…their performance warmed the packed house, especially in the propulsive finale. Throughout, the playing was plausibly proportioned, diligently balanced and full of pulse. This spirited accord carried over into their singularly appropriate encore—the Scherzo *from* Frei Aber Einsam (*Free but Lonely*) Sonata in C Minor *which Brahms composed with Schumann and Destrich.*

The success of that event occasioned another four concert season for '80-'81 with Pro Musica collaborating in a Detroit Symphony Bartok Festival. The year began with a recital by violinist Cho-Liang Lin. A scholarship pupil of Dorothy DeLay at Juilliard, he was receiving rave reviews in concerts from coast to coast. His concert for us was a showcase of virtuosity.

Ruth Carlton covered that one in the *Detroit Free Press*.

Lin was born in Taiwan in 1960. Before coming to this country in 1975 as a scholarship student at Juilliard, he had concertized extensively through Southeast Asia. He is still a Juilliard student but don't let this mislead you. He is a full fledged artist.

He has effortless virtuoso equipment and the musicianship that controls it. With intense concentration he builds in long, purposeful shaped phrases. To all this add his youthful joy in performing, his good looks and his infectious grin.

Pro Musica, which has a unique record for introducing musicians who become world famous, can congratulate itself for booking another major artist.

Prokofiev, whose Sonata No. 2 in D was listed first in the program, had himself played for Pro Musica in its early years. He should have been pleased with Friday's presentation which did equally well by his violent, gutty, abrasive phrases and the rare measures of shining melody.

James Gemmell, also a Juilliard student, was the eminently satisfactory pianist. He tackled the Prokofiev with the same intensity and fearless risk-taking as the violinist. He gave no feel of holding back, but matched passion for passion. In fact, no one need hold back for fear of covering Lin. He draws a big, round tone and when occasion demands can slash out a fortissimo.

Prokofiev wrote this big, rough hewn sonata in 1944. The first movement, Moderato, for all its quicksilver changes emerged as a tightly knit, dramatic unit on the grand scale. The young performers slammed into the Scherzo, sang the Andante with wistful tenderness and built up to the final Allegro con brio in breathtaking fashion.

Beethoven's Sonata No.7 in C Minor received a strongly contrasted, powerful performance. When the stormy opening theme gives way to the quiet secondary theme it came through poignantly childlike. For the Adagio cantabile, Lin spun a shining, silken tone without sacrificing any of its warmth. The Scherzo sparkled and the finale whirled by with passion and brilliance.

It was fascinating to watch this young Asian turn Spanish Gypsy when he took on Manuel de Falla and Sarasate after intermission with fire and wild abandon. The de Falla was an arrangement by Paul Kochanski of Suite Popular Espanol *whose six short dances exploit all the sounds the violin can make—pizzicato, double stops and dazzling showers of harmonics.*

Sarasate was represented by the Introduction and Tarantella. *After a schmaltzy start it breaks into the mad dance. This is, of course, a war horse with which its violinist composer thrilled 19th century audiences.*

Wieniawski's Capriccio Valse *is of the same period and lineage— virtuoso fireworks and Viennese pastry. Absolutely delicious.*

The series continued in February '81 with a trio of pianist Joseph Kalichstein, violinist Jaime Laredo and cellist Sharon Robinson. Their conventional program of Beethoven, Mendelssohn and Schubert was beautifully performed and particularly memorable for their concert attire. Like Crumb's trunk of percussion, their personal luggage had gone astray and they appeared on stage in blue jeans. It was just one more reminder of the changing times.

Taking part in Dorati's Bartok Festival was especially meaningful as it reminded us that the Hungarian genius had appeared on Pro Musica's very first concert in 1928. It also revived the practice dating from the 1930s of having Detroit Symphony musicians join other guest artists on our concert stage. Among them were DSO concertmaster Gordon Staples and a quartet from the orchestra along with pianists Ilse von Alpenheim, Bela Szilagy and Fedora Horowitz, founder and director of Detroit's Lyric Chamber Ensemble. The program was an enlightening array of transcriptions by, music dedicated to and original works of Bartok. Once again, the society won new friends and prestige with an outstanding musical offering.

The third regular concert for 1980-81 brought soprano Ruth Welting at the peak of a rapid rise from Juilliard, New York City Opera, San Francisco Opera and New York's Metropolitan Opera where she sang the role of *Sophie* in *Rosenkavalier*. As they enjoyed Welting's artistry, no one noticed that there was no gesture toward the mission of new music.

Chapter 21
The Best of Times and
the Worst of Times – 1981

<hr>

As the 1980-81 season was ending, I received a call from Dr. Audley Grossman, Performing Arts Curator at the Detroit Institute of Arts. A newly installed director of the museum was implementing his priorities. He wanted to focus on exhibits of fine art and presentations about them to the exclusion of the museum's extensive program of puppet shows, children's theater, films, concerts and other performing arts. Grossman informed me with obvious regret that Pro Musica was to be a casualty of this change. Even our lecture-recital hall was to be renovated into a small theatre suitable for films, slide shows and lectures. As a part of a wider renovation of the museum, the air ducts to the recital hall would also be out of use for an extended period making it difficult to control temperature and air circulation in the hall. A serious consequence for us was that the acoustics would become less suitable for a live musical performance. On top of all that, the charges for rental of the facilities by outsiders, even the long sponsored Pro Musica, would become prohibitive. We had to look for a new site for concerts.

We had already found a new location for our annual meeting. The dinner, business meeting and election were held in the Eleanor and Edsel Ford house in Grosse Pointe Shores. It gave us a sense of satisfaction to recall that Eleanor Ford had been a founding patron of Pro Musica. Her and Edsel's home had only recently been dedicated as a museum and opened to the public. Its change in status to a tax exempt public institution was engineered by attorney Pierre Heftler, one of Pro Musica's stalwart advisors. His association with the Ford family naturally made us particularly welcome and we were able to enjoy unlimited use of the public areas of the house. Dinner for the 60 members attending was in the spacious Gallery with its vaulted ceiling, followed by our election meeting in the large drawing room. The evening ended with a return to the Gallery for a musical afterglow with Mischa Kottler at the piano. While everyone else was seated on comfortable folding chairs set out for the occasion, I moved to the side of the room to the last empty seat—a tapestry upholstered armchair. Heftler later asked me how it felt to sit in a 200 year old antique. I responded that the elegant Cotswald style mansion and the chair were just right for Pro Musica. Everyone agreed that we should return there the following year.

While efforts to select artists for 1981-82 proceeded, an even more intensive exploration of recital halls in the city was going on. One Board member described it as wandering in a desert of makeshift concert halls. For a while it was discouraging, but the experience taught us to trust our luck and gave us an appreciation of the importance of two features that make a good recital hall: ambiance and acoustics. The DIA recital hall was rich in the first. Located in a beautiful museum, attractively decorated and with comfortable seats and an intimate atmosphere, it endowed our audience with a sense of ease and togetherness. Acoustically, the hall was not outstanding. There was minimal reverberation. But its small size meant that there was no seat where one could not hear everything in a performance, clearly and undistorted. The Romanesque Hall for the afterglow was unmatched as a gracious area for a reception. We found no other facility in the city that was as satisfactory, yet ultimately we found acceptable alternatives.

Then fate stepped in. The Friends for Orchestra Hall committee, continuing their campaign to finish the renovation of the original and acoustically brilliant home of the Detroit Symphony and restore it as a fine concert hall, asked Pro Musica to join them in presenting the new Gold Medalist of the Van Cliburn competition of the previous year. It was Andre-Michel Schub who had thrilled our audience with his Detroit debut concert only two years earlier. The board and I jumped at the opportunity. To appeal to the widest possible audience and fill the hall, the program bypassed our special emphasis on new music; the cause took precedence. Pro Musica's 54th season opened late, on February 12, '82, with Schub's performance in the great acoustics of Orchestra Hall. The program was a crowd pleaser and the artist lived up to the rave reviews he had received in New York. An audience of more than 1,000 filled the main floor providing funds for the continued restoration of the hall.

Meanwhile our search for recital spaces zeroed in on Old Christ Church in the city's center. There were vibrant acoustics in the church, an attractive Parish house for the afterglow and ample parking. Mezzo soprano Alteouise DeVaughn came from the Houston Opera and Pavorotti master class to give our first concert there with excellent results. The atmosphere of the beautiful old church seemed especially suitable as she concluded her performance with a group of spirituals sung with deep feeling. In accompanying her, Detroit pianist Bernard Katz exercised exceptional control to prevent the piano sound from becoming overwhelming in the resonant nave.

When the Gabrieli String Quartet on tour from England performed there for us on April 23 they sounded wonderful in that space. Reporting in the *Detroit Free Press*, Ruth Carlton found the tone "incredibly big, round and bright…Their unity in dynamics, phrasing and style was near perfection, but I was still marveling at the size of the tone… one might have suspected amplification…Whether they are Britain's most renowned quartet, I wouldn't know but it's certain they are among the world's finest."

The concert experience and Carlton's comments impressed on us the importance of good acoustics, which are often overlooked in favor of other considerations. It was a special benefit that the Gabreli's program included the *Quartet in C minor, No. 8* by Shostakovich. This was only the fourth time the Russian composer's name had appeared on a Pro Musica program and the first presentation of one of his string quartets. The one complaint voiced about the evening was the discomfort of sitting in hard wooden pews to listen to music (one of those other considerations). We decided to try another hall.

There was one change we did not have to make. For the annual dinner meeting in June 1982 we returned to the Ford House and the word had spread. This time, 85 members came for a very upbeat gathering facing the future with determination and confidence. They wrestled with the news that membership was only 265 and there was a $600 deficit. The membership mobilized to bring the subscriptions back to 400. Meanwhile, I announced the launch of a campaign to establish an endowment fund.

Such a fund, the Board agreed, would provide a cushion for possible deficits and income to help the budget. It would also allow a break from the total volunteer tradition whereby we would retain the services of a public relations firm to issue professional press releases, get publicity, perhaps even advertise, and promote our concerts. However, the most fundamental reality was that fewer people were buying memberships and more were buying single tickets. The concert market had changed and we had to change with it.

One thing did not have to change. We retained our commitment to having a good time at our annual meetings. The end-of-evening musical offering was provided by pianist member Ruth Burczyk who gave a program of Chopin and Gershwin.

Despite all the distractions, artists we were able to book for the '82-'83 season were right on the mark for Pro Musica's mission to bring emerging stars. First, from Hungary, came the Takacs Quartet on its first U.S. tour. Winners of the Evian, Bordeaux Festival and Budapest International competitions, they had already recorded all of the Schumann and Schubert quartets and were working on Bartok. Sandwiched between Haydn, Webern and Schumann on their program was their choice of Bartok's *Quartet No. 2, Opus 17*. It could not have had a more inspired and authoritative treatment. Meanwhile, as Pro Musica likes to brag about its artists, the Takacs has gone on to be hailed as one of the preeminent quartets in the world.

While it was not possible for anyone to entertain the quartet as house guests, Janice and Zoltan Janosi took up our campaign for the care and feeding of artists. They chauffeured them around town, invited them to dinner at their home and threw a post concert party for the quartet and key members of the Society. It was a gala weekend.

Our exploration of alternative halls occasioned the one unhappy moment of their visit. We were able to book the Fries Auditorium at the Grosse Pointe War Memorial. About the size of our traditional recital hall, its acoustics were passable. However, a wedding was scheduled in the ballroom above and at a critical moment in the *Six Bagatelles* by Webern, the wedding party danced a polka. The auditorium ceiling throbbed in a contrapuntal rhythm while the Takacs players forged bravely ahead. This too finally passed and the concert concluded with a sublime reading of Schumann's first quartet. We could only look ahead to the next hall we intended to try.

Through the intervention of Dr. Hershel and Lois Sandberg, prominent alumni of Wayne State University and leaders of the University's Anthony Wayne Society, our next concert hall was the Community Arts

Jerry Hadley

Auditorium at the McGregor Memorial, adjacent to the University's Music School. Again the size was right, parking could be arranged, there was an attractive space for the afterglow and the acoustics were good. Moreover, the Alumni Association staff was more than cordial in its cooperation.

The artists were tenor Jerry Hadley and his pianist wife Cheryll. His career had been enjoying a meteoric rise through regional opera companies and music festivals across North America. He sang several famous roles at the Washington D.C. and New York City Operas. Not long after he agreed to the contract with Pro Musica, he was signed by New York's Metropolitan Opera.

In a letter to me six months before the concert, he tentatively accepted our invitiation to be our house guests and gave his rationale for the program.

Although three of the four groups on the program are works by romantic composers, we have chosen songs of infinite variety and subject matter. Moreover, the juxtaposition of Liszt and Brahms in the second half is in no way musical redundancy even though these two composers are often lumped together in the history books. The Britten work is among his most unusual and thought-provoking pieces...I believe we have a program which is both interesting and accessible.

He later replaced the Brahms with four songs by Richard Strauss but retained Britten's *Holy Sonnets of John Donne* and Liszt's *Tre Sonnatti del Petrarca*.

Once the Hadleys' travel schedule was cleared, they confirmed their acceptance of our invitation to be our house guests. The process of getting acquainted and becoming good friends moved quickly ahead. On arriving, he complained of an incipient sore throat and showed us his antidote, which was to peel and chop eight fat cloves of garlic, sauté them briefly in olive oil, and crunch them down in a gulp.

With the garlic aromas still in the air, Marybelle helped them settle in their bedroom explaining that our children had hamsters which occasionally escaped. If the Hadleys heard sounds like mice in the night, they should simply call for the family to catch them and put them back in the cage since one hamster had been known to bite.

The next morning, the Hadleys reported that they had indeed heard an escapist in their room. Instead of calling for the hamster catchers, however, Jerry said to Cheryll, "You catch it because I have to sing tomorrow."

Cheryll replied, "You catch it because if I get bitten on a finger, I won't be able to play tomorrow." Eventually, while we slept, they trapped their intruder in a shoe and returned it to its cage. The next night the Hadleys gave Pro Musica an inspired performance.

The Community Arts Auditorium proved to be a comfortable venue. Lois Sandberg with her connections to the Alumni Association took charge of catering the afterglow. The board agreed that we had at last found a satisfactory location. An extra benefit was Hershel Sandberg's ability to promote the concert to other members of the Anthony Wayne Society making one of the rare occasions where we were able to attract audience from an affiliate group.

There were special sentiments associated with the appearance of pianist Cynthia Raim for the last '82-'83 concert. She had grown up in Detroit and began her studies here with Pro Musica's Mischa Kottler. The local Music Study Club gave her scholarship awards She debuted with the Detroit Symphony at age nine and moved on to study with Rudolf Serkin at the Curtis Institute. She made headlines in the music press when she won the Clara Haskil International Piano Competition in Switzerland and won engagements with leading orchestras and concert series.. Pro Musica would not miss the chance to bring back one of our own.

While finances were still precarious, life seemed more stable at last. We returned again to the Ford House in June for the annual meeting and the musical offering was even more lavish. Special guest was composer Karl Meister from Germany, stepfather of Inge Vincent whose husband George was a stalwart member of the Board. Meister's composition for solo piano *Berg Op Zoom* was performed by Fedora Horowitz following a brief talk by the composer. Treasurer Ed Frolich then joined Ruth Burczyk in their locally famed rendition of *Rhapsody in Blue* on two pianos. There was a record attendance of 100 members that evening.

The annual meeting seemed to be turning into another concert in the series with a good meal and a little business thrown in. Part of that business was Endowment Chairman George Vincent's announcement that a preliminary gift of $2,500 had been received and would fuel the formal opening of the drive in September. In spite of all our difficulties, the mood remained upbeat.

The '83-'84 season opened in October with the Silver Medalist of the Van Cliburn competition, Santiago Rodriguez. He had placed second after Andre Michel Schub in a race that was still hotly debated. Reporting from the competition in Fort Worth, Texas, Harold Schoenberg wrote in the *New York Times*: "Mr. Rodriguez is a crowd pleaser, a virtuoso, a colorist, a dashing, cocky performer who has thought out every element of his interpretations. Fortunately he is much more than a technician. His interpretations have had taste at all times and his virtuosity is always employed for legitimate musical devices."

Seeking some privacy, Rodriguez declined our home hospitality but we still had time to get acquainted. In conversation while I brought him to his hotel from the airport, he mentioned how he had met his Russian wife while a student in Moscow. I responded that Prokofiev was the only Russian composer on our past roster. This elicited an excited reaction. He took special pride in appearing on a series where Prokofiev had performed. Later he appeared to have called his wife and passed along that information. At the afterglow he reported that she learned of Prokofiev's visit to Detroit years earlier in the process of writing the composer's biography. His visit here was mentioned in one of his letters home from his U.S. tour. Rodriguez' wife reported that Prokofiev had not been very impressed with Detroit. Regardless, Pro Musica remained as proud as ever of having presented the temperamental composer on his only tour of the U.S. After all, he faced a much grimmer experience when he returned to Stalin's Soviet Union.

The concluding work on Rodriguez' program caused us a twinge of regret. It was the first sonata of Argentine composer Alberto Ginastera. We had tried a few times to bring the Argentinian to Pro Musica but the right opportunity never came up. Rodriguez' performance did receive a glowing review from Nancy Malitz in the *Detroit News*.

The Arden Trio which followed on December 2 was an all American ensemble. It had been formed only five years earlier at the Yale University

Music School and was already performing a full schedule of concerts. Only a month before their Detroit appearance, the *Washington Post* raved about their "awesome technique, expressive range and almost palpable love for the works they play." Their program, including works of Beethoven, Shostakovich, Wuorinen and Ravel, was just right for us. Once again, we missed an opportunity, however. Wuorinen had delivered a lecture preceding the concert in Washington. It would have fit our tradition perfectly. Becoming aware of this only after our concert, I realized that it is important always to ask the artists in advance if they have associations with composers.

The final concert that year was to have presented Mezzo Soprano Kathleen Segar. Her last minute cancellation due to a throat infection prompted a performance by bass-baritone Nicholas Solomon instead. It was no disappointment. Accompanied by Detroit's reliable pianist Bernard Katz, Solomon delivered a fine performance of a broad baritone repertory including arias from *The Rake's Progress* and *The Ballad of Baby Doe*. While it was still early in his career, no one worried about Solomon's progress to stardom; they just enjoyed an excellent performance.

At the annual dinner that year, the important news from George Vincent was the receipt of more gifts to the endowment fund and a goal of $100,000. Once again, the meeting was at the Ford House and came to an exceptionally congenial conclusion. The music was a singalong of traditional and popular American songs with the Society's Secretary Alice Haidostian improvising at the piano. We passed out sheets with the texts and everyone joined in.

Chapter 22

Homecoming and a Fresh Start – 1984

T he really good news came during the summer of 1984. The director of the Detroit Institute of Arts whose policies had driven us out of the museum resigned under a cloud of controversy. Audley Grossman, Curator of Performing Arts, called me to say, "Alex, Pro Musica can come home now." We looked forward to our friendly recital hall and the afterglow in the gracious Romanesque hall. We were eager to regain the congenial ambience we had enjoyed there for nearly 60 years. The happy return to the DIA for the 1984-85 season was celebrated with a sparkling recital by pianist Christopher O'Riley. "He has temperament and a big style" wrote Arnold Schonberg in the *New York Times*. What made us choose him, however, was Ruth Laredo's recommendation that he was the most exciting emerging pianist in America. His program was unusually interesting in that he alternated works by Chopin and Scriabin pointing out similarities and contrasts between them.

The series continued in March 1985 with the Los Angeles Piano Quartet, four musicians from the staffs of California universities and music schools. A piano quartet by Copland honored our new music mission. A Beethoven trio and a piano quartet by Dvorak pleased our traditionalists.

That season ended with our postponed recital by mezzo soprano Kathleen Segar enhanced by her prestigious accompanist, Martin Katz from Ann Arbor. A late addition to the program was composer Dr. David DiChiera, Director of Michigan Opera Theater. He had come to the concert to honor the singer who had starred in recent MOT productions. Unwilling to miss a good opportunity, we persuaded the charismatic opera impresario to give an impromptu talk about his less well known composing career. He then introduced Segar by presenting a group of his songs. They were added to her program only the day before the concert.

Ten years had flown by since I had taken over the Presidency and a new Pro Musica team finally crystallized. The annual dinner, again at the Ford House, recognized people who had shown the desire and ability to play active roles on the board and committees. Officers were the same as in 1975 continuing Pro Musica's long standing tradition of letting officers succeed themselves indefinitely. The rationale was that with longer service they became more effective in their duties and established a valuable institutional memory. But other new people were moving up. Jim Diamond, who had helped us obtain our tax exempt status, became assistant to Treasurer Ed Frohlich. Seven of the eight directors were new on the Board: Paula Barthel and Helene Colbeth for bringing in new members; Pierre Heftler for helping us with his Ford House and DSO connections; Ann Kondak for her diligent work in managing ticket sales for the Jessye Norman concert; John Miller for his uncanny knack for picking special artists. Julia Knoth and Mary Anne Pilette teamed up to issue publicity releases and Sara Rainey became membership secretary.

Second in importance only to the concert was the afterglow. Having taken it over while we were at Wayne University, Lois Sandberg continued with a team made up of Margaret Heftler, Sara Kapetansky, Alice Haidostian , Maxine Zeitz and Jerry Meadows who became permanent helpers for recruiting hosts and hostesses and serving regularly in those roles themselves.

Most revolutionary was the formation of an artist search committee made up of the most avid hunters of new talent: Alice Haidostian, John Miller, Hixie Sanford and myself. Sanford, a former piano teacher, was ready to take on a major role in Pro Musica. Her personal agenda was to bring more women pianists. The committee broke new ground. Never again would artists be chosen by the President alone. There was competition and debate and the results were more interesting. The existence of the committee seemed to bring back a stronger sense of the original mission: new artists, new music and contemporary composers. It was increasingly notable in the changing times that the organization was still run completely by volunteers except for Alice Coleman, our
one-woman secretarial service. She typed up the membership list, mailed out our letters and handled door sales at the concerts. We had become a comprehensive team with a heightened level of enthusiasm.

That year, responding to requests for a program of our Viennese songs, Marybelle and I provided the musical offering to end the annual meeting.

Leonard Pennario

For a while that evening everyone felt that the Ford House Gallery had turned into a cabaret in Austria.

The doors of opportunity were never closed to anyone. Enthusiastic member Phil Leon won approval from the Artist Search Committee to arrange for an artist to open our 1985-86 season. It was his close friend and one of America's best known pianists, Leonard Pennario. Unlike most of our artists, Pennario was near the end of his career. It was a sentimental evening to listen to Pennario's sensitive interpretations of works by the great composers including two of Pro Musica's—Milhaud and Ravel. A somewhat critical report from Nancy Malitz in the implied that Pennario was past his prime. Leon was livid. The Pro Musica audience, on the other hand, recognized the sensitive artistry that shone in Pennario's playing and did not look for the ebullience of a more youthful performer.

Youth highlighted the second concert that year as Pro Musica came up with one of its more miraculous strokes of luck. It was 17 year old violinist, Joshua Bell, already displaying his outstanding talent and reflecting the brilliance of his famous teacher, Josef Gingold. We acted on faith in his recently acquired management who promised that Bell would one day be famous. By the end of his concert no one doubted it. His performance of Bloch's *Nigun* displayed a depth of feeling that belied his youth. De Sarasate's *Carmen Fantasy* meanwhile quickened everyone's pulse.

Having only one guest room at the time, we housed Bell and his mother at the home of one of Pro Musica's generous benefactors, Steven Stackpole. Living in one of Grosse Pointe's few remaining grand estates, an elegantly understated American Georgian mansion, Stackpole personified the great tradition of aristocratic patrons of the arts.

Surrounded by antiques and a ten acre park, Bell mother and son were regaled with lore, puns and witticisms about dinosaurs which were among the eccentric Stackpole's consuming interests. True to our philosophy of unique hospitality, the distractions seemed to put the young virtuoso at ease. We listened in amazement at this youth's performance. In subsequent visits to Detroit appearing with the DSO or on other concert series, he has always asked to be remembered to Mr.Stackpole.

We were even more on track as we wound up the 1985-86 season with composer and pianist Ned Rorem and baritone William Parker. They chose to stay at a mid-town hotel and Rorem arrived early by himself. I met Parker at the airport and arranged to reach the hotel in time for lunch when we could all get acquainted. After calling Rorem's room to announce our arrival, Parker and I waited in the dining room. I was unprepared for what ensued.

Rorem burst through the door of the nearly empty restaurant, saw us and strode briskly to our table. Parker rose to greet his fellow artist. They embraced ardently and kissed with obvious passion. Without conscious thought, it came over me that this was no time for any prudish compunction on my part even though I was put completely off balance. Shaking hands, then, with Rorem, I urged them to be seated and after a deep breath, proceeded to have a very satisfying luncheon conversation. The topics ranged from music and writing (Rorem is a successful author) to art and politics, and then to anecdotes about other creative acquaintances encountered in travels to Europe and North Africa. Needless to say, I missed no opportunity to fill them in on Pro Musica history. Even by the end of the luncheon, however, I realized that I had not completely recovered my composure. I later discovered I had not recovered my credit card, either. To my relief, the cashier who knew who I was and had even attended Pro Musica called me later in the day to tell me she was saving it for me and wondered if she could get tickets to "that handsome composer's concert." Of course—I gave her a pair.

In speaking to our audience, Rorem credited his time in France with major influences on his muse. While there he had become particularly well acquainted with Jean Cocteau and acquired a deep appreciation of Debussy's music. After an opening cycle of songs by Debussy, he and Parker launched into four groups of Rorem's songs. His settings of *War Scenes* by Walt Whitman

Ned Rorem

made the big dramatic impact of the evening. For some they were shocking. Whitman's poetry describing Civil War battlefield gore enhanced by Rorem's gaunt, compelling settings was devastating. As members asked me if we were turning the Pro Musica stage into a platform for anti-war politics, I thought of Coolidge defending tone clusters a few decades earlier. I replied rhetorically with the question: "What is art after all if not an expression of life's experience?" As they had done to a greater or lesser degree throughout our history, some members wanted only to experience sweet and comforting familiar music. Others were thrilled with Rorem's power of expression and asked for more. All of which was evidence of a highly successful concert as far as I was concerned. Everybody was talking about it. I do not recall that we lost any members over it and the cashier from the restaurant thanked me for one of the highlights of her young life.

Even though Rorem was not our house guest, he did give me a brief dedication and his autograph. They are on the fly leaf of his latest book of the time. His visit was the occasion of one more important event. For the first time, we were able to obtain a grant to bring in a composer. It was from the Michigan Council for the Arts. Decades later the $500 seems like small change but it balanced Pro Musica's books that year.

More changes were in the air. As we set out to plan our annual dinner we learned that the Ford House was being treated totally as a museum. No more dinners there. An activities hall had been constructed on the property for that kind of event but it had all the charm of a business meeting room, no view of the lake and the acoustics of a padded cell. Our dinner, on September 8, 1986, moved back to the Grosse Pointe War Memorial.

Musical entertainment for the annual meeting was a separate event this time and one that was both sad and distinguished. Patrons of Pro Musica, Leo and Eleanor Cooney, had lost their only son to a tragic illness. They were former professional musicians. Both had trained at the Juilliard School. Leo was a tenor working in opera, chorus and radio in New York. Eleanor Jannsen was a brilliant violinist, pupil of the concertmaster of the Berlin Philharmonic, a soloist with major orchestras in the U.S. She gave that up when she married and became a mother. They were an artistic family. Their son Ron, a promising young businessman, was also a poet whose work had been praised by author Joyce Carol Oates.

In Ron's memory, friends of the Cooneys made many impressive gestures of respect and sympathy. A book of Ron's poetry was published.

Mike Whorf, the producer of a life experience program called Kaleidoscope on a local radio station, aired a series of programs about the young man's life and writing. Composer James Hartway, on the staff of the Music Department at Wayne State University, set many of Ron's poems to music. He titled one large cycle *Songs for Ronnie*. Then, in the flow of sympathy, a friend and former artistic associate of the Cooneys from New York volunteered to come to Detroit to give a recital honoring Ron's memory with a performance of those songs. The friend was Robert Merrill, famed baritone of the Metropolitan Opera.

Robert Merrill

The concert was produced by the Lyric Chamber Ensemble under the direction of its founder, Fedora Horowitz. Pro Musica joined in promoting the event and more than half of our membership accepted the invitation at the annual dinner to attend. The concert, on Sunday, September 28, 1986, was performed before a sellout audience in Orchestra Hall. No one ever had a more beautiful eulogy.

Change continued even in the makeup of the volunteer staff of Pro Musica. Membership Chairman Sara Rainey passed her duties to Michelle Drake. In place of Franziska Greiling, Detroit electrical contractor and avid music lover Ray Litt began to write and mail press releases to the media. Elizabeth Soby took on the role of historian and Lois Sandberg's social committee was down to just Betty Jane Barnes and Jerry Meadows.

Two truly dedicated members assumed the key activities of recruiting new members and reminding existing members to renew. Ann Kondak took on the renewals committee while Louise Papista brought a Grecian flair in her buffet lunches to inspire the new member promotion team.

Life at the museum was changing, too. While we were welcomed back to our traditional stage and afterglow location, we were stopped short by the Founders Society. They officially owned the large silver tea and coffee service and the giant Russian Samovar that we used at our afterglow. One tea service, in fact, had been donated by Pro Musica. But these pieces, through long service, were wearing out and needed costly repairs. The ladies of the Founders decided that their equipment would now be off limits to outside groups. Only Pro Musica's unique status at the museum and an intercession with officers of the group won back our privileges.

A new food concessionaire at the museum also presented a problem. An exclusive contract was the excuse to end Pro Musica's privilege to bring in its own finger sandwiches and doughnut balls for the afterglow. Again, diplomatic contacts with influential figures at the museum won recognition of our grandfathered rights to bring in our own food. The cost was, of course, a major factor. Using the caterer would have tripled the expense. That did not end the issue, however. Every year it came up again.

On the positive side, our new treasurer, Jim Diamond, reported our most successful season in a decade and a small but helpful income from the endowment fund. The impediments that appeared in our path were dealt with and we moved ahead.

The 1986-87 season opened in October with the Vienna Schubert Trio, from Vienna, of course. Along with superb musicianship, they brought us an awareness of a less well known force in 20th century music. We heard the *Trio in D Minor* by Alexander von Zemlinski and learned from the artists that he was best known as the teacher and brother-in-law of Arnold Schoenberg. He was also a colleague of Alban Berg, Kurt Weill and Gustav Mahler. In spite of his close association with these leading avant garde figures, Zemlinsky's music is romantic and lyrical. Along with trios by Schostakovitch and Brahms, it made an informative, well balanced and satisfying program.

Hosts for the trio were Inge and board member George Vincent who could offer three guest rooms and a living room with a piano where the artist could practice. Inge recalls that they had an unanticipated but considerate audience.

> The trio— a cellist, a pianist and a violinist— practiced separately in three different rooms. Sharing our home at that time was a very excitable, long-haired dachshund. To our amazement Fritzi did not vocalize, but went quietly from one closed door to the next, ears cocked and listening attentively to prove that music also "charms the beast."

The series continued in March with the appearance of a good friend, pianist Ralph Votapek. He had appeared a decade earlier in recital and at one of our anniversary banquets. On this occasion he gave us a big program of great though not revolutionary works, elegantly performed.

Being able to bring in our own food for the afterglow paid a dividend at this concert. Recent new member Kathy Schmidt donated a generous supply of a special treat from her business: Kathy's New York Cheesecake Shop. We licked our chops.

The composer appearance at our third concert was serendipitous. In a last minute plan, we sought to honor once more the memory of Ron Cooney. We asked baritone Gordon Hawkins to include one of the songs on his program for us and invited Hartway, the composer, and the young poet's family to the concert. Hartway spoke briefly. Hawkins programmed the song between Wagner's Aria O *Evening Star* from *Tannheuser*, Griffes' *Sorrow of Mydah* and a group of spirituals. It was a touching presentation.

Hawkins himself was a great success. He was a national winner of the Metropolitan Opera National Council Auditions and young veteran of the Wolf Trap, Washington, Virginia and Boston Concert Operas with an impressive roster of roles to his credit.

His accompanist was pianist Bob McCoy.

Chapter 23
After 60 years, Change is a Way of Life – 1987

T he DIA's Kresge Court was packed on September 29 with nearly 100 members and friends celebrating the society's 60th anniversary at a gala banquet and concert at the Museum. That was our annual meeting. After dinner, Toastmaster Jack Barthel (his wife Paula was a board member) had the party chuckling over his commentary about Pro Musica's windsurfing President (I had just taken up the sport) and glowing with pride as he introduced long-time members Pierre Heftler, Tom LoCicero, Ed Frohlich and Alice Haidostian to recall past joys and triumphs of our concerts.

Our music for the evening followed in the Recital Hall. Mischa Kottler performed an elegant program of Chopin, Medtner, Rachmaninoff, Liadow and Ravel. Thanks to generous reports in the press, there was a capacity crowd. By this time, Kottler was widely acknowleged to be a great surviving exponent of the Hoffman-Paderewski-Rachmaninoff-Rubinstein era of piano. He had left Russia as a youth to pursue serious piano studies in Vienna with Emile von Sauer, the most eminent pupil of Liszt. Moving to New York, he became accompanist to the famed violinist Leopold Auer. But Auer saw greater talent in the young Kottler and introduced him to Sergei Rachmaninoff. The composer spent one entire afternoon with Kottler giving him what we now call a master class.

Kottler recalls that he played the entire 2nd piano concerto without orchestra for Rachmaninoff who alternately praised and corrected him. The composer expressed regret that his concert career did not permit him to take Kottler on as a pupil. He advised the young man to return to Europe to study. Kottler went to Paris and was accepted as a pupil by Alfred Cortot.

The year before Pro Musica was formed, Kottler came to Detroit.

Entering the city's musical circles he sought opportunities to perform and began accepting pupils. He became a charter member of Pro Musica attending the society's first two concerts by Bartok and Ravel and many more in succeeding years. His pupils often won top local and even national awards. Three of them—Seymour Lipkin, Ruth Laredo and Cynthia Raim—became famous international artists. At this late stage in his career, Mischa was official pianist of the Detroit Symphony, artist in residence at Wayne State University, and an active teacher of promising young pianists.

Kottler was known as well as a raconteur and he spiced his presentation with reminiscences of his one day master class with Rachmaninoff and hearing Ravel play at Pro Musica's opening season. His personality and performance brought a standing ovation and a spontaneous audience performance of "Happy Birthday." He had celebrated his 85th only nine days earlier. He responded with three encores—a piece by Ibert, Rachmaninoff's *Variations on Liebesleid* (by Fritz Kreisler) and a piece of his own which he called *A Little Viennese Waltz*. The air was thick with *gemütlichkeit*. There was a universal feeling that evening that Pro Musica was supreme and immortal.

A month later, the Auryn Quartet from Germany officially opened our '87-'88 season. They were already stars in Europe and major competition winners. We were inspired to bring them by a *Washington Post* review of their debut concert in the U.S. the previous year. Their program of Beethoven, Berg, Mozart and Schubert proved their mastery of the complete repertory and certainly satisfied us.

A particularly rare experience that season was to hear the true contralto voice of Mira Zakai in February. Her program, too, included music of Berg along with Purcell, Schumann, Mahler and De Falla. The *Seven Popular Spanish Songs* brought the already impressive program to a stirring close.

For the finale that year, we had another example of a choice by a dynamic member of the Board. Hixie Sanford, in her support of women pianists and her enormous admiration of Ruth Laredo, persuaded us to bring Ruthie for a third time. As it turned out you can't have too much of a good thing, especially with a spacing of several years in between. Ruth's many hometown fans and friends were able to admire the superb, mature artist she had become. One of her preoccupations at the time was the music of Rachmaninoff which made up a large part of her program. There was much interest and significance for Pro Musica in her presentation of a new piece, *Song and Dance 1987*, by Ned Rorem. Concluding with Ravel's *Valse Noble et Sentimental* and *La Valse* was a nice tip of the hat to our history.

Concert after concert and artist after artist were exceptional and conversation at the afterglows invariably included many questions on how Pro Musica managed to present such outstanding concerts so consistently. Actually, that was the easy part. We were finding crowds of wonderful artists ready to come and give us stunning concerts. The problem was in trying to choose only three. The other big challenge was filling the house. Our membership had leveled off at about fifty percent capacity.

We had to use every possible device to generate door sales in order to have a good audience and make ends meet. Urging members to bring friends had results as limited as the circle of members' musical friends. Free public service publicity in the media was becoming increasingly difficult to get in a way that singled us out as something singular. Paid advertising was economically impractical for an audience as small as ours and there was no changing that. Also, there was no thought of a drastic change in philosophy. The Pro Musica Board and membership was totally committed to the intimate character of our concert evenings and our mission of everything new—new artists, new music, new composers. Big name stars in a big hall were not for us. So we kept our expenses low, kept reminding our friends to come and bring friends to enjoy one of the best kept musical secrets in town.

If the public were fully aware of the party atmosphere at our annual meetings it is possible that attendance at both the dinner and our concerts might have improved. The meeting in September '88 found a new home. It was a gracious English manor house on the shore of Lake St. Clair. Mado and Dr. Kim Lie were our hosts and the atmosphere was, as usual, congenial and festive. Once again, Marybelle and I ended the evening with a sentimental reprise of our repertory of Viennese Songs.

On the artist search committee, Hixie Sanflord continued to take a leadership role in finding great artists and programs for us. The '88-'89 season opened with her choices of soprano Benita Valente and pianist Cynthia Raim. *Cindy's* Detroit origin and Kottler training made her special for us. She had only recently won the Clara Haskil Award in Switzerland and appeared to have her career on its way. The distinguishing feature of Valente's part of the program was her spirited performance of songs by the Catalonian composer Roberto Gerhard. A student of Schoenberg, he had left his native Barcelona for England in1939 and composed a highly respectable collection of music in all forms.

Mid-season, Marybelle and I eagerly welcomed Uruguayan guitarist Edouardo Fernandez as our house guest. It was a very

Eduardo Fernandez

congenial time as we drained him of information about South America and he and I exchanged lore and knowledge of guitars. I proudly showed him my favorite of my three guitars, one made for me by French Luthier Robert Bouchet. Just as Segovia had done before him, he snorted unhappily as he tried to tune when he discovered that the machine heads worked the reverse of the Spanish ones on his guitar. But again like Segovia he praised its tone quality and action. I was especially pleased when he played the Sonata by Ginastera from his program.

There was another surprise. I had forgotten that a year earlier, when we signed the contract, his manager asked permission to book him at a concert in Bloomfield Hills on the same trip, less than the traditional 50 miles away. Our concert was on the usual Friday and the other on the following Monday. We did the other series a major favor. John Guinn reviewed the Pro Musica performance with a very flattering report of Fernandez' artistry and mentioned the second performance. If the double booking was what motivated him to review our concert, I was ready to do it again. Meanwhile, the Monday concert had to turn people away from its small venue. Fernandez was an impressive artists and Pro Musica booked him for one of our rare repeats the following year.

The Alexander String Quartet completed our season with one of the most remarkable quartets we have ever heard. It is *The Kreutzer* by the Czech composer Leos Janacek. This amazing piece of music, based on a

The Alexander String Quartet

short story of the same name by Tolstoy, chronicles a murder by a jealous husband incited by the passionate playing of his wife and a male friend violinist. Janacek and the Alexander Quartet took us on an emotional rollercoaster ride even more startling that Tolstoy's tale. The quartet changes tempo and meter repeatedly and has players execute startling special effects on their instruments that increase the sense of drama. It made me regretful that Pro Musica had never been able to book Janacek, but his life had ended the year Pro Musica's began. Quartets by Mozart and Brahms gave balance to the program.

Once more the movable feast of the annual meeting found another site. This was the home of Ed and Jessie Frohlich on a cul de sac in Grosse Pointe Farms. It was formerly the mansion of one of the founders of Detroit's auto industry. Pianist Frohlich was known to have two grand pianos in his living room which made possible a very special musical treat. He and Mischa Kottler gave us a two piano recital after the brief business meeting was done. The graciously furnished mansion mirrored the timeless, traditional style that characterized most of what Pro Musica did. The Museum, the Ford House, and private mansions like the Frohlich's put Pro Musica events in a setting that conjured a sense of turning back the clock to times when such entertainment was the privilege of aristocrats in their palaces. The locations, in fact, tended to increase the attendance.

A pianist with a fast rising career opened the '89-'90 season. Stephen Hough won the Naumberg Competition in '83 and since appeared with a dozen of America's leading orchestras. His recording of the Hummel Concerto was named *Gramaphone Magazine's Recording of the Year*. Music by Swiss composer Rolf Liebermann added the desired contemporary touch to his program.

Honoring a Detroit born artist, we presented lyric soprano Janet Williams. Educated at the city's Cass Technical High School, she was a finalist in the '86 Metropolitan Opera Great Lakes Auditions and spent the following years as artist in residence at the San Francisco opera. With family in Detroit, she naturally stayed with them but at a dinner with Mischa Kottler at our home there were intriguing explorations of Russian songs that Kottler was eager to accompany.

In our publicity and promotion, we made a special effort to invite William's family and friends to the concert and even to reach out to other members of the city's African-American community who might enjoy her recital. Many of them came to hear her. We had high hopes that this might significantly integrate and build the Pro Musica audience, but unfortunately this did not happen.

I suppose my own enthusiasm for the classical guitar influenced us to bring back Eduardo Fernandez a second year in a row. But there was no denying the splash he had made in Detroit the year before and his recognition by leading U.S. critics. Writing in the Detroit Free Press, John Guinn praised his "Total technical command…clean articulation, beautifully shaded dynamic contrast, wide tonal variety, impeccable phrasing…a great musician who happens to play the guitar…one of the most satisfying recital experiences of the season." The *Guitar Review* commissioned him to transcribe several important works by Alberto Ginastera. Pro Musica savored his second appearance playing a mixture of traditional guitar classics and modern pieces by Giulio Regondi and one by the guitarist's wife, Anna.

As we looked forward to the '90-'91 season we were aware of more changes that we would have to adapt to and more devices to help the budget. A search for a new Director at the museum finally ended with the appointment of Dr. Samuel Sachs II, a fellow Harvard alumnus. We contacted him and made him aware of Pro Musica's long relationship and distinguished programs, especially that Pro Musica was the museum's oldest tenant. Meanwhile the roster of Museum personnel with whom we worked to produce our concerts was experiencing turnover. Following an accident that took the life of Dr. Audley Grossman, we depended on Christopher Claypoole to reserve our dates and handle the details of our meetings and afterglows. There were new people to deal with in catering, audio visual services and the security staff. The museum's institutional memory was short when it came to Pro Musica. We had to help it out. It was important to acquaint new staff members at the museum with the history and unique status of Pro Musica; that we alone among museum tenants were allowed to bring in our own food for our reception and that instead of rent, we simply paid the costs for services and personnel on duty at our evenings. We were advised always to include on our program that we were sponsored by the Department of Performing Arts which provided an endorsement of our special privileges. We even arranged to use the staff parking lot on Kirby Street for reserved member parking on the evenings of our concerts and parking in the circular drive at the Woodward Avenue entrance as a perk for our new category of Patron members. The privilege of parking right in front of the main entrance provided an incentive for our most loyal members to pay double for a season subscription. Patrons could also deduct the premium cost (half the doubled price) on their income tax as a gift to Pro Musica.

These were important news items for discussion at the annual dinner that year which was held once again at the home of Dr. Kim and Mado Lie. Equally important, in addition, Treasurer Jim Diamond reported that income from the endowment fund again balanced the budget in the season just ended but he also made it known that inflationary increases made it desirable to continue building that fund. Membership secretary Florence Arnoldi was able to help the finances, too. She had sold enough parking passes to the Kirby Street lot to more than pay for the attendant which created another small source of revenue for us.

Taking it all in stride, nearly 90 members in attendance enjoyed their dinner, re-elected five directors and listened to music by the Essex Trio from the Music Department at Wayne State University. New member of the Board, Harold Arnoldi, husband of our Membership Secretary and a Professor at the University's music school, secured the trio of students for our meeting. Music of Beethoven, Dvorak and Mendelssohn was on their program.

A brother-sister team opened our season in October. Originally from Canada, Violinist Corey Cerovsek and his pianist sister Katja both had attended Indiana University. Corey studied with Josef Gingold and earned graduate degrees in Music and Mathematics. He was already performing regularly with major orchestras in North America and Europe. Katja graduated at age 13 from Canada's Royal Conservatory before moving on to Indiana and later studies with Menahem Pressler of the Beaux Arts Trio. She was also studio accompanist to cellist Janos Starker. Corey's program ranged satisfyingly from Bach to Schoenberg and Katja provided a mid-program piano solo of *Islamey* by Balakirev.

The New World String Quartet

The popularity of ensemble programs was easy to understand when we brought the combination of the New World String Quartet and clarinetist David Shifrin. Naumberg Award winner and Quartet in residence at Harvard University, the foursome enjoyed enviable recognition in both Europe and America. Shifrin's reputation and his status with the Chamber Music Society of Lincoln Center was equally illustrious. After quartet performances of Schubert, Bartok, and Wolf, the program brought the Mozart Clarinet Quintet. I was sitting near the back of the hall nearly in a trance at the beauty of Shifrin's performance. A friend in the next seat whispered to me at a break between movements, "How do you like them?" My response required no thought. "I think I've died and gone to heaven."

Flutist and youthful composer Gary Schocker closed our season that year. We had determined to bring him on hearing the combined virtuosity and expression on the tape that his manager sent. He had been a hit at the New Jersey Symphony the previous year when he substituted for an ailing Jean Pierre Rampal and dazzled the audience with his own cadenzas for the Mozart Flute Concerto. Our audience was similarly impressed and several members commented afterwards that his playing of Debussy's *Syrinx* for solo flute was nothing less than sublime.

Schocker and his pianist Dennis Helmrich were exceptionally congenial house guests and with one daughter away at college, we were able to accommodate them both. As we relaxed at home on the evening before the concert, questions inevitably arose over the guitar and accordeon cases in the corner. Hearing about our devotion to the somewhat obscure tradition of Viennese songs, Schocker insisted on hearing us perform. Marybelle struck a bargain whereby we would trade performances. He played Debussy's *Syrinx* for us and we played and sang *Vienna, City of My Dreams*. It turned into a very personal session of house music and a bond of friendship. We were very much aware the next day that there was a new devotion to his performance for Pro Musica.

By this time in the course of the Society's inner workings, the Board and the Artist Search Committee were holding a joint, midwinter meeting to plan the next season well before the present one was completed. From year to year, the location of the meeting alternated between different areas of metropolitan Detroit where various members lived. The membership was thinly spread over a three county area so that wherever a meeting was held, some had to make a long drive. This time it was at the home of Board member Jean North in Birmingham. We Grosse Pointers took the long drive.

The usual routine was for me to present suggestions received from members and artists' agents. We listened to tapes recorded at concert performances and commercial recordings, if they were available. For the '91-'92 roster, we read biographies and reviews and quickly narrowed the choices down to a piano duet, three solo pianists, seven ensembles, a tenor and a baritone. As preferences began to focus on a few artists, Ken Collinson recommended a package of three. Pianist Seung-un Ha was a fast rising attraction from one of New York's leading managements. She had given well received recitals at the Ravinia and Aspen Festivals and soloed with Chicago's Grant Park Symphony and at Avery Fisher Hall in New York under Leonard Slatkin. Ciosoni was a trio of clarinet, flute and double bass from the University of Illinois offering an early form of what we now call a cross-over program. Switching between arrangements of classics and jazz, their presentation was an interesting synthesis of traditional and contemporary. Tenor Keith Mikelson, originally from the Detroit area, was developing his career singing heldentenor roles with European opera companies. Our group voted unanimously for the combination.

The annual dinner in September moved to an impressive new location. New Board member Harold Arnoldi arranged for us to meet in the architecturally stunning McGregor Memorial at Wayne State University (the architect was Minoru Yamasaki). Meeting facilities, quality catering, parking and even musicians eager to perform were readily available.

When the season got under way, the concerts were highly satisfactory as usual. Ms. Ha played a conventional recital brilliantly while the Ciosoni left a number of members bemused. After opening with music by Bach and John Cage the trio moved to *Iberique Peninsulaire (1970) for solo bass* by Francois Rabbath, *Curtains for Felix: to the demise of a rubber plant (1940)* by Allan J.Segall, and *Trio plus audiotape: Jest Fa-Laffs (1991)* by Salvatore Martirano. A trio by Jelly Roll Morton completed the journey. One member resigned. The rest displayed a good humored readiness to subscribe to Pro Musica's adventure mission, just as their predecessors had in the early days. At moments like that, I was always impressed with how special our audience is. Most of the artists were impressed, too. They often commented on it.

Keith Mikelson was a learning experience in more than one way. He explained that he was actually what is called a *Jugend Heldentenor* (young noble tenor) and would not mature into full voice for another ten years. In our intimate recital hall, the young voice was already overwhelming. He migrated easily from lyric roles by Puccini and Smetana to the more powerful arias by Weber and Beethoven and concluded with Wagner, the Prize Song from *Die Meistersinger* and Tristan's *Denkt dich das?* We all developed a new appreciation for the demanding art of the *Noble Tenor*.

Since we had to bring Mikelson from his busy schedule of bookings in European opera houses, we also got an expensive lesson on the air fares of the time. Roundtrip was more expensive when it originated in Europe. There were none of those bargain tourist flights that we had been taking out of New York. The plane fare busted our budget. We shrugged and started planning how we might make it up next season.

NEW WAYS FEED ON THE OLD

1988–2006

Chapter 24
Serendipitous Fund Raising
and Artist Selection – 1992

M arybelle and I decided to celebrate our 25th wedding anniversary at the end of the summer (the date was September 2). We reserved the ballroom at the Grosse Pointe War Memorial and planned a party program that rivaled the best of Pro Musica's celebrations.

More than 200 guests came to share the fun. A tape of keyboard stylings from my jazz pianist nephew, Thomas Suczek in California, opened the music followed by live improvisations by Pro Musica's Vice President Alice Haidostian. Wines and champagnes from the New York Finger Lakes and California's Napa Valley flowed to accompany a banquet centered on a Chicago Steamship Round of Beef. The meal climaxed with Viennese Walnut Rum Tortes with lime icing, 20 of them turned out by Marybelle and our daughters Hedi and Yohanna.

The entertainment followed with a Mozart Duo for violin and viola played by Beatriz and Gregg Staples, widow and son of the late Gordon Staples, DSO Concertmaster and my collaborator in the Grosse Pointe Summer Music Festival. Alice Haidostian accompanied our friend, soprano Johanna Gilbert in two Viennese Lieder and the Anniversary Waltz. Everyone joined in.

Nonagenarian Mischa Kottler played *Polchinelle* by Rachmaninoff and then Chopin's Waltz in A flat minor with exquisite style. Experiencing a memory lapse, he kept us in rapturous suspense as he played the repeat at least three times before he finally remembered the coda. Following the genuinely warm applause, we cautiously declined his offer to play more.

Marybelle and I shared the limelight with a joyously sentimental rendition of our favorite duet from Viennese operetta, *Meine Liebe, Deine Liebe* from *Land of Smiles* by Franz Lehar. As we sang, we danced a simple pantomime choreographed by Jud Sheldon, Dance Director at the Center for Creative Studies. Our orchestra leader, violinist George Steppula, and a small ensemble from the orchestra, provided the accompaniment. We did not need to translate the last line: *Ich liebe dich und du liebst mich und da liegt alles d'rinn.* Everyone understood.

After waltzing, tangoing and polkaing to the Strauss-style salon orchestra, countless departing guests observed that it was truly a Pro Musica party. That was particularly apt since the invitation had declined personal gifts and suggested instead donations to the Pro Musica Endowment Fund. In fact, we more than paid for Mikelson's plane fare that evening.

At that year's annual dinner, Treasurer Jim Diamond was able to announce a new high in the assets of the Endowment Fund. The meeting's location had moved back to the Crescent Sail Yacht Club in Grosse Pointe Farms where 80 members enjoyed the usual congenial evening.

Meanwhile, the active participation of members in the artist selection process was producing interesting results. The opening attraction for the '92-'93 season was the Ames Piano Quartet from the University of Iowa. They were suggested by Board member and historian Penny Soby because the pianist in the group was William David, a native of Grosse Pointe. The quartet was winning recognition as a leading ensemble. Surprisingly, while they had already toured North America, Asia and Europe, they had not yet appeared in Detroit. Recognizing hometown artists who were on the road to success was certainly part of our mission.

Exposure to a new composer was another aim and their opening presentation was *Phantasy Quartet, 1910* by Frank Bridge. Bridge was a graduate of England's Royal Conservatory, violist with the Joachim Quartet and a teacher of Benjamin Britten. His music is characterized by a highly expressive Romantic idiom. The Ames group followed that with the even newer *Quartet dated 1976* by William Bolcom. He was already known for juxtaposing ragtime and electronic music and his interest in popular American song of the 19th and early 20th century which he has performed and recorded with his wife. At the time of this concert Bolcom was already on the music faculty at the University of Michigan and undoubtedly available to us. However, it would be another 10 years before we arranged his appearance at Pro Musica.

The Ames' concert closed with a very satisfying performance of the G minor piano quartet by Brahms which provided David his opportunity to shine in the work's final movement, *The Gypsy Rondo*. At the afterglow, old school friends and teachers were there to congratulate him.

Recommendation for the second artist that season came from former Treasurer Ed Frohlich who was always alert to promising artists who were not getting the attention they deserved. Pianist Tian Ying, a pupil of Russell Sherman at the New England Conservatory, was a finalist in the '89 Van Cliburn Competition and winner of the '85 Stravinsky Awards International Piano Competition. As was usual in those years, no critics attended but the members found Ying's interpretations intensely imaginative and beautiful. As his hosts, we found him somewhat ascetic. He slept on the floor and was exceedingly polite and soft spoken. Then, as he warmed up on our parlor grand Steinway, we were aware of the unusual degree of sensitivity in his playing. The opportunity to listen to such practice sessions was one of the privileges of having the artists stay with us in our home.

Although we were not bringing composers very often in the the '80s and '90s, our artists did recognize our interest in having some new music on every program. Mezzo soprano Phyllis Pancella gave us *Psalm of the Distant Dove* by Czech composer Hugo Weisgal who had come to the U.S. to study at the Peabody Conservatory and Curtis Institute with Fritz Reiner and Roger Sessions. She ended her program with Leonard Bernstein's light hearted song cycle "La Bonne Cuisine" from *On the Town*. Having won the Metropolitan Opera National Council Auditions and the MacAllister Competition, Pancella was alredy a major figure in opera and concert yet this was her first appearance in Detroit.

For the previous four years, I had been writing a column in the *Grosse Pointe NEWS* to review the theater performances at Canada's Stratford Festival. Now I had branched out to include coverage of Detroit Symphony concerts with the new music Director, Neeme Jarvi, on the podium. On hearing his performances, I felt immediately that Detroit had acquired a truly great and inspired conductor. Since our local paper was providing no coverage, I undertook to review most of his performances over the course of that year.

My approach to reporting on the DSO performances caught the Maestro's attention. The intent was to explain the nature of the experience of hearing his performances and what I felt he was trying to achieve rather than simply to criticize or praise it. His wife would send my reviews for

Neeme Jarvi with the author

republication in the Estonian newspaper in New York and then to Talinn. My commentary must have struck a responsive chord in him because when we were finally introduced after a concert, he recognized my name at once and said, "Oh, you are the critic. Very good. Very professional." It was the basis for a cordial friendship and a valuable relationship with the symphony organization. I learned from him of his plans to bring to the states the young Norweigian pianist Leif Ove Andsnes at about the same time that a New York management offered us a Royal Norwegian Embassy sponsored piano quartet of Norway's most eminent players. Violinist Arve Tellefsen and violist Lars Anders Tomter were then, and still are world class artists. Cellist Truls Mork and Andsnes meanwhile were just beginning to win recognition although they were already impressive. Since Andsnes was booked to play the Grieg Concerto later in the same season, I had to persuade a sympathetic DSO management that a chamber music appearance would not conflict with their presentation of Andsnes. It was simply another of Pro Musica's serendipitous coups.

The Quartet arrived on Thursday and stayed, by preference, in a hotel near the Fisher Building. However, we met them and extended all the cordial welcome that we could. Andsnes asked if he could have access to a good piano so that he could practice the Mozart Concerto No. 21 for a concert in Los Angeles a few days later. I offered him the piano in our Recital Hall, or the parlor grand Steinway in our home. He chose the latter. That evening, while Marybelle and I had a late supper on our enclosed terrace, we drank in Leif's run through of the entire piano solo part in the connecting room. It was heavenly dinner music.

We found him a gentle, sensitive young man who poured all his considerable passion into his playing. It was a joy to converse with him and a blossoming friendship had formed that we hoped would continue.

The next morning, the day of their concert, the Detroit Symphony was performing under the baton of Finnish conductor Paavo Berglund, who was a respected and much loved friend of the quartet. So I contacted Jill Woodward at the DSO and arranged to take them to the 10:30 a.m. concert. Somewhat truculently, Truls Mork observed that it was too early for him to get up but the others persuaded him that he should make the effort. After the performance, Marybelle and I invited them and the conductor to lunch. There was animated conversation in which they brought each other up to date on their respective careers.

We were especially interested to learn that Arve Tellefsen had been Concertmaster of the Vienna Symphony for several years and Lars Anders Tomter was an eminent viola soloist in Europe. Our theory regarding the benefit of congeniality with artists in terms of getting an inspired performance was amply verified that evening. The Grieg Festival Quartet opened our 93-94 season with stunning performances of violin and cello sonatas by Grieg, *Maerchenbilder* for viola and piano by Schumann, and the Brahms *Werther* piano quartet in C minor.

When Andsnes returned to play again with the DSO, we never missed a concert and the visits backstage. On the weekend when he performed the Rachmaninoff 3rd we had the opportunity to give him a ride back to his hotel after the performance. Learning that he was hungry, we offered him a visit to *Bert's in the Marketplace,* a soul food restaurant where Detroit's Jazz musicians gathered after their regular gigs for midnight jam sessions. There we feasted hungrily on blackened catfish, barbecued ribs and improvisational performances of Detroit's unique jazz tradition. A pianist, bassist and saxophone player were on the stage. Shortly a clarinetist arrived and simply stepped up on the platform to join in. More came later. Leif found it a memorable evening. When we finally brought him to his hotel and wished him luck on his forthcoming performance of the Rachmaninoff 3rd with Jarvi and the New York Philharmonic, his reply was characteristically modest: "With Maestro Järvi's help I think it could go well." In fact, that performance a week later won him rave reviews and a new high in world class status. I watched eagerly for his return engagements in Detroit.

The series continued in February with French pianist Jean Yves Thibaudet. With the support of George and Aphie Roumell, we persuaded the Alliance Francaise to make an event of it for their membership so that we anticipated a full house. For his two days in Detroit, Thibaudet was our house guest. Then, at dusk on Friday evening, it began to snow heavily. With a little more advance warning, we might have cancelled the concert but it was late and it still appeared that most people could come. As I drove I-94 from Grosse Pointe to the Museum, I found the freeway filled with snow and nearly void of cars.

Thibaudet's excellent program of Ravel and Schumann was a rich treat for less than 100 intrepid members who braved the elements. As I drove him to the airport the next morning on well cleared pavement we exchanged vows for another concert in the near future so that everyone could hear him. Regrettably, I could not seek a new date for almost ten years. By then, his fee had skyrocketed and his schedule was full.

Soprano Camellia Johnson attracted the attention of a number of members when she sang Aida at MOT and soloed at a Detroit Symphony concert. For our spring program in 1994, she offered songs by Handel, Debussy, R. Strauss and Liszt, winding up with a group of songs by her close friend, torch song composer Ricky Ian Gordon. Two of the songs, "Harlem Night Song" and "Port Town" were written for her. She concluded with a group of spirituals. As the audience gave her an ovation, someone in the front row sang out a heartfelt "Bravo." Ms. Johnson replied "You are very kind." Her fan responded "You are very good!" For us, it was another very good Pro Musica evening, but we had come to expect them to be that way. Their exchange made it into one of the few reviews, a very praiseful one to be sure, of Pro Musica concerts by John Guinn in the *Detroit Free Press*.

Following our announcement of the coming year at the annual dinner that September (once again at the Crescent Sail Yacht Club) Guinn gave Pro Musica another nice mention in his rundown of the season's attractions: "Pro Musica Snags a Winner... the venerable local society that has a knack for bringing up-and-coming performers of considerable potential will present the Detroit debut of Austrian baritone Wofgang Holzmair." That was to be the season's second concert and we appreciated Guinn's recognition of our long-term and somewhat tricky mission.

The first artist for the 1994-95 season was pianist Armen Babakhanian, fifth prize winner at the 9th Van Cliburn competition. James Keller of *The New Yorker* hailed him as the overwhelming talent of that event and predicted world class status for him. In another example of getting support from an affiliate group, Alice Haidostian persuaded nearly 50 members of the Armenian community to support one of their own and had the afterglow catered ethnic Armenian delicacies like *choloreg* (sweet bread), *pakhlava* (filo dough filled with honey and ground nuts), and *khurabia* (white sugar cookies). The program boasted two modern composers. There were *Six Pictures for Piano* by fellow countryman Babajanian and *Ghost Waltzes* by Morton Gould which had been commissioned for performance at the competition.

Hosting baritone Wolfgang Holzmair provided an exceptional insight into the concept of taking good care of the artists. When I met him and pianist Thomas Palm at the airport, Holzmair was very reserved and formal. At home we sat on our glassed in terrace surrounded by blooming plants inside and heaps of snow outside and he relaxed. We discussed the stresses of touring and the music business in general. He called our terrace a winter garden and seemed to be reminded of winter in Austria with all the snow outside. Our impromptu performance of a Viennese song drew favorable suggestions from him for concertizing that repertoire. When I pointed out that I had only a light voice, he noted that he, too, had a light voice. There was a feeling of camaraderie. Gradually, he revealed how different our encounter was compared to his previous concert that week.

The presenting organization was a university near a large city where a hotel at the airport donated the accommodations in support of the arts program. The concert manager picked him up, took him to the concert and returned him to the airport hotel. Holzmair had an extended layover, however, since his Pro Musica date was several days later so he spent the next three days at the airport with no further contact from the university. Meanwhile, the hotel had only donated one night's accommodations and charged him for the next three. It was obviously a depressing experience. I told him I wished he had come to us for those three days. He wished he had known he could.

As I described to him my favorite Viennese songs, he showed amazement that he and his generation had no awareness of that repertoire. It comes from the operettas and a very large literature of popular songs—a sort of Viennese tin pan alley— from Vienna's heyday of a century ago. I first learned the songs from my Viennese grandmother and then heard them sung in recital by soprano Lotte Lehman. That was before Holzmair was born. The music is artistic and the texts offer sentimental praise of the charms and eccentricities of the city, the wine, the sense of humor and the people. Holzmair speculated that his unfamiliarity was partly due to the fact that he came from a village near Linz and moved to Vienna only as an adult to pursue his singing studies and career. By then, the *Weiner Lieder* tradition had already faded into history. On hearing the text of *Heut' kommen d'Engerln auf Urlaub nach Wien* (Today, the Angels take vacations in Vienna), he roared with laughter and twitted the Viennese for unparalleled arrogance. But when he wrote a note of appreciation for our hospitality, he suggested that, like the angels, we should come to Vienna and pay him a visit.

Along with high praise for his roles in opera and as soloist with Europe's leading orchestras, he was most highly regarded as a recitalist and interpreter of art songs. The *New York Times* ran a euphoric report on his three volume recording of Schubert lieder. By then, he had moved to a newer repertory. The centerpiece of his program for us was Schumann's *Dichterliebe, Op. 48*.

His visit was not without suspense, however. On the day of the concert, we had scheduled a radio interview only to be informed by Palm that Holzmair does not speak at all on the day of the concert. After some deliberation, he agreed to a half hour of conversation on the air since it was important for promotion.

It was even more suspenseful the morning after. As I merged on to the freeway toward the airport, a harsh Michigan February sleet storm began and the pavement was instantly coated with ice. Cars ahead of us were spinning out. The road was cluttered with a new cluster of collisions every few miles. With caution and skill acquired over years of driving north to ski, I threaded our way through the wreckage each time only to face more down the road. Between incredulous utterances that he had never seen anything like it, not even in snowy Austria, Holzmair expressed the hope that he could make his plane and have a day of rest and silence before his next recital at University of California, Berkeley.

Looking ahead, with still a long way to go, I could see that the curve just beyond the Michigan Avenue exit was impassable. It was the only choice, however, and on the surface street we finally reached Telegraph road and a convoy of salt trucks. We made the airport with minutes to spare and later learned that the flight was also delayed. Holzmair dashed for the plane with a hasty farewell. Palm was more relaxed expressing a hope that I would understand the singer's mood. I certainly did. Two years later when I visited him after a performance at the University Musical Society in Ann Arbor, we recalled that hair-raising ride with amusement.

To close our season, the new Orion Quartet reminded us of one of our important composer appearances. In between quartets by Mozart and Beethoven, they presented the second string quartet by Leon Kirchner (composer in residence at Harvard). He had appeared for us in 1963 with the Lenox Quartet performing the same work. The Orion came with impressive credentials. It had just collaborated with the Guarneri Quartet in the Mendelssohn Octet, and was Quartet in Residence at the Chamber Music Society of Lincoln Center. We would see its violist, Steven Tenenbom, again in a few years in another ensemble with his wife, Ida Kavafian (another former Detroiter).

In the continuing task of replacing members and attracting door sales, a Committee of the Whole was organized. The entire membership was enlisted to promote the 1995-96 season. Chairman Elaine Weingarden distributed scripts and materials, and members were urged to telemarket. Each was given a small, manageable list. The response was helpful but limited. Telephone solicitation and selling concert tickets is not an activity that many people feel comfortable with. I recalled our late president Dorothy Coolidge's success in that field with envy.

On another issue, we met with Joseph Bianco of the DIA Founders' Society and Rudy Lauerman, the museum's Audio Visual Manager, to discuss how we could improve the acoustics of the Recital Hall. Important measures that needed to be taken were to remove the draperies on the back wall and replace the acoustic tile with a hard surface on the ceiling. Both conditions were created during the *worst of times* from 1981 to 1983 when we had to leave the museum for two seasons. Out of our slim resources, Pro Musica agreed to share in the expense. It made a noticeable difference.

The passage of time was punctuated by the passing of Dr. Berj H. Haidostan, husband of 1st Vice President, Alice, in March, 1993. Her donation to the Endowment in his memory set an important example for other members but the event also reminded us of the constant attrition in membership. Among the loyal core, membership was a lifetime commitment. Losing one was like an alert to recruit more actively. Nonetheless, we were slowly winning new devotees and the ranks of working members changed and grew. New on the committee roster were Stan Beattie, publishing the programs; Seymour Kapetansky writing and distributing press releases; Daniel Herman, florist donating arrangements for the afterglow tables; Scott Ferris, endowment committee. It was never easy but we never fell short. Moreover, as leaders, we kept up our own efforts. First Vice President Alice Haidostian and I represented Pro Musica wherever we could and however we could. It was fun and fulfilling, for example, for us to present a program of French cabaret songs for the Alliance Francaise. I sang, Alice accompanied at the piano, and several entertained Alliance members joined Pro Musica.

The process of acquiring new members is not a well defined formula, however. Adherents are won by the experience of attending a brilliant performance in the ambience of an intimate hall and with old or new-found friends in music. Along with a superior listener impact, the salon atmosphere creates a closeness and congeniality that contributes power-fully to the quality of the total experience. The graciousness and good fellowship at the afterglow round off the evening with a pleasant oppor-tunity to unwind after the concert. Luring friends and acquaintances to try it with a personal invitation seems to yield a higher success rate than the conventional devices of direct mail, telemarketing or advertising.Even so, it is always important for Pro Musica to be acknowleged in the media. That provides background awareness that supports a personal invitation to attend. But good exposure in the media has become harder and harder to get.

The Parisii String Quartet

In the fall of 1995, The French Insti-tute and the Alliance Francaise made special arrangements for their members to purchase tickets for our opening pre-sentation of the Parisii String Quartet. Aphie and George Roumell, who were also members of the Alliance, agreed to host two members of the quartet while Marybelle and I hosted the other two. Lots of French conversation was overheard at the afterglow that Friday following a generous program of four quartets. The fact that two were by Pro Musica composers, Milhaud and Ravel, was not lost upon the crowd or the Pari-sian musicians. And the composition by

Webern was eminently satisfying for the new music enthusiasts. Nor could the traditionalists complain. They had to be delighted with an eloquent rendition of the late Beethoven *Quartet in F major, Opus 135.* Everyone went home well satisfied.

The vocal program came second that season with soprano Susan von Reichenbach. Sharing the hospitality privilege, Inge and George Vincent acted as hosts . Her program of infrequently heard art songs expanded our appreciation of the repertoire. Songs by Reynaldo Hahn, a Venezuelan contemporary composer of operas who spent most of his life in France, were new to most of us.

To close the season that year, we were at last able to bring another composer, Robert Helps. He was an important figure in American music even though he remained mostly in the background. A pupil of Roger Sessions, he taught at several leading conservatories in the East and worked closely with Aaron Copland on concert projects. In our tradition, he spoke from the piano and played examples of his compositions. It gave us a lively musical picture of the life of an American composer in the 20th century who divided his energies between composing and his position as Professor of Music at South Florida University.

A letter from Europe then led us into a new routine for the summer. The daughter of friends in Germany, Isabel Gabbe, and her fiancé, Laurent Boullet, were coming to the Aspen Festival in Colorado. Both were pianists invited to perform, teach, and take master classes there. Knowing about Pro Musica, they hoped we might be able to produce a concert for them en route to earn money for their transportation.

With the help of Alice Haidostian, Marybelle and I enlisted the collaboration of Tuesday Musicale and sent out invitations for a concert and buffet supper in our home, co-sponsored by Pro Musica. Our capacity of 40 people was filled so quickly that we scheduled a second performance the next evening. That sold out, too.

The music alternated between solo and four-hand pieces by the pianist sweethearts. Each played a Schubert sonata. Brahms waltzes and Dvorak Slavonic dances were played four-handed. The food almost caused a crisis, however. Grateful for our enterprise on their behalf, Isabel and Laurent insisted on helping in the kitchen where he undertook the slicing operation on the very sharp *mandolin* utensil to prepare the *potatoes Anna* and almost took a slice off the end of his finger. He played that evening with a band aid and no one knew the difference. It was, like so many other Pro Musica events, a really nice party. Everyone had a good time and the proceeds paid Isabel's and Laurent's passage home.

We attended their wedding the following year at the Mozarteum in Salzburg where they had met as students. Most flattering to Marybelle and me, they asked us to take part in the family music-making at the reception by performing a few of our Viennese songs. Relatives and friends had come from four continents for the wedding and most of them were amateur or professional musicians. Isabel's sister, Sabine, joined us to play the violin parts. As the only Americans in that cosmopolitan assemblage, our authentically styled performance of a uniquely Viennese art form occasioned considerable surprise.

Pro Musica's annual dinners in recent years had been such good parties with no new problems to solve that events at the 1996 meeting created a pleasant stir. First, the Endowment Committee announced that two members had made the first gifts of stock shares to our fund. Then our treasurer, Jim Diamond, who had recently undergone surgery, suggested that we should name an assistant treasurer. The nominee was Shahe Momjian who was promptly elected. Lastly, Alice Haidostian made a donation to start a fund in memory of Tom LoCicero, who had recently passed away. The loss of another stalwart end-ed the evening on a sad note.

Promoting our opening concert in September of 1996, we used an unusually successful device in advertising on the local classical music station of the time. There was a moment of absolutely sublime cello playing on a CD given us by our soloist, Suren Bagratuni. It stood out even in an already superb performance. We selected that ten-second passage to insert in a 60-second commercial promoting his concert. The magic of beautiful music was proven beyond doubt. A number of callers for tickets admitted to being captivated by that spot on FM radio and we had an exceptionally good turnout for his recital.

Suren Bagratuni

Bagratuni showed himself to be a quick wit as well as a great cellist. I took him to the Detroit Symphony to be auditioned by the artistic administrator for a possible concerto performance. She listened and then asked him if he would be interested in the job of principal cellist with the orchestra. "Oh, I couldn't," he replied. "I am trained only to be a soloist."

Italian pianist, Fabio Bidini, did yeoman service for us. We dedicated his concert to the memory of our late vice president, Tom LoCicero, who had always taken great pride in his Italian heritage. Bidini, a Busoni Competition winner and Van Cliburn finalist, for all his youthful 20 years, gave an intensely satisfying performance. Recalling the previous summer, we then persuaded Bidini to play for a house concert. This time it was to benefit the Pro Musica Endowment. The formula of music and an appetizing meal created a special ambience. There seemed to be a distinct affirmation of music by delectable food and of food by exquisite music. Sonatas by Scarlatti and Chopin, mouth-watering appetizers preceding a buffet of shrimp poached in white wine with a light tomato sauce, Tubetti pasta, Florentine salad and Hazelnut Torte combined to create an atmosphere that was very congenial. With the collaboration again of The Tuesday Musicale, it was an unqualified success.

We seemed to be on a popularity roll, in fact. Newspaper articles that winter called us "Champions for music" and a "Stop on the Road to the Top." Better yet, the David M. Whitney Fund responded to an application we made earlier in the year with a major grant to be added to the endowment. At that point, I persuaded myself to stop worrying about not selling out the membership and perpetually precarious finances. The endowment was now more that $100,000. That provides a small income and protects us against a catastrophe. We should concentrate on doing exciting, creative programs and bringing absolutely the best new artists we could find. If we are good, I felt, and get the word out, people will come.

Our 1996-97 season concluded in April with Canadian bass-baritone Nathan Berg. The engagement provided a bonus for him in being able to have a session with, and be accompanied by, Ann Arbor's highly respected pianist and vocal coach Martin Katz. Berg made the most

Nathan Berg

of the opportunity by staying with Katz instead of accepting our invitation and the recital certainly made it seem worthwhile. *Songs of Travel* by Vaughan Williams that opened the program and *Old American Songs* by Copland that closed it were much appreciated additions to the Pro Musica repertoire.

The annual meeting that summer featured an unusual musical treat. We had recently become friends with Peter A. Soave who was a virtuoso on the *bayan*, the Russian button accordion known in Argentina as the *bandoneon*. Soave had recently captured first prize at the international competition in Moscow competing with champion Russian artists who had previously dominated the event. After our dinner and brief election, his two most gifted students, Mady Dessimoulie and Guillaume Hodeau, joined him in a program of Tango music by Astor Piazzola. In the nautical atmosphere of the Crescent Sail Yacht Club meeting room, with sounds of the water lapping at hulls in the harbor and halyards slapping against masts, the music transported us into a fantasy world. Recalling the story of how Piazzola's last teacher, Nadia Boulanger, had encouraged him to forget about classical forms and write the music he knew and loved the best, we knew that evening we were the beneficiaries.

A few weeks later, Pro Musica's 70th season opened in October, 1997, with the Artis Quartet from Vienna. Our home hospitality program was possible by housing three players with us and the fourth with our Austrophile neighbors Ed and Jeannie Smith. The Smiths had never attended Pro Musica but they had skied in Austria and were enthusiastic hosts. Our hospitality skills were tested in a new way, however. At the previous booking in Florida, Cellist Othmar Mueller had found time to go swimming in the surf. Caught in a dangerous undertow he had struck the sand in shallow water and came up with pain and numbness in his bowing arm and shoulder. Frantic calls to our best health care contacts got him an immediate x-ray and consultation with a neurologist. The diagnosis was reassuring and Mueller played that evening, although it was without the doctor's approval. The elegant Viennese style of the quartet's performance of music by Mozart and Schubert was even more reassuring and Mueller left for their next engagement confident that he would be all right. When I happened to encounter first violinist Peter Schumayer in Vienna's Dorotheum auction house two years later, he assured me that the cellist was fully recovered.

Chapter 25

Creativity in Programming and Marketing

Pianist Frederic Chiu is an example of the surprising ways that artists sometimes get a publicity break and influence our program. As a finalist in the Van Cliburn competition he played a virtuoso transcription as his optional selection and for that the judges disqualified him. A columnist from the *New York Times* rushed back to his paper and published a feature in the performing arts section that described Chiu as the audience favorite at the competition and decrying the jury's action. It gave Chiu national celebrity.

Our audience did not need any encouragement to appreciate the pianist's artistry and intelligent musical insights. He performed three cycles of music for or about children and the complete *Chopin Etudes Opus 10*. His brief notes published in the program provided succinct and perceptive commentary.

> *The Prokofiev cycle was composed by a grown-up child for children to play.*
> *The Debussy cycle was composed by an adult for children to listen to.*
> *The Schumann cycle was composed by an adult for adults to reminisce about their childhood.*
> *The Chopin cycle was composed by a teen-ager, and adults can spend their whole lives practicing and only attempt to play it.*

Frederic Chiu

Many came to me at the afterglow with the suggestion that we bring Chiu back. I proposed this to him and asked what kind of program he would offer. He responded immediately: "I would play the Liszt transcriptions of Schubert's settings for his Schwannengesang song cycle with an actor reading the poem of each song in English before I play that transcription."

Chiu's idea was to make the audience fully aware of the sentiments and imagery in the poetry that Schubert was expressing in his justly famous accompaniments. These were superbly enhanced by Liszt's conversion into virtuoso concert showpieces. Chiu expressed the opinion that these may be Liszt's finest transcriptions. The whole concept struck me as brilliant. My immediate reaction was that I wanted to read the poetry myself but I realized that a well-known actor would be much better box office. I sought the agreement of members of the board and began to plan. It would take more than a year to find and sign the right actor.

Meanwhile, the season ended in April 1998 with lyric soprano Theresa Santiago, a graduate of Juilliard who placed first in the 1994 Naumberg competition. Her opening group consisted of the *Hermit Songs* by Samuel Barber. It reminded us wistfully that Pro Musica had missed including that composer on its roster because he was preoccupied with the production of his opera, *Vanessa*. Santiago also introduced us to rarely heard music by Richard Hundley and Fernando Obradors, whose songs in Spanish provided welcome opportunities for vocal fireworks.

That fall, the moveable feast that was our annual dinner meeting was held in a unique location. Former Pro Musica members Sara and Melvin

Theresa Santiago

Maxwell Smith had built a home designed by Frank Lloyd Wright on an open woodland site with a pond in Bloomfield Hills. After their death, the Smiths' children put the property in a trust and dedicated it to public use for selected non profit groups. It is a fascinating house to visit. The Smiths were small in stature and Wright designed the house in proportion to their size. A long display shelf in the salon is filled with a fine collection from the arts and crafts movement. The house itself has the feeling of a miniature and the individualistic style of the architect is unmistakable. The terrace and lawns sloping down to the pond create a beautiful setting. In balmy September weather we dined and held our meeting at tables out of doors.

The report by treasurer, Shahe Momjian, revealed how we were managing financially in sharp contrast to Coolidge's *Hay in the Barn* policy. Income from ticket sales was $19,926 and expenses were $25,177. The biggest cost items were fees and expenses of $11,849 for the artists, followed by $9,399 for staff and services at the museum. Postage, printing and advertising accounted for the rest. The operating deficit of $5,250 was covered by income and capital appreciation from the endowment fund.

Not included in the reckoning was the value of volunteer hours spent by officers, board and committee members of the Society. We audited the time spent for management, negotiating contracts, record keeping, writing and mailing out publicity, designing and distributing fliers, chauffeuring and hosting artists, and all the other activities involved in producing concerts. Valuing them at a conservative $20 per hour, we estimated more than $50,000 in these services. This was an important factor in our being able to offer our concerts and afterglows with great artists and composers at the modest price of only $50 for the three-concert season.

One other important device had been instituted as well. Each year, nearly 100 members subscribed to Patron Memberships at double the price of a regular season ticket. The patrons were and still are a critical factor in enabling us to meet expenses from year to year.

In another significant development, a recently recruited Board member, Patrick Broderick, helped us open a tax-sheltered brokerage account for the deposit of securities that had been given to the endowment fund. Invested in a mutual fund, a GNMA fund, gifted equities and some cash, the endowment that year was worth $108,000 bringing Pro Musica's total assets to $115, 306. It was a far cry from the unincorporated group with $1,000 in the bank of only 13 years earlier. The challenge of selling enough tickets to eliminate operating deficits still remained, but the business meeting adjourned with a satisfying sense of security and achievement.

For the meeting's usual musical finale, the group of nearly 50 members barely fit cozily in the salon and adjacent dining area of the house for a program of light classics and Gershwin played on the Smiths' parlor grand piano. The artist was local musical celebrity David Syme. A few members, remaining out of doors, enjoyed hearing the music floating through open windows across the landscape.

Julian Rachlin

Recommendations from DSO Music Director Neeme Järvi, who had brought violinist Julian Rachlin as soloist the previous year, influenced us to open our 1998-99 season with him. A native of Lithuania, Rachlin moved with his parents to Austria to continue his studies. As he began to perform publicly, he was described by other musicians as evoking feelings of the old Russian School that he had learned from Boris Kuschnir. But he was also credited with an impressive interpretive approach that he acquired growing up in Vienna. By the time we presented him, his career already sparkled with starring appearances with such important orchestras as the Philadelphia, Baltimore, Detroit and Minnesota Symphonies. He had performed chamber music with past Pro Musica artists, cellist Truls Mork and violinist Cho-Liang Lin. He was the youngest soloist ever to appear with the Vienna Philharmonic.

His conventional but nonetheless brilliant recital program included impressive treatments of sonatas by Beethoven and Brahms and virtuoso displays of Saint-Saens' *Rondo Capriccioso* and Waxman's *Carmen Fantasy*. For my personal taste, special moments came with Kreisler's *Liebesleid und Liebesfreud*, and then *Rosamarin* for an encore which he dedicated to Marybelle and me. That was a bonus of the camaraderie we enjoyed having Rachlin as our house guest. I could never conceal my fondness for my Viennese heritage.

Our next artist guest, Brazilian pianist Arnaldo Cohen, was similarly congenial. We picked him because his recorded performances of the Schumann Fantasy and Brahms Handel Variations were unexcelled. His status in Europe where he won attention substituting for Martha Argerich with the Concertgebuow in Amsterdam was already firmly established. His studies in Brazil with Jacques Klein, a disciple of Willam Kapell, and in Vienna with Bruno Seidhover and Dieter Weber, bypassed the influences and style of the great American music schools that were most familiar to us. As we welcomed him to Detroit, he burst upon our scene like a new form of energy. His program choices—by Debussy, Chopin, Schumann and Liszt—were practiced in our living room and performed in recital with drama, flair, romance and high energy. It was a refreshing perspective on keyboard artistry.

Our friendship blossomed during his three-day visit. He professed genuinely to enjoy our performances of the Wiener Lieder, which he recalled fondly from his days as a student in that musical city. My ambitions to make a quality recording of our performances struck a sympathetic chord and we phoned a record producer friend of his in London to discuss the idea. Cohen even offered us his London flat as a home base while we carried out the plan. Our inability to schedule the availability of a suitable violinist to complete the trio was our principal impediment. But we had a good time exploring the scheme and Pro Musica presented a memorable pianist.

Plans for the final concert brought back memories of Coolidge's comments on the headaches of presenting opera stars. In our unsuccessful efforts to book soprano Inessa Galante, we had discovered a Detroit-born bass-baritone by the name of Christopher Schaldenbrand who had made it as a member of the Metropolitan Opera company. We even saw him on a TV broadcast of the Met's production of *Carmen*. We jumped at the opportunity to bring a hometown artist but finding a date was not easy. His manager kept juggling new bookings to appear in regional opera companies as well as at the Met. Finally we settled on the opera slow season in May and began our promotion campaign. But only weeks before his concert, he was offered a major role in the premiere of a new work at the Houston Opera. His management sent us soprano Bridgett Hooks in his place. She had a lovely voice, had sung extensively on the Community Concert Series and gave us a beautiful recital. We had built up so much anticipation for bringing a hometown artist, however, that the mood at the end of the season was inevitably anti-climactic. I was tempted to repeat Coolidge's angry cry of "no more opera stars," not to mention their managers.

Chapter 26
The Inspiration of Obstacles
and Adversity – 1999

D uring the season just ended, in the search for a suitable actor to read the poetry from the Schwannengesang songs, I recognized the man we needed while attending a play at the Stratford Festival in Ontario, Canada. Star actor at Stratford, winner of New York's prestigious Tony Award, matinee idol of Michigan fans of the Festival, Brian Bedford was the answer to my quest. Using my contacts as board member of the Michigan Friends of Stratford and arts columnist for the Grosse Pointe News, I broached the idea with Stratford's Director of Press Relations. The problem, as usual, was finding a date when Bedford, Frederic Chiu, and our recital hall were all available. Bedford was the most difficult.

After receiving his private phone number from a supportive Festival executive, I spoke to him at his home in Stratford. The idea interested him and the possibilities that the program could be taken on tour and recorded added to the appeal. But there was very limited time available during

Brian Bedford

the Stratford season which ran from April to November. He normally played two or three starring roles in repertory which left him only occasional days off. The rest of the year, he wintered in North Africa. I had to wait for the next season schedule to be confirmed before we could look for an opening.

At the end of the season, the hit production of Shakespeare's *Much Ado About Nothing*, starring Bedford as Benedick, was taken for a limited run to the New York City Center. Going to see it, I contacted Bedford at his hotel. He had his schedule. We agreed on Wednesday, October 13. I offered a modest fee that Pro Musica could afford. He countered that he should be paid the same as the pianist. Recognizing that this could be the clincher, I agreed immediately. We had a date.

When I contacted the museum to reserve the hall, I had another surprise. Due to planned renovations, the Recital Hall would not be available to us for the next two seasons. Our solution was to move to the large auditorium which was not available on weekends when the highly popular film theater used it. By a stroke of luck, our Wednesday date with Bedford fit the situation. We were able to move the Pro Musica concerts to the auditorium on Wednesdays. Now we had 1,100 seats to fill. It seemed that one problem solved led to another.

Reporting Pro Musica's forthcoming concert with Bedford to a Board meeting of the Michigan Friends of Stratford, I caught the ear of the Festival's development staff who considered it to their benefit to jump on the bandwagon. The Festival offered to chauffeur Bedford to and from Detroit for the concert and, when asked, they agreed to let us promote it to all the Stratford fans on their Detroit area mailing list. In fact, they were ready to do a mailing themselves and sell the tickets with a commission scaled to cover just their costs.

Meanwhile, other challenges were looming. Life at the Detroit Institute of Arts was becoming more expensive and more difficult. Drastic reductions in state and city subsidies, the reorganization of the museum management with a change in director, and the transfer of control from the city to a governing board, necessitated many changes in operating systems and policies. The effect on Pro Musica was the erosion of privileges that had been in place for more than 70 years. There were increases in costs for space and services that we had enjoyed at nominal or no charge. Items like piano rental, audio visual services, stage set up, parking attendant, and management fee were now appearing on our bill for the first time. In effect, the museum had formerly used its subsidized status to extend subsidies to Pro Musica. It could no longer do so.

There was a lesson for us in this. The Museum had never been encouraged to build its own endowment to free it from the need of subsidies. This made us increasingly aware of the need to build our own endowment so that gradually we would be able to pay our own way fully. Meanwhile, we had to compensate the museum for services that had once been free.

Even so, the museum management accommodated us to the fullest extent possible. We were, after all, its oldest tenant and a non-profit arts organization, not a business that could afford to pay thousands of dollars to rent a gallery for a reception. And we brought to the museum the prestige of our distinguished artists and audiences who were actual or potential museum patrons. Our relationship remained cordial and the museum staff helped us as much as they could.

Returning to the home of Dr. Kim and Mado Lie for our 1999 annual meeting, several developments were topics for discussion. Stan Beattie announced the creation of a Pro Musica computer network between himself, treasurer Shahe Momjian and myself. Stan's membership data base and Shahe's financial records were backed up in three locations. Lynnette Iannace and Seymour Kapetansky were coordinating publicity releases with the Stratford Festival for the Chiu-Bedford concert. Bill Harmon had made contact with an organization of young, single professionals and was working out a plan to promote Pro Musica with that group. Ken Collinson provided a dedicated phone line that people could call for a message that he would record about Pro Musica. Ken was also working with me to research translations of the texts from *Schwannengesang* for use in the upcoming performance. The dramatically improved appearance of our programs and brochures was credited to a new chairman of graphics. Kyo Takahashi had retired with me from the advertising business where we had become good friends. He took over the design and layout of Pro Musica's printed materials with dramatic impact.

Adapting to the new regime at the museum, we took other advantage of their facilities. As a way to enhance the experience of a Pro Musica evening, we arranged to open a gallery of the museum's permanent collection for a short, free tour before each concert. We also persuaded the catering staff to open the Gallery Grill for dinner. The idea was inspired primarily by Bill Harmon's experience in discovering Pro Musica. He told us:

My parents gave me their tickets for one concert and I took a date. She was really impressed with the fact that I knew of such a great thing to do in Detroit. Then I felt that it would be even more attractive to people like myself in the young professionals group if they could come for cocktails and dinner, and maybe a little gallery tour to make a package evening.

Overcoming the museum catering department's misgivings about attracting enough customers to meet expenses, we instructed our members to
make reservations and come for dinner. To everyone's delight, the restaurant was sold out. For a few seasons, the catering department tolerated
the suspense of waiting to see if their tables would be filled and trying
to stock just enough food to meet the demand. Remodeling inside the
museum was to make it impossible to continue these dinners. The gallery
tours remained an unqualified success with large enough crowds to require
two and sometimes three docents for guides. They seemed well worth the
extra costs for guards which are kept at a minimum as long as a docent is
present.

With characteristic enthusiasm, the '99 annual meeting discussed,
improved and approved all these undertakings, held an election and was
eager for the expected musical surprise. It is well described in secretary
Ann Kondak's minutes.

*Charles Mason, who had no children or heirs, was a writer/composer of
popular songs in the 30s and 40s and was employed for a while by the
Jerome Remick music publishing house whose owner helped found Pro
Musica. Mason had many songs that were copyrighted but never sold
commercially. He was a friend of the Suczek family and before he died,
he gave his manuscripts to Alex who loved the songs. Alex sang several
of Mr. Mason's songs accompanied on the piano by Alice Haidostian.
The program was delightful and enjoyed by all present.*

October was drawing near. Marketing of the Chiu-Bedford concert was on
a roll. The Stratford Festival marketing department reported selling more
tickets than Pro Musica did. The Canadian Consulate donated $1,000
to help pay for a greatly expanded afterglow in the museum's spacious
Prentis Court.

The texts of the poetry posed a problem, however. Having read all
the available translations, I found them accurate but awkward for reading
aloud so I decided to set them aside and write new ones in blank verse. My
goal was to express the true meaning of the German originals in graceful
phrases that would be clearly understood when spoken by a skilled actor.
Meter and rhyme were secondary. Chiu and Bedford accepted the new
texts without reservations.

On the evening of the concert, a few glitches reflecting disorganization at the museum in a time of change did occur. Callers left voice mail reservations for dinner which could not be honored. Hopeful diners were turned away hungry.

Brian Bedford arrived around lunchtime to rehearse with Chiu in the afternoon. It went well. They agreed on staging and timing and even added a few creative touches such as alternating the reading of lines of text and playing segments of the music where there were extended transitions and changes of mood. Then, after having a museum dinner which we had fortunately arranged in advance, Bedford asked for his couch where he could rest before the performance. My request for that accommodation, days earlier, had been overlooked. Nothing could be arranged. Marybelle finally found a quiet room where she could only lay her coat and a make-shift cushion on the floor. Our actor was obviously and rightfully irritated, but he took it like a trooper.

The concert was a triumph. A thousand people filled the auditorium's main floor. The performance was immensely moving and the prepared encore Liszt transcription of Schubert's famous song *Die Forelle (The Trout)*, with a reading of the poem, was acknowleged with an extended ovation. It seemed as though everyone stayed for the afterglow.

Two newspapers covered the concert. Lawrence B. Johnson summarized the program succinctly in the *Detroit News*. "As Bedford limned each sentiment of yearning or regret, of love rekindled or lamented, Chiu followed with Liszt's probing and dazzling restatement for keyboard alone."

Mark Stryker wrote a perceptive commentary in the *Free Press*.

Wednesday's recital…surely ranks among the most novel in the society's 73 seasons…The clever twist was that to better understand Schubert's skill in realizing in music the imagery of the text, Bedford, on loan from the Stratford Festival, preceded each song (transcription) by reading the translation. Often the idea worked superbly. Bedford, his diction as precise as an etching, would speak of flowing tears and eternal grief and Chiu would enlarge the metaphor through a despairing funeral march. Chiu wisely reordered the songs to form a more compelling dramatic arch, the narrator moving from an idealized nostalgia for past love through a weather-beaten present and concluding with a premonition of death…Chiu typically avoided overt sentimentality. He opted for a muscular lyricism, speckled by brawny attacks and stony tone, that often added welcome virility to Liszt's rosewater surfaces…an unusual concert experience…and at its best—as in …Heinrich Heine's delectable words and Liszt's lilting music in the song The Fisher Girl—*the results were sweet and moving.*

A year later, I realized my ambition to do the reading myself. From my windsurfing hideaway on South Padre Island, I arranged with the music department at the University of Texas in nearby Brownsville to bring Frederic Chiu, by now a really good friend. He flew down for a modest fee and I did the reading for the fun of it. It was again a successful evening. While on the island as our guest, Chiu tried windsurfing and I took snapshots of him in action on the water. After he left us to go on a concert tour in Europe, he showed the pictures proudly to amazed friends.

Once again, arrangements at the Detroit Institute of Arts changed. Delays in the renovations made it possible for us to return to the smaller Recital Hall for the rest of the season. Unfortunately, with contracts and dates all committed, we had to stay on the Wednesday evening schedule even though we were losing some long-time regular subscribers who could not attend mid-week. On the other hand, the smaller hall was better suited to the artists and the size of audience we could attract to their special programs. Our loyal members appreciated the new artists we discovered and much preferred the intimate hall.

Barely a month after the *Schwannengesang* program, we presented Canadian soprano Isabel Bayrakdarian. Once again, board members Alice Haidostian, Mado Lie and Hershel Sandberg had recommended her after hearing her on Canadian radio. Like other singers, Bayrakdarian engaged Martin Katz to accompany her so that she could coach with him. The concert was outstanding and nostalgic as it included such works as Barber's *Hermit Songs* and *Spanish Songs* by Obradors. No one was surprised when a year later we heard that Bayrakdarian had been cast in an important role at the Metropolitan Opera.

Isabel Bayrakdarian

After our season had already been booked, Alice Haidostian brought news that a new piano quartet called Opus One had been formed by violinist and former Detroiter Ida Kavafian, violist Steven Tenenbom, cellist Peter Wiley and pianist Anne-Marie McDermott. Considering the prestige of the artists and our past connections with Kavafian and Tenenbom, the board agreed that we should be the first to present Opus One in Detroit. We were especially eager to hear McDermott whom we knew then only by reputation. For the same reasons, The Tuesday Musicale agreed to Alice Haidostian's suggestion that they co-sponsor a special concert in January and our marketing machinery went into action. Knowing Pro Musica's mission for new music, Kavafian programmed Hartke's 1988 Tableaux for violin, cello and piano, *The King of the Sun*, along with a Haydn trio and a Brahms piano quartet. McDermott made such an outstanding impression that members urged us to bring her back for a solo recital.

While no critic reviewed the concert, Mark Stryker published some worthwhile insights regarding the ensemble's unusual status which made it all the more appropriate for Pro Musica.

> *Opus One balances the usual repertoire of Mozart and Brahms with a commitment to such new American composers as Stephen Hartke. It has no professional management because it doesn't need it. According to Kavafian, they organized the quartet because we love making music together. But the group is not looking for a career. None of us have time... Opus one will play no more than 20 concerts annually. The irony is that the group could perform more than 100 given the reputation and resumes of the players...*

Their independence is also important for their artistic freedom, Kavafian explains:

> *When speaking with an agent, presenters often balk at contemporary music like Hartke's quartet. But if we talk directly to the presenter I can say...it's really a great piece and right for your audience...All of a sudden it's not too modern anymore. At least not with a group like Pro Musica.*

Chapter 27

An Object Lesson for Impresarios – 2000

T he final, regular concert of our season was even more exceptional and was scheduled for Tuesday evening May 2, 2000. That was a story in itself. It began two seasons earlier with Leif Ove Andsnes' most recent appearance as soloist with the DSO. Meeting him after the concert we asked if he would come back to give Pro Musica a solo recital. He assured me that he would and asked me to call his management. When I did, his manager told me that Andsnes was too busy. There was absolutely no opening in his schedule. His fee had also skyrocketed. Not to be dismissed so easily, I urged him to ask Andsnes which he agreed to do. A week later the manager called me back to say, with some surprise in his voice, "Leif wants to play for Pro Musica but he wants to bring you a trio program with violinist Christian Tetzlaff and his cellist sister, Tanya. The date they are available is Tuesday May 2."

This was possible because the three of them were appearing at the Gilmore Foundation in Kalamazoo, Michigan, on Monday May 1. It was a part of Andsnes' acknowledgement of the generous award the Foundation had given him the previous year. The trio had a program that Andsnes wanted very much to play for Pro Musica. At that point, I had barely heard of the Tetzlaffs, but I quickly learned that Christian was the most highly praised young violinist in Europe at the time. It was certainly an offer we could not refuse.

On Monday May 1st, Marybelle and I, Pro Musica Secretary Ann Kondak and her husband Nick drove in two vehicles to Kalamazoo to attend the concert there. The plan was to bring the trio to Detroit on Tuesday. All three would be our house guests. To be able to handle the trio, the cello and their luggage, Ann and Nick Kondak followed us in their sports van.

The concert in Kalamazoo was an object lesson for impresarios. It was held in the auditorium of an arts center that had been a school building. The hall is attractive, but too large and not acoustically live enough for chamber music. It was far from full and the audience, while polite and considerate, was only moderately responsive. Possibly as a reaction, even though the performance was technically expert, it never seemed genuinely inspired.

After the concert, the trio expressed their own misgivings. Leif complained about the piano which had been specially brought from Steinway in New York. Christian asked me doubtfully, "What did you think?" No one could put their finger on any specific shortcoming but there was an air of disappointment. Recalling other ensembles I had heard made up ad hoc of soloists that did not project a convincing musical magic, I became concerned about Pro Musica's concert.

The next morning, on the drive across Michigan, we had pleasant conversation about music and Leif's career progress and plans. Arriving at our home soon after noon, the trio settled in their rooms while Marybelle and I prepared a luncheon banquet. The Tetzlaffs relaxed with just a sip of wine and everyone feasted hungrily on one of Leif's favorite entrees— broiled salmon filets. Then, mid afternoon, they all took my suggestion to go upstairs and have a nap.

That evening, we arrived at the hall barely an hour before concert time. They tried the piano and the acoustics, then ran through key entries and passages. Leif was pleased with the piano which had been worked on by our technician, Tom Pettit, that afternoon. The program was all Schumann: *Six Pieces in Canon Form and Trios No. 2 and 3.*

By concert time, the audience filled the little hall and there was excitement in the air. I delivered my usual brief greeting and sat down nervously with Marybelle, side stage, second row. Moments later Leif, Christian and Tanya walked on stage to welcoming applause. A hush of anticipation fell over the talkative crowd and the trio began to play.

The chemistry of the Recital Hall, the Pro Musica audience and the inspired playing of the trio resulted in a totally different performance from the previous evening in Kalamazoo. The dynamics of their very first phrases of music were electrifying and the waves of silent reaction of the audience behind me made the back of my neck tingle. What I originally intended to be a piano recital turned into one of the most superb chamber performances I ever heard.

Christian Tetzlaff's note in our guest book put into words what I had hoped to achieve. *Great hospitality, great audience, great food, and thanks for the sleepover.*
The lone press report, by Ruth Crystal-Zaromp in the *Detroit Monitor*, began with the information that Pro Musica Detroit was founded "before most of us were born" and continued with a slightly inaccurate compliment. "Its president for many years, Alex Suczek, can be credited with its track record of excellence—but even he is younger than this

Leif Andsnes and the Tetzlaffs

series, now in its 73rd season." In truth, Pro Musica Detroit and I were born in the same year and I felt challenged every season to maintain the standard that had been set before me.

She continued with much more important observations.

The hall was totally sold out and one could notice many younger faces, which is not the norm in classical music events these days...Andsnes...is among the select few who can combine ferocious technique with refined art...Both Tetzlaffs...seem to be well versed in the universal language of music...This program...was combined with a private tour of the DIA's Van Gogh: Face to Face exhibit...a rare appetizer for the musical program.

Schumann and Van Gogh...both suffered from mental illness...Their affliction proved to be the moving force behind their art. Schumann's affliction is manifested in the works on this program. Some of the structure and the rhythms are ...hard to fathom. However, as Van Gogh demonstrated in his art, madness and art need not be mutually exclusive. Indeed, the three gifted performers...not only found a method in Schumann's madness, but turned his obscure and neglected works into a refined and sublime art, making one wonder why such music is not performed more often.

My own answer to the critic's concluding question is that few musicians could match that remarkable performance. It could be achieved only by the masterful artistic leadership of the pianist and the equally masterful response of the violinist and cellist. To hear such a performance is a rare privilege indeed.

Meanwhile, more changes were taking place at the museum. Graham Beal had been recruited to take over as director and I met with him to make him aware of our history, our special relationship with the museum and Pro Musica's needs. He was understanding and sympathetic but obviously preoccupied with his assignment to revitalize the museum and rebuild attendance while working to restore the institution's funding. One positive step for Pro Musica was Beal's assigning a single staff person to work with us in setting up arrangements for our concerts. In recent years we had found ourselves dealing individually with the different staff members responsible for reserving the hall, security, parking, food service, audio-visual equipment and stage set up. Now we could do it all through Dianne Abel, Director of Visitor Services, and still enjoy much of the privileged access to the facilities of past decades. She has proven to be a particularly skillful coordinator of the museum's diverse resources.

What we could not avoid, however, was the constantly changing schedule of renovations that forced us to change from Friday to Wednesday evening dates and from our intimate Recital Hall to the too spacious auditorium. It also would occasion the temporary closing of the museum dining room and put an end to pre-concert dinners. But we had to adapt. So with the success of the *Schwannengesang* concert fresh in our memory, we decided to look for attractions that would take advantage of being in the auditorium. As a marketing strategy to help fill the house, Pat Broderick used his connections with the museum staff to help us arrange to sell tickets through the museum box office. Phone orders could be taken on credit cards which could boost sales. Our concerts would also be listed in the Museum calendar.

As we considered the possibilities, two very enticing opportunities arose. The U.S. management of the 18-member Berlin Chamber Orchestra offered us a date in the fall of 2000 at a fee that was reduced because the group would already be traveling in our area. We also remembered learning from Neeme Järvi of his younger son's crossover orchestra, *The Absolute Ensemble*. A group of 17 outstanding, classically trained musicians, Kristjan Järvi's ensemble was making a big impression in New York and Europe with programs of what some observers were calling "Third Stream Music—jazz, rock, Broadway, funk fusion and Latin Licks," all played with symphonic virtuosity. Having both groups in the same season would make a stunning contrast in programs. The Berlin group specializes in such classic composers as Haydn, Mozart and Boccherini; *The Absolute* in the music of John Adams, Charlie Mingus, Steve Reich, Charles Coleman and Michael Daugherty with a few classicists like Bach, Beethoven and Debussy thrown in. At a meeting in January 2000, the board voted to take the plunge.

We had reason to be confident. Thanks mainly to the success of the *Schwannengesang* concert the past season had been profitable. A preliminary report from treasurer Shahe Momjian showed $50,998 gross income and a net of $8,395. That was almost double the highest previous gross and an unheard of net operating profit. Total assets of the endowment had risen to $131,725. I suspected we could not duplicate the success of the *Schwannengesang* concert but we decided to press our advantage.

Bringing two large ensembles in one season posed a new level of financial commitment and logistics, however. It was deemed prudent to seek a subsidy for the increased budget. We would have to arrange accommodations and local transportation for both groups. The logistical costs alone would be significant.

Hershel Sandberg, with the help of his son Daniel, identified the Michigan subsidiaries of three German automotive parts suppliers that might be interested in sponsoring the Berlin Chamber Orchestra. We obtained the names of executives to contact. I wrote letters and made phone calls. The Robert Bosch Corporation, a company with a long tradition of supporting the arts, generously responded to our invitation with a $10,000 grant. Gratefully, we felt able to proceed with confidence.

Then it occurred to me to extend the hospitality tradition to involve more of Pro Musica's loyal membership in housing the large group. I sent a letter to members inviting them each to host one or two members of the Berlin Chamber Orchestra for the fall concert. It was amazing how eagerly they responded and how smoothly it worked out. We hired a bus to bring the orchestra and its instruments from the airport to the museum. There, members met and picked up their guests along with instructions for bringing them back for rehearsal, performance and finally to catch the bus back to the airport.

An invitation to the chief executives and foundations of local businesses for sponsorship of our Absolute Ensemble concert was not successful. Even the local distributor of Absolut Vodka turned us down. However, the support of the Robert Bosch Corporation for the first concert gave us enough security to proceed and we counted on improvements in our marketing to attract a larger audience.

As a result of building our data base, Stan Beattie reported 1,500 qualified names and addresses in our mailing list. A handsome brochure for the upcoming season, designed by Kyo Takahashi, was ready for Susanne McMillan to send out under our third class, non-profit permit. A team led by Elaine Weingarden would maintain stocks of the brochure at pickup points like churches, libraries, and bookstores throughout the metropolitan Detroit area. We engaged a public relations and marketing service to issue press releases, arrange media interviews and set up cooperative deals with restaurants. They would provide a dinner-and-concert package with transportation between restaurant and museum. The releases publicized the availability of tickets by credit card through the museum box office.

Board member Ann Greenstone arranged for our annual dinner in September 2000 at the Birmingham Athletic Club. Members reviewed plans for the coming season with considerable enthusiasm and agreed to renew individual efforts to promote the concerts. The musical entertainment was a video of Canadian Baritone James Westman who would present our final concert of the season. It had been filmed at the International Vocal Competition in Wales where he had taken a gold medal. It was agreed to advise the Canadian Consulate in Detroit of the concert and seek assistance in promoting it.

Everyone seemed energized by the new scale of our programs but an important question had been raised. Hershel Sandberg expressed the feeling of many long time members that the intimate ambience of our concerts and afterglows was part of Pro Musica's identity. They hoped we would return to the smaller recital hall with its salon atmosphere and the beautiful Romanesque Hall and Kresge Court for the afterglow. That was an important part of what had attracted them to Pro Musica in the first place. Difficult as it is to produce concerts of such special quality on a small scale, I was nonetheless in total agreement.

As the date for the Berlin Chamber Orchestra approached, the musicians' management raised another requirement that we rarely had to deal with. Their double bass was shipped separately and in case it went astray, they wanted us to have a spare available. It took only a few phone calls to local bass players to make the arrangement, but it added to my apprehensions regarding all the complicated arrangements. Fortunately, my concerns proved to be unwarranted. The orchestra's plane arrived on time and so did their double bass. The bus was at the airport waiting. The Pro Musica hosts eagerly fetched their house guests and brought them punctually to rehearsal and concert. Even before the event was over I was hearing about new friendships formed and the pleasure of entertaining the artists.

At the museum, we discovered a new food service in the Crystal Gallery at the balcony level of the auditorium. It was open regularly on weekend evenings for the film theater. We arranged to have it open the evening of our concert so that both musicians and members of our audience could eat there before the performance. We learned later that since it was catered by an outside service, it represented unwanted competition for the museum's contracted restaurateur. We did not press the issue.

The Berlin Chamber Orchestra concert on Wednesday, November 15, 2000, was an unqualified success. The responsible executive from our benefactor Robert Bosch Corporation was there and proud of what he had helped us accomplish. Nearly 900 people filled the auditorium's main floor and enjoyed a virtuoso performance. True to an old tradition, the orchestra members played standing up to have optimum freedom of expression. The concert ended with an ovation and again it seemed as though everyone joined us in the Prentis Court for the afterglow. There a manager of the orchestra sold out his supply of CD recordings of the Mozart selections the audience had just heard in the concert.

Our efforts were directed immediately to promoting the Absolute Ensemble's appearance in February. Kristjan Jarvi described his group as "a catalyst for changing prevailing notions of what constitutes a serious concert in the tradition bound world of classical programming." It amounted to a complete antithesis of the Vienna Classics just presented by the Berlin group. His stated goal was "to perform programs that are meaningful for contemporary audiences and provide a perspective on the evolution of music in our time." It is a concept that fit the Pro Musica mission. Kristjan and his musicians appeared to be emerging stars. Their program would take us on a tour of a musical frontier. And the concert would be their debut in Detroit.

We struck a responsive chord in a new segment of the press and the public. The alternative newspaper in the city, The *Detroit Metro Times*, which rarely even mentions a classical music event, published a feature length interview with the young Järvi. There were several photos and a plug on the cover. Inside, an article described the programming concept in depth. Reaching an entirely different public made the concert another of those occasions when a significant number of new people, many of them much younger, appeared in our audience. It gave us a great sense of accomplishment, but also one of frustration as we wondered how we might bring them back. Future programs, lacking the jazz content, would inevitably appear to return to the tradition-bound classical category. Moreover, the midweek schedule was already discouraging attendance. We had even lost a few of our regulars because of it. The rest took it in stride and shared the enthusiasm of our new, younger audience with a spirit of adventure that was reminiscent of the membership in Pro Musica's early days.

We caught attention in another important area, however. Aware that we were bringing the son of DSO Music Director, Neeme Järvi, the symphony's chairman, Peter Cummings, attended the concert and gained a first-hand awareness of Pro Musica. I already knew that it would be important to cultivate his acquaintance. In a brief conversation, asked if he could make time to meet with me. In time, that would prove to be an important step.

James Westman

The on-again, off-again remodeling at the museum made our recital hall available that spring. It was possible to hold the season's final concert there. Canadian Baritone James Westman finished our series with a distinguished recital of art songs by Ravel, Rachmaninoff and Beethoven, concluding with Butterworth's settings of poems by A. E. Housman from *A Shropshire Lad*. Westman is a native of Stratford, Ontario, and rising star after winning an international vocal competition in Wales. Once again, the Canadian Consul General in Detroit supported the afterglow.

The annual meeting on September 14, 2001, at Crescent Sail Yacht Club glowed with the accomplishment of a revolutionary season dimmed only by the lingering shock of the terrorist attack three days earlier in New York. We rekindled our spirits with memories of the three concerts that year. They had been artistic triumphs and with the help of our corporate sponsor we ended the season in the black while the endowment fund crept up to a new high.

That was beginning to change, however, as we felt the impact of the decline in the stock market. Most of the money was invested in a conservative *Growth and Income Fund*. While it was invested defensively, it was still subject to the downward trend.

But there were other important developments as well. Member Sarah Snow initiated a program for bringing music students from Detroit's Cass Technical High School which has an excellent musical curriculum. They were students who might otherwise not have the opportunity to attend a classical music performance. A letter to the membership brought funds to supplement her seed gift so that for the season just ended we had been able to invite 16 students to each concert. Members endorsed her efforts and several offered to help with the understanding that this small beginning could be an important new effort in developing future audience.

On the organizational side, with Shahe Momjian moving to Chicago, Stan Beattie agreed to step up to the treasurer's role and asked for assistance in maintaining the Society's data base on the computer. Health problems of membership secretary Florence Arnoldi and her husband Harold made it necessary for her to turn her job over to Margaret Beck. I had to report that our relationship with the DIA was continuing to change. Pro Musica could no longer bring in its own donated finger sandwiches and other treats for the afterglow. The critical issue was having liability insurance coverage for catered food. The museum insisted that whoever provided the food had to have at least $1,000,000 in coverage. In addition, since the management of the museum is now an independent entity, there is no more Founders' Society to be our sponsor. We needed to work out an up-to-date relationship with the museum's chairman and new Director.

My own tenure was another question that I felt obliged to discuss. My presidency was about to match Dorothy Coolidge's longevity on the job.

New Ways Feed on the Old

Breaking her record was never my desire. I asked a search committee to find someone who could work with me and be able to take on executive leadership or to succeed me. My hope was that whenever someone took over, it would be a smoother and easier transition than I had experienced. Amid protestations, I promised that I would always be around to help, no matter what.

The musical surprise that evening was to have been a video of a young soprano under consideration for a future concert. When the club's VCR refused to function, Alice Haidostian and I filled the breach with French cabaret songs and a tune by Charlie Mason. Secretary Ann Kondak reported that members enjoyed the impromptu program and gave us an enthusiastic hand.

Chapter 28

New Opportunities and New Challenges
— 2001

For some time, The Detroit Symphony Orchestra under the leadership of its board Chairman Peter Cummings had been planning a very ambitious enlargement of its facilities at Orchestra Hall. When built in 1919, it was simply a concert hall with great acoustics and minimal public amenities. After being abandoned for several decades, it had been restored and was again the home of the orchestra. The scope of the proposed expansion was visionary including many long needed features such as elevators, extra rest rooms, a members' lounge for important supporters, rehearsal rooms, and catering facilities. Of the greatest interest to Pro Musica was the plan for a recital hall with the best possible acoustics. There was no question in my mind, and board members all agreed, that we would at least try that recital hall when it was finished. It might even provide a basis for reviving the intermittent collaborations between Pro Musica and the DSO that had occurred from time to time throughout our history. To germinate the idea and explore the possibilities, I met with key figures at the DSO.

In a luncheon conversation with the new President, Emile Kang, he described to me the policies and ambitious plans for the addition and I outlined major aspects of Pro Musica's achievements and mission—living composers, new artists and programs balanced with new and old music. I suggested that our two organizations should have a cooperative relationship. He responded that several other series might like that, why should it be Pro Musica? To my immediate retort, "Because we're better," he admitted, "Well, you certainly have the most creative programs." For the time being, that was where we left the subject.

I made more progress in a visit with Peter Cummings. He expressed no reservations and agreed at least in principle to all sorts of concepts like coordinating programs, and sharing artists and publicity. At the very least it opened the door for Pro Musica to seek more specific arrangements with the DSO's working management and staff. I moved on to the people who were planning how the new facilities would be run. In that role I found Maude Lyon. We worked out a tentative agreement for a first concert in the new recital hall during the inaugural period when it would first open in the fall of 2003. We discussed costs and picked a tentative date. She introduced me to her staff.

Then an important new volunteer with a skill we needed landed literally out of the blue into Pro Musica's welcoming arms. Local public radio host, Celeste Headlee, interviewed me about Pro Musica emphasizing its creative programming and its continuing success in bringing to Detroit a remarkable roster of performing artists and composers. Meanwhile Mark Domin, son-in-law of Secretary Ann Kondak, undertook to serve as webmaster and set up our web page. Within a day after hearing that interview, Kent Flowers visited www.promusicadetroit.com, found my phone number, and called. He was so impressed with the society's goals and achievements that he volunteered for any job we needed done. It was no time before he informed me of his computer skills. For the moment, I filed that information in the back of my mind.

With the 01-02 season upon us, we opened, still at the museum, with our eagerly awaited recital by pianist Anne-Marie McDermott. For her program she set up an intriguing comparison of two works by Bach and two by Prokofiev. As we listened to her high energy performance, we were struck by the analogies between the development styles and rhythmic patterns of Bach's *Baroque English Suite* and *Partita No. 1* and Prokofiev's totally modern, and often percussive *Sonatas Opus 14 and 84.* McDermott exceeded our expectations and provided a special insight into Prokofiev's music and its ties to the past.

Anne-Marie McDermott

At the next concert, the Artemis Quartet, another group from Vienna, accomplished a similar feat, alternating quartets by Mozart and Beethoven with music of Kurtag and Bartok. The music of Hungarian composer Gyorgy Kurtag was of special interest. Born only two years before Bartok's first appearance at Pro Musica, he was a student of Bartok's successors, Messiaen and Hindemith. From the classical predictability of Mozart and Beethoven, the Quartet took us on a journey through Bartok's harmonic and rhythmic complexity of 1927 (*Quartet No. 3*) to mid 20th century serial techniques of Kurtag's *Hommage a Mihaly Andras*.

With the mid season compulsion to complete plans for the coming year, I picked up the threads of negotiation with the Detroit Symphony as they began to publicize plans for opening the extensive addition to Orchestra Hall and its promised recital hall. Juggling my multiple roles, I took a tour of the facility still under construction and devoted my newspaper column, *State of the Arts*, to a description of the new facility, its possibilities, and the DSO's plans for its use. I revived the negotiations for Pro Musica to hold a concert there as a part of the inaugural season.

The new facility was to be called the Max M. Fisher Music Center and its recital hall was expected to have outstanding acoustics. It would also provide well coordinated amenities like a spacious atrium, a Patrons' reception room, a green room, rehearsal rooms, and such conveniences as additional check rooms and rest rooms. The feature that most aroused our interest was the new recital hall which was to hold approximately 400 seats.

Before I could pursue the idea further, the cast of players in the DSO management changed. President Emile Kang had resigned in the wake of a financial crisis. Maude Lyon left for another project. In their places I found myself working with two imaginative and practical executives: Ross Binnie and Steven Millen. It became evident quickly that together we could make things happen.

With responsibilities for DSO marketing and house management, Ross Binnie was able to work out terms for Pro Musica to use the facilities. We picked a date for our opening concert in November, 2003, and Ross demonstrated how interested they were in having Pro Musica appear in their new facility by granting us every possible concession.

Catering the afterglow and finding a suitable location for it in the new facility were real challenges. We needed food to meet historic standards and an ambience that would maintain the traditional congenial atmosphere. Audience and artists had always been able to socialize warmly and comfortably in the DIA's Romanesque Hall and Kresge Court. And the cost had to be manageable. A caterer oriented to lavish receptions for high roller patrons was not interested in Pro Musica's usual menu of low budget finger sandwiches and doughnut holes. Moreover, donated food was totally out of the question.

I called in Pro Musica's reserves for afterglow planning, Alice Haidostian and new board member Moira Escott who had been elected at the latest annual meeting. They finally negotiatied a workable plan.

Meanwhile, in the background of our negotiations with the new staff at the MAX, as the new facility was being nicknamed, we renewed contact with the other key DSO man, Steve Millen, General Manager. He was doubling in the role of the unfilled position of Artistic Administrator to help the Music Director select soloists and plan programs. He and Binnie together were also filling the leadership void created by Kang's departure. In the little time they had available to meet with me as they carried all these extra responsibilities, we seemed to make a congenial trio.

The 2001-02 season ended with Pro Musica still at the DIA and in our

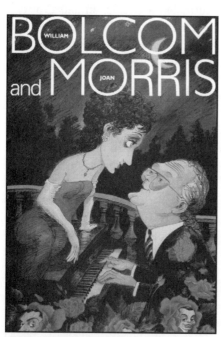

Flyer for William Bolcom and Joan Morris

favorite recital hall with the afterglow in the timeless atmosphere of the Romanesque Hall and Kresge Court. The artists were pianist-composer William Bolcom and his wife, Joan Morris, mezzo soprano. They agreed to give us the Michigan premiere of his complete cycle of Cabaret Songs. While light and entertaining, the songs revealed highly sophisticated musical settings for the utterly contemporary texts. Bolcom and Morris demonstrated the engaging stage presence that had long since established their reputation in the field of American song. Less obviously, Bolcom's fascinating musical settings confirmed the awareness that here, too, was the highly praised composer of the new opera, *View from the Bridge*. An appreciative crowd filled the Recital Hall and buzzed with approval at the afterglow.

A Board meeting held later that May considered the effect that current developments would have on our on operations. I reviewed the work of our publicity agents, Frank and Melissa Bunker at Marketwrite, Inc. in placing news releases in the newspapers and on public radio. Alice Haidostian and Lois Sandberg described how they had worked with Lauri Phillippo at the DIA catering staff to have hot hors d'oeuvres and more interesting fare at the social hour. We noted that the DIA Director of Visitor Services, Dianne Abel, arranged for listing of our concerts in the monthly DIA brochure. And I played a recording of my interview with Celeste Headlee at WDET. Everyone agreed that she had done an outstanding job of editing our one-hour conversation down to an engaging, 5-minute sketch of our concert society.

A sad and important step was the acknowledgement of the opening on our Board left by the resignation of Harold Arnoldi due to ill health. We voted to fill his unexpired term with CPA Harry Pevos who was ready to help Treasurer Stan Beattie with the books and give us an informal annual audit. With annual income in excess of $50,000, we needed accurate financial management with checks and balances. At that point the board formally asked Kent Flowers to take over data base management. Kent is the surprise recruit who had heard my interview with Celeste Headlee, looked Pro Musica up on the internet and called me to volunteer his services in any capacity. In no time we put him to work on his home computer as manager of our information systems. Our new Treasurer, Stan Beattie, transferred the membership and mailing list files and was accordingly able to concentrate his energies on his duties as treasurer. These are considerable in as much as they include filing the IRS forms for a tax exempt organization and keeping track of Pro Musica's endowment fund. Pro Musica had acquired some important new management talents and opened the door to a new era.

That board meeting took place at the home of another new board member, Lee Barthel, and his wife Floy. It was a spacious and gracious setting and as we discussed the question where to hold our annual meeting in September, Lee and Floy volunteered their home. He offered to move his collection of antique autos out of their showroom garage creating a display on his lawns so that we could use the showroom for the meeting. No offer was ever accepted more promptly.

That 2002 annual dinner proved to be a grand fulfillment of Pro Musica's often mentioned tradition of always having a good time while it carried on its mission. The weather was Michigan's best, a balmy September evening. More that a dozen antique autos of various makes, models and vintages were on display scattered around the Barthels' spacious lawns and gardens. Tables were grouped outdoors on the apron of the showroom where the buffet afforded easy access to a tasty dinner. There was an air of gracious patronage for a great musical tradition notwithstanding our constant awareness that every season was a new financial challenge. As usual, conversation flowed along with the champagne punch.

While the business meeting was brief, care was taken to acknowledge all the important volunteer work carried out by loyal members over the past season. Mark Domin kept the web page up to date. Penny Soby deposited historical records in the Detroit Public Library. I reported our new coordinator at the DIA in the person of the Director of Visitor Services, Dianne Abel, and that we could expect to return permanently to our Recital Hall in the near future. In his role as treasurer, Beattie reported that higher costs for artists and DIA services resulted in an operating deficit that year of $9,200. It was made up with income and asset growth of the endowment fund. He projected another loss for the next season unless members and the marketing team increased efforts to bring in new members.

Press Agent Melissa Bunker in her third season working for us reported increased media coverage and that partnerships have been established with restaurants who would give patrons shuttle service to the concerts after dinner. Susanne McMillan turned out several promotional mailings. Design chairman Kyo Takahashi reported tentative designs for the anniversary history book and of our brochures and programs. Efforts by Lois Sandberg and Alice Haidostian to improve the quality and variety of the afterglow refreshments were explained by Haidostian who urged members to send cards to Lois Sandberg who was then in hospital. Elaine Weingarden, along with running a program to place brochures at free pickup points, helped Sarah Snow in the distribution of tickets for our concerts to high school music students and thanked members for the private cash gifts that made this possible. Ken Collinson continued to update the message on the Pro Musica information telephone line and respond to voice mail on that line. Four board members were re-elected and Harry Pevos graduated from appointed status to being elected to a full, three year term.

With all that accomplished in less than one hour, we moved to our musical treat. It was provided by Celeste Headlee who had interviewed me on Public Radio. She is also a lyric, coloratura soprano and granddaughter of the eminent African-American composer William Grant Still. Accompanied by DSO pianist Robert Conway, Headlee sang operatic arias, art songs and tunes by her grandfather including a few from his opera, *Troubled Island*, with a libretto by Langston Hughes. It had premiered at the New York Music Center more than a half century earlier attended by mayor Fiorella LaGuardia and with the support of Eleanor Roosevelt. Members at once began to speculate on a concert version for Pro Musica.

At the quick board meeting that followed, officers were all re-elected and Board members brought up a few key issues. Lorraine Lerner offered her expertise in contacting foundations to replace the funds borrowed from the endowment and make up the deficit. Alice Haidostian proposed using the restaurant that catered the inexpensive buffet in the museum's Crystal Gallery to provide a reasonably priced pre-concert food service. A possible increase in season and single ticket prices was discussed and postponed. Bill Harmon expressed concern over the irregular telephone response at the museum's box office which was supposed to take ticket orders by credit card over the phone in the weeks before a concert. By 10:30 p.m. we were thanking our hosts and heading home. Along with providing an enjoyable evening, Pro Musica's meetings were expeditious.

When our 2002 season opened on October 23, involved members described the program as not just a concert. "It was an event." DSO composer in residence and Professor of Composition at the University of Michigan, Michael Daugherty, gave us his inside story as a composer, with a slide show explaining how his music is inspired by American icons. We heard of his fascination with Las Vegas neon signs, Cadillac tail fins, Harley Davidson Motorcycles, Spaghetti Westerns, and Route 66. He explained his use of rigorous, polyrythmic counterpoint with a playful and pointed use

Michael Daugherty

of pop music from his youth combined with a wry sense of timing, deft orchestration, and a sensitivity to the spatial dimension of music. Step by step, his revelations were illustrated with pieces whimsically titled *Jackie's Song, Firecracker, Sinatra Shag, Venetian Blinds, The High and Mighty for Piccolo and Piano* and *Egyptian Time*. The performances were deftly handled in solos and ensembles by the University of Michigan Contemporary Directions Ensemble under Jonathan Shames, the group's Artistic Director.

Among the various members of the audience who were drawn to a Pro Musica concert for the first time, our guest music students from Detroit's Cass Technical High School were most enthusiastic. They cheered at the end of *Sinatra Shag* which Daugherty had carefully explained in advance as referring to a kind of rug. While the press did not attend, The DSO's Chairman Peter Cummings did, much to his credit. Daugherty was simply impressed with the turnout and asked how we managed to get so many people to listen to contemporary music. Recalling Pro Musica's history and mission, we mentally compared the frontier status of Daugherty's music to what early Pro Musica members heard in concerts by Bartok, Honneger, Tansman, Hindemith, Copland and, more recently, George Crumb. If we can keep our audiences in the avant-garde like that for 77 years, we must be doing something right.

What seems to be right about it is that we don't try to stay exclusively on the frontier. Our next concert in February 2003, presented one of the world's great mezzo sopranos in a program that was tuneful, emotional and traditional. Irina Mishura had come to Detroit as a hopeful immigrant

Irina Mishura and author

from Russia and supported herself initially in a menial job. But a voice like hers can't be hidden and in no time she was invited by Neeme Järvi and the DSO to be soloist in a performance of Tchaikovsky's *Snow Maiden*. They then recorded it on the Chandos label. She sang *Amneris* in *Aida* at Michigan Opera Theater and soon was in demand at all the great opera houses of North America and Europe.

At our concert in the DIA auditorium, her Russian songs and her arias from *Carmen*, *Samson and Delila*, *Cavalleria Rusticana* and *Don Carlo* brought to mind what Detroit *Free Press* critic Herman Wise had said of Russian soprano Olga Alverino after a Pro Musica concert in 1935. "The drama that lies in Russian song requires a woman who is both emotional and intellectual to make its meanings clear." The singer also needs a velvety, resonant voice. Mishura had it all including a tenor husband, Jack Morris, who could appear from the wings to join her in the duet from *Samson and Delila*.

A new hitch at the DIA brought a sudden crisis. I was informed at the last minute by the auditorium manager that our afterglow, scheduled to be in the auditorium's balcony level Crystal Gallery, had to be limited to 100 guests due to fire laws. I delivered an embarassed apology from the stage restricting the afterglow to members only. Mishura saved the day by graciously offering to meet with her fans in the lobby for a while after the performance. The effect was to leave the crowd's enthusiasm undimmed.

With the 2003-04 season looming on the horizon, I returned to the offices of the DSO to finalize plans for being a part of the inauguration of *The Max*. It was delicate negotiating on many levels. We needed to keep our expenses at a manageable level and we knew that costs at the new facility were inevitably higher. We were powerfully tempted by the promise of superior acoustics in the still unfinished Music Box Recital Hall. Expecting them to be outstanding, we were eager to try them out. On the other hand, our historic relationship with the museum, as difficult as it had been in recent years, was still important. The museum is a beautiful and gracious venue for Pro Musica and an integral element of our tradition. Only a handful of concerts had ever been held at other locations. Moving Pro Musica to a new home was not a decision to be taken lightly.

The DSO's new marketing director, Ross Binnie, was the picture of cordiality and accommodation. We came to terms on basic arrangements comparable to those at the museum and found common goals as a basis for meeting other needs such as where to hold the afterglow, catering it, patron parking and having the DSO box office sell Pro Musica tickets. The important factor is that the DSO management wants quality musical programs in its new facility and none fit the bill better than Pro Musica. Our decision was to hold our first concert there the following November when the Max opened. The other two

Pro Musica concerts would be back at the museum to complete the season. Our two organizations would decide on the future thereafter. Another important change was to return to weekend performance dates. Our traditional Fridays were no longer possible at the museum since it was now staying open on Friday evenings and the sounds of people in the hallways would be a distraction for concert attendees. Saturdays there, however, were possible. We had lost a number of regular members when conditions at the museum required us to hold concerts on Wednesday evenings. So plans were set for our first concert in November 2003 to be at the MAX and the other two at the museum, all on Saturday evenings.

While these arrangements were pending, the 2002-03 season came to

Mark Kosower

a close with cellist Mark Kosower and his pianist wife Jee-Won Oh in the museum Recital Hall. It was a long awaited event. We had him on our high prority list for several years but with only three concerts a year and too many excellent attractions to choose from, we delayed in setting the date. His performance was worth waiting for and his program filled our bill offering in its second half a striking work by Ginastera and Kodaly's unique unaccompanied Sonata for Cello Solo.

The return to weekend dates seemed like a good opportunity to try to regain members that had withdrawn when remodeling at the museum made it necessary for us to hold concerts on Wednesdays in the large auditorium. We had managed to turn this to our benefit by having such events as actor Brian Bedford reading poetry with the Liszt transcriptions of Schubert's *Schwannengesang* settings, as well as the Berlin Chamber Orchestra and the Absolute Ensemble. The concerts that attracted only our smaller, loyal following had lost our cherished intimacy by being held in the larger hall and discouraged members who had conflicts on a mid-week evening. We aimed to bring them back.

At this time we were talking earnestly with the Community Foundation for Southeastern Michigan about opening an endowment account with them. With a strong recommendation by Alice Haidostian, the

Board agreed to transfer $10,000 of endowment funds to an account at the Foundation. This led to the idea of a grant to fund a campaign for rebuilding membership. Going through the steps of meeting criteria, we obtained the pro bono services of Rob Gold, Director of Marketing at Meadowbrook Theater and former marketing manager at two regional symphony orchestras. He outlined a plan, with numbers, for a highly focused direct mail campaign. The projection was for a return of slightly less than one percent and a two year grant from the Foundation made it possible. While the results met the projection, we had hoped it would do better and began to wonder how we could improve the second year's results. At the same time we joined the cooperative Michigan ArtsList for access to the mailing lists of other musical organizations in the area and began to think about how we would select the most appropriate names from their lists.

The saddest form of membership attrition then struck once again. The death of Lois Sandberg was a tragic blow to our organization. Her resourceful management of the Afterglow had been a source of pride and confidence to us along with her enthusiastic devotion to our musical undertakings. Once again, the ranks closed. We still enjoyed the support of Dr. Hershel Sandberg as 2nd vice president, and Alice Haidostian and Moira Escott assumed full responsibility for the post-concert social hour.

The 2003 annual dinner in September took place at the Grosse Pointe Hunt Club through the sponsorship of George and Inge Vincent and changes continued. Plans were discussed for our first concert in the Music Box Recital Hall at the MAX and I announced the support of the Harvard Club of Eastern Michigan eager to honor their fellow alumnus Richard Kogan who would appear as pianist.

There was much discussion of the impact of our move to the MAX for that concert and for the future. For that occasion, the intent was to remind ourselves and our audience of Pro Musica's long, intermittent relationship with the DSO. Back in the 30s, The DSO had twice presented concerts with Pro Musica programs. In one concert, pianist and Pro Musica member Eduard Bredshall had played the Detroit premiere of Ravel's new piano concerto. In another, the program was made up entirely of Detroit premiere performances. Both concerts were highly praised by critics and audiences. Over the years, DSO musicians often performed in concerts to complete ensembles performing a visiting composer's music. And in the 70s, when Antal Dorati was Music Director of the DSO, Pro Musica produced chamber music concerts as events in his festivals of music by Bartok and Brahms.

Holding our opening concert of the 2003-2004 season during the inaugural festivities at the MAX was an important way to emphasize this long standing relationship. It was also a good excuse for us to try the acoustics and to see how we could function in the new facility and if we could replicate the congenial atmosphere of our traditional afterglow. These were all important considerations for the board, for the members, and for me.

Meanwhile, the election gave us the opportunity to add a new member replacing Board member Ann Greenstone who had limited time to work for the society and had offered to stand aside. With a spontaneous nomination from the floor, Moira Escott agreed to run and Pro Musica gained an eager, active new board member. As a staff member at the Canadian Consulate General in Detroit, she brought important links to Windsor, Ontario, the community across the Detroit River, and we were about to discover the energy and initiative she would bring to our efforts.

It was Moira, working closely with Alice Haidostian, who finalized menu details for the November afterglow with the caterer at the MAX. Thanks to their efforts the food was satisfactory and the budget manageable. While logistics of serving and seating audience members needed to be improved, the afterglow was well attended and enjoyed.

The concert itself made the greatest impact. Pianist Richard Kogan, a former classmate and performing associate of violinist Lynn Chang and cellist Yo Yo Ma at Juilliard High School and Harvard College, brought a unique concert format. In addition to being an outstanding concert pianist, Kogan is a graduate of Harvard Medical School and is a practicing psychiatrist. Combining his two professions, he studies the records of the mental health and behavior of composers and interprets their impact on the composer's music. Cellist Yo Yo Ma and violinist Lin Chang credit him with providing important insights that help in their interpretations when they play as a trio.

His lecture at our concert on the personality and psychiatric profile of Robert Schumann was startling and revealing. The audience acknowleged gaining a deeper understanding of Schumann's music, which is unusual in its structure and often mystifying. They also found Kogan's performance of such works as *Carnaval* exceptionally meaningful and moving. Many members commented at the afterglow that it was the most interesting concert they had ever attended and urged the Board to bring him back.

The fact that he is a Harvard graduate caught the interest of officers of the Harvard Club of Eastern Michigan. A contingent of 62 alumni made the evening a club event and attended the concert. Several were impressed with Pro Musica's mission and announced their intent to join. We realized that this could be an important new avenue of gaining members and decided to ask our members to suggest other affiliate organizations whose members we might persuade to attend as a group.

Those who were motivated to come to the next concert were not disappointed. The violinist Philippe Quint had defected from the former Soviet Union in 1991. He had studied at Moscow's Special Music School for the Gifted. In New York he attended Juilliard, studying with Dorothy Delay, to graduate in 1998. His career here has already garnered important recognition and his performance for Pro Musica was dazzling, including music by three composers who had appeared for the Society: Cowell, Foss and Ravel. Members also noted the outstanding collaboration of pianist David Riley and suggested him as a candidate for a solo recital.

Moving from triumph to triumph, the final concert of the season with lyric tenor Manuel Acosta proved to be another winner. The youthful singer amazed opera fans in the audience with his confident opening aria, *Una Furtiva Lagrima* from Donizetti's *Elisir d'Amore* with its challenging high notes. He went on to give virtuoso and impassioned interpretations of the heroes from *Carmen*, *Eugene Onegin*, *La Boheme* and Lehar's *Land of Smiles*. His second half included six arias from the very special *Zarzuelas*, Spanish equivalents of Viennese Operetta and in their unique Iberian idiom, they were received with enthusiasm.

Our efforts to promote the concert through the Mexican Consulate and in the Spanish speaking community were minimally successful. However, generous advance coverage in the *Detroit Free Press* reached a number of Detroit area Hispanics. They joined our audience for the first time and promised to come again.

We were faced with a surprise change of venue for the Afterglow. Our Romanesque Hall and Kresge Court were rented out from under us to a business client that obviously was able to pay the Museum a welcome rental fee. Our move into the new DIA Café passed as an interesting, though less atmospheric new location.

On the other hand a pre concert gallery tour was a very successful bonus. Honoring our artist's Mexican origin, we viewed the Diego Rivera Detroiot Industry Murals led by Docent Irving Berg for a highly informative exploration of Rivera's remarkable representation of Detroit Industry and glorification of the working man. Everyone seemed to find the evening a glowing example of Pro Musica's high quality, creative programming.

Meanwhile, I had been working behind the scenes to find artists to recommend to the Board for the coming seasons and to continue to develop synergies with the DSO. As so often happens in seeking new programs, opportunities came from unexpected sources.

Celeste Headlee at WDET Public Radio, who had interviewed me a year earlier and who publicized our concerts, suggested a remarkable young operatic basso that she had met at Michigan Opera Theater. We contacted Valerian Ruminsky, read his bio and reviews, and listened to tapes and CDs of his singing.

A youthful musician named Mitchel Nelson who was representing an outstanding string quartet approached me with a suggestion for a special program with fast rising clarinetist Alexander Fiterstein. Their recordings and a new suite based on the score from an award winning film proved well worth our attention.

Then longtime member and President of the Rackham Symphony Choir, Ray Litt, suggested tenor Rodrick Dixon who had performed recently with the choir. We met and explored more new exciting ideas.

Those three were agreed to by the Board for the 04-05 season but as we were doing that, I encountered a member of the Contrasts Quartet and learned that the pianist is married to the important American composer Aaron Jay Kernis. I recognized his name but needed to confirm my impressions with a look at his biography. Almost breathlessly I scanned the following on the internet:

> One of the youngest composers ever to be awarded the Pulitzer Prize, Aaron Jay Kernis is among the most esteemed musical figures of his generation. With his fearless originality [and] powerful voice (The New York Times) each new Kernis work is eagerly awaited by audiences and musicians with intense anticipation. He is one of today's most frequently performed composers. His music, full of variety and dynamic energy, is rich in lyric beauty, poetic imagery and brilliant instrumental color.

Bringing Kernis as a Pro Musica composer, could be as important as the society's most prestigious events with Bartok, Ravel, Copland, Boulanger, Poulenc and the others. It was potentially important enough to be the basis for launching the new collaboration with the DSO. I made an appointment with Ross Binnie and Steve Millen and proposed it for the 2005-06 season.

To my surprise and delight, Millen's immediate response was: "As a matter of fact, I was thinking of trying to bring Kernis for a concert of his music." I proposed that we should plan a weekend when Kernis and the Contrasts Quartet would appear on a Friday evening in the MAX for Pro Musica. The DSO could then have Kernis for concerts of his music on Thursday, Friday morning, Saturday and Sunday. It would be a Kernis Festival Weekend.

I left the DSO offices with a portfolio of plans to work out and visions of a whole new future for the society. Pro Musica would retain its autonomy but enjoy the recognition and prestige of sharing artists and composers whenever possible with the DSO. We would hold concerts as much as possible in the excellent, new Music Box recital hall, and Ross Binnie proposed that he would work out an arrangement for us to hold our Afterglows in a suitable space in the building. In the meantime, we had the 2004-05 season to produce. At the moment, I could only dream where all these plans would lead.

Chapter 29

What Does It All Add Up To? – 2004

Anyone active in the field of serious music can appreciate the accomplishment that this history represents. But there is a depth of feeling about Pro Musica that has been the key inspiration behind the loyalty and support of a cadre of devoted, longtime members who have worked for the society in many ways as well as being loyal supporters through all its ups and downs. Stimulated in part by reading this book in manuscript and by efforts to research and recall details of the history, two couples wrote their own impressions of the Pro Musica experience. They convey a spirit that no list of artists and programs can express quite so eloquently.

Pro Musica has been a part of our lives since we married in 1957. Prior to our marriage, however, Leonard had become a member on his own as a result of a suggestion made to him by a fellow chamber music lover.

Leonard was searching for an opportunity to hear live chamber music. He had been attending concerts given by professional and amateur musicians in a carriage house behind the Smiley Brothers piano company in the old Hecker mansion near the museum. The group was called the Chamber Music Workshop. One of its members suggested to Leonard that he might be interested in Pro Musica because of its variety of programming and the high caliber of musicians it attracted.

Leonard sought information about Pro Musica and after his first concert he became a member. I think it was also a good place to take a date!

Soon after our marriage the Pro Musica season began. Leonard took me to my first chamber music concert. Up until that time I had gone only to symphony concerts and to an occasional recital while I was in college.

The whole experience was very new to me.

That first exposure to chamber music has continued to be a very special memory. The concert was played by a chamber orchestra (I Solisti di Zagreb) and I was thrilled with the intimacy of the group, the place and the chance to sit as close to the music as I wanted.

Leonard has had a life long passion for classical music and our children, to this day, feel its calming, reassuring tones as a reminder of their home, wherever they are in the world.

Our earliest memory of Pro Musica was the formal dress of the audience: evening gowns and tuxedos. In addition, they all seemed to know each other! We knew no one at these concerts. It never bothered us being outside of the group because the programs were very satisfying. It felt like Pro Musica was our little secret.

The program began with a warm welcome by Mrs. Coolidge, President of Pro Musica to all the people in attendance. She let us all know that the three concerts for the season were all in place and that "the hay was in the barn." An invitation to join the afterglow was extended to everyone. We were told it would be a good opportunity to meet that evening's performers. That tradition made us feel comfortable and also made all the Pro Musica concerts very special. Later on, I participated in the afterglow by pouring coffee in the Kresge Court. Sometimes Leonard served tea sandwiches.

We discovered that in each season there was at least one memorable concert that made the whole season worthwhile. We also loved the variety of programming including composers, singers, soloists and chamber groups.

We knew that the musicians were chosen with care. So many of the performers were beginning their careers and we heard them before their talents were recognized by the general public. There are many examples of great performances in the years past.

The composers were always a treat. We had lots of challenges in hearing music we had never heard before. At the same time we appreciated the talents of those people presenting their music to us.

There was never a question about maintaining our membership in Pro Musica. As our family was growing up we would take one child at a time to a concert. They remember the evenings well because of the intimacy of the hall and feeling so close to the performers. They also loved being in the Art Institute at night and being in the Kresge Court afterwards. It was very charming to them.

The mission of Pro Musica has always been clear to everyone who ever attended a concert. It is stated often and Pro Musica has stayed the course in this regard.

Lorraine Lerner

June 29, 2004: Nick had been invited to a Pro Musica concert in the spring of 1957 (Lois Marshall, soprano with Weldon Kilburn, piano). He came home and said, "We need to join Pro Musica! That is a wonderful series in an intimate setting." We joined and have been members since. Our daughter was born in September 1957 and the first concert was my first outing after her birth (I Solisti di Zagreb). Pro Musica has always been a priority for us. It puts on the type of concerts we enjoy with an excellent balance of chamber music, instrumental and vocal programs. The opportunity to visit with the artists after the concerts and to socialize with other members adds to our enjoyment.

Early on I was recruited to work on renewals. We met at Alice Lungershausen's home. The committee met in the summer and we diligently contacted all recent members and tried to sign up new members as well. Sure enough, in those days all memberships were sold so that we had a full house by the first concert. As Dorothy Coolidge would say, "The hay is in the barn."

Our neighbor Ruth Roth was social chairman and we were recruited for another volunteer activity. In those days we had hot hor d'oeuvres that were much sought after. Pro Musica had its own service pieces at the museum. The person who made coffee for us, Wilfred, was steady but imbibed somewhat during the evening. However, he always came through for us. Mrs. Roth ran the operation like a sergeant, making sure everything proceeded in clockwork order.

A later assignment was membership chair, a position I held for some years. This was in the days before computers. A.l records were typed or handwritten. Ed Frohlich was treasurer and I often delivered membership checks to his home and had a chance to visit with him. Pro Musica was able to hire Alice Coleman who did secretarial work for us, keeping records, sending out notices and preparing programs. An advantage for me was that she would handle the membership table when the concerts started so that I could go into the hall as soon as the program started. Alice took care of latecomers. I continued this position until I became secretary.

Nick and I were too busy in the early years to attend annual meetings. Once we realized the importance of these meetings in the governance and member participation we started going to all of them. An extra bonus was the special entertainment that was provided.

Some years ago I became secretary which involves, among other duties, taking minutes and arranging special meetings. We have always had a dedicated board that has worked to make sure that Pro Musica is successful in its mission. Board members always stepped in to handle assignments.

The special treatment for artists instituted by AlexSuczek has provided many bonuses and added a special dimension to membership. We have had the opportunity to meet artists when they had to be transported to or from the airport or in town, or taken out for a meal. Many performers spend a lot of time away from home. They miss their families and they appreciate the personal attention.

One of my special memories is the George Crumb concert. This was an exciting evening. Many young people who do not usually attend classical concerts came from communities many miles away to see Mr. Crumb. His approach was quite novel including music notation on a circular staff. It was interesting to see how some of the long-time members would react. During a period when Mr. Crumb spent a good deal of time explaining his music and answering questions, Mary Topalov, a long-time member, stood up. I wondered what she would say about the unusual music we were hearing. Mary said in a very firm voice, "Enough talk. Let us hear more music." Right on! That is the Pro Musica spirit!

When we were part of the Grieg Festival and sold individual tickets to a special concert, I had received many requests for tickets, more than the number of people the Recital Hall could accommodate. Alex said, "Go ahead and sell the tickets."

When it appeared that there would not be enough seats, we asked the museum staff to provide extra seats. They were concerned that we had oversold the hall but did bring in extra chairs. It worked out all right.

Ann Kondak

New Ways Feed on the Old

With many members having expressed similar sentiments to me over the years, it seems almost a foregone conclusion that Pro Musica will survive all difficulties and continue to thrive. Perhaps it is summed up best by a friend who reported taking his father to a concert only three days before he passed away. As they were leaving the hall, the father said, "That's what makes life worthwhile."

Chapter 30

Postlude – May 2006

Another season has passed and this book is almost ready to go to print. There is just enough time to report what appears to be another new departure for Pro Musica, one that looks like it will carry Pro Musica into a new era of great musical experiences.

It is powered by our renewed relationship with the Detroit Symphony Orchestra. In the season just completed we successfully created joint presentations of pianist Antii Siirala and composer Aaron Jay Kernis. Recognizing the potential of our collaboration, DSO management invited Pro Musica to produce fliers promoting those two concerts for insertion in DSO programs at concerts two or three weeks preceding our events.

Our audiences on those evenings were noticeably increased. Siirala gave a balanced program with suitably recent and important compositions by Janacek and Szymanowski. That satisfied the new music fans. Schumann and Beethoven's three outstanding *Sonatas No. 24, 26 and 27* pleased those with more traditional taste. And Siirala's especially sensitive interpretations impressed every one.

The concert with Kernis satisfied the other half of Pro Musica's mission to bring a composer with a performance of his music. Kernis explained the personal background to his pieces which were performed by various combinations of quartet of piano, strings and clarinet. The pianist, Evelyne Luest, was his wife giving further authority to the performance. And again the audience showed special appreciation of having a Pulitzer Prize winning composer appear for us.

Then, even without a collaboration with the Symphony, we were able to insert a flier for the third concert featuring the young award-winning baritone Thomas Meglioranza with pianist Reiko Uchida. The program insertion proved to be a highly effective and cost effective promotion device. Door sales at the DSO box office got a significant lift.

Baritone Meglioranza delivered his program of "Reflections of Italy" with beguiling artistry while pianist Uchida revealed brilliant technical virtuosity along with her sensitive accompaniments. She was absolutely dazzling in one of the extra additions to the program at its end when Meglioranza announced from the stage a group of short songs by young composer from the University of Michigan. Derek Bermel's setting for his ethereal song "Spider" was a showpiece. A number of new music enthiasts expressed special satisfaction over the number of songs they had never heard before. There was a feeling of being included in a private joke when the baritone gave as his final encore the satirical number "The New Suit" by Mark Blitzstein—a song that was a favorite of Leonard Bernstein that had been performed mainly at private parties by Bernstein himself.

Always looking for ways to improve the ambience, we made important changes in the way we used the hall. Recognizing our audience's dissatisfaction with the folding risers that opened up to form a raked array of seating, the DSO management suggested we seat the audience at cabaret tables. It reminded me immediately of the informality we had always enjoyed and I agreed at once.

It was well received except that with musicians and audience all on a single flat floor level, the sight lines were poor for people not in front. The stages hands stepped in with another solution: put the musicians up on a platform stage. They gamely met the challenge of lifting the concert grand on the stage and another problem was solved. The audience loved it.

Then the catering staff that serves the Afterglow added another improvement. At the end of the concert, a movable wall opened on to the Atrium where we found our buffet and beverages already set up and ready to serve. We were able to visit the buffet and return to our cabaret tables to enjoy the conversational end of the evening. Everyone loved it.

Meantime, I recognized that it was an appropriate time to plan for the following season. It would be Pro Musica's 80th and we again had a lot to celebrate. Reflecting on the fact that 80 years earlier in the winter of 1927-28 two of the greatest composers of the 20th century had appeared in Pro Musica's opening season, I decided to commemorate their concerts. For Bela Bartok, I was able to engage the young Hungarian violinist, Barnabas

Kelemen, who had won Josef Gingold's prestigious Indianapolis International Violin competition two years earlier. He plays Bartok's music with the flair of a son of Budapest.

For a commemorative Ravel program, we turned to the source of artists that served Pro Musica in 1928 –the DSO. Under the leadership of the Symphony's solo cellist Robert deMaine, we formed a septet of strings, flute, clarinet and harp. They will perform the stunning "Introduction and Allegro" in which Pro Musica's founder, Djina Ostrowska, who was harpist of the DSO back then enchanted the society's founding audience. It is a fitting celebration of our revived relationship with the Symphony, recreating a historic performance. It was received so enthusiastically that the Allegro had to be repeated as an encore and may well again.

Acting Artistic Administrator of the orchestra, Steve Millen, admitted after our meeting that he had intended to ask Pro Musica to include DSO musicians in some of our concerts. For us, it is a natural.

A third concert to complete the series and serve as opener, is a recital by the fast rising young pianist Mihaela Ursuleasa. That choice serves as a reminder that it is also our mission to bring the rising new artists to our series.

This book is about to go to print. An appealing 80th anniversary season is scheduled. A cordial and successful collaboration with the orchestra that helped Pro Musica come into being, in spite of its skeptical Music Director, is in full swing. And I have served as President for 32 years. It adds up to my opportunity to make an important move. At my urging, the Board has designated a successor to step in at the end of next season and I am suggesting that they name me Artistic Advisor. I look forward to the kind of guided, smooth transition in leadership that evaded me 32 years ago and most importantly, a rewarding continuation of Pro Musica's mission to carry the torch for new music and new artists.

Appendix A
Chronological Listing of Concert Artists and Programs

This appendix supplements the main text which provides general information about the concerts and artists in the context of the society's overall history. It is cross referenced with this appendix by date. Artists and their programs are listed as appearing in the surviving copies of programs in the Burton Historical Collection and Music and Performing Arts Department of the Detroit Public Library, and in the Pro Musica archives. There were normally three concerts per season. In a few seasons, there were four concerts. Special concerts co-sponsored with the Detroit Symphony Orchestra or Tuesday Musicale, benefit concerts and musical offerings at anniversary banquets and at some annual dinner meetings are included.

1927-28
February 19 Bela Bartok, Hungarian Composer, Pianist & Musicologist
    (Program preceded by a 10 minute talk in English)
Bartok: Suite, op. 14 (1916)
    Rumanian Christmas Songs (1915)
Kodaly Epitaphe (from op. 11, 1918)
    Allegro molto (from op. 3, 1909)
Bartok Sonata (1926)
    Burlesque, 2 (un peu gris, 1908-10)
    Dirge 1
    Bear dance
    Evening in the Country
    Allegro Barbaro

March 28 Maurice Ravel, French Composer, Pianist, Conductor
    Assisted by: Lisa Roma, soprano; Djina Ostrowska, harp, John Wummer, flute; Marius Fossenkemper, clarinet; Joseph Gorner, 1st violin; Otis Iglemann, 2nd violin; Valbert Coffey, viola; Georges Miquelle, cello.
All Ravel Program
    Sheherezade (Three poems for voice and piano)
    Sonatine (for piano)

Histoires Naturelle (voice and piano)
> Le Paon, Le Grillon, Le Cygne, Le Martin-Pecheur, La
> Pintade

Pavane pour une Infante defunte (piano)

Habanera (piano)

Rigadoun (from Le Tombeau de Couperin) (piano)

Chansons Grecques (voice and piano)
> Le Reveil de la Mariee; La-bas vers l'Eglise; Quel gallant
> Chanson des cueilleuses de lentisques; Tout gai!

Introduction et Allegro (Harp with string quartet, flute and
clarinet)

April 20	Povla Frisch (Danish Soprano); Celins Dougherty, Accompanist Assisted by: Gizi Szanto and June Wells, piano; John Wummer, flute; Joseph Gorner, violin; Georges Miquelle, Julius Sturm, Ray Hall & E. Borsody, celli.
Stuart Mason	Quartet for Celli
	Songs for Soprano
Benati	Credi nell' alma mia
Rameau	Menuet
Schubert	Die Stadt; Rastlose Liebe
Faure	Au Cimitiere
Hue	Le petit Ane blank
Ravel	Le Paon
Hahn	Infidelite
De Falla	Seguidilla
	Music for Two Pianos
Manuel Infante	Ritme, danse Andalouse
Arnold Bax	Moy Mel, Irish Tone Poem
Edwin Burlingame Hill	
	Jazz Study
Goossens	Suite for Flute, Violin and Harp
	Songs for voice and piano
Krika	L'Abatros
Moussorgski	O, raconte Nianioushka
Cesar Cui	La Fontaine de Czarskoe-Zelo
Sibelius	Var Det en Droem

1928-29

December 2	Ottorino Respighi, Composer, Pianist, Conductor with Mme. Elsa Respighi-Oliveri Sangiacomo, vocalist assisted by Joseph Gorner, violin and members of the Detroit Symphony Orchestra

Appendix A

Pizzetti   *Songs for voice and piano*
Pizzetti   Sonetto del Patrarca; I pastori
Malipiero   Dai sonetti delle fate
Castelnuovo-Tedesco
                   Piccino, piccio
Cuest   Giro tondo dei golosi
Respighi   Sonata for violin and piano
                   Five Songs
                   La notte; Non e' morto il figlio tuo;
                       La mamma e'come il pane caldo; La Madre; Pioggia
                   Canzoni Popolari
                       Spagnole; Americane del Sud; Italiane
                   Three Botticelli Paintings for small orchestra
                       La Primavera; L'Adorazione Dei Magi; La Nascita Di Venere (conducted by the composer)

January 26   Arthur Honegger, composer-pianist; Mme Andree Vaurabourg; Mme. Cobina Wright, soprano assisted by Dirk van Emmerik, A. Witteborg, John Wummer, George Miquelle, R. Schmidt and Joseph Gorner

All Honegger Program
                   Toccata and Variations for piano (1916) (Mme. Vaurabourg)
                   Trois Poemes de Paul Fort for voice and piano (composer at the piano)
                   Trois Contrepoints
                   Prelude a deux voix (cell0 and oboe)
                   Chorale a trios voix (violin, cello and English horn)
                   Canon sur basse obstinee a quatre voix (piccolo, violin, English horn and cello)
                   Rhapsodie for two flutes, clarinet and piano (1917)
                   Chanson de Ronsard for voice and piano (1924)
                   Trois Chanson de la Sirene for voice and piano (1927)
                   Suite for two pianos (1928)

April 2   Greta Torpadie, soprano; Wilbert P. Coffey, composer; Richard Dolph, tenor; assisted by Ilya Schkolnik, conductor; Fred Paine, Percussion; Margaret Mannebach, piano; Allan Farnham, violin; Messrs. Van Emmerick and Wittman, oboe and viola; and a chamber ensemble of the DSO.

Albert Spalding
                   Studies for violin and piano
Ernest Bloch   Studies for violin and piano.
Louis Gruenberg

"Daniel in the Lions Den" for soprano and chamber orchestra with brass and percussion.

Griffes, Withorne, Copland, Mannes, and Ornstein
        group of Songs by American composers for soprano and piano.

Virgil Thompson
        Five excerpts from the Song of Solomon for soprano with Chinese drum, gong, sticks and cymbals.

Valbert P. Coffey
        Three songs for tenor and chamber orchestra

Charles M. Loeffler
        Two Rhapsodies for oboe and viola.

1929-30

November 22   Gabriel Leonoff, tenor; The Detroit String Quartet: Ilya Schkolnik, 1st violin, William Grafing King, 2nd violin, Valbert P. Coffey, viola, George Miquelle, violoncello; Margaret Mannebach, piano.

        In Honor of the visit to Detroit by Alexander Glazounoff

Glazounoff   Prelude and Fugue for string quartet

Sokoloff, Glazounoff & Liadow
        Polka for string quartet from "Les Vendredis"
        Songs for tenor and piano

Glazounoff   Song of Masha (manuscript); A Dream

Scriabine   Devotion (Detroit premiere)

Medtner   Serenade (ms, Detroit premiere)

Cesar Cui   Miniature

Rimsky-Korsakoff In Spring

Waldo Warner   The Pixie Ring: A Fairy Miniature Suite for string quartet
        Songs for tenor and piano

De Falla   Jota; Seguidilla (from Murcia)

Joaquin Nin   Suffer My Soul (Old Spanish); El Gilguerito

Casella   Pieces for String Quartet
        Preludio; Ninna Nanna (Berceuse); Valse Ridicule; Fox Trot

January 22   Alexander Tansman, composer-pianist, with Ilya Schkolnik, violin, Jeanette van der Velpen Reaume, voice and John Wummer, flute.

All Tansman Program
        Sonata Rustica for piano
        Cinq Melodies for voice and piano
        Trois Impromptus for piano
        Cinq Mazurkas for piano
        Sonata for violin and piano

Andante et Scherzo de la Symphonie en la-mineur for piano
March Militaire de la Nuit Kurde for piano
Sonatine for flute and piano

March 2   Sergei Prokofiev, composer and pianist; Beatrice Griffin, violin;
Lina Llubera-Prokofiev, mezzo-soprano; Roy Schmidt, clarinet
and the Detroit String Quartet of the DSO.

Prokofiev   Andante from the Fourth Sonata, op. 29 for piano solo
Three melodies for violin and piano
Piano solos: March and Scherzo from the Opera, "Love for the
Three Oranges;" Allemande, op. 12; Prelude, op. 12; Gavotte, op.
12; Gavotte, op. 25; Gavotte, op. 32; Grandmothers Tale, Op. 31,
No. 2; Suggestion Diabolique, op. 4.

Five Russian Songs for voice and piano
Miaskovsky   Circles
Prokofiev   An Incantation for Fire and Water
Lament, Russian Popular Song
The Mulberry Tree
Strawinsky   A Song of the Dew
Prokofiev   Overture on Yiddish Themes op. 34 for four strings, clarinet and
piano.

1930-31
January 16   Hans Barth, composer-pianist (presented through the National
Music League)

Compositions for Harpsichord
Scarlatti   Sonata
Corelli   Gigue
Rameau   Gavotte
Haydn   Minuet
Gossec   Tambourine
Compositions for Piano
Barth   Sonata No. 3;   The Violet Muses; Thoughts of a Looking-glass
Compositions for Quarter-tone Piano
Barth   Shadows of a Cathedral; Prelude and Fugue; Spirit of Dawn
Gershwin   Prelude
Barth   North Wind

February 24   Laura Littlefield, Soprano, Joachim Chassman, violin, Mischa
Kottler, piano, Detroit String Quartet (see Nov. 22, 1929) Miss
Mannebach, piano, and Mssrs. Miquelle, Beaume, Hall and Bach-
mann, celli.

H. Matheys   Violin Sonata (Chassman and Kottler)

	Songs for soprano
Eric Satie	Dapheneo; La Statue de Bronze
F. Poulenc	Le Bestiaire
	Le Dromadaire; La Chevre; La Sauterelle
	Le Dauphin; L'Ecrevisse; La Carpe
V.P. Coffey	Three Characteristic Pieces for string quartet
	French; Spanish; American
	Compositions for piano solo (Kottler)
Vuilemain	Carillon dans la Baie
Fr. Poulenc	Trois Mouvements perpetuels
Eric Satie	Prelude Flasque
P. Wladigeroff	Autumn Elegy
Eugene Goosens	Three songs for soprano and string quartet
	The Appeal; Melancholy; Philomel
Stuart Mason	Four Pieces for Four Celli
	Prelude Triste; Guitare; Orientale; Chanson at Danse Negre

April 17	Hans Kindler, cello, assisted by Djina Ostrowska, Dr. Mark Gunsburg, John Wummer, Ilya Schkolnik, Valbert Covvey, Georges Miquelle
Debussy	Sonata for Cello and Piano
	Prologue, Serenade Fantastique, Finale
Roussel	Serenade for flute, violin, viola, cello and harp
	Allegro, Andante, Presto
Hindemith	Sonata, op. 25 for cello solo
	Allegro Marcato, Moderato, Lento, Allegrissimo, Allegro molto moderato
	NOTES: Hindemith is without doubt the most prominent and talented composer among the younger generation in Germany. This sonata was written shortly after the war (WWI) and has the same despair and bitterness as Erich Remarque's "All Quiet on the Western Front." ... The entire sonata takes only ten minutes and because of its conciseness and comparatively unfamiliar idiom will be played twice.
Pierne	Sonata da Camera, op. 8 for flute, cello and piano

1931-32

December 4	Yoshida Trio: Seifu Yoshida, Shakuhachi; Madame Yoshida, Koto and Shamisen; Tomiko Chiba, Koto and vocal; Mitsumi Bando, dance.
Seifu Yoshida	Pray to God, duet for Shakuhachi and Koto taken from the Gagaku, said to be the oldest Oriental music written about the year one thousand.

Appendix A

Yatsuhashi	Rokudan, a classical melody for Koto, Shamisen and Shakuhachi written ca. 1500 AD by Koto virtuoso and an icon of Japanese music still popular today.
Miyagi	Dances for Koto, Shamisen and voice. Composer is a contemporary, blind Koto virtuoso.
	Hatsudayori (New Message); Itako-Deshima, (Island Melody)
Miyagi	Contemporary Songs for two Kotos and voice
	Flower Garden
	Spring is calling. Duo for Shakuhachi and Koto
	Beyond the Clouds—Boat Song for Koto and Shakuhachi and voice.
Anonymous	Classical Dances with Shamisen and Song accompaniment
	Musume Dojoji (from Kabuki drama of a girl who put an end to her life because of her unrequited love for a young priest in Dojoji Temple from the 18th century.)
	Asazumafune (from Kamakura Era in 13th century, a girl dances with a Tambour on her breast, enjoying peace of mind on a Spring night.)
Yoshida	Shakuhachi Solos with Koto Accompaniment
	Cradle Song; Mountain Pass

January 22	Eva Gauthier, soprano, Celius Dougherty, piano
	Songs from French Classics
Rameau	Recit et air, Les oiseaux d'alentour (from L'Impatience)
Lully	Air des songes, O tranquil sommeil (from Persee)
Monsigny	Air de Betzy, Il regardait mon bouquet (from Le roi et le fermier)
Lully	Recit de la galanterie, Soyez fidele
Gretry	Air d'Isabelle, Je suis fille (from Le tableau parlant 1769)
	Austrian Composers
Joseph Marx	Wie Einst
Arnold Schoenberg	
	Maedchenlied
Gustav Mahler	Ich atmet'einen linden Duft
Alban Berg	Nacht; Schilflied
Joseph Marx	Die Nachtigall; Valse de Chopin from "Pierrot Lunaire"
	Compositions for Piano Solo
Alban Berg	Sonata op. 1
Arnold Schoenberg	
	Klavierstueck op. 23
Maurice Ravel	Laideronnette, Imperatrice des Pagodos
Manuel de Falla	Spanish Dance, "La Vida breve"
	Settings of Amy Lowell Poems

Henry Hadley	When I Go Away
Alexander Lang Steinert	Four Lacquer Prints Vicarious; Temple Ceremony; Storm on the Seashore; A Burnt Offering
Carl Engel	Opal

Modern French Songs

Faure	La parfum imperissable (poesie de Leconte de Lisle) Tristesse (Poesie de Theophile Gautier)
Debussy	Le Promenoir des deuxs amants (poesie de Tristam Lhermite) Aupres de cette grotte somber Crois mon conseil, chere Climene Je tremble en voyant ton visage
Ravel	D'Anne jouanat l'espinette (poesie de Clement Marot)
Debussy	Ballade des femmes de Paris (poesie de Francois de Villon)

April 8   Dr. Ernst Toch, composer-pianist, assisted by Retta Richter, soprano, and Georges Miquelle, cello.

All Toch Program

Piano Sonata
Five Songs, op. 41
   Der Abend, Heilige; Spaetnachmittag; Kleine Geschichte;
   Was denkst du Jetzt?
Capricetti, op. 36 (piano solo)
Kleinstadtbilder, op. 49 (piano solo)
Sonata for Cello and Piano, op. 50
   Allegro commodo, Intermezzo: "The Spider," Allegro
Burlesken for piano solo

1932-33

December 2   Florent Schmitt, composer-pianist, assisted by Mrs. Cornelius K. Chapin, soprano, Georges Miquelle, Mme. Jeanne Reol, Walter Poole, Gilbert Beaume and Henry Siegel

All Schmitt Program

Four Preludes for Piano: Cloitre; Lac; En revant; Glas
Chante Elegiaque for cello and piano op. 24
Three songs
   Il pleut dans mon Coeur (poesie de Paul Verlaine)
   Lied (Poesie de Camille Mauclair
   Fils de la Vierge (Poesie de Maurice Ganivet)
Quintet op. 51: Lent-Anime, Lent, Anime

January 24   The Detroit Symphony Orchestra, Victor Kolar, cond. Edward Bredshall, piano

Dubensky	Fugue for Violins and Violas
Sibelius	Seventh Symphony (one movement) op. 105
Ravel	Concerto for Piano and Orchestra (Detroit premiere)
Weinberger	Polka and Fugue from "Schwanda" (Detroit premiere)

March 10 Georges Miquelle, cello, Mischa Kottler, piano, Mark Gunzberg, piano, Loretta Petrosky, piano.

Saint Saens	Sonata in C minor op 32 for cello and piano (Kottler)
Rachmaninoff	Suite for two pianos op. 17 (Gunzberg, Petrosky)
Chopin	Introduction and Polonaise, op. 3 for cello and piano (Miquelle, Kottler)

March 17 Beatrice Griffin, violin, Mabelle Howe Mable, piano, Ilya Schkolnik, violin, Mischa Kottler, piano, Georges Miquelle, cello, Cameron McLean, baritone

Handel	Sonata No. 5 in G minor for two violins and piano (Griffin, Schkolnik, Kottler)
	Compositions for violin solo (Griffin)
Spalding	Alabama (Melody and Dance in Plantation Style)
	Bygone Memories; Air and Negro Dance from Tallahassee Suite; *Songs for baritone and piano* (McLean, Mable)
Respighi	Nebbie
Erlebach	Long Dog
Oberstadt	Un Grand Sommeil Noir; Chansons après et douce; Mana Zucca; O Mighty Ocean
	Compositions for piano solo (Kottler)
Tausman	Mazurka; Berceuse; Mazurka
Castelnuovo-Tedesco	
	"Vitalba e blancospino"
Kottler	Gavotte
Rhene-Baton	Fileuse de Carantec
Ropartz	Sonata in G minor for cello and piano (Miquelle, Kottler)

1933-34
December 1 Henry Cowell, composer-pianist-lecturer
All Cowell Program

Informal Discourse on Modern American Music
Compositions for piano solo
The Tides of Manaunaun; Exultation; The Aeolian Harp;
Whirling Dervish; The Snows of Fujiyama; Sinister Resonance;
Reel; The Voice of Lir; The Fairy Answer; Gig; The Banshee;
Advertisement; The Harp of Life

January 19	The Detroit Symphony Orchestra, Victor Kolar, cond., Ilya Schkolnik, violin, Albert Mancini, trumpet.
	Concert Program of Detroit Premieres
Malipiero	Concerti for Flutes, Oboes, Clarinets, Bassoons, Trumpets, Drums and Double Basses.
Castelnuovo-Tedesco	
	Concerto Italiano for Violin and Orchestra
Kolar	Canzone della Sera with Trumpet solo
La Monaca	Three Hindoo Dances from the opera "La Festa di Gauri."

April 6	John Goss, baritone accompanied by Miss Margaret Mannebach and Duo pianists Edward Bredshall and Mischa Kottler
	Old English Songs
Arne	Come Away Death
Wigthorp	Am Not, I, of Such beliefs
Boyce	Song of Momas to Mars
Gamble	A Kiss I Begged
Purcell	There's Not a Swain
Songs by Peter Warlock	
	As ever I Saw (16th century); The First Mercy (Bruce Blunt); Elore-lo (17th century); Jillian of Berry (16th century)
Brahms Lieder	
	In Waldeseinsamkeit; Geheimnis; Auf dem Kirchhove; Komm bald; Staendchen
	Compositions for two pianos
Vuillemin	Pavane
Dana Suesse	Dansa a Media Noche
Infante	Three Andalusian Dances: Ritmo, Sentimiento, Gracia
Ravel	Cinq Melodies Populaire Grecques
	Le Reveil de la Mariee; La-bas vers l'Eglise;Quel gallant!; Chanson des cueilleuses de lentisques; Tout gai!

1934-35

December 7	Jeanne Laval, contralto; Miss Harriett J. Ingersoll, accompanist
Franceso Santoliquido	
	Tre Poesie Persiane (Negi de Kamare, Omar Khayyam, Abu Said)
Ralph de Golier	
	To a Sleeping Child
John Ireland	Tryst
Arnold Bax	Cradle Song
Rutland Boughton	
	Immanence
Armstrong Gibes	
	The Orchard Sings to the Child

Appendix A

Arnold Schoenberg
        Traumleben; Waldsonne; Erwartung; Hochzeitslied
Negro Spirituals
        Steal Away Jesus
(Trans. Louis Gruenberg)
        Didn't My Lord Deliver Daniel?
Louis Gruenberg
        Caravan Song; The Temples
        Animals and Insects
            The Lion
            The Explanation of the Grasshopper
            Two Old Crows (Vachel Lindsay)

February 1   Paris Instrumental Quintet: Rene Le Roy, flute; Pierre Jamet,
                harp; Rene Bas, violin; Pierre Grout, viola; Roger Boulme, cello
Francois Couperin
                Concerts Royaux for violin, cello and harp
W. A. Mozart   Quartet in D major No 28 for flute, violin, viola and cello
Gabriel Pierne   Variations Libres et Finale, op. 51 for flute, violin, cello and
                    harp (dedicated to the Paris Instrumental Quintet)
Claude Debussy
                Sonata for flute, viola and harp
Joseph Jongen   Concert a cinq, op 71 for flute, violin, viola, cello and harp
                (dedicated to the Paris Instrumental Quintet)

March 29   Filip Lazar, composer-pianist; assisted by Ann Dick, soprano; Gaston
                Brohan, double bass; Joachim Chassman, violin; Marius Fossenkem-
                per, clarinet; D. Von Emmerick, oboe; J. Mossbach, bassoon.
All Lazar Program
                First Suite for Piano
                    Berceuse; The Drunkards; Dance; By the River; The Ox Cart
                Two Roumanian Folk Dances
                Songs for Soprano and piano
                    Three Pastorales; Two Love Songs; Gay Song
                Three Dances for violin and piano
                Bagatelle for double bass and piano
                Second Suite for piano
                Pieces minuscules pour les enfants
                Trio for oboe, clarinet and bassoon

1935-36
November 15 Mme Olga Averino, soprano; Miss Margaret Mannebach,
                accompanist

Gluck	Adieu d'Iphigenie;Vieni che poi sereno
Orlando Lassus	
	Mon Coeur se recommande a vous
Lully	Revenez, revenez amours
Liszt	Ich Liebe dich; Comment disaient-ils
Mary Howe	Schlaflied
Loeffler	Petite Priere
E. Bloch	Psalm 114
Ravel	Habanera (vocalize); Kaddisch
Casella	Tre Canzoni Trecentesche
	Giovane bella; Fuor de la bella Gaiba; Amante sono
Alban Berg	Lied des Lulu
Stravinsky	Forget me nots; The Dove
	Trois petits chansons (Souvenirs de mon enfance)
	Le Petite Pie, Le Corbeau, Tchitcher-Iatcher
Borodin	Song of the dark forest
Levine	Two Nursery Rhymes: A Wand, A Christmas Tree
Olenine	From the Haystack
Moussorgsky	Death the Commander; Gathering Mushrooms

February 7	Detroit Woodwind Ensemble: John Wummer, flute; Dirk Van Emmerik, oboe; Marius Fossenkemper, clarinet; Joseph Mosbach, bassoon; Albert Stagliano, French horn; Edward Bredshall, piano.
Mozart	Quintet in E flat for piano, oboe, clarinet, horn and bassoon
Jacques Ibert	Trois Pieces Breves for flute, oboe, clarinet, horn and bassoon
Prokofieff	Deux Vision Fugitives for flute, oboec clarinet, bassoon
	Compositions for piano solo
Scriabine	Sonata No. 9
Schoenberg	Gavotte
En Auto	Poulenc
Le Gibet	Ravel
Fireworks	Debussy
	Flute Solos
Bernhard Heiden	Suite for flute and piano
Enesco	Cantabile and Presto
Honegger	Goat Dance
Paul Juon	Divertimento for flute, oboe, clarinet, horn, bassoon and piano

May 10	Jesus Maria Sanroma, pianist
Mateo Albeniz (1760-1831)	
	Sonata
Padre Antonio Soler	
	Two Sonatas

Debussy	The Interrupted Serenade; La Puerta del Vino; Tocatta
Krenek	A little Suite
Shostakowitsch	
	Five Preludes, op. 34
Villa Lobos	The Little Rubber Dog
Ravel	Alborado del Gracioso
Hindemith	Introduction and Lied
Schoenberg	Six little piano pieces
Malipiero	Homages: To a Parrot; To an Elephant; To an Idiot.
Toch	The Juggler

1936-37

October 25   Special Concert: Recital of Modern Music: Edward Bredshall, pianist and the Detroit Woodwind Ensemble. Charles Frederick Morse, speaker.

Jacques Ibert	Trois Pieces Breves
Prokofieff	Deux Vision Fugitives
Walter Piston	Sonata for flute and piano
Honegger	Goat Dance for solo flute
	Compositions for solo piano
Scriabine	Sonata No. 9
Aaron Copland	Sentimental Song
Ravel	Le Gibet
Debussy	Fireworks
Paul Juon	Divertimento for flute, oboe, clarinet, horn, bassoon and piano

December 14   Budapest String Quartet: Josef Roismann, Alexander Schneider, Boris Kroyt, Mischa Schneider.

Albert Roussel	Quartet in D major, op. 45
Bela Bartok	Quartet op. 17 no. 2
Paul Hindemith	
	Quartet, op. 22, no. 3

February 26   Eunice Norton, pianist

Aaron Copland	
	Piano Variations
Maurice Ravel	Gaspard de la nuit
Paul Hindemith	
	Three Etudes, op. 37
Charles E. Ives	Thoreau (from Piano Sonata No. 2)
Stravinsky	Petrouchke suite

April 2   Povla Frisch, soprano; Celius Dougherty, piano.

Bach	If you were near
Schubert	The Butterfly
	Sunset
Faure	A Cemetary in Brittany
Dupont	Mandoline
Ravel	The Peacock
Koechlin	Winter
Debussy	The Colloquy

1937-38
December 10   Jesus Maria Sanroma, pianist

J. S. Bach	Six pieces from Anna Magdalena Bach Notebook
Haydn	Sonata No. 7 in D major
Hindemith	Sonata No. 3 (1936)
Albeniz	From the Suite Iberia

Edward Ballanchine

Ten variations on "Mary Had A Little Lamb" in the styles of ten composers

Mozart	Agnelleto in C
Beethoven	Adagio
Schubert	Demi-moment Musical
Chopin	Nocturne (posthumous)
Wagner	Sacrifical Scene and Festmahl
Tchaikovsky	Valse Funebre
Greig	Mruka Klonh Lmbj
MacDowell	At a Lamb
Debussy	The Evening of a Lamb
Liszt	Grand Etude de Concert

February 18   The Roth Quartet: Feri Roth, Jeno Antal, Ferenc Molnar, Janos Scholz assisted by Johana Harris, piano.

Debussy	Quartet, op. 10
Casella	Three Pieces
Roy Harris	Piano Quintet

March 11   Paul Hindemith, composer and violist with Mme Lydia Hoffman-Behrendt, piano; Miss Margaret Mannebach, piano; Mr. Eugene Conley, tenor; Mr. James D. Barrett, violin.

All Hindemith Program

Violin Sonata (1935), Barret/Mannebach
Viola Sonata op. 25, no. 1, (Hindemith)
Piano Sonata No. 1, (Hoffman-Behrendt)
Three Songs to poems by Friedrich Hoelderlin (Conley)

Viola and Piano Sonata, op. 11, no. 4 (Hindemith/Hoffmann-Behrendt)

1938-39

December 2   Mme. Olga Averino, soprano; Alexei Haieff, accompanist; Mme Lydia Hoffman-Behrendt, piano solo.

Hindemith   Reihe Kleiner Stucke, op.37 for piano solo
Songs and Arias

Hindemith   Geburt Maria and Argwohn Josephs from "Das Marienleben."
Igor Stravinsky   Pastorle; Tilimbom; Three Little Songs
Moussorgsky   In the Vale; Death the Commander

Prokofieff   Sonata No. 2 for piano solo
Songs and Arias

Darius Milhaud   Chansons Hebraiques Populaires
Francis Poulenc   Bonne Journee; Une Herbe Pauvre; Carte Postale; Attributs
Claude Debussy   Extase; Pierrot; Chevelure; Rondel Chinoise
Compositions for piano solo

Francis Poulenc   Pastorale et Toccatta
Darius Milhaud   Saudades de Brazil
Debussy   La Dance de Puck; General Lavine
Maurice Ravel   Jeux d'Eau

January 27   Mlle. Nadia Boulanger in a Lecture Recital with piano illustrations: WHAT IS FREEDOM IN ART?
Mlle. Boulanger is the most distinguished living woman lecturer, teacher, inspirer and conductor; former lecturer on harmony at the Paris Conservatory and teacher of theory and composition at the Conservatoire Americaine de Musique at Fontainebleau.

March 3   The Pro Arte Quartet: Alphonse Onnou, Laurent Halleux, Germann Prevost, Robert Maas.

Milhaud   String Quartet in B flat, no. 2
Malipiero   String Quartet no. 3
Walter Piston   String Quartet no. 2
Ravel   String Quartet in F major

1939-40

December 8   TRIO: Frank Sheridan, piano; William Kroll, violin; Victor Gottlieb, cello.

J. B. Loeillet   Sonate a trios, B minor
Frank Bridge   Sonata for violin and piano, A minor
Claude Debussy

Suite, "Pour le Piano"

Maurice Ravel   Trio, A minor

January 12   Aaron Copland, American composer and pianist
Lecture demonstration on modern piano music with illustrations
selected from the works of Stravinsky, Schoenberg, Hindemith,
Milhaud, Prokofieff, Poulenc, Chavez, Thomson, Copland.

March 15   Yves Tinayre, Recital of Vocal Music, Harrison Potter at the
piano

I. PRIMITIVE MASTERS OF OCCIDENTAL MUSIC

Composer unknown Xth century	Ode (Boetius) *
Magister Leoninus (late XIIth century)	Organum duplum: "Deum time"
Perotin le Grand (?-1236)	Conductus: "Beata viscera" *
	Lai pieux: "Agniaus douz" *
Composer unknown (XIIIth century)	Motet: "Flos de virga nascitur"
II. Composer unknown (XIVth century)	Ave Mater (Venetian School)
Konrad Paumann (1410-1473)	Two Early Kirchenlieder (German School)
Josquin de Pres (1450-1521)	"Eia Mater fons pietatis"
III. Ernest Chausson	Hebe (Louise Ackermann)
	Les Heures (Mauclair)
Debussy	L'echlonnement des haies (Verlaine)
Pierre de Breville	La Petite Ilse (Jean Lorrain)
Ravel	Le grillon (Jules Renard)
IV. Johannes Wolfgang Franck (1641-1688)	
	Two sacred Lieder
Andreas Hammerschmidt	Motet: "De profundis clamavi"
*voice unaccompanied	

1940-41

December 6   The Coolidge Quartet: William Kroll, Jack Pepper, Nicolas Moldovan, Victor Gottlieb

Darius Milhaud
        Quartet no. 10 (1940)
Eugene Goossens
        Quartet no. 2, op. 59 (1940)
Beethoven   Quartet in C major, op. 59, no. 3 (1806-7)

January 31   John Kirkpatrick, pianist: American music of the past, present, future.

Roger Sessions (1896-)
        Sonata (1928-30)
Edward MacDowell (1861-1908)

Woodland Sketches; Fireside Tales;
New England Idyls
Carl Ruggles (1883-)
Angels (1920); Marching Mountains (1924);
Evocations; Five Chants for piano
Hunter Johnson (1906-)
Sonata (1934)
Charles E. Ives (1874-)
The Alcotts (1915)
Louis Moreau Gottschalk (1829-69)
The Union (variations on The Star Spangled Banner, Yankee
Doodle and Hail Columbia.)

March 28   Bela Bartok, composer and pianist, Ditta Pasztory Bartok, piano,
George Miquelle, cello.
Bartok   Rhapsody for cello and piano
Debussy   Jardin sous la pluie, L'Isle joyeuse (Mme Bartok)
Kodaly   Two pieces from Op. 11 (Mr. Bartok)
Bartok   Five pieces from "Mikrokosmos (Mr. Bartok)
Bach   Two Fugues from "Kunst der Fuge"
Mozart   Fugue in C minor
Bartok   Four pieces from "Mikrokosmos"
Debussy   En blanc et noir – three pieces (Mr. and Mrs. Bartok)

1941-42
December 5   Belgian Piano-String Quartet: G Momaerts, piano;Albert Rahier,
violin; C. Foidart , viola; J. Wetzels, cello
J. S. Loeillet   Sonate a Quatre
Alexandre Tansman
Suite-Divertissement (Dedicated to the Quartet)
Jean Absil   Quartet (Dedicated to the Quartet)
Gabriel Faure   First Quartet in C minor, op. 15

January 30   Duo Pianists: Celius Dougherty and Vincenz Ruzicka
Mozart   Sonata in D major
Schubert-Bauer
Andantino Varie; Rondo Brilliante
Stravinsky   Concerto per due pianoforte soli
Casella   Marcetta
Bizet   Trompette et Tambour
Ravel   Les entretiens de la Belle et de la Bete
Respighi   Canto di caccia siciliano

Warlock	Mattachins (Sword Dance)
Ravel	La Valse (transcribed for two pianos by the composer)

March 27 Elsie Houston, Brazilian Soprano; Vincent de Sola, accompanist

S.L.M.Barlow	The Cherry Tree (old English)
A. Perilhous	Complainte de St. Nicloas (traditional)
Lully	Atys (from opera Atys)
J. Tierson	Margoton (18th century)
Eric Satie	Dapheneo
M. Ravel	Sur L'herbe
Stravinsky	Three Little Songs
Joaquin Nin	Tres Villancicos; El Vito
Camargo Guarnieri	
	Sae Arue
Jayme Ovalle	Berimbao
Lorenzo Fernandez	
	Toada pra voce
Villa Lobos	Carreiro
Arr. L. Gallet	Tayeras
Arr. Villa Lobos	
	Tu passaste per este jardim
Arr. H. Tavares	Dansa de caboclo
Arr. Villa Lobos	
	Ena mokoce ce maka
Arr. Elsie Houston	
	E ora so
Brazilian Voodoo	
	Four Magic Themes from Candomble (with percussion)

1942-43

December 4 William Primrose, violist, Arthur Benjamin, pianist.

Nardini	Sonata in F minor
Hindemith	Sonata, op. II, no. 4
Arthur Benjamin	
	Sonata for Viola and Piano (1942)
Brahms	Sonata in E flat, op. 120, no. 2

January 29 The Roth Quartet: Feri Roth and Samuel Siegel, violins, Julius Shaier, viola, Oliver Edel, cello

Boccherini	String Quartet in G minor
Ravel	String Quartet in F major
Shostakovich	String Quartet opus 49

Appendix A

March 26   Povla Frijsh, soprano, Celius Dougherty, piano
Dvorak   Drei Zigeunermelodien sung without pause
Brahms   Wie Melodien
Wolf   Der Gaertner; Dass doch gemalt
Schumann   Mein schoener Stern
Stravinsky   La Rosee Sainte
Poulenc   Air Champetre
Milhaud   Chand de Nourrice (Poemes Juifs)
Debussy   Fleurs de bles
Ravel   Chanson Romanesque
Hahn   Offrande
Ennemond Trillat
    Une recette (porc a l'espagnole)
Faure   Nell
Virgil Thompson
    Dirge
Rebecca Clarke
    The Donkey
Sinding   Kjarlikhet (Love Song in Norwegian)
Alnaes   Selma (sung in Norwegian)
Heise   Igennem Boegeskoven (sung in Danish)
Naginski   The Pasture
Castelnuovo-Tedesco
    Recuerdo
Grieg   Der Gynger en Baad paa Boelge (sung in Danish)

1943-44
December 3   Mary Burns, contralto; Arthur Kaplan, piano
Handel   Scene from the Opera "Julio Cesare'
Marx   Selige Nacht; Der Ton
Strauss   Wasserrose; Caecilie
Granados   La Maja Dolorosa
Manuel de Falla
    Jota
Servantsdiantz   Ma bien Aimee (Melodie Armenienne)
Szulc   Dansons la Gigue
Bartok   Two Hungarian Folk Songs
M. Kennedy Fraser
    Two songs of the Hebrides
Griffes   The Sorrow of Hydath
Bax   Cradle Song
Winter Watts   Entreat me Not to Leave Thee; Joy

January 14   The Budapest String Quartet: Josef Roismann, Alexander Sch-
neider, Boris Kroyt, Mischa Schneider
Samuel Barber   Quartet
Paul Hindemith
                Quartet in E flat major (1943)
Beethoven   Quartet in F major, op. 135

April 21   Claudio Arrau, Chilean pianist
Debussy   Images; Estampes
Ravel   Gaspard de la Nuit
Poulenc   Caprice Italien (from the Suite Napoli)
Villa Hobos   Choros No. 5
Bartok   Allegro; Barbaro
Stravinsky   Trois Mouvements de Petrouchka (adapted from the ballet)

1944-45   The Britt String and Piano Trio: Viola Wasterlain, violin; Conrad
Held, viola and piano, Horace Britt, cello.
J. B. Loeillet Sonate a trios
Jean Francaix   Trio (1933)
Bloch   Three Nocturnes (violin, cello, piano)
Dohnanyi   Serenade, op. 10

January 19   E. Robert Schmitz, pianist
Shostakovich   Second Sonata, op. 64, B minor
Ravel   Jeu d'eau
                Rigaudon, Menuet and Toccata from "Tombeau de Couperin"
Strawinsky   Danse Infernale du Roi Kastchei et Berceuse from "Firebird"
Prokofieff   Sonata No. 7, op.83
Debussy   La Puerta del Vino, Ce qu'a vu le vent d'ouest, La Terasse des
audience du clair de lune, Etude pour les arpege, Etude pour le
octaves

April 6   Martial Singher, baritone, Paul Ulanowsky, piano
French XI century
                La Chanson de Roland
French XV century
                En venant de Lyon; L'amour de moi
Lully   Aria de Caron from Alceste
Rameau   Aria de Thesee from "Hippolyte at Aricie
Martini   Plaisir d'Amour
Mozart   Serenate de Don Giovanni
Berlioz   Serenata de Mephistofeles
Goudoud   Serenata

Appendix A

Moussorgsky	Serenata from "Songs and Dances of Death."
Brahms	Serenade: Vergebliches Staendchen
Chabrier	Ballade des gros dindons; Pastorale de cochons roses; Vilanelle des petit canards

Two Songs of the French Underground

Anna Marly	Chant de la liberation; Complainte du Partisan
Ravel	Don Quichotte a Dulcinee

1945-46

November 30 Duo Pianists: Dougherty and Ruzicka

Schubert	Fantaisie, op. 103
Stravinsky	Sonata (1943-44)
Czerny	Grande Fantaisie Concertante, opus 797
Rieti	Chess Serenade (1945)
Dougherty	Sea-Calm (1945)
Stravinsky	Scherzo a la Russe (1945)
Milhaud	Le Bal Martiniquais (1944)
Strauss	Rosenkavalier Waltzes

January 23 The Guilet String Quartet: Daniel Guilet, Jac Gorodetzky, Frank Brieff, Lucien Laport Kirsch

Schubert	Quartet, op. 125, no. 1 in E flat major
Milhaud	Quartet No. 12 (1945) Detroit Premiere,
Randall Thompson	
	Quartet no. 1 in D minor

April 22 Martial Singher, baritone & Paul Ulanowsky, piano

Lully	Bois epais, from Amadis
Rameau	Invocation et Hymn au Soleil from Les Indes Galantes
XVIII century	Tambourin
Handel	Where ere You Walk
Schubert	An die Lieder; Der Doppelgaenger; Der Jungling an der Quelle; Du bist die Ruh
Moussorgsky	Air du Tsar, from Boris Godounoff
Faure	Poeme d'un jour (Recontre, Toujours, Adieu)
Debussy	Trois Ballades de Francois Villon (a s'Amye, Requeste de sa Mere, Dame de Paris)
Ravel	Quatre chants populaires: Hebraique; Italienne; Francaise; Espagnole

1946-47

November 15 Rose Dirman, lyric soprano & Donald Comrie, piano
Johann A. Hasse
          Nel mirar qiuel sassso amato, "Sant Elena al Calvario

Pietro D. Paradies
        M'ha presa alla sua ragna
Charles Gounod
        D'un bout du monde, "The Mock Doctor"
Alban Berg   Die Nachtigall
Joseph Marx   Selige Nacht; Und Gestern hat er mir Rosen Gebracht;
        Hat dich die Liebe beruht
Gabriel Dupont Mandoline
Leo Delibes   Eglogue
George Bizet Pastorale
Debussy   Lorsqu' autour de sa tete, "La Damoiselle Elue"
Enrique Granados
        La Maja y el Ruisenor, "Goyescas"
Henry Hadley The Time of Parting
Paul Bowles   In the Woods
Elie Siegmeister
        The Ballyboo Zoo
Howard R.Thather
        Summer Evening
Rhea Silberta You Shall Have Your Red Rose

January 31   Pasquier Trio
Beethoven   Trio in G, Op. 9, No. 1
Dohnanyi   Serenade No. 10
Jean Cras   Trio

March 28   Gold & Fizdale, duo-pianists
Mozart   Theme and Variations K. 501
Paul Bowles   Sonata for Two Pianos (1945)
Schumann   Impromptu
Alexei Haieff Sonata for Two Pianos (1945)
Erik Satie   Morceaux en Forme de Poire (1903) originally written for one
          piano, four hands.
Copland   Danzon Cubano (1943)
Milhaud   Braziliedra (1937)

1947-48
December 10 Jacques Abram, pianist
Bach   English Suite No. 6 in D minor
Mozart   Sonata in A minor
C. Guarneri   Tonada Triste
R. Morillo   Cancion Triste y Danse Alegre
N. Medtner   Fairy Tale in B minor

P. JHindemith	Sonata No. 2
Villa-Lobos	Polichinelle
S. Prokofieff	Prelude in C; Sarcasm
M. Ravel	Alborado del Gracioso

January 23 Paganini Quartet: Henri Temianko & Gustave Rosseels, violins, Robert Courte, viola, Gabor Rejto, violoncello

Vivaldo	L'Estro Armonico (Concerto 5) in A major
Mozart	Adagio and Fugue in C minor, K.V. 546
Debussy	Quartet in ;G minor, op. 10
Bartok	Quartet in A minor, Op. 7

April 2 Martha Lipton, Mezzo-soprano; James Quillian, piano

Mozart	Parto, Parfto from "La Clemenza di Tito"
Moussorgsky	Cycle of 7 songs from "The Child's Nursery."
Wolf	In der Fruehe (Eduard Morike); In dem Schatten Meiner (anon. Spanish)
	Mignon (Goethe); Ich hab' in Penna Einen Liebsten Wohnen (Heyse)

Maurice Thirtiet

Deux Ballades Medievales from the film "Les Visiteurs de Soir"

Demons et Merveilles; Le tender et dagereux visage de l'Amour

Arr. Canteloube

Le Coucou (chants d'Auvergnes)

Debussy	La Chevelure; Noel des enfants qui n'ont plus de maisons
Britten	The Rape of Lucretia
Hindemith	The Whistlin' Thief
Chanler	The Dove
Villa Lobos	Cancao do Carreiro

1948-49
November 26 Francis Poulenc, composer-pianist; Pierre Bernac, baritone

Lully	Mercure's Aria from Persee; Rafrina's aria "Ballet"; Cadmus Aria from "Cadmus et Hermione"
Duparc	Elegie; Le Manoir de Rosemonde; Soupir; L'Invitation au Voyage
Debussy	Beau Soir; Mandoline; Colloque Sentimentale; Ballade des Femmes de Paris
Faure	Apres un Reve; Le Secret; Aujrore, Claire de Lune; Les Berceaux
Poulenc	Pieces pour piano: Mouvement Perpetuels; Nocturne en ut majeur; Intermezzo en la bemol; Pastourelle
	Chansons Villageoises: Chanson du clair Tamis; Les Gars qaui Vont a la Fete; C'est le joli Printemps; Chanson de le Fille Frivole; Le Retour du Sergent

March 2	The Juilliard String Quartet:Robert Mann, Robert Koff, violins; Raphael Hillyer, viola; Arthur Winograd, cello
Beethoven	Quartet, Opus 59, NO. 1
Webern	Five Movements for St;ring Quartet, Opus 5
Bartok	Fourth Quartet

April 1	Arthur Gold and Robert Fizdale, duo-pianists
De Manziarly	Sonate (1947)
Rieti	Suite Champetre (1948)
Bowles	Concerto for Two Pianos Alone
Mozart	Sonata in D (K. 448)
Tailleferre	Valse Lente (1948)
Milhaud	Carnaval a la Nouvelle Orleans (1947)
	Mardi Grax! Chic a la Paille!
	Domino Noir de Cajun
	Les Mille Cent Coups

1949-50

November 16	Benjamin Britten, composer and pianist; Peter Pears, tenor
Anonymous	Have You Seen but a White Lily Grow?
Dowland	In Darkness Let Me Dwell
Purcell	I'll Sail Upon the Dog Star (from Orpheus Brittanicus)
	There's not a Swain (from Orpheus Brittanicus)
	Sweeter than Roses (from Orpheus Brittanicus)
Purcell- Britten	Three Divine Hymns (from Harmonia Sacra)
	Evening Hymn; Job's Curse; Alleluia!
Britten	Seven Sonnets of Michelangelo

Folk Songs of the British Isles arranged by Benjamin Britten
>Down by the Sally Garden (Irish)
>The Ploughboy (English)
>The Bonnie Earl O"Maroy (Scottish)
>Sweet Polly Oliver (English)

February 3	New Friends of Music Quartet: Hortense Monath, piano; Bronislav Gimpel, violin; Frank Brieff, viola; Jascha Bernstein, cello.
Brahms	Pianol Quartet in A Major, Op. 26
Hindemith	String Trio No. 1, Op. 34
Faure	First Piano Quartet in C minor, Op. 15

March 31	Grant Johannesen, pianist
Bach	Prelude and Fugue in A minor
Poulenc	Eight Nocturnes (first performance in Detroit)
Rameau	Two "Pieces de Clavecin"
	L'Egyptienne, Les Sauvages

Appendix A

Hindemith	Sonata No. 3, in B flat Major
Ravel	Gaspard de la Nuit (Ondine, Le Gibet, Scarbo)
Mennin	Partita 1949 (first performance in Detroit)
	Introduction, Aria, Variation-Canzona, Canto,
	Allegro vivace e Vigoroso

1950-51
December 7 Louis Kaufman, violin and Annette Kaufman, piano

Tartini	Sonata Di Camera in B flat (ms. uncovered in Vienna in 1937)
Poulenc	Sonata for Violin and Piano
Guarnieri	Canto I
Prokofieff	Gavotta (arr. By Jascha Heifetz)
Kodaly	Adagio
Milhaud	Danses de Jacaremirim (Sambinka, Tan, Chorinko)
Copland	Waltz and Celebration "Billy the Kid"
Bennett	Nocturne and Allemande
Triggs	Danza Braziliana (dedicated to the Kaufmans)

February 2 Norman Dello Joio, composer-pianist; Gladys Kuchta, soprano;
      Robert Goss, baritone
All music by Norman Dello Joio
     Five Songs: Mill Doors, The Assassination, Lament, The Dying
      Nightingale, There is a Lady Sweet and Kind
     Sonata No. 3 for Piano
     From the Opera "St. Joan"
     The Maid's Soliloquy, Song of the Sentry, Dance of rthe Dau-
     phin's Tumblers, Joan's Dress Aria, The Creed of Pierre Cauchon,
     Meeting at Night, following "The Assassination."

March 2 Suzanne Danco, soprano; Paul Ulanowsky, piano

XIII century	Three Laudi from Laudario 91 di Cortona
Monteverdi	Ecco di dolci raggi, from "Scherzi Musicali"
	Con che soavita, from "VII ;;Libro del Madrigali"
Bononcini	Deh, piu a me non v'axcondete
Grandi	Motet-Quam pulchra es
Ariosti	Vuoi, che parta, from "Lucio Vero."
Mortari	Le Carnaval de Venise: Dans la Rue, Sur les Lagunes, Carnaval,
	Clair de Lune Sentimental
Debussy	Ariette Oubliees: C'est l'extase langoureuse, Il pleure dans mon
	Coeur, L'ombre des arbres, Chevaux de bois, Spleen, Green
Milhaud	Chants populaires hebraiques: Le Chant du veilleur, Berceuse,
	Chant Hassidique
Poulenc	Le Bestiare ou Cortege d'Orphee: Le Dromedaire, La Chevre du

Thibet, La Sauterelle, Le Dauphin, La Carpe
Aiar Chantes: Air Romantique, Air champetre, Air grave, Air vif

1951-52
November 30   Gold and Fizdale, duo-pianists
Satie   En Habit de Cheval: Choral, Fugue Litanique, Autre Choral, Fugue de Papier
Bizet   Jeux d'Enfants: L'Escarpolette (The Swing) Reverie; La Toupie (The Top) Impromptu; La Poupee (The Doll) Berceuse; Les Chevaux de Bois (The Merry-Go-Round) Scherzo; Le Volant (Battledore and Shuttlecock) Fantaisie; ATrompette et Tambour (lTrumpet and Drum) Marche; Les Bulles de Savon (The Soap Bubbles) Rondino; Les Quatre Coins (Puss in the Corner) Esquisses; Colin-Maillard (Blind Man's Bluff) Nocturne; Saute-Mouton (Leap Frog) Caprice; Petit Marie, Petite Femme (Little Husband, Little Wife) Duo; Le Bas (The Ball) Galop
Strawinsky   Concerto Per Due Pianoforti Soli (1935): Con Moto, Notturno, Quattro Variazioni, Preludio e Fuga
Hindemith   Sonata (1938): Maszig Bewegt, Lebhaft, Ruhig Bewegt
Milhaud   Les Songes (1933) Scherzo, Vales, Polka

February 1   Gerard Souzay, baritone; James Shomate, piano
Scarlatti-   Chi vuole innamorarsi
Dorumsgaard   Caldo Sangue fromOratorio The 16th King of Jerusalem
                  Bellezza che s'ama
                  Toglietemi la vita ancor
Faure   Four Songs: Spleen, Green, Tristesse, Mandoline
de Machaut   Douce Dame Joli
Anon.   Tambourin
Poulenc   Priez pour paix
Leguerney   A son Page
Ravel   Histoires naturelle: La Paon (The Peacock); Le Grillon (The Cricket); Le Cygne (The Swan); Le Martin-Pecheur (The Kingfisher); Le Paritade (The Guinea Hen)
                  Don Quichotte a Dulcinee: Chanson Romanesque; Chanson Epique, Chanson a Boire

April 18   Albeneri Trio: Erich Itor Kahn, piano; Giorgio Ciompi, violin; Benar Heifetz, cello
Martinu   Trio in D minor (1950: Allegro moderato, Adagio, Allegro
                      Bohuslav Martinu was born in 1890 at Policka, Czechoslovakia. He was a pupil of Suk in Prague and Roussel in Paris and has

produced a great deal of chamber and orchestral music. He came to the United States in 1940 and teaches at the Mannes Music School in New York.

Faure   Trio in D minor, Op. 120: Allegro, ma non troppo; Andantino Allegro vivo.

Gabriel Urbain Faure was born in Pamiers in 1845 and died in Paris aged 79. He held a series of positions in church music culminating as organist at the Madeleine. Among his most important works are his songs, Requiem, Opera "Penelope" and his chamber music.

Piston   Trio in E: Allegro, Adagio,Allegro con brio, Allegro moderato

Walter Piston was born in Rockland, Maine in 1894. He studied at Harvard and in Paris and then became a member of the Harvard music faculty. He tends to new harmonies and approaches atonality in his orchestral and chamber works.

Ravel   Trio in A: Modere; Pantoum-Assez Vif; Passacaille-Tres Large; Final-anime

Maurice Ravel was born in 1875 at Ciboure, near St. Jean de Luz, and died in Paris in 1937, aged 62. He was a pupil in composition of Faure and Gedalge at the Paris Conservatory who taught him the value of classic form. Chabrier, whom he met and admired, taught him the charm of vivacious melody, bright rythms and clear orchestration. Another influence was Erich Satie.

April 20   Jennie Tourel, coloratura mezzo-soprano; George Reeves, piano
Pro Musica's 25th Birthday Program

Purcell	From rosie Bowers (Purcell's last composition)
Beethoven	An die ferne Geliebte
Debussy	Trois Poemes de Charles Baudelaire: Le Balcon, Recueillement, La Mort des Amants
Respighi	Nebbie
Gretchaninoff	Roman Sonnets: Sunset over Pincio, Piazza di Spagna
	Amour Eternel
Dougherty	Barcarolle
	Weathers
Villa Lobos	;Modinha
	Cancao do Marinheiro
	Cancao do Carreiro

1952-53
November 14 Berkshire Quartet: Urico Rossi, Albert Lazan, violins; David Dawson, viola; Fritz Magg, cello; John Langstaff, baritone
Malipiero   Rispetti e Strambotti

Anonymous	Early French Chansons: L'Amour de Moi (15th century, arr. Tiersot); Le Cycle du Vin (arr. Ferrari); Chanson deThibaut de Champagne (13th century, arr. Ferrari); Les Filles de la Rochelle (16th century, arr. Tiersot)
Barber	Dover Beach (Matthew Arnold)
Prokofieff	Quartet No. 2, Op. 92: Allegro sostenuto, Adagio, Allegro

February 6	Robert Goldsand, piano
Handel	Suite in F major
Prokofieff	Sonata No. 7, Op. 83
Berg	Sonarta in B minor, Op. 1
Scarlatti	Three Sonatas
Copeland	Passacaglia

May 22	Blanche Thebom, mezzo soprano; William Hughes, piano
Bach	Of Great Jehova Will I Be Singing
	Komm Susser Tod
	Prepare Thyself, Zion
Debussy	Chevaux de bois
	La Chevelure
	Le Faune
	Les Berceaux
	Tojours
Verdi	Aria of Abigail from Nabucco
	Songs without Words
Stravinsky	Pastorale
Ravel	Habanera
Prokofieff	Melody No. 4, Op. 35
Rachmaninoff	Vocalise
Panofka	Tarantella
Dougherty	Five Songs: A Lady; Weathers; The K'e; An Essay!; Listen! The Wind

1953-54

November 20	Quartetto Italiano: Paolo Borciani, Elisa Pegreffi, violins; Pierro Farulli, viola; Franco Russi, cello.
Giardini	Quartet, Opus 23, No. 4 in C minor: Allegro, Adagio, Rondo Allegro
Busoni	Quartet, Opus 19 in C Major
Turina	Oracion del Torero
Wolf	Italian Serenade

Appendix A

Debussy	Quartet, Opus 10, in G minor: Anime et tres decide; Assez vif et bien rhythme, Andantino doucedment expressif; Tres modere-Tres Mouvement et avec passion – Tres vif.
February 12	Eugene List, piano, Carroll Glenn, violin; assisted by Oberlin Conservatory Quartet: Nathan Gottschalk and Larry Moore, violins; Paul Collins, viola; Pewter Howard, cello
Ravel	Le Tombeau de Couperin (Mr. List)
Prokofieff	Sonata for Solo Violin, Opus 115 (Miss Glenn)
Vivaldi	Concerto, Il Riposo for violin
Bartok	Duets for Two Violins (Miss Glenn and Mr. Gottschalk)
Haydn	Concerto for Violin and Piano, and strings
Dello Joio	Sonata No. 3 for Piano (Mr. List)
March 19	Aaron Copland, composer-pianist; Patricia Neway, mezzo-soprano.
	The concert opened with a talk by Mr. Copland: The Composer's Experience. He then accompanied Miss Neway in a recital of songs.
Copland	Twelve Poems of Emily Dickinson
Berlioz	Three Songs from Nuits d'Ete: Absence, Au Cimitiere, Villanelle
Menotti	Magda's Aria from The Consul (1950)

1954-55

December 3	New Music Quartet: Broadus Erle and Matthew Raidmondi, violins; Walter Trampler, viola; David Soyer, cello.
Purcell	Chacony in G minor for viola
A. Scarlatti	Sonata a Quatro in D minor
Sammertini	Concertino a 4 Stromenti Soli
Bartok	Five Pieces from "Mikrokosmos"
Villa Lobos	Quartet No. 7
December 10	Darius Milhaud, composer. Zadel Skolovsky, piano. Milhaud reviewed his "Forty years of Music Life" illustrated with explanations of the works performed by Mr. Skolovsky
Milhaud	Saudades do Brazil
	Printemps
	Automne
	Hymne de Glorification (World premiere performance)
May 13	Phyllis Curtin, soprano; Gregory Tucker, piano
Handel	Solo Cantata: Lucrezia

John Blow	Venus' Lament on the death of Adonis
Ginastera	Five Argentinian Songs: Chacarera, Triste, Zamba, Arrorro, Gato
Barber	Hermit Songs to poems translated from anonymous texts of the 8th to 12th centuries
Tucker	Lullaby; The Drummer
Pinkham	Sing Agreeably of Love

1955-56
November 18 Martial Singher, baritone; Edward Mobbs, piano

Rossi	Lamento of Orfeo
Lully	Aria of Charon from " Alceste"
Rameau	Castor et Pollux
Anon.	Musette (XVIII century)
Mozart	Cantata: "Die ihr des unermesslichen Weltalls"
De Falla	Retablo de Maese Pedro (scene of Don Quixote)
Milhaud	Chants Populaires Hebraiques
Poulenc	Three songs from "Chansons Gaillardes": Serenade, Invocation aux Parques, La Belle Jeunesse
	Priez pour Paix
	Fetes Galantes

January 27 Roman Totenberg, violinist, and his ensemble of two violins, viola, cello, bass, piano flute and clarinet

Vivaldi	Concerto in G minor, Opus 8, "Winter"
Bach	Brandenburg Concerto No. 5 for violin, flute, piano and strings
Hindemith	Funeral Music (Music of Mourning)
Bartok	Five Rumanian Dances
Milhaud	Suite for violin, clarinet and piano
Ravel	Tzigane

March 9 Moura Lympany, piano

Bach	Chromatic Fantasy and Fugue in D minor
Debussy	Three Studies from Book I
	L'Isle Joyeuse
Ravel	Ondine
	Toccata (from Le Tombeau de Couperin)
Shostakowitch	Three Fantastic Dances
Katchaturian	Two Dances: Valse-Caprice, Dance
Prokofiev	Toccata

1956-57
November 16 I Solisti di Zagreb, Antonio Janigro, conductor and cello soloist with seven violins, three violas, two cellos and one double bass.

Boccherini	Cello Concerto in B flat. Soloist: Antonio Janigro
Kelemen	Concertante Improvisations (1955)
Hindemith	Funeral Music for viola and strings. Soloist: Stefano Passaggio
Lhotka	Scherzo (1931)
Britten	Simple Symphony Op. 4 (1934)

January 11 Lukas Foss, composer-pianist, assisted by The Detroit Symphony
String Quartet: Mischa Mischakoff and Gordon Staples, violins;
William Preucil, viola; Paul Olefsky, cello

Foss	String Quartet in G (1947)
	Three Two Part Inventions (1937) for piano solo
	Capriccio for Cello and Piano (1946) A

"Some Thoughts on the Writing and Understanding of Modern Music:" Mr. Foss

Bach	Concerto in F minor for piano and strings

March 22 Lois Marshall, soprano; Weldon Kilburn, piano

Purcell	The Queen's Epicedium (Elegy for Queen Mary, 1695)
Debussy	Four Songs: C'est L'extase, Green, Il p[leure dans mon Coeur, Cjevaux de bois.
Mozart	Constanza's Aria from "Die Entfuhrung aus dem Serail"
Barber	Three songs: Rain has fallen, Sleep Now, I hear an Army
De Falla	Seven Popular Spanish Songs

1957-58
November 1 I Solisti di Zagreb, Antonio Janigro, Conductor and cello soloist
(see previous season)

Corelli	Sarabande, Gigue, Badiniere
Vivaldi	Cello Concerto in D Major, Antonio Janigro, soloist
Roussel	Sinfonietta Opus 52
Kelemen	Three Dances for Viola and Strings, Stefano Passaggio, soloist
Hindemith	Eight Movements Opus 44
Rossini	Third Sonata for Strings in C

January 31 Grant Johannesen, piano

Bach	Fantasia in C minor
Copland	Piano Variations
Castro	Tangos (1942) (American Premiere)
Prokofieff	Sonata No. 7, Opus 83
Poulenc	Suite Francaise
Debussy	Two Etudes: Pour les sonorities opposes; Pour les cinq doigts (après Czerny)
	L'Isle Joyeuse

March 21	Paul Creston, composer-pianist, assisted by Marjorie McClung, soprano.
Bach	Komm in mein Herzenshaus from Cantata No. 80
	Bist du bei mir
Vivaldi	Aria del Vagante from Oratorio "Juditha triumphans"
Durante	Vergin tgutto amor
Lully	Air de Rafrina
	Air de Sangaride
Gluck	Recitatif et Air d'IUphigenie en Tauride

A short talk by Mr. Creston

Creston	Sonata for piano, Op. 9 (1936)

Piano compositions by Paul Creston

Lydian Song, Op. 55 (originally for harp solo)
Prelude and Dance, Op. 29 No. 1
Prelude and Dance, Op. 29 No. 2
Six Preludes, Op. 38

Songs by Paul Creston

The Bird of the Wilderness
Four Songs to Death (Poems from Gitanjali by Tagore)
A Song of Joys (Poem by Walt Whitman)
Psalm XXIII
Three Songs Op. 46: A Serenade; Lullaby; Fountain Song

1958-59

December 5	John Browning, Pianist
Bergsme	Four Tangents: Prologue, Unicorns, Fishes, Epilogue
Bach	Partita No. 2 in C. minor
Hindemith	From "Ludus Tonalis": Praeludium, Fuga; Interludium
Ravel	Sonatine: Modxere, Menuet, Vif
Cumming	Alleluja for a Joyous Occasion
Poulenc	Trois Mouvements perpetuels
Barber	Sonata, Opus 26
January 23	Reverend Russell Woolen, pianist-composer; Leslie Chabay, tenor
Monteverdi	Salve Regin
Da Viadana	O dulcissima Maria
Schuetz	Bringt her dem Herren
	Eile mich Gott zu erretten
Woollen	Suite for High Voice on Poems of Gerard Manley Hopkins. (composed for this occasion and dedicated to Pro Musica of Detroit.)

A talk by Russel Woollen: Problems of the Composer

Bartok/Kodaly	Hungarian Folksongs

Appendix A

Woollen	Sonatina for piano solo

March 14   I Musici: Six violins, two violas, two cellos, one bass, piano and cembalo.
Following a 17th century tradition, these 12 musicians play without a conductor, each one taking turn in solo and ensemble parts. Hearing them in 1952, Arturo Toscanini called I Musici "a perfect chamber orchestra." This is their third North American tour.

Vivaldi	Concerto in C minor for Strings and Cembalo
	Concerto in B flat Major for Violin, Cello, Strings and Cembalo
	Concerto Grosso in A minor, Opus 3 No. 8
Bucchi	Concerto Lirico for Violin and Strings
Britten	Simple Symphony

1959-1960
November 6   Camera Concerti, Joseph Eger, Director and French horn; Charles Treger, concertmaster with five violins, two violas, one cello, one double bass, two oboes, two French horn, and piano and cembalo. The group is focused largely on great concertos for horn and viola or viola d'amore.

Bach	Concerto in C minor for Violin and Oboe (Karen Tuttle and Henry Schuman)
Kurka	Ballad for French Horn and String Orchestra (Joseph Egger)
Hindemith	Trauermusik for Viola and String Orchestra (1936)
Delano	Ofrenda Musical (1959) (in memory of Luis Pales Matos)
Mozart	Ein Musikalischer Spasse (A Musical Joke) K. 522

February 26   William Masselos, pianist

A. Scarlatti	Four Sonatas (E minor, L24; E Major, L23; G Major, L487; D minor L422)
Schumann	Kreisleriana
Chavez	Polignos and Solo (from Seven Pieces for Piano)
Hovhaness	Jhala
Copland	Variations
Schoenberg	Opus 33 A and B
Webern	Variations
Ben Weber	Fantasy
Griffes	Sonata

March 25   Michel Senechal, Tenor; Charles Wadsworth, piano

Rameau	L'Impatience-Cantate pour tenor
Purcell	Fairest Isle; Music for a While; Man is for Woman Made
G. A. Rossini	Musique Anodine; U'UltimoRicordo; La Fioraia Fiorentina

Traditional	Three French Songs arranged by Benjamin Britten: Eho! Eho!; La Bells Est au Jardin d'Amour; Quand J'Etais Chez mon Pere
Tomas	Mignon: Elle ne croyait pas
Berlioz	Rondo
Duparc	Four Songs: Lamento; Extase; L'Invitations aau Voyage, Soupir

1960-61

November 18	The Royal Danish String Quartet: Arne Svendsen and Palle Heichelmann, violins; Knud Frederiksen, viola; Pierre Rene Honnens, cello
Haydn	Quartet in G Major, Opus 77,N0. 1
Niels Bentzon	Quartet, Opus 24, No. 6
Bartok	Quartet No. 6

January 20	Arthur Gold and Robedrt Fizdale, duo-pianists
K.P.E.Bach	Little Duet for Two Pianos
Schubert	Grand Duo, Opus 140
Debussy	Six Epigraphs antiques
Poulenc	Sonata for Two Pianos 1953 (dedicated to Gold & Fizdale)

March 18	Jennie Tourel, coloratura mezzo soprano; Allen Rogers, piano
Monteverdi	Lamento di Arianna
Monsigny	La Sagesse est un tresor from "Rose et Colas."
Duparc	La Vie Anterieure (text by Baudelaire)
Debussy	Fetes Galantes, Vol. 1: En Sourdine, Fantoches, Clair de Lune
Satie	Le Chapelier
Poulenc	Violin
Dargominsky	Love Song
Gretchaninoff	Two Songs: The Snowdrop, On Golden Fields
Rachmaninoff	Two Songs: Before my Window, Floods of Spring
Ginastera	Two Songs: Triste, Chacarera
Bernstein	Four French Recipes: Plum Pudding, Ox-tails, Tavouk Guenksis, Rabbit Stew in a Hurry (dedicated to Miss Tourel)

1961-62

December 1	Seymour Lipkin, pianist
Bach	Concerto after the ItalianTaste
Carter	Sonata 1945-46
Bach	Suite No. 5 in G. Major, "French."
Stravinsky	Four Etudes, Opus 7
Prokofiev	Sonata No. 3, Opus 28.

Appendix A

January 30   The Netherlands Chamber Choir of Amsterdam, Felix de Nobel,
                   conductor
Jacobus Clemens Non Papa
                   Sanctus
Antonius Brumel
                   Sicut Lilium
Loyset Compere
                   O Bone Jesu
Orlando di Lasso
                   Jubilate Deo
John Farmer   Fair Phyllis
Thomas Weelkes
                   Phyllis Go Take Thy Pleasure
Thomas Morley
                   Come Lovers Follow Me
Peter Philips   The Nightingale
Thomas Morley
                   Hard by a Crystal Fountain
Herman Strategier
                   Cantica Pro Tempore Natali
Rudolf Mengelberg
                   Antiphona de Morte
Manuel Palau   Hermosita
Francis Poulenc
                   Soir de Neige
Folk Songs   Het Kwezelken (Flemish); De Drikusman (Dutch); Down in the
                   Valley (American); Skotse Trije (Dutch)

February 23   The Beaux Arts Trio of New York: Menahem Pressler, piano,
                   Daniel Guilet, violin, Bernard Greenhouse, cello
Robert Casadesus
                   Second Trio, Opus 53
Boris Koutzen   Trio
Maurice Ravel   Trio in A minor

1962-63
November 9   Jaime Laredo, violin; Ruth Meckler Laredo, piano; David Soyer,
                   cello
Bach   Sonata No. 6 in G Major for violin and piano
Hindemith   Sonata in E for violin and piano
Barber   Sonata for piano, Opus 26
Kodaly   Duo Opus 7 for violin and cello

January 22	Leon Kirchner, composer-pianist in residence at Harvard University with The Lenox Quartet: Peter Marsh and Theodora Mantz, violins; Paul Hersh, viola; Donald McCall, cello.

Three works by Kirchner with commentary by the composer
String Quartette No. 1
Trio for violin, cello and piano
String Quartette No. 2

March 1	John Boyden, baritone; Eugene Bossart, piano
Schubert	Five Lieder: Dem Unendlichen, Nachtviolen, Seligkeit, Der Wanderer an den Mond, Der Musensohn
Frank Martin	Six Monologues from Everyman by Hugo von Hoffmannstahl: Ist all zu End das Freudenmahl?; Ach Gott, wie graust mir vor dem Tod; Ist als wenn eins gerufen hatt; So wollt ich ganz zerrmichtet sein; Ja! Ich glaub: solches hat der vollbracht; O ewiger Gott! O gottliches Gesicht!
Debussy	Three Ballads of Francois Villon: Ballade de Villon a s'amaye; Ballade que feit Villon a la requeste de sa mere pour prier; Ballade des femmes de Paris.
Gerald Finzi	Let Us Garlands Bring (Texts by Shakespeare): Come Away, Come Away Death; Who is Sylvia?; Fear No More the Heat o' the Sun; O Mistress Mine; It was a lover and His Lass

1963-64

December 13	The Paul Kuentz Paris Chamber Orchestra with Christian Larde, flute, and Gabin Lauridon, contrabass.
Rameau	Concert No. 6 for orchestra
Dittersdorf	Concerto in E Major for Contrtabass and Orchestra
Pergolesi	Concerto in G Major for Flute and Orchestra
Casterede	Prelude and Fugue for String Orchestra (1961)
Lesur	Serenade for Strings (1954)
Bartok	Six Rumanian Folk Dances

February 7	Charles Rosen, pianist
Bach	The Goldberg Variations: Aria, 30 variations, Aria da Capo
Ravel	Suite: Gaspard de la Nuit: Ondine, Le Gibet, Scarbo

April 4	Regina Sarfaty, Mezzo soprano; David Stimer, pianist
Bellini	Three Songs: Quando incise su quell marmot; Dolente Immagine di Fille mia; Per pieta bell'idol mio.
Poulenc	Four Songs: C'est ainsi que tu es; Amoureuses; Hotel; Adelina a la promenade.
Stravinsky	Jocasta's Aria from "Oedipus Rex"

Appendix A

| de Falla | Seven Popular Spanish Songs: El pano moruno; Seguidilla murci-ana; Asturiana; Jota; Nana; Cancion; Polo. |
| Rorem | Nine Songs: What if Some Little Pain; To You; O You; Stop All the Clocks; The Air is the Only; Do I Love You; In the Rain; Rain in Spring; Alleluia. |

1964-65
November ? Ronald Turini, pianist (program missing)

February 12 The Paganini Quartet: Henri Temianka, Stefan Krayk, violins; Albert Gillis, viola; Lucien LaPorte, cello.
Hindemith   Quartet No. 3, Opus 22
Prokofiev   Quartet No. 2, opus 92
Ravel   Quartet

April ? Coro do Brasil, national chorus of Brazil (program missing)

1965-66
November 12 Theodor Uppman, baritone; Allen Rogers, piano.
Four Songs from Shakespeare
Vaughan-Williams
       Orpheus with his Lute
Peter Warlock   Sigh No More Ladies
Roger Quilter   Fear No More the Heat O' the Sun
Marc Blitzstein   Vendor's Song
Charles Ives   Walking, The Greatest Man, Cannon, Charlie Rutlage
Kirk Mechem   The Greed Blooded Fish, Inferiority Complex, July Rain, A Farewell
Ravel   Don Quichotte a Dulcinee
Aubert   Trois Chansons Francaises: Les Charpentiers du Roi, Le Nez de Martin, Les souliers de l'avocat.
Poulenc   Four Songs: Atgtributs, Chanson a Boire, Montparnasse, La Belle Jeunesse.

February 4 The Clebanoff Strings: Herman Clebanoff, conductor
Vivaldi   Concerto in G minor, Opus 12, No. 1 for solo violin and strings. Herman Clebanoff, soloist
Mozart   Symphony in D Major, K. 136 (Salzburg)
Vivaldi   Concerto in A Major, Opus 3, No. 8 for two violins and strings. H. Clebanoff and Arthur Tabachnick, solo violins
Hindemith   Trauermusic for solo cello and strings
Keleman   Improvisations Concertantes
Barber   Adagio for Strings, Opus 11

Shostakovich	Two Pieces for String Octet, Opus 11: Prelude, Adagio; Scherzo, Allegro Molto
March	Richard Cass, pianist, program missing.

1966-67

November 11   Helen Vanni, Mezzo-soprano; Richard Cumming, pianist and composer

Purcell-Edmunds	
	Four Songs: We Sing to Him; Strike the Viol; Music for a While; Hark How All Things in One Sound Rejoice
Mahler	Fruehlingsmorgen; Ich atmet' einen Lindenduft; Hans und Grete; Liebst du um Schoenheit.
Cumming	The Sick Rose; Memory, Hither Come; London; The Little Black Boy
Debussy	Ariette Oubliees: Green; C'est l'extase langoureuse; Il pleure dans mon Coeur; Chevaux de bois.
Chanler	The Rose
Hindemith	The Moon
Edmunds	O Death, Rock Me Asleep
Barber	The Monk and His Cat
Rorem	Bedlam

January 20	The Zurich Chamber Orchestra, Edmund De Stoutz, conductor; John
Bacon, violin;	Andre Lardrot, oboe
Frank Martin	Etudes pour Orchestre a cordes (1956)
Bach	Concerto in D minor for violin, oboe, strings and continuo
Stravinsky	Concerto in D
Bartok	Divertimento for strings (1939)

April 22	Mischa Kottler, pianist (40th anniversary banquet)
Bach	Chromatic Fantasy and Fugue
Schumann	Fantasy in C Major

1967-68

November 10	Charles Bressler, tenor, program missing.
January 19	Abbott Lee Raskin, pianist, program missing.
March 1	Munich Chamber Orchestra, program missing.

Appendix A

1968-69
October   Jean Paul Sevilla, program missing.

November 15   Stecher & Horowitz, duo pianists
Schumann-Debussy
                   Etude in the form of a canon, Opua 56, No. 4
Schumann   Andante and Variations in B flat, opus 46
Chopin   Rondo in C Major, Opus 73
Piston   Concerto for Two Pianos Solik
Debussy   EnBlanc et Noir
Rachmaninoff   Fantasy, Opus 5, (Suite No. 1)

January 17   Lili Chookasian, soprano; Max Walmer, piano
Gluck   O Stygian Gods (from "Alceste")
R. Strauss   Allerseelen, Staendchen
Brahms   Die Mainacht
Hugo Wolf   In dem Schatten meiner Locken, Mignon
Poulenc   Fleurs, Air Champetre, Violin, Air Vif.
Arr. Copland   Three Old American Songs: Long Time Ago, Simple Gifts, At the
                   River.
R. Hundley   Maiden Snow;The Astronomers; Some Sheep are Loving (poem
                   by Gertrude Stein, song written for Miss Chookasian)
                   Armenian Songs
Komitas   Apricot Tree (Dsirani Dsar)
Ghevontian   The Spinninig Wheel (Jakarag)
Servantsdiantz   The Crane (Groong)
Spendiarian   Almast's Aria (fom "Almast")

March 1969   Chicago Symphony Quartet, program missing.

1969-70
November 21   Guarneri String Quartet: Arnold Steinhardt and John Dalley,
                   violins; Michael Tree, viola, David Soyer, cello.
Mozart   Adagio and Fugue in C minor, K. 546
Berg   Lyric Suite for String Quartet
Ravel   Quartet in F major

January 30   Karan Armstrong, soprano; Anastasios Vrenios, tenor; Thomas
                   Schilling, piano.
Donizetti   E tutti parla barbaro (duet from L'Elisir d'Amore)
Schubert   Four Songs: Libesbotschaft; Die Liebe hat Gelogen; Nacht und
                   Traeume; Staendchen (Mr.Vrenios)
Poulenc   C; A Sa Guitarre. (Miss Armstrong)
Rabey   Tes Yeux (Miss Armstrong)

Debussy	Fantoches (Miss Armstrong)
Massenet	Le Reve (from Manon, Mr.Vrenios)
Tomas	Je Suis Titania (from Mignon, Miss Armstrong)
Donizetti	Ternami a dir che m'ami (duet from Don Pasquale)
Puccini	Che gelida manina; Si, mi chiamano Mimi; O soave fanciulla (duets from La Boheme)
Ravel	Cinq Melodies Populaire Grecques (in Greek) Wake up my Dear; Down Below, The Church Tower; Which Gallant can Compare with Me?; Song of the Lentisk Gatherers; Be Gay! (Mr.Vrenios)
Bernstein	I Hate Music (Cycle of Five Songs, Miss Armstrong)
Wright-Forrest	Stranger in Paradise (duet from Kismet)

March 6	Jeffrey Siegel, pianist
Mozart	Sonata in F Major, K. 332
Brahms	Variations and Fugue on a theme by Handel, Opus 24
Ravel	Valses Nobles et Sentimentals (Adelaide)
Stravinsky	Three Dances from Petrouchka

1970-71

November 20	Malcolm Frager, pianist
Handel	Aria and Variations
Beethoven	Sonata in E flat major, Op. 27, No. 1
Prokofieff	Prelude and March from Op. 12 (two of 10 short poems in this opus)
Prokofieff	Sonata No. 3
Brahms	Variations and Fugue on Theme of Handel, Opus 24.

January 22	Helen Boatwright, soprano; William Dale, piano.
Ernst Bacon	Three Songs: Eternity; She went as quiet; A Spider (poems by Emily Dickinson).
Sessions	On the Beach at Fontana (James Joyce)
Lockwood	The Pasture (Robert Frost)
Howard Boatwright	
	At the Rouhnd Earth's Imagined Corners (John Donne)
Schumann	Frauenliebe und leben
Mozart	Recitative: E Susanna and Aria: Dove Sono (Marriage of Figaro).
Debussy	Four Songs: Cheveaux de Bois; C'est l'extase; Green; Mandoline.
Ives	Six Songs: Walking; The Side Show; Wiegenlied; The Seer; Down East; Judge's Walk.

Appendix A

March 12 The Orford Quartet: Andrew Dawes and Kenneth Perkins, violins; Terence Humber, viola; Marcel St. Cyr, cello.
Mozart   Quartet No.l 19 in C Major, K. 465 (Dissonant)
Bartok   Quartet No. 2, Opus 17
Schubert   Quartet No. 14 in D minor (Death and the Maiden)

1971-72
November 19 Guarneri String Quartet: Arnold Steinhardt and John Dalley, violins; Michael Tree, viola; David Soyer, cello
Mozart   Quartet in D minor, K. 421
Sibelius   Quartet, opus 56, "Voces Intimae"
Mendelssohn   Quartet in E flat major, opus 44 no. 3

January 21 Ronald Holgate, baritone; Frederick Popper, piano
Carissimi   Vittoria, Vittoria
Torelli   Tu lo sai
Beethoven   An die ferne Geliebte
Tchaikovsky   Yeletsky's aria from The Queen of Spades
Ravel   Don Quichotte a Dulcinee: Chanson Romanesque, Chanson Epique, Chanson a Boire
Floyd   Aria from Susannah
Menotti   Aris from Old Maid and the Thief
Moore   Aria from The Devil and Daniel Webster

March 10 Ruth Meckler Laredo, pianist
Scriabin   Sonata No. 3 opus 23 (1903)
Schumann   Kinderscenen Opus 15
Scriabin   Sonata No. 5 Opus 53 (1907)
Debussy   Reflets dans l'eau
Ravel   La Valse

1972-73
November 17 Ronald Holgate, baritone; Frederick Popper, piano
Arr. Britten Folk Songs from the British Isles: O Waly, Waly; The Miller of Dee; The Foggy, Foggy Dew; Oliver Cromwell
Schubert   Lieder: Der Doppelgaenger; Das Fischermadchen; Die Stadt; Der Atlas
Moussorgsky   Songs and Dances of Death: Lullaby; Serenade; Trepak; Commander in Chief
Bernstein   Sam's Aria from "Trouble in Tahiti"
Duparc   French Art Songs: Phidyle; Chanson Triste; Extase; Le Manoir de Rosemonde
Mozart   Count's Aria, Un Bacio di Mano, from "Le Nozze de Figaro"

January 19	Gold and Fizdale, duo pianists
Mozart	Introduction (K375) and Fugue (K448) in C minor
	Sonata (K448) in D Major
Poulenc	Sonata for Two Pianos (1953) Dedicated to Gold & Fizdale
Brahms	Waltzes, Opus 39 for piano, Four Hands
Debussy	Capriccio D'Apres le Bal Masque (1952)

March 30	Guarneri String Quartet: Arnold Steinhardt, John Dalley, violins;
	Michael Tree, viola; David Soyer, cello.
Mozart	Quartet in D Major, K. 499
Bartok	Quartet No. 6
Smetana	Quartet, "From My Life."

1973-74

November 16	Senofsky-Mack-Lesser Trio: Berl Senofsky, violin; Ellen Mack,
	piano; Laurence Lesser, cello.
Mozart	Trio in Blat Major, K. 507
Ravel	Trio in A minor
Schubert	Trio in B flat Major, Op. 99

January 18	Eugene List, piano
Bach	Toccata In C minor
Paradisi	Toccata in A Major
Schumann	Toccata in C Major
Brahms	Sonata No. 1, Opus l
Chopin	Sonata in B flat minor
Debussy	Feux d'Artifice, Soiree dans Grenade
Ravel	Toccata

March 15	Indiana Opera Trio; Grace Trester Jones, soprano; Jean Deis,
	tenor; Roy Samuelson, baritone; Carl Fuerstner, piano.
Schuetz	Das Blut Jesu Christi, trio from :"Kleine Geistliche Konzerte."
Purcell	Hark My Damilkar, duet from "Tyrannic Love: by Dryden 1670
	Sound the Trumpet, duet from Welcome Songs to Charles II ahd
	James II 1687
	My Dearest, duet from Oroonoko, by Thomas Southerns 1695
Handel	Italian Chamber Trio, dated Naples, 1708, accompaniment by J.
	Brahms.
Mozart	Trio from "The Magic Flute"
Donizetti	Spirto Gentila, from "La Favorita"
Rossini	La Calunniua, from "Barber of Seville"
Bellini	Qui la voce, from "I Puritani"
Donizetti	Trio from "Elixir d'Amore."
Verdi	Duet from "La Forza del Destino"

Appendix A

Borodin	Igor's Monologue, from "Prince Igor"
Britten	Embroidery Aria, from "Peter Grimes"
Cilea	Lamento de Federico, from "L'Arlesienne"
Gounoud	Trio from "Faust"

1974-75
November 15   Gail Robinson, Soprano; Donald Hassard, piano.
Handel   O Had I Jubal's Lyre, from Joshua
Mozart   Alleluja, from Exsultate, Jubilate
Arr. Weckerlin   Four Bergerettes (18th century
       O ma tender musette; Bergere Legere; Philis, plus avare que tendre; Jeune fillete
Lehar   Liebe, Du Himmel auf Erden
J. Strauss   Fruhlingstimme Walz (Voices of Spring waltz)
Granados   La Maja y el Ruisenor (The Maiden and the Nightingale)
       Favorites of Famous Favorites
Donizetti   Chacun le Sait (from "La Filled u Regiment") Jenny Lind
Bishop   Lo, here the Gentle Lark, Amelita Galli-Curci
Bachelet   Chere Nuit, Lili Pons
Herbert   Italian Street Song (from "Naughty Marietta") Jeannette Mac-Donald

January 31   Orford String Quartet: Andrew Dawes, Kenneth Perkins, violins; Terence Helmer, viola; Marcel St.Cyr, cello
Haydn   Quartet in D Major, Op. 76, No. 5
M. Schafer   Quartet No. 1, 1970
Mendelssohn   Quartet in A minor, Op. 13, No. 2

April 25   Gary Graffman, piano
Mozart   Sonata in F Major, K. 332
Beethoven   Sonata in C minor, Op. 111
Ravel   Sonatine
Moussorgsky   Pictures at an Exhibition

1975-76
November 21   Ralph Votapek, piano
Beethoven   Sonata in A Major, Op. 101
Chopin   Barcarolle, Op. 60
Copland   Piano Sonata (1941)
Rachmaninoff   Four Etudes Tableaux, Op. 39: No. 1 in C minor, No. 8 in D minor, No.5
       In E flat minor, No. 9 in D Major
January 23*   Eugene Fodor, violin; Stephen Swedish, piano

Bach	Sonata No. 1 in G minor
Prokofieff	Sonata No. 2 in D Major, Op. 94a
Penderecki	Three Miniatures for violin and piano, 1959
Bloch	Baal Shem 1923, Simchas Torah
Kreisler	Tambourin Chinois
Paganini	Caprices Nos. 17 and 24
Bazzini	La Ronde de Lutins (Scherzo Fantastique)

April 2*   Sofia Steffan, mezzo soprano; Eugene Szabo, piano

Purcell   If Music be the Food of Love; Man is for the Woman Made; There's not a Swain of the Plain; Sweeter than Roses.

Brahms   Von ewiger Liebe; Ach, wende diesen Blick; Das Marchen spricht; Nicht mehr zu dir zu gehen; Wie froh und Frisch.

Stravinsky   Jocasta's Aria (from "Oedipus Rex")

Honneger   Petit Cours de Morale: Jeanne; Adele; Cecile; Irene; Rosemonde.

Poulenc   Hotel; Les Gars qui vont a la Fete.

Joaquin Nin   Diez Villancicos Espanoles: Asturiano; Gallego; Vasco; Castellano; de Cordoba; Murciano; Aragones; Segundo Catalan; Jesus de Nazareth; Andaluz.

   ** These two dates differ from the dates on the programs in the archives. The dates were switched at the last minute to avoid a conflict between Fodor's concert and Artur Rubinstein appearing with the Detroit Symphony.

1976-77

November 5   The Tashi: Peter Serkin, piano; Ida Kavafian, violin; Fred Sherry, cello; Richard Stoltzman, clarinet.

Stravinsky   Three pieces for Solo Clarinet

Brahms   Sonata in G Major for Violin and Piano

Messian   Quartet for the End of Time (1941)

January 28   Leslie Guinn, baritone

Schubert   Fischerweise; An Sylvia; Im Fruehling; Abschied.

Schoenberg   Die Aufgeregten Op. 3; Verlassen Op. 6; Warnung Op. 3; Der Verlorene Haufen Op. 12.

Wolf   Morgentau; Der Feuerreiter; Neue Liebe; Zur Warnung.

Schumann   Die Fluechtlinge; Widmung; Aus den oestlichen Rosen; Schneegloeckchen; Du bist wie eine Blume; Schlusslied des Narren.

Brahms   Zigeunerlieder Op. 103; Lieber Gott, du weisst; He, Zigeuner; Brauner Bursche fuehrt zum Tanze; Hochgetuermte Rimaflut; Roeslein dreie in der Reihe; Wisst Ihr, w;ann mein Kindchen; Kommt dir manchmal in den Sinn; Rote Abendvolken ziehn am Firmament.

Appendix A

March 11   Juliana Markova, piano
Beethoven   Sonata in F minor, Op. 57 "Appassionata"
Brahms   AThree Intermezzi, Op. 117
Prokofiev   Old Grandmother's Taless Op. 31
    Sonata No. 7, Op. 83

April 22   Golden Anniversary Musical Banquet
    Ralph Votapek, piano
    Musical Offering: All Gershwin program in Fries Auditorium at Grosse Pointe War Memorial followed by dinner in the Ballroom.
    Dedication: Bach Chaconne by Gordon Staples, violin
    Musical Afterglow: Viennese Songs by Alex Suczek baritone & guitar, and Marybelle Suczek, accordion.

1977-78
Fall 77   Lydia Artimew, piano
Mozart   Sonata in D major, K 311 (1777)
Schubert   Sonata in A minor, Op. 42 (1825)
Schumann   Fantasiestuecke, Op. 12 (1837)
Chopin   Ballade in A flat Major, Op. 47 (1841)
    Polonaise in F sharp minor, Op.44 (1840)

February 3   The Marlboro Trio: Charles Libove, violin; itchell Andrews, piano; Charles McCracken, cello.
Haydn   Trio in E flat Major, H. XV, 10
Dvorak   Trio in E minor, Op. 90 "Dumky"
Ravel   Trio in A minor (1914)

April 7   Valerie Girard, soprano; Lawrence J. LaGore, piano
Handel   Care Selve
Haydn   On Michty Pens (from "The Creation")
Brahms   Die Mainacht; Das Maedchen Spricht; Serenate; Meine Liebe ist Gruen.
Moore   The Willow Song (from "The Ballad of Baby Doe")
Puccini   Musetta's Waltz (from "La Boheme")
Debussy   C'est l'Extase; Mandoline
Faure   Prison; Fleurs Jetee
Schoental   From the Roadside (a cycle of poems by Walt Whitman): Mother and Babe; Thought; Visor'd; To Old Age; A Farm Picture; A Child's Amaze.
Turina   Tu Pupila Es Azul

| Sandoval | Vocalise (written for Bidu Sayao) |
| Obradors | El Vito |

1978-79

October 27 George Crumb, composer; The Aeolian Cahmber Players: Lewis Kaplan, violin Thomas Hill, clarinet; Ronald Thomas, cello; Jacob Maxin, piano; assisted by Ervin Monroe, flute.

Speaking extemporaneously from the Recital Hall stage, George Crumb gave brief comments before each of his three works on the program.

Eleven Echoes of Autumn (1965) Commissioned by Bowdoin College for the Aeolian Chamber Players.

Dream Sequence, 1976, commissioned by Ambassador and Mrs. George J. Feldman for the Aeolian Chyamber Players

Voice of The Whale (Vox Balaenae) 1971 for electric flute, cello and piano.

February 23 James Tocco, piano. (Composer John Corigliano was scheduled to appear with Tocco but cancelled at the last minute)

Beethoven	Sonata in C major, Op. 2, No. 3
Corigliano	Etude Fantasy (1976)
Chopin	Sonata in B minor, Op. 58

April 28 Cesar-Antonio Suarez, tenor; Frank DiGiacomo, composer and piano.

Paisiello	Nel Cor Piu Non Mi Sento
Antronio Lotti	
	Pur Dikcesti a Bocca Bella
Pergolesi	Nina
Torelli	Tu Lo Sai
Perez Freire	Ay, Ay, Ay
Rossini	La Danza
Donizetti	Fra Poco a me Ricovero from "Lucia di Lammermoor"
Verdi	Dei Miei Bollenti Spiriti from "La Traviata"
DiGiacomo	Alla Sua Donna
	(Commentary on composing opera illustrated at the piano)
Hageman	Do not go My Love
Eduardo Sanchez de Fuente	
	Mirame Asi
Verdi	La Donna e Mobile from "Rigoletto"
Donizetti	Deserto in Terra from "Don Sebasiano"
Puccini	Che Gelida Manina from "La Boheme"

Appendix A

1979-80

November 9   Andre Michel Schub, piano, replacing Alexander Toradze, piano,
                      who cancelled because his travel visa was refused by the Soviet
                      Government.
Beethoven   Sonata in C Major, Op. 2 No. 3
Mendelssohn   Variations serieuses, Op. 54
Brahms   Variations and Fugue on a Theme of Handel
Liszt   Etudes No. 2 and No. 6

February 29   Musica Camera: John Anderson, clarinet; Tanya Remenikova,
                      cello; Alexander Braginsky, piano; with Barney Childs, composer.
Beethoven   Trio Op. 11
Franck   Sonata in A Major for cello
Childs   Trio for Clarinet, Cello and Piano, (1972)
Brahms   Trio in A minor, Op. 114

March 28   Jessye Norman, soprano; Dalton Baldwin, piano (at Orchestra Hall).
Haydn   Cantata for Soprano and Pianoforte from "Arianna a Naxos."
Brahms   Botschaft, Op. 47 No. 1; Wie Melodien zieht es mir, Op. 104 No.
                      1; Alte Liebe, Op. 72 No. 1; O komme holde Sommernacht, Op.
                      58 No. 4; Von ewiger Liebe, Op. 43 No. 1.
Poulenc*   Trois Poemes de Guillaume Apollinaire: Voyage a Paris; Montpar-
                      nasse; La Grenouilliere.
                      Valse Chantee: Les Chemins de L'Amour.
R. Strauss   Heimliche Aufforderung, Op. 27 No. 3; Ich trage meine Minne,
                      Op. 32 No. 1; Mit deinen blauen Augen, Op. 56 No. 4; Seitdem
                      dein Aug', Op. 17 No. 1; Cacelie, Op. 27 No. 2.
                      *Poulenc performed at Pro Musica as pianist and composer in
                      1948.

April 11   Joint concert in Brahms Festival of the Detroit Symphony, Antal
                      Dorati, Music Director: Ilse von Alpenheim, piano; Igor Ozim,
                      violin.
Brahms   Sonata No 2 in A Major
                      Sonata No. 1 in G Major
                      Sonata No. 3 in D minor
                      Encore: Scherzo from Frei Aber Einsam Sonata in C minor com-
                      posed jointly by Brahms, Schumann and Destrich.

1980-81

November 7   Cho Liang Lin, violin; James Gemmel, piano
Prokofiev   Sonata No. 2 in D Major, Op. 94a
Beethoven   Sonata No. 7 in C minor, Op. 30 No. 2

De Falla	Suite Popular Espanol (arr. Paul Kochanski)
Mozart	Adagio in E flat Major
Wieniawski	Capriccio Valse
Sarasate	Introduction and Tarantelle

February 20	The Kalichstein-Laredo-Robinson Trio: Joseph Kalichstein, piano; Jaime Laredo, violin; Sharon Robinson, cello.
Beethoven	Variations in G Major, Op. 121a on Wenzel Muller's "Ich bin der Schneider Kakadu"
Mendelssohn	Trio in D minor, Op. 49
Schubert	Trio in B flat Major, Op. 99, DK 898

March 15	Bartok Festival concert in cooperation with the Detroit Symphony: Ilse von Alpenheim, piano; Fedora Horowitz, piano; Bela Szilagy, piano; Gordon Staples, violin; Detroit String Quartet with James Waring and Inez Redman, violins; David Ireland, viola; John Thurman, cello.
Zipoli	Pastorale, transcribed by Bela Bartok
Marcello	Sonata in B flat Major, transcribed by Bela Bartok (Fedora Horowitz, piano)
Kosa	Hommage a Bela Bartok
Soproni	Hommage a Bela Bartok (Bela Szilagy, piano)
Bartok	Five Pieces from Mikrokosmos arranged for string quartet by T. Serly: Jack in the Box; Harmonics; Wrestling; Melody; From the Diary of a Fly
Dorati	Variations on a Theme by Bartok (Ilse von Alpenheim, piano)
Bartok	For Children, arr. E. Zathureczyka
	Sonatine for Piano, transcribed for violin and piano by A. Gertler (Gordon Staples, violin; Bela Szilagyi, piano)
	Tempo di ciaccona and Fuga, transcribed for piano from the Sonata for Violin Solo by G. Sandor (Bela Szilagyi)

April 10	Ruth Welting, soprano
Handel	Endless Pleasure, Endless Love, from "Semele."
	O Sleep, Why dost Thou Leave Me?
Bellini	from "Composizione da Camera": Per Pieta, bel idol mio; Malinconia, Ninfa gentile; Vanne, o Rosa fortunate.
Schubert	from "Ausgewahlte Lieder": Nacht und Traeume; Neidenroslein; Die junge Nonne.
Debussy	Quaatre Chansons de Jeunesse: Pantomime (Verlaine); Clair de Lune (Verlaine, 1st version); Pierrot (de Banuille): Apparition (Mallarme).

Appendix A

Adam	Bravour Variationen on a ATheme by Mozart (with solo flute)
	Old English Melodies
	A Pastorale; My Lovely Celia; Shepherds Thy demeanour vary'
Carpenter	Gitanjali song offerings (poems by Rabindranath Tagore): When I
	Bring to You Colored Yoys; On the Day when Death will Knock at
	Thy Door; The Sleep that Flits on Baby's Eyes; Light, My Light
Folk Songs	The Lass from the Low Country (English)
	Black is the Color of my True Love's Hair (Southern U.S.)
	Virgin Mary (Spiritual)
Moore	The Willow Song from "The Ballad of Baby Doe"

1981-82
March 26 Alteoiuise DeVaughn, mezzo soprano; Bernard Katz, piano
Stradella Pieta, Signore!
Gluck O del mio Dolce Ardor
Marcello Il mio bel fuoco
Mozart Parto, Parto from "La Clemenza di Tito"
Saint Saens Mon Coedur souvre a toi voix from "Samson et Delila"
Bizet Seguidilla from "Carmen"
Handel O Thou That Tellest Good Tidings from "Messiah"
Hall Johnson Give me Jesus; Honor ! Honor!; Goin' to Shout All Over God's
Heab'n; My Lord, What a Morning; Ride on King Jesus.

April 23 Gabrieli String Quartet: Kenneth Sillito & Brendan O'Reilly,
violins; Ian Jewel, viola; Keith Harvey, cello.
Mozart Quartet in C Major, No. 19, K 465 "Dissonant"
Shostakovich Quartet in C minor, No. 8u, Op. 110
Tchaikovsky Quartet in F Major, Op. 22, No. 2

1982-83
November 19 The Takacs String Quartet: Gabor Takacs-Nagy & Karoly Schranz,
violins; Gabor Ormai,viola; Andras Fejer, cello.
Haydn Quartet in D Major, Op. 64, No. 5 "The Lark"
Bartok Quartet No. 2, Op. 17
Webern Six Bagatelles, Op. 9
Schumann Quartet in A minor, Op. 41, No. 1

March 4 Jerry Hadley, tenor; Cheryll Drake Hadley, piano
Faure Chanson d'Amour; Mandoline; L'Hiver a cesse; Apres un Reve;
Notre Amour.
Britten The Holy Sonnets of John Donne, Op. 35
Liszt Tre Sonetti del Petrarca
R. Strauss Zueignung; Allerseelen; Befreit; Cacilie

April 8   Cynthia Raim, piano
Bach   Italian Concerto
Brahms   Piano Pieces, Op. 76: Capriccio in F sharp minor; Cappriccio in
          B minor; Intermezzo in A flat Major; Intrermezzo in B flat Major;
          Cappriccio in C sharp minor; Intermezo in A Major: Intermezzo
          in A minor; Cappriccio in C Major.
Bartok   Sonata
Ravel   Le Tombeau de Couperin

1983-84
October 7   Santiago Rodriguez, piano
Bach   Chromatic Fantasy and Fugue,BWV 903
Schumann   Carnaval,Op. 9
Chopin   Nocturne in C minor, Op. 48, No. 1
          Nocturne in F sharp Major, Op. 15, No. 2
Ginastera   Sonata, Op. 22, No. l

December 2   The Arden Trio: Suzanne Ornstein, violin; Clay Reude, cello;
          Thomas Schmidt, piano.
Beethoven   Trio in D Major Op.l 70, No. l, "Ghost"
Shostakovich   Trio in E minor, Op. 67
Wuorinen   Trio 1983
Ravel   Trio (1915)

March 16   Nicholas Solomon, bass-baritone; Bernard Katz, piano (substitut-
          ing for Kathleen Segar who cancelled due to illness)
Handel   Sorge infausta una procella from "Orlando"
Rameau   Puissant maitre des flot from "Hippolyte wet Aricie"
Pergolesi   Sempre in contrasti from "La Serva Padrona"
Schubert   Gruppe aus dem Tartarus; Du bst die Ruh; Erlkonig
Paulis   Frank's Road Song from "The Postman Always Rings Twice"
Stravinsky   The Panting Slave from "Rake's Progress"
Moore   Tabors Love Song from "Ballad of Baby Doe"
Floyd   Blitch's Prayer from "Susannah"
Fine   Childhood Fables for Grownups: Polaroli (to Arthur Berger);
          Tigeroo (to Harold Shapero); Lenny the Leopard (to Leonard
          Bernstein); The Frog and the Snake (to Lukas Foss)
Barber   Dover Beach

1984-85
November 9   Christopher O'Riley, piano
Debussy   Images Book II: Cloches a travers les feuilles; Et la Lune descend
          surf le Temple qui fut; Poissons d'or.
Schubert   Sonata in D Major, Op. 53

Scriabin	Prelude in C Major, Op. 11, No. 1
Chopin	Mazurka in A minor, Op. 17, No. 4
Scriabin	Poeme, Op. 59, No. 1
Chopin	Mazurka in D Mojor, Opus Posthumous
Scriabin	Prelude in B flat Major, Op. 17, No. 6
	Prelude in B flat Major, Op. 17, No. 16
Chopin	Polonaise in F sharsps minor, Op. 44
Scriabin	Sonata No. 10, Op. 70
Chopin	Barcarolle,Op. 60

March 15	Los Angeles Piano Quartet: James Bonn, piano; Clayaton Haslop, violin; Ronald Copes, viola; Peter Rejto, cello.
Beethoven	String Trio Op. 8, "Serenade"
Copland	Quartet for Piano and Strings (1950)
Dvorak	Piano Quartet in E flat Major, Op. 87

April 19	Kathleen Segar, mezzo soprano; Martin Katz, piano; with Dr. David DiChiera, composer (and Director of Michigan Opera Theater).
Bononcini	Per La Gloria D'Adoravi
Durante	Vergin, Tutto Amor
Schumann	Fraunliebe und Leben
Faure	Poeme d'un Jour
Barber	The Daisies; Sure on this Shining Night
DiChiera	Selected songs preceded by a brief talk by the composer about his work.
Copland	Long Time Ago; At the River
Mozart	Recitative: Ah Scostati! Aria: Smanie Implacabili from "Cosi Fan Tutte"
Rossini	Aria: Non piu Mesta from "La Cenerentola"

1985-86	
October 25	Leonard Pennario, piano
Debussy	Five Preludes: La terrasse des audiences du clair de lune; Ondine; Ce qu'a vu le vent d'Ouest; La Cathedrale engloutie; Minstrels.
Schubert	Sonata in A Major, Op. posthumous.
Barber	Excursions
Scriabin	Nocturne for the left hand alone
Milhaud	Saudades do Brasil
Ravel	Pavane pour une Infante defunte
Chopin	Scherzo in B flat minor

February 28	Joshua Bell, violin, Angela Cheng, piano.
Brahms	Sonatensatz in C minor (1853)
Faure	Sonata in A Major, Op. 13
Bach	Ciaccona from Partita in D Minor s. 1004
Bloch	Nigun (Improvisation)
De Sarasate	Carmen Fantasy, Op. 24

April 18	Ned Rorem*, composer/piano; William Parker, baritone.
Debussy	Le Promenoir dex deux Amants (1904-1910) Tristan L'Hermite; Aupres de c ette grotte somber; Crois mon conseil, chere Climene; Je Tremble en voyant ton visage.
	Trois Ballades de Francois Villon (1910): Ballade de Villon a s'amaye; Ballade quie villon feit a la requeste de sa mere pour prier Notre-Dame; Ballade des femmes de Paris.
Rorem	Four songs from "Flight for Heaven" (Robert Herrick) 1950: To Music, to becalm his fever; Upon Julia's Clothes; To the Willow Tree; To Anthea, who may command him anything
Rorem	War Scenes (Walt Whitman) 1969: A Night Battle; Specimen Case; An Incident; Inauguration Ball; The Real War Will Never Get in the Books.
Rorem	Settings of Poems by Walt Whitman: To a Common Prostitute (1982); Look Down Fair Moon (1957); Oh You to Whom I Often and Silently Come (1957); To You (1957); Sometime with One I Love (1957)
Rorem	The Lordly Hudson (Paul Goodman, 1947)
	*Mr. Rorem's appearance was made possible by a grant from The Michigan Council for the Arts.

1986-87

October 31	The Vienna Schubert Trio: Claus-Christian Schuster, piano; Boris Kuschnar, violin; Martin Hornstein, cello.
Zemlinsky	Trio in D minor, Op. 3
Schostakovitch	Trio No. 1 in C Major, Op. 8
Brahms	Trio No. 2 in C Major, Op. 87

March 6	Ralph Votapek, piano
Mozart	Sonata in CMajor, K 330
Schumann	Kreisleriana, Op. 16
Prokofieff	Third Sonata in A minor, Op. 28
Scriabin	Fourth Sonata in F sharp Major
Debussy	Three Preludeds: Bruyeres; La serenade interrompue; Les collines d'Anacapri
Ravel	La Valse

Appendix A

April 3   Gordon Hawkins, baritone; Bob McCoy, piano; (with composer
                James Hartway)
Handel   Sitraiceppe from "Berenici"
Duparc   Chanson Triste; Extase; Phidyle
R.Strauss   Morgen; Allerseelen; Zueignung
Wagner   O du mein holder Abendstern, Wolfram's aria from
                "Tannhaeuser"
Griffes   The Sorrow of Mydah
Hartway   Autumn (poem by Ron Cooney)
Trad.   Negro Spirituals
Ravel   Don Quichote et Dulcinee

1987-88
September 15 60th Anniversary Banquet at the Detroit Institute of Arts
                Mischa Kottler, piano
Chopin   Ballade No. 4 in F minor
                Sonata No. 3 in B minor
Medtner   Two Fairy Tales
Liadow   Barcarolle
Rachmaninoff   Two Preludes
                Etude
Ravel   Sonatine

October 23 The Auryn String Quartet; Matthias Lingenfelder & Jens Op-
                permann, violins; Stuart Eaton, viola; Andreas Arndt, cello.
Beethoven   String Quartet in D Major, Op. 18 No. 3
Berg   Lyric Suite for String Quartet (1925-26)
Mozart   String Quartet in B flat Major, K 589
Schubert   Andante movement from a Quartet as encore

February 3 Mira Zakai, Contralto; Mikael Eliasen, piano
Purcell   Lord, What is Man?
Berg   Four Songs, Op. 2: Schlafen, Schlafen; Schlafen'd traegt Mann
                mich; Nun dich der Riesen starksten; Warm die Luefte.
Schumann   Frauenlieve und Leben Op. 42
Mahler   Lieder und Gesaenger aus den Jugendzeit: Fruehlingsmorgen; Erri-
                nerung; Hans und Grethe; Serenade aus Don Juan; Fantasie aus
                Don Juan.
De Falla   Siete Canciones Populares Espanoles

April 15   Ruth Laredo, piano
Chopin   Three Mazurkas, Op. 6: No. 1 in F sharp minor; No. 2 in G sharp
                minor; No. 3 in E Major.
Beethoven   Sonata in F minor, Op. 57, "Appassionata"

Rachmaninoff Prelude No. 5 in G Major, Op. 32
Prelude No. 10 in G flat Major, Op. 23
Moment Musicale No. 2 in E flat minor, Op. 16
Moment Musicale No. 3 in B minor, Op. 16
Prelude No. 4 in D Major, Op. 23
Prelude No. 5 in G minor, Op. 23
Rorem* Song and Dance (1987)
Ravel * Valse Nobles et Sentimentales
La Valse
*Ned Rorem appeared at Pro Musica as pianist and composer in
1986 and Maurice Ravel in 1928.

1988-89
October 21 Benita Valente, soprano; Cynthia Raim, piano
Schubert An die Musik; An die Nachtigal; Nacht und Traeume; Rastlose
Liebe
Wolf Mignon Lieder: Heiss mich nicht Reden; Nur wer die Sehnsucht
kennt; So lasst mich scheinen bis ich wserde'
Chopin Andante Spianato and Grande Polonaise Brilliante for piano
solo
Rachmaninoff Variations on a theme of Corelli for piano solo
Debussy Ariette Oubliees: C'est l'extase; Il pleure dans mon Coeur; L'ombres
des arbres; Chevaux de Bois; Green; Spleen
Roberto Gerhard (1896-1970)
Seis Canciones: La Ximbomba; La Mal Maridada; Laieta; Soledad;
Farriquino; Corrandes.

January 27 Eduardo Fernandez, classical guitar
Elizabethan Music for lute
Anna Torres 1001 Faces (U.S. Premiere performance)
Villa Lobos Choros
Ginestera Sonata

April 7 The Alexander String Quartet: Eric Pritchard & Frederick Lifsitz,
violins; Paul Yarbrough, viola; Sandy Wilson, cello
Mozart Quartet in D Major, K 575, "The Prussian"
Janacek Quartet No. 1, "Kreutzer" (1923)
Brahms Quartet No. 1 in C minor, Op. 51, No. 1

1989-90
October 22 Stephen Hough, piano
Liszt Ave Maria; St. Francis Preaching to the Birds
Schumann Davidsbuendlertaenze, Op. 6

Appendix A

Liadov & I. Friedman	Musical Snuff Boxes
Liebermann	Four Apparitions
Chopin	Two Mazurkas
Moszkowski	Valse mignonne; Serenata; Caprice espagnol

March 9   Janet Williams, lyric soprano, Lawrence Frank Gee, piano.

Metastasio	L'Amero Saro Costante from Il Re Pastore
Wolf	Der Knabe und das Immlein; Auch Kleine Dinge; In dem Schatten meiner Locken; Er Ist's; Elfenlied; Das Verlassene Maegdelein; Ich hab' in Penna einen Liebsten.
Bizet	Comme Autre Fois from "Les Pecheeurs de Perles"; Ouvre ton Coeur
Faure	Reve d'amour; Mandoline; Notre Amour
DiChiera	Time Does not bring Relief; Loving you Less than Life; I Being Born a Woman; What Lips My Lips Have Kissed
Stravinsky	No Word From Tom from "The Rakes Progress."

April 20   Eduardo Fernandez, classical guitar

Sor	Les Adieux, Op. 21; Gran Solo, Op. 14, Introduction & Allegro
D. Scarlatti	Six Sonatas (arr. Edouardo Fernandez) K 430, 403, 462, 175, 513 & 141
Giulio Regondi	Notturno, Op. 19
Anna Torres	Mil y una caras
Albeniz	Cadiz (trans. E. Fernandez); Sevilla from Suite Espaniola Op. 47 (trans. Miguel Llobet

1990-91

October 26   Corey Cerovsek, violin; Katja Cerovsek, piano

Bach	Sonata in E minor, S. 1023
Beethoven	Sonata in A Major, op. 47 (Kreutzer)
Balakirev	Islamey
Schoenberg	Phantasy, Op. 47
Kreisler	Menuett (in the style of Porpora); Berceuse Romantique
Ravel	Tzigane (1924)

March 15   David Shifrin, Clarinet; with The New World String Quartet: Curtis Macomber & Vahn Armstron, violins; Benjamin Simon, viola; Ross Harbaugh, cello

Schubert	Quartetsatz in C minor, D 703
Bartok	String Quartet No. 3 (1927)
Wolf	Italian Serenade
Mozart	Clarinet Quintet in A Major, K 581

April 12	Gary Schocker, flutist and composer; Dennis Helmrich, piano
LeClair	Sonata in G Major
Schocker	Figments (1990)
Martinu	Sonata (1945)
Debussy	Syrinx for solo flute
Bach	Sonata in B minor, BWV 1030
Schocker	Regrets & Resolutions (1988)

1991-92

November 1	Seung Un Ha, piano
Bach	Toccata in G minor, BWV 915
Beethoven	Sonata in C minor, Op. 13 (Pathetique)
Chopin	Ballade No. 1 in G minor, op. 23
Schumann	Fantasie in C major, Op. 17

February 28	Ciosoni: Michael Cameron, bass: Tim Lane, flute; Eric Mandat, clarinet
Bach	Excerpts from A Musical Offering
John Cage	Sonata for Two Voices (1933); Composition for Three Voices (1934)
Luciano Berio	Sequenza for Solo Flute, 1959
Francois Rabbath	
	Iberique Peninsulaire (1970) for solo bass
Salvatore Martirano	
	UIUS & Jest Fa'Laffs (1991); Trio plus audiotape
Allan J. Segall	Curtains for Felix (1940) dedicated to the demise of a rubber plant.
Charles Wuorinen	
	Turetsky Pieces (1961)
Eric Mandat	Folk Songs (1986) clarinet
Michael Cunningham	
	Capriccios, Opus 142 (1989)
Jelly Roll Morton	
	Buddy Bolden's Blues; Jelly Roll Blues

May 1	Keith Mikelson, heldentor; James Wilhelmsen, piano
Weber	Durch Die Waelder from "Der Freischutz"
Beethoven	Gott! Welch Dunkel hier from "Fidelio"
Smetana	Wart, nur Wart, Hans' aria from "The Bartered Bride"
Tchaikovsaky	Frag nicht danach, was Mutter ist from "Panatoffelchen"
Puccini	Ch'ella mi creda libero e lontano from "Fanciulla del West"
	Recondita Armonia from "Tosca"
Leoncavallo	Vesti la Giubba from "Pagliacci"
Wagner	Walthers Preislied from "Die Meistersinger"
	Duenkt dich das? From "Tristan und Isolde"

Appendix A

1992-93
November 20   The Ames Piano Quartet: William David, piano;Laurence Burkhalter, viola; George Work, cello; Mahlon Darlington, violin

Frank Bridge   Phantasy Quartet (1910)
Wm.Bolcom   Quartet (1976)
Brahms   Quartet in G minor, Op.25

March 5   Tian Ying, piano
Mozart   Rondo in A minor, K 511
Cholpin   Mazurkas, Op. 67: No. 1 in G Major; No. 2 in G minor; No. 3 in C Major; No. 4 in A minor
Rachmaninoff   Sonata No. 2, Op. 36 (revised 1931)
Schubert/Liszt   Soiree de Vienne
Liszt   Sonata in B minor

April 30   Phyllis Pancella, mezzo soprano; Hal France, piano.
Dowland   Shall I sue (2nd Book of Ayres); Come Away, Come Sweet Love (1st book of Ayres).
Argento   Dirge (from Six Elizabethan Songs); Diaphenia
Schumann   Frauenlieve und Leben, Op. 42
Weisgal   Psalm of the Distan Dove
Dvorak   Gypsy Songs, Op. 55
Ildebrando Pezzetti da Parma
   La Madre al figlio lontano (from Cinque Liriche); Passeggiata.
Bernstein   La Bonne Cuisine: Plum Pudding; Oxtail Soup; Tavoik guenksis, Rabbit at top speed; I can cook too, from "On The Town."

1993-94
October 15   The Grieg Festival Quartet: Arve Tellefsen, violin; Lars Anders Tomter, viola; Truls Mork, cello; Leif Ove Andsnes, piano
Grieg   Sonata in C minor for violin and piano
   Sonata in A minor for cello and piano Op. 36
Schumann   Maerchenbuilder for viola and piano: Nicht Schnell; Lebhaft; Rasch; Langsam
Brahms   Piano Qujartet in C minor, Op. 60, No. 3, "Werther"
February 25   Jean Yves Thibaudet, piano
Ravel   Pavanne pour une infante defunte (1899)
   Jeu d'eau
   Miroirs (1905): Noctuelles, Oiseaux tristes, Une Barque sur l'Ocean; Alborado del gracioso; La Vallee des cloches
Schumann   Arabesque; Etudes Symphoniques in C sharp minor, Op. 13

April 29	Camellia Johnson, soprano; Neal Goren, piano.
Handel	V'Adoro, pupille from "Giulio Cesare
Debussy	Nuit d'etoiles; Romance; Mandoline.
R.Strauss	Breit Ueber mein Haupt; Einerlei; Befreit; Zueignung.
Liszt	Comment, disaient-ils; Oh! Quand je dors.
Ricky Ian Gordon	
	Harlem Night Song *; Kid in the Park; Will There Really be a Morning?; Port Town* (* composed for Miss Johnson)
Spirituals	Ride On, King Jesus (arr. HallJohnson); This little Light of Mine (arr. Jacqueline Hairston); He's Got the Whole World in His Hands (arr. Margaret Bonds)

1994-95

September 14	Annual Meeting entertainment: Alex & Marybelle Suczek- The Grosse Pointe Schrammel, voice, guitar and accordion.
Benatzky	Ich Muss Wieder Einmal in Grinzing Sein (I must go once more to Grinzing.)
Sieczynsky	Wien du Stadt meiner Träume (Vienna, City of my Dreams)
Arnold	Da Draussen in der Wachau (Out there in the Wachau).

October 7	Armen Babkhanian, piano
Haydn	Sonata in B minor, Hob. XVI/3
Franck	Prelude, Chorale and Fugue
Babajanian	Six Pictures for Piano: Improvisation; Folk Theme; Toccatina; Intermezzo; Chorale; Dance of Sassoun
Morton Gould	Ghost Waltzes (1993) commissioned for the Ninth Van Cliburn International Piano Competition.
Mussorgsky	Pictures at an Exhibition

February 3	Wolfgang Holzmair, baritone; Thomas Palm, piano.
Mendelssohn	Allnaechtlich im Traeume Op. 86, No. 4; Gruss Op. 19a, No. 5; Reiselied Op. 34, No. 6; Auf Fluegeln des Gesanges Op. ;34. No 2 (poems by Heinrich Heine).
Schumann	Dichterliebe Op. 48:
	Im wunderschoenen Monat Mai
	Aus meinen Traenen spriessen
	Die Rose, die Lilie
	Wenn ich deine Augen seh'
	Ich will meine Seele tauchen
	Im Rhein, im heiligen Strome
	Ich grolle nicht
	Und wuessten's die Blumen
	Das ist ein Floeten und Geigen
	Hoer ich das Liedchen klingen

	Ein Juengling liebt ein Maedchen
	Am Leuchtenden Sommermorgen
	Ich hab' im Traume geweinet
	Allnaechtlich im Traeume
	Aus alten Maerchen winkt es
	Die alten, boesen Lieder

Duparc Chanson Triste (Lahor); Extase (Lahor); L'invitation au voyage (Baudelaire)

Faure Chanson de Shylock; Prison; Poeme du jour.

Ravel Cinq melodies populaire Grecques: Le Reveil de la Mariee; La-Bas, vers l'eglise; Quel Galant!; Chanson des Dueilleuses de Lentisques; Tout Gai!

April 21 Orion String Quartet: Daniel Phillips & Todd Phillips, violins; Steven Tenenbom, viola; Timothy Eddy, cello.

Mozart String Quartet in D minor, K 421 (Daniel Phillips, first violin)

Kirchner* String Quartet No. 2 (1958) (Daniel Phillips, first violin)

Beethoven String Quartet in C Major, Op. 59, No. 3 (Todd Phillips, first violin)

*Leon Kirchner spoke at Pro Musica with the Lenox Quartet performing this quartet in 1963.

1995-96

November 10 Parisii Quartet: Thierry Brodard & Jean-Michel Berrette, violins; Dominique Lobet, viola; Jean-Philippe Martignoni, cello.

Milhaud Quartet No. 4, Op. 135

Beethoven Quartet in F Major, Op. 135

Webern Quartet, Op. 28, (1938)

Ravel Quartet in F Major

March 8 Susan von Reichenbach, soprano; Douglas Martin, piano.

Brahms Sapphische Ode; Feldeionsamkeit; Wie Melodien zieht es.

Wolf Verborgenheit; Auf ein altes Bild; In dem Schatten meiner Locken; Morgenstimmung.

Hahn D'une Prison; Si mes vers avaient des ailes!

Chausson Les papillons; Le charme; Le temps des lilas.

R. Strauss Amufer; Malven; Einerlei.

Joseph Marx Und gestern hat er mir Rosen gebracht; Waldseligkeit.

May 3 Robert Helps, composer-pianist

Helps Portrait (1960)

Nocturne (1973)

Hommages: a Faure; a Rachmaninoff; a Ravel.

Sessions	Sonata No. 2
Helps	Two Songs for voice and piano freely transcribed for piano solo
	"Shilflied" (the Reed Songs) by Felix Mendelssohn (1988)
	"Love is a Sickness Full of Woes" by John Ireland (1995)
	Shall We Dance (1994)

August 28 & 29

Isabel Gabbe & Laurent Boullet, solo and duo pianists in a scholarship benefit concert at the home of Alex & Marybelle Suczek. Co-sponsored by Tuesday Musicale.

Dvorak	Slavonic Dances Op. 72 (Ms. Gabbe & Mr. Boullet)
Schubert	Sonata in A Major, Op. posth. 120 (Mr.Boullet)
Schubert	Sonata in A minor, Op. posth. 143 (Ms. Gabbe)
Brahms	Valses Op. 39 (Ms. Gabbe & Mr. Boullet)

1996-97

September 27	Suren Bagratuni, cello; Adrian Oetiker, piano
Debussy	Sonata in D minor
Brahms	Sonata in F Major, Op. 99
Khudoyan	Sonata No. 1 for Cello Solo (1961)
Shostakovich	Sonata in D minor, Op.40

February 27	Fabio Bidini in a concert with buffet supper at the home of Alex & Marybelle Suczek to benefit the Pro Musica Endowment.
Scarlatti	Sonata in F minor, L. 118
	Sonata in D Major, L. 465
Chopin	Sonata No. 3

February 28	Fabio Bidini, piano.
Beethoven	Sonata in A Major, Op. 101
Chopin	Ballade No 3 in A flat Major, Op. 47
	Scherzo No. 2 in B flat minor, Op. 31
Schumann	Carnaval, Opus 9

April 11	Nathan Berg, bass-baritone; Martin Katz, piano
Vaughan Williams	
	Songs of Travel: The Vagabond; Let Beauty Awake; The Roadside Fire; Youth and Love; In Dreams; The infinite Shining Heavens; Whither Must I Wander?; Bright is the Ring of Words; I have Trod the Upward and the Downward Slope.
Ravel	Don Quichotte a Dulcinee: Chanson Romanesque; Chanson Epique; Chanson a boire.

Ibert	Quatre Chanson de Don Quichotte: Chanson du depart; Chanson a Dulcinee; Chanson du duc; Chanson de la mort.
Duparc	Lamento; Soupir; Chanson Triste; La Vie Anterieure.
Copland	Selections from Old American Songs: The Boatman's Dance; Long Time Ago; At the River; Ching-a-ring Chaw.

1997-98

September 27 Peter A. Soave, bayan (Russian button accordeon) with two of his students, Mady Dessimoulie and Guillaume Hodeau performed music of Astor Piazzola at the conclusion of the Pro Musica annual dinner meeting at the Crescent Sail Yacht Club in Grosse Pointe Farms.

October 22 The Artis Quartet: Peter Schuhmayer & Johannes Meissl, violins; Herbert Kefer, viola; Othmar Mueller, cello.

Schubert	Overture in C major
Mozart	Quartet in D Major, K 499, "Hoffmeister."
Schubert	Quartet in D minor, D. 810, "Death and the Maiden."

March 25 Frederic Chiu, piano

Prokofiev*	Music for Children: Morning; Promenade; Fairy Tale; Tarantella; Regrets; Waltz; Parade of the Grasshoppers; Rain and the Rainbow; Tag; March; Evening; Moonlit Meadows.
Debussy	Children's Corner Suite: Doctor Gradus and Parnassum; Jimbos Lullaby; Serenade for the Doll, The Snow is Dancing; The Little Shepherd, Golliwog's Cakewalk
Schumann	Kinderscenen, Op.15 (Scenes from Childhood): Strange Lands and People; By the Fireside; Curious Story; The Knight of the Rocking Horse; Blind Man's Bluff; Almost Too Serious; Pleading Child; Frightening; Perfectly Contented; Child Falling Asleep; An Important event; The Poet Speaks; Reverie
Chopin	Twelve Etudes, Op. 10: No.1 in C Major; No. 2 in A minor; No. 3 in E Major; No. 4 in C sharp minor; No. 5 in G flat Major; No.6 in E flat minor; No. 7 in C Major; No. 8 in F Major; No. 9 in F minor; No. 10 in A flat Major; No 11 in E flat Major; No. 12 in C minor

*Sergei Prokofiev performed at the piano for Pro Musica in 1930, his only appearance in Detroit.

April 24 Theresa Santiago, lyric soprano; Eunmi Lee Moon, piano

Barber	From Hermit Songs: At St. Patrick's Purgatory; Saint Ita's Vision; The Heavenly Banquet; The Crucifixion; Sea Snatch; The Desire for Hermitage.

R. Strauss	Allerseelen; All mein Gedanken; Morgen; Zueignung.
R. Hundley	Strings in the Earth and Air; Seashore Girls; Postcard from Spain; Maiden Snow; Moonlight; Watermelon.
Duparc	L'invitation au voyage; Le manoir de Rosamonde; Chanson Triste
F.J.Obradors	Al Amor; Corazon, porque pasais; Con amores, la mi madre; Del cabello mas sutil; Chiquitita la novia.

1998-99

September 13   David Syme, pianist, performed a program of popular music and light classics at the conclusion of the annual dinner meeting. It was held at the former home of Sara and Melvyn Maxwell Smith in Bloomfield Hills. Designed by Frank Lloyd Wright, the home is now in trust as a historic building. The meeting was held both in the house and on the terrace.

October 23	Julian Rachlin, violin; Rohan de Silva, piano
Beethoven	Sonata No. 5 in F Major, Op. 24, "Spring."
Brahms	Sonata No. 2 in A Major, Op. 100
Prokofiev*	Melodies for Violin and Piano, Op. 35 (1925)
Saint-Saens	Introduction and Rondo Capriccioso, Op. 28
Kreisler	Leibesleid und Liebesfreud
Waxman	Carmen Fantasy
Kreisler	Rosamarin (encore)
	*Prokofiev performed at the piano for Pro Musica in 1930, his only appearance in Detroit.

January 29	Arnaldo Cohen, piano
Debussy	Images (Book I): Reflets dans L'eau; Hommages a Rameau; Mouvement.
Chopin	Ballade No. 4 in F minor, Op. 52
	Three Etudes: Opus 10, No. 10 in A flat Major; Opus 10 No. 11 in E flat Major;
	Opus 25, No. 12 in C minor.
	Scherzo No. 1 in B minor, Op. 20.
Schumann	Arabesque in C Major, Op. 18
Liszt	Sonata in B minor.

May 14	Bridgett Hooks, soprano; Susan Nowicki, piano. Replacing bass Christopher Schaldenbrand who cancelled due to a pressing commitment at the Houston Opera.
Wagner	Dich Teure Halle
Faure	Mandoline, La Lune blanche Luit dan les Bois

Appendix A

Duparc   Chanson Triste
Verdi   Pace Pace
Barber   Nocturne, Sure on this Shining Night
Strauss   Zueignung, Morgen, Caeceilie
Rachmaninoff Oh Never Sing To Me Again; How Fair This Spot
Traditional   This Little Light O'Mine; Here's One; Ride On Jesus
              He's Got the Whole World in His Hands

1999-2000
September 15 Alex Suczek, baritone; Alice Haidostian, piano
Charles Mason Original Songs in the Tin Pan Alley style of the decades of the
               30s, 40s and 50s written, set to music and copyrighted by profes-
               sional song writer Charles Mason who bequeathed the manu-
               scripts to Alex Suczek in the 1960s Performed as entertainment at
               the conclusion of the 1999 Annual Dinner Meeting in the Grosse
               Pointe Lakeside home of Dr. & Mrs. Kim Lee

October 13 Frederic Chiu, piano; Brian Bedford, actor/narrator
Schubert/Liszt Schwanengesang D 957 transcribed for piano solo: Die Stadt;
                Das Fischermädchen; Aufenthalt; Am Meer; Abschied; In der
                Ferne; Ständchen; Ihr Bild; Frühlingssehnsuht; Liebesbotschaft;
                Der Atlas; Der Doppelgänger; Die Taubenpost; Kriegers Ahnung
                    English text of each song was read before the performance of
                the Liszt transcription of that song setting in a format conceived
                by pianist Frederic Chiu. Texts were translated from the German
                and adapted by Alex Suczek for reading at this world premiere
                performance of Mr. Chiu's format.

November 16 Isabel Bayrakdarian, soprano; Martin Katz, piano
Vivaldi   Piango, gemo, sospiro e peno; La Pastorella; Sposa son disprezzata
              (from "Bajazet"); Agitata da due venti (from "Griselda")
Granados   Las quejos o la maja y el ruisenor (from "Goyescas")
Tchaikovsky   Sred' shumnovo bala, Op. 38, No. 3;   Kalybel'naya pesnya, Op.
              16, No. 1; Serenada, Op. 63. No. 6; Kukushka, Op. 54, No. 8
Barber   Hermit Songs, Op. 29 (1952-53): At St. Patrick's Purgatory;
              Church Bell at Night; St. Ita's Vision; TheHeavenly Banquet;
              The Crucifixion; Sea-Snatch; Promiscuity; The Monk and his
              Cat; The Praises of God; The Desire for Hermitage
F. Obradors   Canciones clasicas espanoles (1921): La mi sola, Laureola; Al
              Amor; Corazon, por que pasais; El majo celoso; Con amoares, la
              mi madre; Del cabello mas sutil; Chiquitita la novia

January 21	Opus One Piano Quartet: Ida Kavafian, violin; Anne-Marie Mc-Dermott, piano; Steven Tenenbom, viola; Peter Wiley, cello. (Special extra concert presented together with Tuesday Musicale)
Haydn	Piano trio in G Major Hob. XV 25, "Gypsy Rondo"
Hartke	"The King of the Sun" Tableaux for violin, cello and piano (1988)
Brahms	Piano Quartet No. 2 in A Major, Op. 26 (1861)
May 2	Leif Ove Andsnes, piano; Christian Tetzlaff, violin; Tanja Tetzlaff, cello
Schumann	Six Pieces in Canon Form
	Trio No. 2 Op. 80 in F Major
	Trio No. 3 Op. 110 in G minor

2000-01

November 15	The Berlin Chamber Orchestra, Katrin Scholz, Music Director & Violin Soloists presented with the generous support of Robert Bosch Corporation.
Haydn	Symphony No. 49 in E minor, La Passione
Mozart	Concerto for Violin and Orchestra in D Major, KV 218
Boccherini	The Night Watch of Madrid, Op. 30, No. 6, G 324
Mozart	Symphony No. 29 in A Major, KV 201
February 21	Absolute Ensemble, Kristjan Jarvi, Director: Valerie Chermiset, flute/piccolo; Vadim Lando, clarinet; Marftin Kuuskmann, bassoon; Ann Ellsworth, French horn; Mike Seltzer, trombone; Matt Herskowitz, piano/keyboard; Shalini Vilayan, violin; Ann Kim, cello; Keve Wilson, oboe/English horn; Michiyo Suzuki, bass clarinet; Monica Ellis, contrabassoon; Charles Porter, trumpet; David Rozenblatt, percussion/keyboard; Vesselin Gellev, violin; Edmundo Ramirez, viola; Mat Fieldes, bass.

ABSOLUTE MIX
Charles Coleman
          Absolution
James MacMillan
          Henry VIII
          T. S. Eliot
Shafer Mahoney
          Dance Machine
Steve Reich   Clapping Music
Michael Daugherty
          Dead Elvis

Appendix A

Mat Fieldes	Cracked Out
Shafer Mahoney	
	Snap
Matt Herskowitz	
	Sewrial Blues
Charles Mingus	
	Goodbye Pork Pie Hat (arr. Ian Frenkel)
Jimi Hendrix	Purple Haze (arr. Daniel Schnyder)
Django Bates	Some More Upsets
Claude Debussy	
	Prelude to the Afternoon of a Faun (arr. Benno Sachs)
John Adams	Road Runner

May 9   James Westman, baritone; John Churchwell, piano. Co-sponsored by the Consulate General of Canada.

Ravel*	Don Quichotte a Dulcinee, 1932-33
Rachmaninoff	Ann kak polden' barasha
	Hristos Vaskres
	O net, mal'u, ne ukhadi
	V malchan'yi nochi taynay
Beethoven	An die ferne Geloiebte, Op. 98: Auf dem Hugel sitz ich spahend; Wo die Berge so blau; Leichte Segler in den Hohen; Es kehret der Maien; Nimm sie hin denn diese Lieder.
Butterworth	Six Songs from A Shropshire Lad: (Poems by A. E. Housman) Loveliest of Trees; When I was One-and-Twenty; Look not in my Eyes; Think no more, Lad; The Lads in their hundreds; Is my team ploughing?

*Maurice Ravel appeared at Pro Musica as composer and pianist in March, 1928.

2001-02

October 24   Anne-Marie McDermott, piano

Bach	English Suite No. 3 in G minor, BWV 808
Prokofiev	Piano Sonata in B flat, Op. 84
Bach	Partita No. 1 in B flat, BWV 825
Prokofiev	Piano Sonata No. 2 in D minor, Op. 14

March 6   The Artemis String Quartet: Natalia Prischepenko and Heime Mueller, violins; Volker Jacobsen, viola; Eckart Runge, cello

Mozart	Preludes and Fugues K. 405 based on fuges from J. S. Bach's The Well Tempered Clavier II
Kurtag	Hommage a Mihaly Andras: 12 Microludes for string quartet, Op. 13
Bartok *	Quartet No. 3 (1927)

Beethoven   Quartet in C sharp minor, Op. 131
*Bartok appeared at Pro Musica as composer and pianist in 1928 and 1936.

May 8   William Bolcom, piano-composer; Joan Morris, mezzo soprano
Bolcom   Complete Cycle of Four Volumes of Cabaret Songs: (Michigan
                 Premiere)
                 I. Over the Piano; Fur (Murray the Furrier); He Tipped the Waiter;
                 Waitin'; Song of Black Max (as told by the de Kooning boys)
                 II. Places to Live; Toothbrush Time; Surprise!; The Actor; Oh
                 Close the Curtain; George
                 III. The Total Stranger in the Garden; Love in the Thirties; This
                 King of Orf; Miracle Song; Satisfaction; Radical Sally
                 IV. Angels are the Highest Form of Virtue; Poet Pal of Mine;
                 Can't Sleep; At the Last Lousy Moments of Love; Lady Luck;
                 Blue

2002-03
October 23   Michael Daugherty, composer; The University of Michigan Con-
                 temporary Directions Ensemble: Jonathan Shames, conductor;
                 Nancy Ambrose King, Oboe; Elizabeth Major, soprano; Catherine
                 Apple, flute/piccolo; Harry Ong, clarinet/bass clarinet; Jill Collier,
                 cello; Kent Craig, percussion; Irena Portenko, piano; Angela We,
                 piano; Nicole Esposito, piccolo; Elizabeth Minnemeyer, violin;
                 Christopher Wild, cello; Veena* Kulkarni, piano; David Schober,
                 piano; David T.Little, Graduate Assistant.
Anecdotes and commentary by the composer illustrated with slides.
                 Jackie's Song for solo cello and ensemble (Mr. Wild).
                 Firecracker, for solo oboe and ensemble (Nancy Ambrose King).
                 Sinatra Shag (Ms. Apple, Mr. Ong, Ms. Minnemeyer, Ms. Collier,
                 Mr. Craig, Ms. Kulkarni).
                 Venetian Blinds for piano solo (Ms Portenko)
                 The High and the Mighty for Piccolo and Piano, (Ms. Esposito
                 and Mr.Schober)
                 Egyptian Time for Voice and Piano, (Elizabeth Major, Mr.
                 Schober)

February 26 Irina Mishura, mezzo soprano; Kevin Bylsma, piano
Rachmaninoff   Vocalese; Again, I am Alone; Lilacs; Spring Waters.
Tchaikovsky   None but the Lonely Heart; Why did I Dream of You?; At the
                 Ball; Does the Day Reign?
Botari   Singing Again
Anon.   Dark Eyes
Cilea   Acerba volutta from "Adriana Lecouvrer"

Appendix A

Bizet	Gypsy Song from "Carmen"
Saint-Saens	Mon Coeur s'ouvre a ta voix from "Samson et Delila"
Mascagni	Voi, Io sapete o mamma from "Cavalleria Rusticana"
Verdi	O don fatale from "Don Carlo"

May 7   Mark Kosower, cello; Jee-Won Oh, piano
Locatelli   Sonata in D Major
Schumann   Fantasiestuecke, Opus 73
Ginastera   Sonata for Cello and Piano opus 49, 1979
Kodaly   Sonata for Unaccompanied Cello opus 8

2003-04
November 15   Dr. Richard Kogan, pianist & psychiatrist
Combining his two professions, Kogan delivers a lecture and concert focusing on the influence of the personality and mental condition of Robert Schumann and how this influenced the music he composed. His performance then becomes a meaningful demonstration of his analysis. He offers similar programs on Beethoven, Gershwin, Mozart and Tchaikovsky. His lifelong friends and musical associates, violinist Lin Chang and cellist Yo Yo Ma, turn to him for guidance on interpretation when they perform as a trio.
Schumann   Carnaval, Opus 9
Widmung (Dedication) transcribed by Franz Liszt
Fantasie in C. Opus 17

February 28   Philippe Quint, violin; David Riley, piano
LeClair   Sonata No. 3 in D Major
Cowell   Suite for Violin & Piano
Tchaikovsky   Valse Scherzo, Opus 34
Foss   Three American Pieces
Gershwin   Transcription from Porgy and Bess
Ravel   Tzigane, Concert Rhapsody

May 15   Manuel Acosta, tenor; Kevin Bylsma, piano
Donizetti   Una Furtiva Lagrima from L'Elisir D'Amore
Puccini   Che Gelida Manina from La Boheme
Tchaikovsky   Lensky's Aria from Eugene Onegin
Bizet   La Fleur que tu mavais jetee from Carmen
Lehar   Dein ist mein ganzes Herz from Das Land des Lächelns
Denza   Funiculi, Funicula
    Zarzuela selections
Serrano   Cancion Guajira from La Alegria del Batallon
Te Quiero Morena from El Trust de los tenorios

Soutullo	Bella Enamorada from El ultimo de los romanticos
Guerrero	Flor Roja from Los Gavilanes
Torroba	De este apacible Rincon from Luisa Fernanda
Sorozabal	No puede ser from La Taberna del Puerto

2004-05

October 23 The Amernet String Quartet, Misha Vinenson and Marcia Littley de Arias, violins; Michael Klotz, viola; Javier Arias, cello; with Alexander Fiterstein, clarinet.

Mozart	String Quartet in G minor, K, 387
Olivera	Sechs Yiddische Lieder und Tanzen for clarinet and string quartet from the film score for "Der Golem."
Arias y Luna	Inemiliz
Brahms	Quintet for Clarinet and Strings in b minor, Opus 115

February 26 Richard Kogan, pianist and psychiatrist.
"George Gershwin by Proxy." A lecture concert (see November 2004)
Swanee
Rhapsody in Blue (for piano solo, arr. By Gershwin)
Love Walked In
"Porgy and Bess" Fantasy (transcription by Earl Wilde)

May 14 Valerian Ruminski, bass; Persis Anne Parshall Vehar, composer and pianist.

Purcell	Arise ye Subterranean Winds
Handel	Fra L'ombre e gl'orrori from Pastoral Acis, Galatea & Polephemus
Schubert	Schwannengesang Lieder: Ständchen, Aufenthalt, In der ferne, Der Atlas.
Brahms	Four Serious Songs: Denn es beget dem Menschen wie dem Vieh; Ich wandte mich; O Tod, wie bitter bist du; Wenn ich min menschen und Engleszungen redete.
Thomas	Two obscure arias: Je t'implore on mon frere from Hamlet, Le Tambour Major from le Caid.
Britten	Claggart's aria from Billy Budd
Puccini	Vecchia Zimarra from La Boheme
Vehar	Out of Absurdity (settings of selected texts by Charles Bukowski, the Skid Row Poet): this moment; trashcan lives; the pack; wind the clock; wearing the collar; roll the dice
Novello	And Her Mother Came Too
Edwards	Into the Night
Foster	Beautiful Dreamer
Gershwin	Just Another Rhumba

Appendix A

2005-06

November 11   Antii Siirala, pianist
Janacek   Sonata 1.X 1905
Schumann   Romanzen, op. 24: Sehr Markiert, Einfach, Sehr Markiert
Szymanowski   Metopes, 3 poemes, op. 29: L'isle des Sirenes, Calypso, Nausica
Beethoven   Piano Sonata No. 24 in F sharp major, op. 78 "a Therese"
   Piano Sonata No. 27 in E minor, op. 90
   Piano Sonata No. 26 in E flat major, op. 81a, "Les Adieux"
February 10   Aaron Jay Kernis, composer, with The Contrasts Quartet: Evelyne Luest, piano; Monica Bauchwitz, violin; Sophie Shao, cell;, Ayako Oshima, clarinet.
Kernis   Ballad for cello and piano (2004)
Beethoven   Piano Trio No. 6, op. 97. "Archduke"
Kernis   Fanfare con Fuoco for clarinet, violin, cello and piano (2003)
   Waltz for piano
   Speed Limit Rag for piano (2001)
   Trio in Red for clarinet, cetto and piano (2000-01)
May 12   Thomas Meglioranza, baritone; Reiko Uchida, piano
Schubert   Three Songs for Luigi Lablache: L'incanto degli occhi D902 No. 1 (Metastasio),
   Il traditor deluso D902 No. 2 (Metastasio), Il modo dip render moglie D902 No. 3 (Metastasio)
Schumann   Zwei Venetianische Lieder: Leis' rudern hier, mein Gondolier, Wenn durch die Piazzetta die Abendluft weht
Barberian   Stripsody
   (Cathy)
Busoni   Goethe Lieder: Zigeunerlied, Schlechter Trost, Lied des Mephistopheles
Ives   Settings of Folgore da San Geminiano: August, September, December
Rossini   La Chanson du Bebe
Songs added to program and sung as extras and encores
Derek Bermel   Nature Calls; Spider Lover; Mushroom; Dog
Aaron J. Kernis
   A Pregnant Dream
Mark Blitzstein   The New Suit

Appendix B
List of Officers and Board Members by Year Elected

Honorary President
Dorothy (Mrs. Frank W.) Coolidge, 1975

President
Louis Ling, 1928
Charles Frederic Morse, 1931
Dorothy (Mrs. Frank W.) Coolidge, 1946
Alexander C. Suczek, 1975

First Vice President
Mme. Djina Ostrowska, 1928
Louis Ling, 1932
Dr. Hugh Stalker, 1949
Alexander C. Suczek, 1964
Thomas V. LoCicero, 1975
Mrs. Berj H. Haidostian, 1991

Second Vice President
Charles Frederic Morse, 1928
Mrs. Wilson W. Mills, 1931
Miss Margaret Mannebach, 1932
Mrs. W. Terrance (Betty) Bannan, 1965
Mrs. George Zeitz, 1976
Dr. Hershel Sandberg, 1987

Secretary (Recording)
Edward G. Kemp, 1928
Roger W. Beebe, 1931
Oliver Spaulding, 1936
John E. Coulter, 1937
John W. Nelson, 1944
Malcolm Johns, 1947
Mrs. William J. Coulter, 1949

Appendix B

Miss Marie Marti, 1960
Mrs. Arnold (Alice) Lungershausen, 1962
Mrs. Berg H. (Alice) Haidostian, 1969
Mrs. Nicholas Kondak, 1991

Secretary (Corresponding)
Mrs. Frank W. Coolidge, 1928

Treasurer
Raymond W. Reilly, 1928
Roger W. Beebe, 1931
Oliver Spaulding, 1936
John E. Coulter, 1937
Frederick. J. Sevald, 1946
Edward P. Frohlich, 1960
James P. Diamond, 1986
Shahe Momjian, 1998
Stanley A. Beattie, 2002

Assistant Treasurer
James Diamond, 1983
Shahe Momjian, 1997

Endowment
James P. Diamond, 1984
Dr. Hershel Sandberg, 1990

Membership Secretary
Mrs. Walter C. Boynton, 1928
Mrs. Frank W. Coolidge, Jr., 1931
Mrs. Florence Adams McKinstry, 1946
Mrs. Arthur L. Miller, 1948
Mrs. John M Chase, 1954
Mrs. Thomas I. Young, 1977
Mrs. John Rainey, 1980
Mrs. George Drake, 1986
Mrs. Harold Arnoldi, 1990
Margaret Beck, 2001

Social Committee Chairman
Mrs. E. W. Austin, 1934
Mrs. Philip C. Baker, 1936
Mrs. J. Leslie Berry, 1947

Mrs. John W. Nelson, 1950
Mrs. Edward (Ruth) Roth, 1962
Miss Margaret McEvoy, 1973
Mrs. George Zeitz, 1974
Mrs. Pierre V. Heftler, 1982
Mrs. Hershel Sandberg, 1985

Program Chairman
Edouard Bredshall, 1937

New Member Chairman
Mrs. Edward Bauman, 1970
Ms. Elizabeth Soby, 1986
Ms. Nicholas Kondak, 1988
Mrs. James North 1989
Mrs. Leonard Lerner, 1991

Renewal Chairman
Mrs. Eugene Karpus, 1970
Miss Charlotte Ann Moore, 1975
Mrs. Manuel Papista, 1976
Ms. Mary Louise Baldwin, 1980
Ms. Inga Callaway, 1986
Mrs. Nicholas Kondak, 1991

Press Relations
Mrs. Daniel Knoth, 1968
Mrs. Franziska Greiling, 1976
Ms. Fran Emmons, 1978
Miss Mary Anne Pilette, 1980
Mr. & Mrs. Ray Litt, 1983
Seymour Kapetansky, 1992
Kenneth Collinson, 1992

Historian
Ms. Elizabeth Soby, 1983

Founding Board of Directors
1928: Willoughby Boughton, Mr. & Mrs. Walter C. Boynton, Mrs. Edwin Hewitt
   Brown, Mrs. Frank W. Coolidge, Jr., John E. Coulter, Mrs. Ernest Haass, Mrs.
   George T. Hendrie, Miss Margaret Holden, Miss Elizabeth Johnson, Mrs. Henry
   B. Joy, Edward G. Kemp, Louis Ling, Miss Margaret Mannebach, Frederick B.

Manville, Henri Matheys, George Miquelle, Charles Frederic Morse, Rene Muller, Mrs. Samuel Mumford, William H. Murphy, Madame Djina Ostrowska, Miss Caroline Parker, Mrs. Franz Prattinger, Mrs. Jeanette van der Velpen Reaume, Mr. and Mrs. Raymond W. Reilly, Mrs. Edwin S. Sherrill, Miss Jennie M. Stoddard, Mrs. Myron B. Vorce, Edward Werner, Francis L. York.

Board Replacements (outgoing board members are not listed)

1931: Valbert Coffey, Mrs. John S. Newberry, M. Hubert O'Brien, Ilya Schkolnik, Mrs. B. E. Taylor, Mrs. Edith Rhetts Tilton, Dr. Harold Wilson.

1932 to 1946: There is no accurate record of changes to the board for this period.

1947: Mrs. Philip C. Baker, Mrs. Terrance W. Bannan, John E. Coulter, Mischa Kottler, Dr. Harry Seitz, Dr. Hugh Stalker, Miss H. Dorothy Tilly, Floyd G. Hitchcock (plus the officers).

1948: Mrs. Warren B. Cooksey, Mrs. W. J. Coulter, Edward Frohlich, Malcolm M. Johns, Dr. Harry Seitz.

1949: J. Leslie Berry, Carl Beutel.

1950: Dr. Cyril E. Barker, Thornton Zanolli

1951: Mrs. Abraham Cooper, Dr. C. E Barker, David Sutter

1952: John R. Phelps

1953: Clark Eastham

1954: Mrs. Hixie B. Hatten, Mrs. Vernon M. Venman

1955: Mr. Frank G. Murch

1957: Mrs. Wendling H. Hastings

1958: Mr. Kurtz Myers

1959: Miss Marie Marti, Alexander C. Suczek

1961: Joseph A. Luyckx

1962: Mrs. Arnold Lungershausen, Mrs. Edward Roth

1963: Mrs. Julian Wolfner, Thomas V. LoCicero

1965: David Kludt

1969: Pierre Heftler, Eugene S. Karpus, Mrs. Sol Q. Kesler, Reginald Thomas

1970: Mrs. Edward Roth, Mrs. George Zeitz

1971: Edward Kroll

1972: Gerald F. Meadows

1973: John P. Miller, Noel F. Duncan

1975: Mrs. Edward Bauman, David Coolidge

1976: James P. Diamond, Mrs. Paul J. Kelly, Mrs. Nicholas Kondak, Mrs. Bert E. Taylor, Mrs. Daniel Knoth

1978: Marvin Bookstein

1980: Mrs. James Ellison

1983: Mrs. John Barthel, Mrs. John F. Colbeth, Mrs. Pierre V. Heftler, Richard E. Smoke, Ms. Elizabeth Soby.

1986: Mrs. Zoltan J. Janosi, Dr. Hershel Sandberg, Ms. Elizabeth Soby, Mr. George C. Vincent, Daniel Herman, Edward P. Frohlich

1987: Kenneth Collinson, Mrs. James North, Mrs. Stanley Weingarden

1991: Mr. Harold Arnoldi, Mrs. Leonard Lerner,

1996: Thomas V. LoCicero emeritus

1998: Bill Harmon, Mrs. Angus McMillan, James P Diamond emeritus, Edward P. Frohlich emeritus.

1999: Patrick Broderick

2000: Ann Greenstone, Elizabeth Soby emeritus

2002: Lee Barthel

2003: Harry Pevos

2004: Moira Escott

2005: Frederick McKenzie

Appendix C

List of Composers, Artists, and Ensembles

Index of Composers

Bartok, Bela. 1928 & '36
Bolcom, William. 2002
Boulanger, Nadia. 1949
Britten, Benjamin. 1949
Carter, Eliot. 1961
Childs, Barney. 1980
Copland, Aaron. 1940 & '50
Cowell, Henry. 1933
Creston, Paul. 1958
Crumb, George. 1978
Daugherty, Michael. 2002
Dello Joio, Norman; 1951
DiChiera, David. 1984
DiGiacomo, Frank. 1979
Foss, Lucas. 1948
Gershwin, George "by proxy." 2005
Hartway, James. 1987
Helps, Robert. 1996

Hindemith, Paul. 1938
Honnegger, Arthur. 1929
Kernis, Aaron Jay. 2006
Kirchner, Leon. 1963
Meister, Karl. 1983
Milhaud, Darius. 1954
Poulenc, Francis. 1948
Prokofiev, Sergei. 1930
Ravel, Maurice. 1928
Respighi, Ottorino. 1928
Rorem, Ned. 1986
Schmitt, Florent. 1932
Schocker, Gary. 1988
Schumann, Robert "by proxy." 2003
Tansmann, Alexander. 1929
Toch, Dr. Ernst. 1932
Vehar, Persis Anne Pershall. 2005

Index of Solo Artists

Abram, Jacques. 1948
Acosta, Manuel. 2004
Andsnes, Leif Ove. 1993, 2000
Armstrong, Karan. 1969
Arrau, Claudio. 1944
Babakhanian, Armen. 1994
Bagratuni, Suren. 1996
Bayrakdarian, Isabel. 1999
Bedford, Brian, 1999
Bell, Joshua. 1986

Berg, Nathan. 1997
Bidini, Fabio. 1997
Boyden, John. 1963
Bressler, Charles. 1967
Browning, John. 1958
Cass, Richard. 1966
Cerovsek, Corey 990
Cerovsek, Katia. 1990
Chiu, Frederic. 1998, '99
Chookasian, Lili. 1969

Cohen, Arnaldo. 1999
Curtin, Phyllis. 1955
DeVaughn, Alteoise. 1982
Fiterstine, Alexander. 2004
Fodor, Eugene. 1976
Frager, Malcolm. 1970
Frisch, Povla. 1928, '37, '43
Glenn, Carroll. 1954
Gold & Fizdale. 1947, '49, '51, '61
Goldsand, Robert. 1953
Graffman, Gary. 1975
Guinn, Leslie. 1977
Ha, Seung Un. 1991
Hadley, Jerry. 1983
Haidostian, Alice. 1999
Hawkins, Gordon.987
Holgate, Ronald. 1972
Holzmair, Wolfgang. 1995
Hooks, Bridgett. 1999
Houston, Elsie. 1942
Järvi, Kristjan. 2001
Johannesen, Grant. 1950, '58
Johnson, Camellia. 1994
Kavafian, Ida. 2000
Kogan, Richard. 2003, '05
Kosower, Mark. 2003
Laredo, Jaime. 1962
Laredo, Ruth. 1968, '72, '88
Lin, Cho Liang. 1980
Lipkin, Seymour, 1961
List, Eugene. 1954, '74
Lympany, Moura. 1956
Markova, Juliana. 1977
Marshall, Lois. 1957
Masselos, William. 1960
McDermott, Anne-Marie. 2001
Meglioranza, Thomas. 2006
Mikelsen, Keith. 1992
Mishura, Irina. 2003
Morris, Joan. 2002
Neway, Patricia. 1954
Norman, Jessye. 1980
O'Riley, Christopher. 1984

Pancella, Phyllis. 1993
Pears, Peter. 1949
Pennario, Leonard. 1985
Primrose, William. 1942
Quint, Philippe. 2004
Rachlin, Julian. 1998
Raim, Cynthia. 1983, '88
Robinson, Gail, 1974
Rodriguez, Santiago. 1983
Rosen, Charles. 1964
Ruminski, Valerian. 2005
SanRoma, Jesus Maria. 1936, '37
Santiago, Theresa. 1998
Sarfati, Regina. 1964
Schmitz, F. Robert. 1945
Schub, Andre Michel. 1979, '81
Segar, Kathleen. 1984
Sevilla, Jean Paul. 1967
Shifrin, David. 1991
Siegel, Jeffrey. 1970
Siirala, Antii. 2005
Singher, Martial. 1945, '55
Solomon, Nicholas. 1984
Stecher & Horowitz. 1968
Steffan, Sophia. 1976
Suarez, Cesar Antonio. 1979
Suczek, Alex. 1999
Tetzlaff, Christian. 2000
Tetzlaff, Tanya. 2000
Thebom, Blanche. 1953
Thibaudet, Jean-Yves. 1994
Tocco, James. 1979
Tourell, Jennie. 1952, '55
Turini, Ronald. 1965
Uppman, Theodore. 1965
Vanni, Helen. 1966
Von Reichenbach, Susan. 1996
Votapek, Ralph. 1975, '87
Vrenios, Anastasios. 1970
Welting, Ruth. 1981
Westman, James. 2001
Williams, Janet. 1990
Ying, Tian. 1993

Appendix C

Index of Ensembles